Finding Pegasus

Terry Church

Llumina Press

Requests for permission to make copies of any part of this work should be mailed to Permissions Department, Llumina Press, PO Box 772246, Coral Springs, FL 33077-2246

ISBN: 978-1-59526-639-2 (PB)
978-1-59526-640-8 (HC)
978-1-59526-641-5 (Ebook)

Printed in the United States of America by Llumina Press

Library of Congress Control Number: 2006908410

Dedication

*This novel has been written with the hope
that the very real Tom Dorrance,
his life and his contributions,
will not be forgotten.*

Acknowledgments

There are many people, especially friends I have known throughout my life, to whom I am indebted for their kindness and/or the life lessons they provided me. Although too numerous to mention individually, I hold all in my heart and memory, and I am grateful.

The following is a list of individuals who have been instrumental in my ability to write this book:

Deborah Davis, who helped me map my way out of the darkness.

Bill Richardson never gave up on my ability to write the truth, even though, for five straight years, I handed in manuscripts filled with complex avoidance at every Wednesday night's writer's class.

Annette Goodheart helped me get the agony out.

Tina McMillan, Annie Calloway, Nanci Jacobs, and the Adult Children of Alcoholics group gave me a place to feel sane, even when I wasn't. You know who you are.

Bill Prange, LAc and friend, applied a sensitivity and understanding that reached far beyond the limitations of conventional allopathic medicine and saved my life.

Susan Terrell sat me down, and through her enthusiasm for this project, managed to commit me to a daily writing regimen, then waved pom poms no matter how bad the first drafts read.

Leslie Keenan's editing expertise along with her confidence in my writing allowed me the inspiration and determination to embark on the many subsequent revisions of this work.

Tessa Fitzgerald and *Siri Larssen* gave me both honest and encouraging feedback on what I had thought was the final draft of this manuscript, until they read it.

Shary Stadler showed me how much it pays to listen to one's intuition. After asking her to read the second, third and fourth "final" drafts, I was delighted and grateful to see her secret editing talents miraculously emerge.

Margaret Dorrance was kind enough to read the entire manuscript and offer key comments about Tom Dorrance and his work.

Brad Straka offered considerable help and support with the book cover.

William W. Walter, Bruce Smith, Susan Chiaventone, Darryl McGuire, and everyone associated with the Eschatology Foundation have helped me realize that putting into practice the marriage of love and truth in daily life is the only renewable and sustainable—or eternal—state of mind, even when I don't seem to feel that way!

Siri Larssen Larry, Stephanie Meux Larry, Abby Hill Larry, Sara Skog Larry, and *Vanessa Watts Larry* are *team originale* forever. I love you more than I can say.

I would also like to give my sincere thanks to Tinker (*Kay Lee*), Pack (*Georgia Dow*), Snaffle (*Carrie di Corsia*), and especially Spurs. Although I was too immature to recognize your significance in my life at the time, letting you slip away, unthanked, I would not be where I am today without you. My hope is that somehow you hear my heart's voice, and know that I still think of you.

And last but most definitely not least, I dedicate this book to my students everywhere. I humbly remain one of yours also.

Chimera was a monster who, legend says, plagued the kingdom of Proteus in ancient Greece. Chimera had three heads: a lion's head that spit lightning and roared smoke, a goat's head that shrieked wildly and wielded sharp horns, and a serpent's head that hissed fire. King Proteus called upon Bellopheron, a young man known for his bravery and athleticism, to kill Chimera. Although Bellopheron stoically agreed, he did not trust his own powers and was afraid he would fail. He went to the temple of the wise goddess Athena to ask for guidance. The goddess appeared to him in a radiant halo of light, a light so bright he could barely look at her.

"Bellopheron," said Athena, "the only way to find Chimera is with the help of the winged horse Pegasus. The only way to tame Pegasus is with a magic bridle. And the only way to kill Chimera is with a magic sword." And then she pointed.

Two objects appeared beside him in the golden light. Sword and bridle, if you could call them that, did not look like ones he had seen or used before, but he knew that was what they must be.

Athena said, "To you these tools have already been granted and are at your disposal whenever you choose, but you will never learn their true meaning or their proper use until you find Pegasus." She held his eyes with her steady gaze. "First, you must find Pegasus."

Prologue

It may at first glance seem peculiar, even exaggerated to many people, to claim that horses, dumb creatures apparently destined only to serve man, should play an important part in his life. If we love and study Nature, however, we soon realize that some animals that are to be our companions through life cannot be carelessly ignored, but deserve a little attention. Their characters, if we learn to understand them, will open the doors of an unknown kingdom, and we might well follow their example of integrity, reliability, and devotion.

Alois Podhajsky
My Dancing White Horses

Spring had come at last to the northeast corner of Oregon, and thirty-three-year-old Tom Dorrance backed a brand new 1943 Dodge truck into the muddy entrance of a holding pen made of post and rail fencing. At five foot, seven inches tall, weighing only 130 pounds in jeans and long-sleeved flannel shirt, he and his ranch hand hoisted custom-built solid wooden railings along two sides of the truck's flat bed. A white cowboy hat shaded Tom's face from the bright sun while he attached a third side that hung off the back end and sloped down to the ground, doubling as a ramp. Softly flapping his arms up and down while adjusting the position of his body, he drove several purebred bulls out of the corner of the pen and watched them lumber up the ramp into the truck's bed. Before they could turn around and run back down, he and his hired hand unhitched the ramp and hoisted it up into the slots that secured its place as a tailgate. Fairly certain it would hold, Tom walked toward the open door of the truck's cab, gauging his steps. As his left foot touched the floorboard, he grabbed the steering wheel and, right leg immediately following, pulled himself up onto the bench seat in one smooth, uninterrupted motion. Practically before the full weight of his slight frame had time to settle he was starting the engine for its very first duty.

Until now, no motorized equipment had ever been used on his family's self-sufficient homestead that, between owned and leased land, encompassed over 20,000 acres. Even with the truck's recent purchase, horses remained his preferred mode of transportation, and the following day, he saddled a bay mare. Donning a slicker that covered his roping saddle and hung past his knees, Tom guided his horse over the slippery slopes in the rain to drive another several hundred head of cattle twenty miles from their protected winter valley to the surrounding windy acres. As spring warmed into summer, it was horses that he used to mow the fields, put up the hay, check fence lines, and rotate the herd over ungrazed pastures too hilly and rocky for the neighboring owners to farm.

Most people wouldn't think twice about the significance of this, he realized, keenly aware of technology's promise of a more advanced and productive life. Nearly everyone he knew was already well accustomed to flipping a switch to a machine that carried out their orders regardless of where they lived, the weather, or their mood on any given day. Their mechanized work horses would not be impacted by the feel of their skin, their internal posturing, or their presence of mind that, in his case, was a matter of immediate survival. Live horses, on the other hand, never behaved in exactly the same way twice, particularly in an environment interfaced with the wild. To act rashly, in a hurried manner, or without thinking could be fatal, or at the very least, enormously inconvenient when, for example, they landed you in the dirt and galloped for home, leaving you to walk five, ten, twenty or more miles home on foot — broken limbs or not.

Similar thoughts filtered through Tom's mind when, ten short years later, well into the burgeoning era of atomic energy and warfare, he drove through town one day and marveled at how he hadn't seen one horse-drawn vehicle. Still, his world remained remote compared to life in the city, particularly one the likes of Los Angeles, an urban mass a thousand miles to the south. Los Angeles had already grown into an endless maze of broad, paved avenues and interconnecting freeways particularly suited to the automobile. Only later would it become relevant to Tom that the daughter of a prominent fashion designer was being born there.

At the time of his daughter's birth, the fashion designer gave excuses for why he didn't come to visit the newborn or his wife during their three days in the hospital, as he had done with his eldest son and two older daughters. Nor did he arrange to pick them up to drive them home — until the last minute when Mrs. Beacon was discharged. Without speaking to her husband, she carried baby Tara, bundled in blankets, out to the asphalt parking lot. All remained silent throughout the nine-mile drive back to their house in the hilly suburbs.

1

~the master~

"Are you a God?" they asked the Buddha.
"No," he replied.
"Are you an angel, then?" "No."
"A saint?" "No."
"Then what are you?"
Replied the Buddha, "I am awake."

— Houston Smith

Tara stood with bare hands curled deep inside her coat pockets, protecting them from a late February afternoon. Most of her dark blonde hair remained stuffed inside the back of her collar for warmth, except for a few renegade curls tossed about by the wind. Overhead, the updrafts chased broken cloud formations across the sun, making the world both hopeful and gloomy in the changing light. Dressed in ordinary blue jeans and hiking boots, Tara leaned her slender frame against the back of a wooden fence post and feigned peaceful repose while her unblinking blue eyes, set between freckled cheekbones and a wide brow, squinted into the distance. She barely breathed, anticipating the arrival of a group of men on horseback. The fence post supporting her solitary weight had been there a while, by the looks of its eroded surface. Yet it remained securely fixed into the ground, acting as a king pin for the line of barbed wire that extended for miles across this rocky pasture.

At last five or six riders, seated in their heavy, western roping saddles, emerged high up on a knoll, steering half a dozen calves along the ridge before sailing down the steep slope at a fast trot, darting between rock outcroppings and oak stands dotting the wide, expansive hillsides. Tara breathed in the sight. California, brittle and brown for much of the year, was now covered in velvety green from winter rains that softened the land into its own harmonious glory from one end of the state to the other, wherever the great sprawls of cement, industry, and population hadn't made extinct the real beauty of this place. A gust of wind made her gasp involuntarily. The calves, uncertain of their fate, broke ranks and ran sidelong.

Unfazed, the riders sat their mounts easily, looking smug in the presence of one elderly cowboy who rode alongside them. Indeed, his casual appearance made him look as if he were one of them. Faded jeans and a dull navy blue wind breaker blended perfectly with the utilitarian garb worn by the rest of the riders, who looked to be somewhere in their mid-thirties, about her age. Only the thicker skin of the elder's leathery face exposed his seniority, and Tara couldn't help wondering what it was like for eighty-year-old Tom Dorrance to ride at such a pace. But the quick and bouncy up-down, up-down stride of his horse didn't seem to make him think twice. He and his mostly male following turned their mounts easily, keeping up with the mistrusting calves that had been compelled to leave the sweet smell of young grass and the comfort of their secluded grazing field. Untidy reddish-brown and white winter coats indicated the herd's Hereford ancestry, and before the calves knew what had happened, they were passing through a narrow gate that led to an enclosed sandy arena, occasionally bawling in bewilderment.

Tara felt her own stomach tighten. Normally, a Sunday such as this would find her at a horse show, competing against other properly groomed mannequins in all-white skintight breeches and black leather knee-high boots, heels strapped with silver spurs polished the night before. A fine wool coat and tails, silk top hat, and white gloves would complete the dress code requirements, along with the close-fitting, contoured saddle and double bridle her horse wore, signifying their passage into international competition. The braided mane of her jet-black Thoroughbred gelding would be accented with white tape and his winter shag meticulously shaved away to give a shine to his well-muscled physique. Even now, she could feel his animated, rhythmic stride as they performed a series of compulsory figures over manicured footing, carefully harrowed and leveled.

But the cowboys before her, sitting in saddles adorned with lariats and saddle horns, rode with abandon in muddy boots and broad-brimmed hats. Their shaggy mounts stretched freely into their stride over uneven terrain. They cared little for her world and ignored her presence.

"Sport of the elite," was how many of their ilk described *her* way of riding.

Sport of snobs, is what they meant, she smiled ruefully to herself. It represented a growing sentiment toward competitive types in her sport who could afford to import expensive show horses from across the Atlantic—horses bred specifically, scientifically, for dressage, the classical European style of riding, originating in royal palaces hundreds of years before.

"Dressage represents the ultimate training for the horse," enthusiasts preached to riders of all other disciplines, exuding an air of superiority in spite of often-inferior skill. Tara tightened her arms around her torso, shifted her position, and felt her face grow hot. *Just walk away,* she told herself, no longer remembering what had compelled her to come all the way out here on this cold, cloudy day in the first place. She ran her tongue over chapped lips, noting the quick and agile steps of the compact Quarter Horses in front of her. Yet her own feet stayed.

The men and one woman, all of whom ranched for a living, were riding in loose formation behind the calves. Tom Dorrance slowed to a walk and carefully filed into the arena with the others.

"Who's he?" she had asked Jolene two weeks before when her friend had told her about him.

"Oh, you know—those cowboys you've heard about who can take a wild horse and tame it without saddle or bridle in a day or so."

Tara had heard of such persons, reading about them in an offbeat equestrian magazine. Their mysterious skill had piqued her fascination, but not enough to distract her from a heavy show schedule.

"Well," Jolene had continued, "Tom is the guru for all those other guys you've read about. He's the one *they* learned from."

"Uh-huh," she'd politely acquiesced, only half believing she could have missed knowing about someone as important as that.

But Jolene hadn't given up. "A lot of people across the country would give their right arm to live so close to Tom." Then she'd handed Tara the simple, homemade flyer with his name, a time and date, and directions to this working cattle ranch in Carmel Valley.

So, here she was. Tom nodded his head at the one woman rider who had stayed behind the others to close the arena gate. She wore a baseball cap and fringed chaps that hung only to her knees. Keeping her horse steady, she leaned sideways out of the saddle to secure the latch. Tom's wordless nod was accentuated by the dip of his hat, a gesture that seemed to define the man. Tara felt a sudden warmth permeate her, as if she already knew him somehow.

Meanwhile the calves, leery of the riders, had huddled together at the far end of the arena. A cowboy moved forward on his horse to cut one out of the herd. When the calf found itself separated from the others, it darted back to the group. The cowboy swung a rope overhead, building a loop before letting it fly from his hands. But he missed noosing the calf's hind legs, and the rope slid free over the animal's rump instead.

Tom sat quietly astride a chestnut gelding who stood evenly on all fours alongside the railing. The horse's ears flicked toward the activity before him, and then back toward his rider, as if waiting for a directive to move. At the same time, he lowered his long neck, jaws occasionally chewing softly. It occurred to Tara that Tom lived somewhere east of here. The horse he rode would be unfamiliar to him, owned by this ranch, and merely on loan for the day's events. Yet already there was a rapport between them. *Calm*, she formed the word in her mind. The horse was calm.

Now she remembered why she had come, her fingers following the edges of the crumpled flyer still in her pocket as unwanted images came to mind of her horse working himself into a frenzy the weekend before at a show.

She turned her gaze away from Tom and the others and chewed on her lip, recalling the sharp buzz of the alarm that had startled her from sleep at 3:30 a.m. seven days earlier. The rush of excitement she used to feel the morning of a horse show had not, on that morning, taken away the groggy ache that infected her senses. Groaning, she'd forced herself to sit up, wondering what had made her think that getting up at that hour was a good idea.

The sudden light emanating from the lamp on her bed stand burned her eyes. Shutting it off again, she made her way to the kitchen table in the moonlight, checking off each item of clothing written on her show list after pulling them on, one by one. White blouse, white breeches, white socks, white stock tie, black belt. She vaguely remembered combing her hair into a braid by feel, pushing tiny shafts of small gold earrings in through a single piercing on each earlobe, wetting her fingers with her tongue to tuck short wisps of hair underneath a hair net. Lastly, she covered herself with an outer layer of street clothes to keep all that white free of hay, manure, and horse snot.

Her watch had read 4:30 a.m. by the time she arrived at the stables to groom her horse and remove the aluminum foil that neatly encased each of the twenty-two finger-width braids in his mane, protecting them from dirt in case he rolled during the night. When she tried to load him into the horse trailer she had to resort to placing a metal chain under his upper lip to get him to follow her inside, his sensitive gums bleeding after he pulled away from her on the first try. By the time he was secured into his compartment, he had already broken into a sweat, and then he bellowed and pawed the sides of the trailer as she pulled down the drive. After a two-hour journey south to Palo Alto, he arrived at the show grounds dripping wet, and a blast of hot air greeted her as she opened the door to his compartment. *Twenty minutes to hand-walk him dry*, she mentally noted as she led him, snorting and kicking, around the parking lot before tying him to the side of her trailer, hoping he'd be content with his hay net and bucket of water while she did a final grooming and tacked him up to ride.

A knot had gripped her stomach when she began her warm-up— walk, trot and canter in each direction—while trainers on the sidelines yelled commands to their students warming up around her. Any last minute instructions had to be given then. Absolutely no talking or coaching was allowed once a competitor entered the show court. She made a point of not watching them, concentrating on her own horse, who had strained against the reins from the onset. Leg yield, shoulder-in, half-pass. The sideways movements, normally her Thoroughbred's forté, were stiff and short strided, the crossing action of his legs anything but fluid or relaxed under her seat. She was glad she'd made the decision to back down to a lower level than his capabilities warranted, hoping to smooth over spots that seemed to have gotten worse, not better, during the previous eight years of his training.

Then there had been the ring steward, waving an arm, calling her to the indoor arena. She pretended to be patient while the gate keeper ran a forefinger inside her horse's mouth, checking to make sure his tongue was not illegally tied in place, and that his bits were free from barbs or twists, a reminder that such methods still pervaded the world of horse training. And then, before she had a chance to accustom her horse to the shadows of the inside court, the whistle shrilled into the air.

At a canter, she entered the 20 x 60-meter rectangular arena through the gate at the far end and rode a straight line directly toward the judge, halting to perform a salute, one white-gloved hand dropping straight down to her hip as her head bowed. After receiving a return nod, she moved her gelding forward into a sitting trot, his rhythmic stride making a swishing sound as the soft footing absorbed the concussion of his steps. Each footfall had to be placed accurately in preparation for a turn or a change of gait. She tried making a smooth transition from a collected trot to an extended trot. But just as she saw his forelegs lift and strike out well in front of his nose, he pulled the reins from her hands and broke into a gallop, not allowing himself to be brought under control until he reached the corner where the tight turn forced him to slow.

On the sidelines, spectators had been cordoned off fifteen feet from the edge of the dressage court, remaining silent lest they distracted the competitors. Seven long, arduous minutes later, she rode her final salute to the judge. The crowd remained hushed before a spattering of polite applause cut the air. She and her gelding walked from the arena, sweat streaming beneath her wool shadbelly. She did not lift her eyes at anyone to smile or nod her thanks, as she once would have done, nor offer her usual "Good luck!" to the other competitors passing her on their way in.

Something slamming into the corner of her eyelid startled Tara back into broad daylight and the bawling of calves. She lowered her head to shield her eyes from the sun and pried out the soft body of a flying insect piece by piece with a fingernail. Better this, she mused, than swallowing it whole, as she commonly did while riding outdoors. When she could look up again, she saw Tom sitting in the same spot on his horse, his lips moving in the distance. The breeze carried his soft, indecipherable tones into her range of hearing. She didn't really care about learning to rope calves for branding or castrations, or any other skill the world of ranching might require. Nevertheless, she worked her way around to the other side of the arena to hear him better, stepping over pockets of native bunch grass that grew in clumps outside the perimeter. But what could he say that would help ease the silent, invisible ache she carried?

She mindlessly felt for the folded flyer inside her pocket. She hadn't told any of her students that she'd taken the day off to drive a hundred and fifty miles to this ranch where Tom had come for the day. Not that they would care where she was. But she had wanted to avoid any sidelong looks asking why she, their classical dressage trainer, had suddenly become interested in an old cowboy. She studied Tom's face, weathered and tanned, yet remarkably free of wrinkles. His nose, softly rounded at the tip, protruded past his brow that was hidden underneath a crisp white hat. His lips curved into a slightly downward smile.

She folded her arms over the wooden railing that enclosed the arena, and renewed her concentration on the scene before her. The calves were fresh and unpredictable, darting to and fro without warning. One in particular had been quick to outrun any approaching horse and rider. The cowboys joked about this amongst themselves in laughing conversation, brimmed hats bobbing up and down. Tom gave little instruction and said nothing to correct their actions. Tara squinted through narrow eyelids whenever he nodded at their tries or murmured some vague encouragement, as if it would help her see what he was so pleased about. Once he mentioned something about the person's angle to the calf, then reminded the riders to alternate which calves they cut from the herd so as not to over-stress any one. It wasn't the kind of "how to" session she had expected. She frowned, not having a clue as to what they were learning.

Another gust of February chill blew directly into her face, stinging the tips of her nostrils. Once again, she wrapped her arms tightly around her torso and breathed in the fresh air recently moistened by rain. The calves' brown and white coat hairs waved and fluttered in the sunlight, revealing young, pink hide underneath. She checked her watch. More than two hours had passed since she'd arrived. Tom had remained quietly astride his horse and out of the way of the other riders the entire time, and although he had a rope coiled on his saddle, he hadn't shown any inclination to use it. She assumed he was too old for that now, but as she was thinking this, he lifted his torso ever so slightly, signaling his mount to move forward. The riders noticed this as well, and lined themselves along one side of the fence. A quiet descended among them. Cowboy hats became still and hands were lowered to rest on thighs and saddle horns.

Tom walked his horse easily on a loose rein, looking down to unfasten the long coil of nylon rope. Coil in hand, he worked the strands in his fingers, sorting them casually. Indifferently. The movement of his horse gently stirred the calves, and they fanned out in front of him. Tom didn't swing a loop overhead the way the others had done, nor did Tara see him do anything to prepare a throw, so when he let the rope fly from his hand, the action was so unexpected it startled her into complete attention. A strange hum, like a low buzzing sound — *was it the rope's unwind?* — filled her head.

The calf that had been quick to flee all afternoon stirred into a run — only now everything appeared to move in slow motion, each single event happening one after another, instead of simultaneously, the way life usually appeared. The calf's legs rotated. His cloven feet churned the sand, straining to get away. Tom leaned forward in the saddle, his right arm reaching out, fingers extended, long after the rope had left their grip. The line of cowboy hats swung slowly left to right, watching it float by. Tara noted their focus, felt their anticipation.

She turned to see the lariat mid-flight. It had been thrown off to the side, nowhere near the calf. Her stomach dropped. No way would it reach its target. But as it extended to its full length, the loop end opened wide and appeared to just hang there, suspended vertically in midair. The calf, still running in slow motion, had turned and was now eerily heading straight to the rope's open middle, as if drawn there by some unseen force. *How had Tom known it would flee in that direction?* Just as the calf reached the lariat, the loop snapped neatly around its neck. Startled, Tara took a quick breath, and suddenly everything was at normal speed again. The other calves scattered.

Barely noticing several cowboys swing off their mounts to help Tom hold the calf, she stood frozen, eyes wide, heart pumping. "Yogi, guru, Zen master, Yoda," all were names that had been recently quoted in a newspaper article, referring to this man who appeared to perform magic—names which he, in that same article, had uniformly rejected. But she had to admit, that's how it felt, not knowing how he had done what he just did. How many years had it taken him to develop that ability?

Tom dismounted. His loosely fitted blue jeans bagged below his seat as he shuffled toward the others through the bare sand, looking as though he'd just done nothing more out of the ordinary than breathing. Two men were already on the ground, muscling the squirming calf. Their efforts to hold it long enough to loosen the rope from its neck suddenly appeared awkward; amateurish in comparison with the elder. But once the noose had been removed, Tom directed one of the men to hold the front legs, the other the hind. The calf struggled against their grip, its tiny cloven hooves dwarfed in huge, calloused, workmen's hands.

"Now if you hold steady as the calf stretches," Tom was saying, "it'll turn *itself*. That way, you won't have to force it to move or to be still." His arms bounced up and down in syncopation with the men as if conducting an orchestra, gesturing his meaning. "It makes a lot less trouble for the calf, and for the person, as well."

The men holding the calf became still and waited. Tara knew that Tom had spent an entire lifetime raising and handling endless numbers of these animals, yet he hovered over this particular calf as if it were his own child in someone else's hands, an uncensored desire for the animal's well being in open view for the muscle and brawn around him to see what he saw, feel what he felt. Tara swallowed back a lump in her throat.

At length, the calf lay still while the men stretched and turned its body the way Tom directed. When he was satisfied, the ropers quietly released the animal back into the herd and remounted. The last of daylight was fading from the sky, and dark silhouettes of horses and riders moved in unison, filling in around the calves to shuffle them back toward the gate and out to familiar pasturelands. It was pitch black by the time they returned to the barn, Tara following on foot. The horses that belonged to the ranch were stabled. The rest were loaded into stock trailers and hauled home. Tara waited in the front yard that doubled for a parking lot until Tom emerged from the shadows of the barn to stand beneath the porch light of the ranch house. She walked in his direction, embarrassed by a sudden urge to throw herself at his feet.

"I wanted to thank you for allowing me to watch you work," was what came out. Composed. Safe.

"Sure," Tom nodded without smiling, kindness showing in his eyes anyway.

She stood tongue-tied. How was she supposed to make this day fit into the rest of her life? Tom waited, nodding his head again, as if encouraging her to speak. She heard herself thank him a second time. He looked around as if there was something he needed to do. A second flush of heat rushed to her face, prompting her to say good-bye, turn on her heel, and walk to the car.

2

~shadows~

To empty mankind of error so that Truth may flow into the mind,
is the work before us;
and those commissioned for this work will suffer tribulation
such as has not been since the beginning.

— Mary Baker Eddy
Science and Health

Damp air clung to her icy hands as Tara reached for the door handle, her pale, white skin looking sickly in the shadows. Shivering beneath her coat, she dropped swiftly into the driver's seat of her faded blue Corolla, started the engine, and pushed the heater knobs up to high. From her position, the yellow porch light was all that could now be seen across the ranch's parking lot, a last reminder, as she steered down the drive, that bodies had once stood there and a day had ended. Darkness met her on the deserted road. Large raindrops splattered intermittently on the windshield, leaving the wipers to smear a fine film of dust to mud. At least she wouldn't have to make light conversation with someone and pretend she wasn't feeling what she couldn't explain. But that thought didn't comfort her.

She shook her head, wishing she had the ability of a wet dog who could, in one swift motion, release billions of water droplets from the grip of its matted fur, and with them its heaviness. She blinked and stared out her windshield. A headache lingered, and the night engulfed her. She couldn't escape it after all. Eight years of discipline, aching muscles, exhaustion, and living like a pauper to make ends meet had merely brought her to where she'd been before she started.

What happened? She often asked herself the question, remembering the feeling of promise the day she'd first laid eyes on her competition horse eight years ago. By that time, she had already spent months scouting for an internationally competitive athlete that could match the rigors of upper level training *and* be within the limits of her price range. Although tempted to give it a rest, she hadn't been able to resist absorbing herself in the classifieds section of the *Los Angeles Times* once more while visiting her parents one weekend.

"I can't tell what it is about this ad that appeals to me," she had dared out loud as she stood by the kitchen phone, her cold fingers hesitating before making the move to pick up the receiver and place the call. Hearing no response, she looked up to see her mother engrossed in the more important activity of wiping down the counter with a sponge. Burying her eyes back in the paper, she took a deep breath and dialed the number.

A man who no longer had time for trying his luck with racehorses had placed a five-year-old on the market. The gelding had strained a tendon while galloping on the track during a training session. The strain meant it would be easier to reinjure the leg in the future, but the next day, she had found herself driving a narrow and dusty lane well outside the county limits to where he was stabled. What was to have been an hour-long trip dragged into two, with nothing but sand, rock, and cactus on either side of the road. Just as she thought of turning back, a tune she had never heard before crackled over the car radio, and the wail of a saxophone climaxed before fading into the background. She strained forward, trying to hear the lyrics. "This city desert makes you feel so cold. It's got so many people, but it's got no soul..." Spellbound, she drove on to hear the rest of the song. A longing welled up inside her. As the last strains of music faded into silence, a cluster of barns emerged out of the desert rock.

It was yet another riding stable in disrepair. Paint peeling off wooden siding that was no longer plumb revealed gray, weathered planks underneath. It was a scene more and more common everywhere she went; a result of the ever rising cost of hay and the land it grew on.

"I'm here to look at the horse advertised in the *Times*," she said after finding the stable manager standing in the barn aisle, a sea of Quarter Horses stalled on either side.

After haltering the one lone Thoroughbred, the manager led the unmuscled, ungroomed gelding out of his stall, and turned him loose in the arena. *Another wasted trip*, she thought—until he moved. With his first trot step, animated and powerful, she knew he was good enough. In the four short years that followed, she and her diamond in the rough had become competitive with the top riders at their level and suddenly, her life was going somewhere.

What happened? Even then, four years into her training, she had felt her horse's tension. His displeasure. But who would have argued her success? Certainly not the judges giving her high scores. And then she had been invited by her coach to ride and train in Germany, followed by a grant from the United States Equestrian Team to make it all possible.

Tara straightened her arms against the steering wheel, pressing her torso into the back of her seat while drawing a deep breath into her lungs. Germany, the dream of a lifetime. Germany, the leading nation in competitive dressage. Her quest to ride in the Olympics had suddenly been given a vehicle. Stable owners offered free board for her horse, enabling her to save money during the remaining months before the trip. Farriers donated free shoeing and veterinarians, medical services. A friend wrote an article about her in the newspaper. Others dropped everything to help prepare for her fundraiser dinner, serving food and washing dishes while she spent the evening going from table to table, shaking hands and expressing her enthusiasm and gratitude like a political candidate at election time.

At her going-away luncheon, she had sat alongside friends and students at the restaurant table, laughing her farewell. The two hour haul with her horse before dawn to the Los Angeles airport the following day, followed by ten hours with him in quarantine had flown by in minutes. He reared and sat back against the ropes inside the horse crate when it was pushed and jostled onto a wide lift, then hoisted to the cargo section of the giant Lufthansa 747. But his sweaty angst had not dampened the thrill of standing with him and two other horses as they were strapped and belted into a locked position just before takeoff.

She had acted as the handler for all three horses in exchange for a discounted fare and a seat with the regular passengers. The pilot gave her a key to the rear of the plane, enabling her to keep hay nets stuffed, water buckets filled, and tranquilizers ready for an intravenous injection should any of them become overly agitated. Adrenaline kept her awake for more than two days by the time they landed in Frankfurt. There they waited another four hours for the computers to come back online at customs. Finally, she loaded her horse onto yet another van, which hauled them several more hours to her trainer's Reitschule in Baden Würtenburg. A tiny compartment made for grooms allowed her to stand next to him and watch his nervous fidgeting as they bumped and swayed over the autobahn. The roar of wind and traffic had been the last thing she remembered while leaning against the siding before finding herself in a heap on the hard metal floor, awakened by the screams of her gelding, who wondered why the person standing beside him only a moment before had suddenly vanished behind the partition.

An onslaught of rain pelting the Toyota's windshield startled Tara back into the night. She leaned forward to keep track of the road, the soft thud-thud, thud-thud action of her wipers useless against the deluge. It would be late by the time she arrived home. Outside, her headlights illuminated silhouettes of oaks and sycamores lining the road. Their long limbs loomed upward into leafy branches, forming a broken canopy overhead. A heavy weight filled her stomach, then lightened again as she realized that perhaps the trees provided just enough connecting branches to allow squirrels and insects to make it from one side of the road to the other. How odd that such a thought should comfort her. But maybe that was all she had done the year she'd trained in Germany, somehow finding intermittent moments of hope that paved a way for her to endure her stay at the riding school.

When she had first arrived at the Reitschule, the privilege of working and training there had made her ignore the fatigue that progressively dogged her, day after day. Whenever she ventured into the small neighborhood post office, bank, or grocery store, people wanted to know where she was from and why she was there.

"I am a dressage rider," she had attempted in her awkwardly developing German. "I am here for training."

"Aaaal-so!" they exclaimed in recognition of one of their nation's most popular sports, the "so" pronounced "zo" and emphasized with lifted eyebrows and a nod of approval.

But it had not taken her long to understand exactly what it meant to have Olympic aspirations in a sport that originated in the military. She and three other apprentices shared a full-sized, single-story house built directly over the barn, a common and practical design in many European equestrian facilities. While her room and board were given in exchange for labor, she paid full price for her training in dollars. She was reminded of this each morning as she and the others, all of whom were German citizens and therefore reimbursed an additional stipend for the same labor, rose early to begin their chores. Sleep being the greatest luxury, they spared only a minute in the predawn darkness to fumble with long underwear, jeans, and top layers before filing groggily down tiled steps to the unheated training complex below. Falling temperatures rudely awakened them in spite of the stables being completely enclosed and warmed above freezing from the heat emanating from the mass of equine bodies stalled along either side of the cement aisle.

Grabbing shovels, pitchforks, and wheelbarrows, they began their day by mucking out forty stalls. If they were quick and finished in an hour and a half, they had twenty minutes to run upstairs, eat breakfast, and change into proper riding breeches and boots before running back down to ready ten horses that their trainer, the Reitlehrer, rode by noontime. Horses were groomed in their stalls or in the corridor and bits of straw meticulously handpicked out of their tails. There was a particular way they were saddled, bridled, led through the aisles, and granted permission to enter the arena. Every action was exacting, every buckle tightened hard and in the right way. At the Reitschule, there was a right way for everything. Every other way was wrong.

At the beginning of the morning's training sessions, Tara and the other apprentices filed into the arena to longe the horses in a circle, or ride for twenty minutes to warm and loosen the muscles of their equine subordinates before handing them over, one by one, to the Reitlehrer. The twenty by forty-meter arena, a large, warehouse-like room made slightly homier by wood-paneled walls, was where they trained. The fact that it was completely enclosed shielded them from the winter wind, but unfortunately, not the cold. By the end of January, salt was brought in and mixed into the footing, a six-inch layer of leather shavings recycled from local saddle shops, to keep its normally fluffy texture from freezing solid.

The Reitlehrer, then in his mid-forties, had been gifted a handsome face with a square jaw, straight white teeth, a broad smile, and blue eyes typical of his German ancestry. His height and stature, another pleasing attribute when combined with his amicability in social situations, only added to his knack for intimidation at the Reitschule. When apprentices weren't nimble enough to deliver a readied mount to the arena in time, his barking screams echoed up from the arena, chasing them up the corridor and ordering them to hurry, *"Schneller, schneller, schneller!"*

If faster motor coordination wasn't possible, greater strain and anxiety were. Tara remembered trying to fasten extra reins and training gear to the saddle with shaky fingers, a mixture of leather oil and mold filling her nostrils. More than once, the screams of the Reitlehrer pressured her to drop a line, still only attached at one end, and march blindly with equine in tow down the aisle to the arena, too frantic to care if huge hooves flattened unsecured buckles or clips scraping the cold, hard floor. On her way there, she walked through clouds of steam rising off incoming bodies dripping with sweat from their exertions in the riding hall. The sound of boots scuffling and steel horseshoes clopping on the cement floor added to the mix as horses and humans wove in clockwork fashion around each other through the dim light and narrow spaces.

Each day, the apprentices rode or warmed up three to five horses apiece under the punishing eye of the Reitlehrer, who sat astride another horse in training and snapped corrections at their imperfect maneuvers. Between rides, they swept barn aisles, cleaned tack, and pitchforked a never-ending regeneration of manure from the stalls. The midday break was usually whittled in half by the time they finished the end-of-the-morning chores. All too soon, Tara needed to prepare for her afternoon rides—and by three o'clock, the hectic pace began all over again. Mothers brought ambitious sons and daughters for riding lessons after school while they passed the time knitting sweaters and caps inside the small, heated viewing room above the arena. Tara could not ever remember seeing a flinch or a break in their polite conversation when the Reitlehrer belted out obscenities to their teenaged offspring, his vocal display wafting up through the glass panes from below.

She, the American, whom the other apprentices resented for diverting the attentions of the Reitlehrer, had never been required to endure the direct assault of actual swear words as she rode alongside them. Perhaps her status as an outsider saved her this open ridicule. But his punitive tone was hardly masked by his feigned politeness, and she felt the impact anyway, her stomach remaining in knots throughout the afternoon sessions.

In the evening, adult men and women came after work to ride and feed their horses stale bread treats from home. The barn aisles filled with their chatter until ten o'clock at night when the Reitschule officially closed, leaving the barn empty and silent, Tara's every limb a heavy brick. It was not merely sleep she craved, but relief that was not forthcoming. In the lull, she often found herself staring at tiny particles of hay and dust floating lightly in the musty air, the previous flurry of activity leaving no trace but this rebounding movement. The cement corridor was made darker by the shadows cast across the floor from metal bars encasing the upper portion of every stall like prison cells, leaving no space for a horse to hang its head to the outside.

Inevitably, she forced herself to look at her Thoroughbred, who stood with his head turned away from her, facing the darkest corner of his stall. He had shown little interest in eating since arriving there—an eerie contrast to the other horses munching their nightly rations. By this time, she had tried every available feed without inspiring his interest, and each day finally ended when she turned away and climbed the stairs, getting what little sleep she could before a repeat of everything the following day.

"Why did you stay?" friends asked her after she had arrived home.

At first, she had given the acceptable, upbeat answer. "There were things I learned there—details about dressage movements, the precision, the methodology—that I don't think I would have learned anywhere else."

Now she knew better. *I wasn't ready to give up hope that things might work out.*

Tara snatched her foot off the accelerator, swerving just in time around a tree limb that had fallen across a blind curve. Along the side of the road, rains had caused great chunks of asphalt to break off and slide over the edge, forcing a single lane. She shifted uneasily in her seat, wondering how many miles she'd have to endure the snail's pace. It made her think of Tom that afternoon, his easy manner and slow movements. The drone of his speech. It might drive her crazy, she realized, trying to learn from someone who said so little. But what could she learn from him anyway? He was not a dressage trainer, and she couldn't just give up everything she'd worked so hard for to follow some octogenarian cowboy.

The Corolla continued to climb an unlit, two-lane highway that opened out onto treeless hillsides. The moon shone briefly before vanishing behind the clouds, lighting up reflector bumps lining the no-passing yellow line in the middle of the road. She slowed down to read a traffic sign, and turned along a route pointing to Interstate 5. Taking in another deep breath, she tried to stretch in the tiny space of her car seat, one hand still on the wheel. In spite of the heater, she felt cold and cramped, her body awkwardly trying to adjust from eight to ten hours of daily exertion to half a day cooped up in a car.

To her relief, the road eventually straightened, and she picked up speed. At the entrance to the interstate, she nearly floored the accelerator while merging in front of another car and watched it slowly fall behind in the rear view mirror. As she settled into her lane, a huge semi roared past, shaking her small car in its wake. Moisture oozed from her palms and she alternately unlocked her grip on the wheel to wipe each hand onto a pant leg. Big transport trucks were common on this thoroughfare where the road was wide, flat, and straight. Engineered for speed. Designed to get there. Wherever there was.

"Where are you?" a teacher once asked her.

"Well," she'd hesitated, wondering why he'd asked the obvious. "I'm here."

"Where is here?"

Duh, here is just here!

"You are where your mind is," he had answered before she could speak.

She wondered at the implications of his statement as she exited onto a feeder overpass that merged with Interstate 280. The long cement corridor was the longest route home, taking her west around much of the Bay Area metropolis. But there was less traffic and the scenery more beautiful, although she couldn't see it now because of the night and the rain. She moved into the left lane to pass other drivers insulated inside their individual cars. They seemed far away, even when they were all boxed in together at the stop and go traffic lights of San Francisco. *A famous city*, she said to herself, thinking of songs written over the years, idolizing the rows of pastel houses lining the streets. But all she saw were sterile walls of unfeeling cement, starkly contrasting the open grasslands of two hours before. *And this is our definition of progress?* Thud-thud. Thud-thud, the wipers droned in mechanical time.

Soon, she passed the toll plaza and drove over the Golden Gate Bridge, moving nonstop and faster than the speed limit. Broad yellow lights illuminated the road that extended high above the wind-swept headlands and surrounding bay. *Detached.* She looked past the railing into a sea of black. *We are all so detached.*

Forty-five minutes later, she was turning into her driveway. She parked the car and, head bowed, closed her eyes briefly before climbing stiffly from her seat. Fatigue followed her across the pavement, up the steps, and into her one-room apartment. She didn't bother to eat, but shed her clothes to the floor, and after unfolding her couch into a bed, wrapped herself in familiar blankets and the dark.

3

~signs~

Tolerance for pain may be high, but it is not without limit. Eventually everyone begins to recognize, however dimly, that there must be a better way.

—*A Course in Miracles*

"Look at the horse, Tara!" The excitement in Jed's voice made her look up. His wide eyes smiled down at her, as if he already knew his toddling sister would like what she was about to see. One of his arms was raised, pointing in the distance. His other hand held hers while they waited for the rest of the family to pile out of the car, having just arrived at the park for a picnic. With her eyes, she looked where he pointed. As she spotted the animal at the far end of the parking lot, a burst of gold and white light shone all around it, and then heated her up inside. She squealed and pulled at her brother's hand, wanting to go to it, touch it, be with it. But Jed's hand held firm. How old he seemed at fourteen. She whined and pulled harder.

"Stop acting like a baby!"

The harsh tone snapped the light out as she swung her head around, silenced mid-whine to see her mother's furrowed eyebrows above her. A dark cloud billowed around the back of the familiar head and shadowed the blue eyes. Tara sagged to the ground, forcing Jed to pull her along.

"Stand up," he complained, but at two years of age, she already felt too heavy to bear her own weight.

Everything went dark, and Tara became aware that she had been dreaming. She felt herself wanting to breathe, but found her lungs unable to take in air. She panicked and sucked harder, stomach pumping in and out. Finally managing a gasp, she jerked her eyes open. Panting, she rolled onto her back, struggling against the heaviness in her body. There was a familiar constriction in her throat, as if she wanted to cry, but couldn't.

The world outside was still dark, and she let her eyes close again. A butterfly appeared above her head, fluttering gaily across the old lawn. The sun was making the ivy on the hill in the back yard shimmer. Diamond-shaped leaves draped thickly, gracefully over a gray brick retaining wall barely visible underneath its blanket of green.

Enraptured by the beautiful, broad orange wings, she leapt after it, flying over the grass with no sense of her four-year-old bare feet touching the ground. Somewhere in the distance a high-pitched sound pierced the air. Coming out of some fog, she recognized her own lungs belting out squeals of bliss.

Then, another sound. Yelling from the back door. Halting abruptly, she turned toward the door and pointed to where the butterfly had been. It would explain everything. But the yelling came closer. She kept pointing, hoping it would come back.

A hand pulled her arm and everything blurred. Stiff and numb, she felt her feet drag through the doorway, then inside the house and into her room. She finally stood where the hand had positioned her, facing away from her bedroom door slammed shut. Without moving or turning her head, she waited until the world stopped spinning, then rolled her eyes left. There sat her bed. Still. Silent. She rolled them right. Her closet was much taller than she, its roof high over her head. Strong. Sure of its place. Instinctively, she crawled beneath the clothes hanging inside. Enveloped by the comforting arms of the dark, she sat on the floor, barely noticing the lumpy carpet of shoes pinching lines into her thighs, while hot tears ran down her cheeks.

She cried so hard, head and torso slumped over her crossed legs, she could barely gasp for air.

"You'd better stop doing that, Tara," the muffled warning of her sisters' voices echoed inside her mind. But she had never been able to imitate their silence, even after she'd learned it was what protected them.

Another dream, that's all it is, Tara told herself, her stomach pumping in and out as she found herself struggling for air a second time. Finally succeeding, she made herself come fully awake. *Sleep apnea,* the words came to her. Isn't that what they called it?

She rolled back to her side, slapped her hands over her face, and rubbed, wanting to squish the fog away. In spite of closed lids, she could now detect daylight oozing its way between the broad wooden slats of her antique window blinds. Reluctantly, she opened her eyes, drifting her gaze over pastel colored walls softened by philodendrons that hung from the ceiling, their leafy tentacles framing the tall windowsills. Another plant sat on the fireplace mantel and flowed to the hardwood floor.

The familiar, cozy walls of her studio had been built in the 1940s as a separate unit attached to a larger, remodeled Victorian, originally constructed in the 1800s. The house was situated outside of town on five acres and owned by her neighbors, who occupied the main section. Although she had her own private entrance directly to the outside, another door on the adjoining wall opened into their hallway. It was soothing to think of their friendly welcome whenever she ventured down the hardwood floors to their living room. On such visits, it was common to see three daughters—ages five, seven, and ten—draped over the laps of their parents on the couch, two longhaired corgis and a golden lab sprawled at their feet. The lack of separateness between children and adults had made her feel awkward when she first moved here two years ago. But somewhere along the way, her mistrust had morphed into captivation. Maybe that was the way families were supposed to be.

She sat up in bed. Judging by the feeling in her body, she would need at least fifteen extra minutes to stretch the soreness out of her legs and thighs before putting ice on her back. There were bagels left in the fridge. She could eat one on the way to the ranch. But with that thought, she fell back onto her pillows, wanting to forget the energy it would take to get through this day.

"When you're old enough to go out and get a job," a history teacher in junior high had said once, "how many days of your life do you lose by living for the weekends?" His eyes had shifted across a sea of desks, neatly aligned in rows. "All that time in between is wasted time."

Pointing her toes, she stretched her arms past her head and extended her body to its full length. For a brief instant, the child in her dream flashed through her mind, and she was again chasing after the butterfly. She stopped mid-stretch, wondering if such ecstasy could ever again be possible. Reluctantly, she turned her head to read her clock. Six-fifteen. Owning her own business meant she could take time off whenever she wanted. Her head rolled back, eyes resting on the ceiling. But there was still the issue of having to earn a living.

Turning onto her side, she swept the bed covers away and swung her feet to the floor. After quickly pulling on sweat pants and a sweatshirt left draped over a chair from the day before, she folded her bed back into a couch. On the remaining floor space, cushioned by an area rug, she began a routine, stretching her muscles through a combination of dance and yoga positions, gathered over the years when time had permitted the active pursuit of such interests.

After the last shoulder stand and stretch of her hamstrings, she got up to retrieve an ice pack from the freezer and laid it directly onto the rug. Covering it with a wet towel to make it colder, she sat facing the opposite direction, pulled up the back of her sweatshirt, and winced as she rolled backward, laying her bare skin directly over the ice. She gritted her teeth for the three minutes it took for her back to go numb, extinguishing the fire that had been reignited after riding nine horses two days before.

"What are you trying to ignore and push behind you?" a massage therapist had asked recently upon hearing about the muscle spasms. Tara, sprawled out on the massage table in a half-dazed stupor, had not even tried to answer the question.

In twenty minutes, the ice pack felt warm. After throwing it back into the freezer, she stood in front of a small closet, one hand reaching back against her cold skin, the other stroking the ultra thin section of suede that lined the tails of the shadbelly she wore at horse shows. Her vision blurred over the fine wool material, picturing herself riding alongside Gene Kelly or Fred Astaire.

Waiting on the shelf above were a stack of skintight breeches in muted colors for everyday use. Several all-white pairs had already been washed by hand, dried, and folded in readiness for this year's competitions. Below them hung long-sleeved cotton shirts in various colors and stripes, giving her a professional look while protecting both arms from the sun and sandy grit, churned into the air by horses' hooves. Suddenly aware of the time, she grabbed one off the hanger, threw it across her shoulders, and pulled her arms through the sleeves. It was already 7:30 when she grabbed a bagel and her pack and pushed through the narrow hallway.

She threw the outer screen wide and let it fall against her back while turning to slam the front door closed. She was racing down the red brick steps when she realized she'd forgotten her keys. Turning around just as the screen slapped shut in her face, she flung it wide, leaned into the solid door, and shoved it open. Her hand froze midway to the wall. The hook that normally cradled her wad of keys was empty. She stopped only a moment to think about where they might be before dropping her pack with a thud. In three strides she was back in the apartment, scanning her desk, kitchen table, entertainment cabinet, nightstands, bathroom sink, closet shelves, and fireplace mantel. The second hand ticked away on the battery clock above the sink. Her place wasn't that big. Where were the keys?

She stopped again in the kitchen, telling herself to be rational, but then slammed her fist into the refrigerator instead. It seemed as though the world was conspiring against her, and she wanted to do something terrible to express it. *How unsightly is that!* It was another voice inside her head.

Unsightly. It was a word her mother would have used. "Being angry is absolutely useless," she had often said while rolling her eyes at one of Tara's periodic "outbursts," as she'd dubbed them.

You were one to talk, Tara said to herself now, thinking how ironic it was for her mother to argue about the proper way to control one's anger—like the time she'd been made to wait for her hair curlers to be removed during a once-a-week visit to the Hollywood beauty salon. Instead of asking for the hairdresser's attention, her mother had simply unpinned the plastic cylinders herself, and after letting them bounce and roll onto the counter, walked out with no explanation. She never returned or spoke to him again, in spite of the fact that he had been a family friend for years.

"Well, I wasn't going to sit there forever," she'd made a point of explaining to Tara later. "My silence should have been enough to make him realize what he'd done."

Tara flew out the front door and, throwing the pack onto the passenger seat, saw her keys dangling in the ignition from the night before. She slammed the door, ran to the driver's side, and flopped into the seat of the nine-year-old, faded blue Corolla. Reaching for her sunglasses on the dash, her eyes lit on a small round metal object teetering halfway over the ledge. She plucked it off, recognizing the message pin at once. She'd purchased it days before and had forgotten to give it to a friend. *Too bad,* she said to herself, thinking the adage, printed on one side, would have suited him perfectly.

Wherever you go, there you are, read the Buddhist saying made popular by Jon Kabat Zinn. She flipped the pin over. A mirror was encased on the other side, and she was now staring herself in the face. She threw it to the floor, put her car in gear, and drove down the drive as fast as she could dodge dogs, soccer balls, and various bicycles left strewn over the asphalt.

It was seven miles by back roads to the ranch where she operated her training business. The streets wound through a residential section before opening out onto wide curves that ran between dairy farms and unpopulated hillsides. In fifteen minutes, she turned off the main road onto the adobe driveway that led into the ranch. Steering around potholes and a row of horse trailers, she parked at the top of the lot, closest to where the horses were stabled.

Grabbing her pack, she headed for the main barn that stood at the foot of three hundred acres of green, hilly pastureland. On one side of the barn stood a row of paddocks, one of which housed her Thoroughbred, now muzzle deep in his morning feed.

She paused to watch the circular motion of his jaw as it ground his hay. When had she begun to dread her rides on him? They'd had difficult training sessions before her trip to Germany. But until she went abroad, she had always remained enthusiastic about her ability to overcome their problems. After the first two months at the Reitschule, however, everything changed.

Wintertime had come, and she would never forget one December morning in particular. She and the German apprentices had sat slumped around the breakfast table after their ritual predawn stall mucking. On that day, the Reitlehrer surprised them all by climbing the stairs to their living quarters, his tall frame towering above them as he announced that Tara's Thoroughbred should be the first horse readied for him to ride. She stared up at him, not wanting to register the threat beneath his smooth tone — or leave her unfinished breakfast.

But leave she did, wincing at her gelding's protruding ribs as she tacked him up and led him inside the arena, his smaller frame even more of a contrast to the heavier European warmbloods. After warming him up at trot and canter on the longe line for twenty minutes, she placed the reins of his bridle into the Reitlehrer's hand, then walked toward the bleachers stationed outside the arena to watch. It was the first time her trainer had agreed to ride him since their arrival that fall. *How interesting it will be*, she thought, *to finally get to see someone else on him.*

She let herself out a side gate stationed along the five-foot-high, solid tongue-and-groove railing, or "stirrup guard," slanted outward at an angle from the ground to make room for the protrusion of a rider's foot as it hung down the horse's side. Although the arena was also completely enclosed, it was separated from the barn by a wall and did not benefit from the living heat of the animals. She seated herself on the hard wooden planks, draping her down coat around her knees and hugging them to her chest for warmth. By the time she looked up, the Reitlehrer had already mounted and was moving her horse forward into a trot. Muscles hardened by the demands of daily gymnastic exercise bulged around the gelding's skeleton, and in spite of the frosty air, it wasn't long before his black coat was covered in sweat.

Tara's eyes followed her horse's every footfall as her trainer moved him rapidly through the simple exercises — walk to trot transitions and changes of direction — to the more difficult flying changes of lead at the canter, in which both front legs and hind legs were supposed to skip in unison across the arena. At the first attempt of that movement, her gelding's hind legs didn't switch with the front. The Reitlehrer gave the cue again, but her horse's head and neck merely strained against the bit.

Tara could still see the way the blood rushed into her trainer's face, the way his jaw clenched tight when he jabbed his spur into her horse's sides. In response, her gelding's muscles became more rigid and his stride shorter and more cramped. Still, the Reitlehrer did not give in, and around and around the arena they went. A swelling appeared over her horse's ribs. A dark trickle oozed down his barrel. Minutes seemed like hours as the sound of her trainer's open-mouthed gasps mixed with her Thoroughbred's raspy breath, forcing billows of white steam from both nostrils flaring red.

Then he bolted, front legs flailing in the air before pounding the earth as he galloped frenetically along the wall. With head and neck straining toward the ceiling, bloodied froth spilled from the sides of his gaping mouth as the Reitlehrer repeatedly jerked on the reins, trying to bring him back under control. For a moment, her horse slowed and it looked as though he would acquiesce, his deer eyes drooping, narrowing. Prey cornered by its predator. But in the next moment, he made a leap toward the wall, a desperate attempt for freedom finally sending him, her prized gelding, her promised vehicle to the prestigious pinnacle of international dressage, running up the slanted stirrup guard like a Fred Astaire horror movie.

Bam, bam, bam! His shod hooves pounded the wooden panels before scraping over their surface as he slid back down to the ground, deftly shuffling his legs to regain an upright carriage on all fours. He would have jumped out had there been an opening in that perfectly enclosed building.

This should not be happening, some far distant voice inside her head cautioned. But she did not say the words aloud. She just sat there, her heart frozen into the pit of her stomach, wondering if she could endure however long it would be before the ride ended. When at last her trainer stopped and brought her horse to stand in the middle of the arena, she bolted off the bench, reaching him just in time to catch the reins the Reitlehrer flung from his hands as he dismounted. Without speaking or looking her in the eye, he simply turned to another mount, already tacked up and waiting for him, leaving her to lead her horse away.

At the exit, she reached for the rubber squeegee that hung from its hook on the wall. She had never seen so much sweat run from a horse's coat as she pressed it over her gelding's sides and down his neck. His breathing was still heavy when she led him up the corridor, through the barn aisles, and outside the big, double doors to the courtyard, walking him cool. Even now, she cringed at the thought of the harried and dazed look in his eyes as he seesawed his jaw while following alongside her, his angst lingering long after the ride had ended.

It had taken a week of nightmares before she'd been brave enough to walk into the Reitlehrer's office and politely attempt a discussion, wanting to know how he had justified his actions that December morning.

"I've seen the way you Americans train," he'd answered. "It's like watching a fairy tale. And you know, your horse is eleven years old. He ought to know better. He needs a firm hand. How else are you going to get anywhere?"

It was a subject rarely discussed openly outside the business. High strung and sensitive horses like hers were usually sold if there was another with "a more suitable temperament for this type of training."

"Be professional about it and don't get so attached," the Reitlehrer had continued. "You could get a good price for him."

Yes, I could get a good price for him, she'd thought to herself when the 747 landed back in Los Angeles late the following summer. His level of training and ability had raised his value as high as the full price on a house in many parts of the country. But by then, he had become nearly impossible for most people to ride, so who would buy him?

Tara let out a deep breath, the sound making her aware of herself still standing at the edge of the ranch's parking lot, staring at the ground. Her pack had slid off her shoulder and now sat by her feet collecting dirt. She looked up to see her gelding with his nose still buried in alfalfa. His ribs no longer showed, and the once startling angle of his shoulder and hindquarter had again rounded into a graceful padding of muscle and flesh. But today this view of natural beauty did nothing to cheer her. She reached for her pack, slung it back over her shoulder, and resumed her way to the barn.

4

~busyness~

The making of time to take the place of timelessness
lay in the decision to be not as you are.

—A Course in Miracles

The smell of dust and rotting lumber greeted Tara as she strode up the sloping walkway to the double sliding doors of the main barn. A few years earlier, the owners of this private boarding and training facility had sold out their family dairy business in a government buyout program. Their intention had been to convert the original milking stanchions into well-constructed box stalls. But somewhere along the way, money had been diverted, and now three rows of half-finished stalls only partially spanned the dirt floor. The barn itself was situated at the base of a hill without proper drainage. Every winter, rainwater flowed directly off higher ground and straight down the aisles, flooding her office and the adjoining tack room. Each morning, this sight of unfinished construction greeted her, exposing one more dream that hadn't come to fruition.

Just inside the entrance, Adon was throwing manure and shavings out of a stall into the wheelbarrow parked outside the door. She couldn't see him behind the plywood walls, but heard his resonant tenor vibrato as he sang his heart out in Spanish. God, she wished she could feel that good.

"Buenos dias," she called, not stopping to hear his reply.

Midway down the aisle, she stopped in front of her office door, set down her pack, and fumbled with her keys in the lock. She turned the knob slowly, a feeling of being watched making her hesitate. She looked up to see Wet Paw, a young tabby cat, stretched out along the barn rafters, head resting between his forearms, staring down at her. The cat had gotten his name from his habit of pawing at his clean water bowl, then lapping at the surface with his tongue while standing

ankle deep, the once clear liquid growing muddy from whatever
stable debris might have been wedged between his toes. He was one of
several cats belonging to another trainer who also worked on the
premises. But because he hadn't gotten along with the other felines
that claimed territory around the ranch, Tara agreed to let him live
near her office.

Now he could often be seen lurking in high, dark places that
offered protection from the wild fox, coyote and the misstep of a
horse's hoof. As long as someone else was buying his food, she didn't
mind feeding him, figuring that a cat's mousing instincts were always
good around the stable. Otherwise, she was too engrossed in her day
to pay much attention.

Once inside her office, she set her planner on top of her desk and
opened it to today's date. The desk was ugly and drab, but made of an
indestructible steel alloy, a fitting design, she thought, for a barn full of
animals known to kick holes through walls, pull down metal feeders,
chew on wood, and lean on automatic waterers until pipes broke and
sent water spewing into the air. Seven needed to be ridden before one
o'clock.

A row of knee-high black boots waited alongside the wall, shiny
from yesterday's end-of-the-day polishing. Tara grabbed her pair and
a set of boot pulls to force the tightly fitted leather over each pant leg.
In less than a minute, she was marching out to the paddocks to halter a
gray mare and lead her back to the crossties. With a brush in each
hand, she groomed the face, neck, barrel and all four legs in less than a
minute, then hoisted a black dressage saddle onto her high back before
securing splint boots around each foreleg for protection from bumps
and bruises. She stood on her tiptoes, reaching to insert a smooth
metal snaffle inside the mare's mouth. The horse lifted her head to
avoid the bridle straps that fit around her sensitive ears, but Tara was
persistent. Once inside the fenced arena, she didn't bother with a
mounting block, but slipped her foot into the stirrup directly from the
ground and vaulted on.

Following a quick warm up, she shortened the reins and rode
eight-meter circles, shoulder-in, haunches-in, half pass, canter-walk
transitions, extended trot, walk pirouettes. In her mind, she checked
off each compulsory movement required in the next show, less than
three weeks away. Sitting solidly on both seat bones, her legs, hands,
and arms exerted separate cues coordinated together, like words in a
sentence that the horse understood by feel. A squeeze of her fingers, a

leg shifted forward an inch, or a brace in her lower back were all cues for a specific response—cues that, hopefully, were subtle enough not to be seen by an onlooker. Meanwhile, the mare's stride expanded and collected through tight turns, straight lines, and circles.

Tara knew how to get a lot from a horse. Years of training had made her strong and adept at multi-tasking her body parts. Germany had taught her how to manage her time and accommodate a higher volume of horses in training. Forty-five minutes later, she was leading the mare back to the barn, just as Lena, her assistant, was walking up from the parking lot.

"How did it go?" Lena paused before asking. Usually Tara's Thoroughbred was ridden first thing every day.

"Not bad," Tara replied, pretending not to notice Lena's stare. She was not prepared to talk about why she had decided not to ride her own horse that day, and the two barely spoke as they saddled two more.

After five horses had been ridden, they took a ten-minute break around noon, standing outside her office inhaling bites of baked tofu and sautéed vegetables while their last two mounts, already saddled and bridled, stood in the cross-ties, waiting to be ridden. She was just finishing her ride on a chestnut Quarter Horse in the indoor arena at the lower end of the parking lot as Carey, her one o'clock lesson, led a horse out of the barn and up to the mounting block. Tara inhaled a deep breath, knowing the afternoon was only just beginning. Wasting no time, she turned and rode out of the gate.

"I'll be back down in one minute," she yelled to Carey as she trotted past, and was already swinging to the ground before her chestnut had come to a full stop in front of the barn doors. She quickly rolled up her stirrups and handed the reins to Lena, who would untack and groom him. She ran to her office to grab a bottle of water, and paused while unscrewing the lid, taking sips in between breaths. She needed to be in a settled frame of mind to teach effectively, she counseled herself, and took a moment to stare at the wall and consider how long she had been involved with horses.

Tara has great enthusiasm for showing the other children how to ride the carousel horses, her nursery school teachers had written in their report to her mother when she was only three, referring to the large metal imitations lined up along the walkway bordering the playground.

"How lucky you are," everyone but her parents had been telling her since then, "that you know your passion—that you love what you do."

She exhaled loudly after a gulp of water. In spite of her parents' affluence and her constant begging for a horse throughout her childhood, they had viewed her interest in riding as superfluous, not an activity with any real value. Certainly not as a potential vocation. It was not until she was almost sixteen that her mother had driven her to the bank to withdraw $400 to buy her first horse—nearly all the money she had saved from the five-dollar-a-month allowance that her grandfather had provided each of his grandchildren from the time they were born.

Only a year had passed before she'd moved away from home, anxious for a life away from the big city and her parents. Finding an apartment a hundred miles north in Santa Barbara and desperate for a job, she called every stable in town, eventually arranging for an interview at Gene's Riding Academy. The sign that hung over the entrance read: "Lessons and Trail Rides," and dangled off its hook at one end. A row of paddocks made of old boards nailed together and reinforced with bailing wire lined one side of the gutted driveway. On the opposite side, a very small riding arena had been carved out of the slope. A workman pushed a wheelbarrow through the gate and dumped a load of fresh manure, gathered from the paddocks, directly over the solid granite base—a perfect recipe, she had found out later, for making the footing too slippery to ride on when the rains came.

Just seventeen at the time, she'd lied about her age to her would-be boss to add two years of credibility to a background only sparsely dotted with professional training.

"There's no money in it," Gene had said to her in his Brooklyn accent after she'd been "hired" as trail guide and assistant to Sidley, an instructor only a year older than she. "But maybe som'im down the road will toyn up an' we can make a deal."

A month passed before she realized that he had never intended to pay her. But even with her savings nearly depleted, she was determined to work doing the one thing she loved. Seven days a week, she tromped behind the barn in rubber boots to retrieve lesson and rental horses from a small dirt "pasture" carved around the trees. During the winter, the number of animals per square inch made it impossible for a blade of grass to grow. Rains that would have normally sprouted seed turned the small area into shin-high mud soup instead, often sucking a shoe straight off a hoof—or her boot off her foot when she waded in to halter a horse. Wooden planks that originally defined the perimeter were left to rot where they fell.

Eventually, they were replaced with electric wire that gave horse or human a disturbingly percussive jolt if either made the mistake of touching it—which she did more than once.

More weeks without pay went by when, one afternoon, she found herself in the tiny arena assisting Sidley at the start of a routine after-school lesson, holding horses for children as young as seven while their small, untrained fingers fumbled with the chinstraps on their crash helmets. How light their bodies seemed when she hoisted them onto English saddles, then adjusted stirrups and untwisted leather reins to be held flat inside the tiny fists.

The lesson had barely begun when Gene called Sidley to him outside the gate. Tara waited in silence as the two of them huddled, conversing in gestures and whispered tones.

"Can you watch them for a minute while I run down to the barn?" Sidley called to her.

"Sure," she waved the instructor on, assuming something important had come up.

She turned back to face the seven children riding around her in a circle, suddenly realizing she was alone. And in charge. She looked back over her shoulder and down the drive toward the barn, but by that time, both Sidley and Gene were nowhere in sight. Turning back to the children, her mind went blank. What in the world was she supposed to say to them?

"Put your knees together!"

It had come out stiff. Harsh. Like an army officer. The kids groaned, but to Tara's amazement, they pulled their feet out of their stirrups and tried to hoist both legs up so that their right knee touched their left knee above the pommel, building inner thigh muscles that would be used for jumping later on. Some couldn't do it, so she went around to each one, supporting their legs until all of them managed to hold the position on their own.

Then she thought of a different exercise. Then another, and another. Their uncensored, awkward efforts filled her with renewed inspiration, and she praised heavily until young frowns of concentration blossomed into open smiles. She had never expected to feel such exhilaration, never imagined that being witness to another human being's self-discoveries could make her forget her own life so completely. And hadn't only a few minutes passed when Gene, back at the gate, waved at her? There was such warmth in his smile. Sidley hadn't returned. Only then did she realize she'd been set up.

"Everyone's parents are waiting. It's past time to quit," Gene tried hard to keep from laughing.

She looked at the parking lot above the arena, startled to see that five or six cars had pulled up only a few feet away. Her watch read 5:15.

"So! You like teaching?" His eyes kept their twinkle as she came through the gate, directing a single-file line of dismounted children, each leading their own horse back to the barn.

Not knowing the first thing about putting what she felt into words, she simply nodded. Vigorously. From then on, Gene gave her the after-school classes. She earned a dollar per head in cash, five days a week. It was barely subsistence living. But she managed to find a room in an elderly man's house for thirty-five dollars a month, a reduced rate in exchange for vacuuming, doing laundry, and washing the dirty dishes left on the counter, piled high with rotten food wedged between plates. The sight and smell repulsed her, but the exchange provided a sanctuary in which to worry over notes and profiles of her classes every night as she searched for ways to better say what she had steadily been learning to say in a hundred different ways, hoping to find the one word or phrase that best helped the child who didn't understand. By the time she actually turned nineteen, she already felt old and longed for a way to explain to her unblemished charges how the adults they were trying so hard to become would never be as good as who they already were.

That was nearly twenty years ago! Tara took a last gulp of water before stepping out of her office and striding down to the arena. Gone were the days when most of her students were children—or even teenagers. Dressage was a serious, exacting sport, requiring in-depth study and concentration. Most kids wanted to be galloping over the hills or jumping fences.

Carey, well into adulthood and a mother of two, was already engaged in a warm-up routine when Tara reached the arena. She stood watching for a moment before commenting. Instructor and student hadn't gotten far into the lesson before the latter burst into tears.

"He's heavy in my hands." Carey forced the words through her teeth.

Tara, taking a deep breath, looked for a way to take the situation at face value. "Turn him in a circle. The bend in his body will help to release his tension." She watched Carey do as asked and saw her horse soften on the reins. "That's better."

"He's still heavy."

"He looks lighter to me."

"Well, he's not."

Without ire, Tara made another suggestion. Then another, and another, doing what she had learned to do so long ago until, finally empty of tears, Carey conceded that something had worked.

"My husband doesn't like it when I spend time here," she confessed after allowing her horse to walk and cool down on a loose rein.

"How come?" Tara kept her voice soft.

"Oh, he's jealous of my time with the horses. And he doesn't have any idea of how much money I spend on training." Tears began filling her eyes again.

"You don't tell him?"

Carey shook her head.

Tara pursed her lips. Appreciation for her student's confession mixed with resentment the way it did every time her job required her to become parent and therapist—on a trainer's salary—to one of her adult students. The responsibility seemed awkwardly misplaced, most of her clients seeming far better off than she. But somehow, she could never quite keep from being the strong one. It was what they needed. And she had finally become important to someone.

After Carey left the arena, Tara stayed to teach three more hour-long sessions. At dusk, she walked slowly back up to the barn. At the crossties, her tired hands reached inside a bucket for a sponge and wiped the sweat and caked mud off her boots, soaped the remaining bridles from her morning rides, and picked up everything left in the aisle to hang neatly inside the tack room. The stable yard was void of activity as she locked the office door and hung the key on a nail hidden on the backside of the building. Grabbing the layers of clothing that accommodated unpredictable weather, she walked out to the parking lot, relieved by the thought of letting the machine on wheels do the work of getting her home again.

5

~secrets~

If the inside of a person is bothered,
it's for sure that the outside of a horse is going to show it.

— Tom Dorrance

Tara walked up the brick walkway, remembering nothing of the drive home from work. Inside the house, she let her belongings lie strewn over the kitchen table and, standing in front of the refrigerator, quickly made a five-minute dinner of leftovers. She left a small pile of dishes and plastic food containers in the sink and made her way to the bathroom. After shedding her clothes and waiting for the hot water to make its way through the pipes, she stood, head bowed, directly under the showerhead, watching the initially clear liquid turn gray and brown against the white porcelain.

She rubbed a towel over muscles now warm and limp, then threw on her sweats before bare-footing it back through the narrow hallway, past the kitchen, and into her living room. Her neighbors had left the day's mail on the corner table and, rummaging through the pile, she caught sight of a folded sheet of paper. Curious, she unfolded it to its full size and recognized the flyer from the day before, the name Tom Dorrance splashed across the front. Mindlessly, she folded it back into the stack of unwanted mail that she tossed into the paper recycle bin stashed underneath the table.

Pressing the play button on her answering machine by rote, she grabbed pen and paper to write down messages and was mildly startled by the sound of her sister's voice.

"Hi, Tara. It's Crystal. Just called to say hi. I was wondering if you'd be coming out for a visit this summer. I'll try you back in a couple of days. Talk to you soon."

She reached forward to press the stop button, silencing subsequent messages. If only it were that easy to put her finger on the vague sense of unease that she felt every time she heard from one of her three siblings. Now living in separate parts of the country, they were quick to remind each other how much they still cared, yet each kept in contact infrequently, usually over the holidays and birthdays with brief cards or letters—or an occasional phone call.

As a child, she had been the closest to Crystal who, in spite of a ten-year age difference, had always been welcoming whenever Tara ventured down the hallway to her sister's bedroom. The cool linoleum tile was soothing underneath her bare feet as she padded them silently through the open door to sit on one of the twin beds. At the time, she hadn't thought to consider the inconvenience she might have caused Crystal, often interrupting her oldest sister's evening studies to beg for colored pencils and a drawing pad. This she eagerly hovered over, awkwardly attempting the shape of a horse—interrupting Crystal several more times just to make sure she'd gotten the head or legs in proportion to the body.

On weekends, she wandered in as well, the way a cat would when craving a loving touch, staring in awe as Crystal's self-taught fingers strummed a guitar. She loved learning the folk songs they sang together, trading off who would sing melody or harmony. The first time her sister placed the pear-shaped wooden box in her own lap, it felt awkward, her hands clumsy in their attempt to pluck its nylon strings. But when Crystal said she could learn to play, she knew she could.

In that room, the two had sometimes stood side by side, tiptoed on the edge of the bed to look out the high windows above, getting a glimpse of the narrow side yard separating their house from their neighbor's. One afternoon, they caught their female cat mating with a stray, Tara's freckled cheek pressing against her sister's smooth complexion while Crystal explained how babies were made. Their contrasting hair color, Tara's blonde against Crystal's dark brown, did little to make Tara feel that there was any difference or distance between them. Crystal had always been there.

She was there in the evenings, as well, when their parents were not, or during the day on weekends. Even when Crystal had her own friends over to the house, Tara was included in many of their activities. Quiet conversations about pet fish, horses, and whether people were born into the world more than once were equally the norm and let her know that, whenever her sister was close, it was okay to be alive.

One day at school, she heard a friend talk about an aunt that had recently suffered a heart attack. By the following morning, she was sure she would die of the same thing, a heavy pain having mysteriously grown around the left side of her chest. Anticipating a scoffing look from her parents, she thought twice about telling them. But by late afternoon, shaky and forlorn, she dared her way through the familiar L-shaped corridor.

"Well, you can lie down in my bed if you like." Crystal looked up reluctantly from high school papers that covered her desk, leaving only lap space for the massive chemistry book lying open on her knees. Blue-gray eyes bordered by long, dark lashes held Tara's gaze with a warning, until a few moments later, a softer expression won over, as it always had, acknowledging the chronic worry that would later leave a solid crease between Tara's brows.

After tucking her youngest sister under the covers, Crystal sat on the edge of the bed. The weight of the familiar body close by made Tara squirm. Should she say it? She looked up again, Crystal's eyes resting on hers. Waiting.

"Do you think it could be my heart?" she blurted in a whisper.

For a moment, the blue gray eyes simply stared back, blank and expressionless. Then the roof of a mouth lined with straight white teeth was all Tara saw as Crystal's head punched back and laughter filled the room. Tara was soon laughing, too, the pain magically dissolving from her chest.

Tara stared at the floor of her apartment, the pen she had grabbed to write down her phone messages lay still in her hand. She had not planned to visit Crystal in Iowa this year, a contrast to her previous efforts to see both sisters in the Midwest every summer. Two years before, she'd wondered what would happen if she stopped being the one to chase after them. Two years ago had been the last time she'd seen either of them.

"It's harder for those of us with families to travel," was what Crystal said. Of course. It made perfect sense. Except that both sisters hadn't stopped flying clear across the country, with or without families or husbands, to see their parents. Or to take vacations. Not even her brother had ever made the fifty-minute flight north from Los Angeles to see her.

She picked up the phone and punched the long distance numbers on her receiver. Six-thirty California time would be eight-thirty Crystal's time — still early enough to call.

"It's Tara," she spoke, hearing her sister's soft "hello" on the other end. "I just got your message."

"Oh, hello. How are you?"

"Fine. How are you?"

"Just fine." There was a pause. Tara took in a breath to fill in the gap, but Crystal beat her to it. "I didn't know what your plans were, but I called to see if you'd be coming out this year."

"It's nice of you to check in." Tara was acutely aware of how polite they were being. "And I'd love to come. But I'm so busy with work and horse shows, it would be hard for me to get away—so I hadn't really planned a trip out there this year."

"Gee, that's too bad. Will you be taking *any* vacation?"

"Well, later in the fall, I might visit a friend who just moved down to LA. It's a quick flight, and fares are cheap these days."

"Oh. Well, that's nice. When are you going?"

"Probably around Thanksgiving."

"Will you be stopping by to see Mom and Dad?"

"I hadn't planned on it."

"I'm sure they'd love to see you."

Tara raised her eyebrows, and then winced.

"Dad's health is failing," Crystal went on. "Did you know that he's on oxygen all the time now?"

"Jed mentioned it."

"I think we're all concerned about what will happen with Mom if he dies."

"Mmm," Tara was trying hard to remain neutral. "Do you think she'll need care?"

"It's hard to say. I think Dad will leave her in good shape financially. But otherwise, I guess we'll have to just wait and see."

"Okay."

There was another awkward silence.

"Well, it's getting late here, and I've got school to teach tomorrow." Crystal seemed ready to get off.

"All right. Thanks for the invitation. Maybe next year."

"Sure. Bye now."

Tara put down the receiver and exhaled with pursed lips, her cheeks ballooning with the compressed air still trapped inside her mouth.

The sound of the alarm the next morning startled her from sleep. Groaning, she flung the covers over her head, and minutes passed before she could convince herself to extend her legs outside the sheets and pull her body out of bed. Throughout the day at the ranch, she couldn't quite bring herself to move at her normal pace, finding herself behind schedule at the end of every hour, all the while pretending as if she was glad to be there. What was happening to her?

The sun hung low in the sky by the time the last of her students finished their post-lesson grooming, stabled their horses, and left for home. Adon had already fed, and the only sound was that of equine molars grinding their hay, a feeling of contentment echoing off the walls as she led her Thoroughbred, saddled and bridled, through the barn aisles to the lower arena.

She began a warm up over the dusty footing, ignoring her gelding's immediate pull on the reins. But in twenty minutes, still working on simple transitions from walk to trot, trot to canter, her hands were cramping, biceps bulging, and the burning sting of salty sweat trickled into her eyes and down her back. She held the reins tighter, determined to out-persevere his resistance until he gave to the bit and softened the contact. But he only pulled harder, his black coat covered in sweat. Her moistened breeches stuck like glue to the saddle as he leaned his weight to one side, torquing his body. She poked him with her spur to straighten him back.

"Obedience," read the official rulebook of the American Horse Shows Association, "is the horse's mental willingness and physical ability to submit to the rider's will."

She had memorized the phrase. But her spur did nothing to cause her horse to submit. Instead, the pungent smell of his exertions increased and mingled with her own as he strained against her grip. Flaring nostrils blew sprays of mucous into the still air. She saw the quickening up and down motion of his front legs as rivulets of sweat ran all the way down to the ground. She had been here with this horse many times before, feeling the familiar ache through her arms. The thought occurred to her that she might not win this battle. She should just stop — do something to circumvent yet another confrontation.

She did not stop. Instead, her horse's escalating defiance only made her more determined to make him soften his pull and maneuver his body the way she wanted him to. Gritting her teeth, she held firm as he flipped his head to free a rein from her grip. She snatched it back, jerking his head straight. He pulled again, harder this time.

As his head turned to the side, she could see his jaw, and then the fiery spark of red that splashed through his deer brown eyes. It was the red spark that made her catch her breath, then recoil with a stabbing pain in her gut as an image of her mother's eyes shot darts into hers. What was she yelling?

In the distance, Tara heard a loud groan and felt a tremendous strain that pulled through her arms and back before she realized that her agile Thoroughbred was leaping high in the air, making her clutch the reins tighter for balance. In his frenzy, her horse had leapt toward the wide steel railing that enclosed the arena. Already the silver pipes were coming at them, and she knew it was all over. In the next instant he would be mangled in steel, and she with him.

She was not aware of making the decision to jump, but felt herself flying out of the saddle, her legs swinging back and over the wide rump as her arms pushed away. In the next moment, she was crouched on the ground, clawing at the sandy footing with her fingers the way she had grabbed the ocean floor many times before when tossed violently by a wave. She sucked in air, and a giddy awe filled her. She had landed on her feet, steady and alive. Then, remembering where she was, she jerked her head up, expecting to see her horse's legs and hooves flailing and broken in the silver railing. But she could only stare in awe. Somehow, miraculously, he had cleared the bars and was already galloping through the parking lot and into the barn.

She had barely stood up when Adon came running down. A horse in flight without its rider often meant serious injury, and he had wasted no time.

"That horse has a screw loose," he said as he climbed through the bars toward her. She nodded solemnly in return. Horses were powerful, dangerous animals. Such behavior was unacceptable.

Knowing she should not end her ride on such a note, her mind wandered over her arsenal of training lines and draw reins in the tack room, equipment she had not used since Germany. She turned to march toward the barn, but after two steps, she stopped. Had it come to that again? Is that what it took to ride dressage?

"I've put him in a stall for you," Adon broke into her thoughts. "I can let him cool off inside this evening, and turn him out for his dinner later tonight."

She looked at him, wondering if he'd read her mind. "I'd be grateful," her voice was trembling.

Instead of following him back to the barn, she walked directly to her car. Without removing her boots, or fetching her driver's license from her pack still in her office, she drove home with a painful knot in her throat. How much less complicated her life would be if only she loved tennis or golf or skiing or any other inanimate thing in the world of sports — the way she used to love to ride.

Early the next morning, she saw at once that Adon had turned her gelding out into his paddock as promised. After filling Wet Paw's food dish and organizing her desk, she went outside to let herself into his paddock. He had his nose to the ground, muzzle deep in a pile of alfalfa, and although he rolled his eye in her direction, he kept perfectly still as she approached. When she was three feet away, she pulled up short. *How ironic*, was the first thought to enter her mind. Adon's kindness in bathing him free of dirt and sweat the night before only made the horror of yesterday's ride more visible in the morning sunlight. The ungloved hand that flew to her mouth in response to sudden nausea, now reached shakily forward against her will, drawing her ever closer until her fingertips landed delicately over the welts and swollen places on his tender sides.

Am I capable of this?

Before this moment, she had not remembered using her whip on him, and even as the proof of it lay in open view, her actions remained a blur. How easy it had been to despise the Reitlehrer's jaw of steel and unyielding hands that morning in Germany three years ago, so clear it was from her detached perspective that his demands of this four-legged creature were entirely unreasonable. How justified she had felt in pointing a finger at the way he rode, at how he acted, who he was. Suddenly, she couldn't fathom why her horse now stood peacefully eating his breakfast, allowing her to be near him; touch him.

She turned and walked back through the gate to her car, turned on the ignition, and drove off the ranch. To somewhere. Anywhere. Surrounding pastures graced with oak trees and the interplay of sloping hillsides alongside the road passed unnoticed. Distant Victorian farmhouses that would normally have been brought to the forefront of her imagination remained tucked back away from the road and invisible. She drove on, vaguely aware of the sky changing from red to pink to light gray as the sun rose higher through a row of clouds.

An hour had come and gone by the time she found her way back. She said nothing to Lena or anyone about her absence and moved mechanically through the rest of her day. When she arrived home from work that evening, she barely paused to set her pack down before going to her answering machine, as habit had trained her. The flashing red light blinked on and off, on and off, on and off. She stared for a moment in silence, her finger hovering over the play button. She then turned abruptly and made her way back through the hallway, out her front door, down the steps, out the front gate, and into the street. She walked. Only when the black of night found her in a place along the road she didn't recognize, did she stop and glance at her wrist. Even if she hadn't already taken off her watch, she wouldn't have been able to see anything.

It's too late to care what time it is.

She turned and headed home again.

6

~kismet~

We don't see things as they are; we see them as we are.

— Anais Nin

Tara reached over her desk in the hallway, glad to be turning the page on her wall calendar to March and the promise of warmer weather. She and Jolene had made plans to get together today, and with breakfast bagel in hand, she threw her duffle bag onto the back seat of her car and sped southbound along a sunny California coast. The odometer on her Corolla read nearly 200,000 miles, but the engine purred smoothly. It was a perfect day for a "weekend" trip—her weekend being midweek to accommodate clients who worked normal jobs and could only ride their horses on Saturdays and Sundays—and she readily found herself soaking in the trees and seashore while letting her mind wander over the endless road, desperately craving the useless hours.

It was midmorning by the time she turned off the inland highway onto the dirt drive to Jolene's training facility. The place was rustic, but tidy and picturesque. Wooden post and rail fencing enclosed the house, outdoor arena, and stable yard. Beyond that were hilly pastures, cross fenced and dotted with horses, necks extending down to graze the lush grass so abundant this time of year. But the sight of the barn looming, suddenly reminded her of her own life—endless sweat dripping off her in one season, frozen to her skin in the next. Frowning, she bounced through the gate.

She drove up to join a row of cars in the parking area. The Corolla remained in idle as she stared out the window. When at last her fingers groped for the ignition and turned the keys to their off position, her body shook with the engine's final rattle. She climbed out of the car onto legs that were lead. Catching movement out of the corner of her eye, she turned, startled by Jolene's energetic demeanor as she strode out of the barn. Embarrassed at herself, Tara smiled and nodded, trying to look normal. Her friend wore the same stretch breeches that she usually wore when dressed for riding—a soft suede horseshoe panel inserted around the seat and inseam for close contact with the saddle—and an added expense on a trainer's salary. Jolene's black leather boots made a soft crunching sound over the thick layer of wood chips spread around the yard to absorb moisture from the rains before the ground turned to mud.

"You chose the perfect time to come down," she called. Her upbeat tone only made Tara feel heavier. "I'm having Tom Dorrance come by and help me with a couple of my horses in—" she checked her watch, "just about half an hour."

Tara nodded politely as Jolene came around the nose of her car to give her a hug.

"How was your drive down?"

"Fine."

"Well," Jolene paused, registering Tara's dull monotone, "you're welcome to just hang out here, or you can watch. You probably came here to get away from training horses."

Tara nodded again, forcing a smile. "It's okay."

"I think you'd find it worthwhile, though. I have a couple of stallions I need help with. One of them's the one I brought back from Germany. You remember?"

"Yeah. I remember." During Tara's year in Germany, she had gone with the Reitlehrer to an international horse show in Aachen and there had met Jolene, who was looking to purchase a competition horse. The one she found and bought had already been going under saddle for some time.

"Well, he's six now. Recently, I started having problems with him rearing."

"Really? What happens?"

"Well, just as I ask him to go forward, he'll plant his feet, then stand straight up on his hind legs, twisting his head around to snap at my boots while his front legs are pawing the air."

Tara's eyes grew wide, imagining the agility it would take a horse to coordinate such a maneuver. She had trainer friends who pulled horses over backwards with the reins to try to cure them of rearing. The challenge was to swing out of the way before being crushed by the mount as both fell to the ground. One person she knew had recently broken a leg, an arm, and a collarbone by not timing things just right.

"It's the only way to really teach them a lesson," he had said. "It makes them afraid to try it again."

Her own gelding had reared over backwards in Germany, making a frantic effort to back away from the confinement of the draw reins — lines that ran from the girth to the bit, acting like a pulley and giving the rider more leverage to keep the horse's head in a tucked position. She was lucky to have already been standing on the ground, lucky he hadn't split his head open or broken his back. She closed her eyes, wanting to erase the thought.

"Then," Jolene said emphatically, bringing Tara back, "I have a three-year-old Lipizzaner stallion. Sometimes he won't let you put a halter on. Other times he'll lunge and strike at you with his front feet when he's led out of the paddock. So he's just been sitting in there for awhile," Jolene stuck her thumb over her shoulder, pointing to several large paddocks behind her.

"Wow!" Tara was incredulous at two such dangerous cases at one time in one place. "Sounds like you've got your hands full. Is the three-year-old yours, too?"

"No. He belongs to one of my customers, but I'd like to be able to work with him. Here, let me help you unload."

Jolene helped Tara carry her bag from the car to the house. They had just come back outside and down the porch steps when a large, once expensive, and still in good condition 1970-something gold Buick crunched its tires over the wood chips and parked in front of the barn. The only thing visible through the car window was a white cowboy hat at the wheel. When the driver's door opened, the rest of a lightly built eighty-year-old frame was revealed. Tom Dorrance looked even more petite than Tara remembered.

He wore a simple, light blue, long-sleeved shirt that buttoned down the front. Baggy blue jeans couldn't hide his bowed legs. In place of boots, he had on tan, mock-suede Hush Puppies. The huge car dwarfed him as he used the doorframe to help pull himself to his feet. Was this aging cowboy going to be able to handle Jolene's stallions?

"Well, hullo there!" He smiled broadly.

"Hi, Tom," Jolene strode over to shake his hand and got a hug instead.

While Tara stood watching, another truck and trailer pulled into the yard. The driver, a man about her age, quietly parked out of the way. She could hardly hear him as he slid from the front seat, closed the door behind him, and went back to unload a Paint gelding left to ride loose in his open stock trailer. He looked down, walking purposefully—as if on a mission—his cowboy hat covering his face and leaving the rest of the world unengaged.

From his western gear, she assumed he had something to do with Tom, and sure enough, once his horse was unloaded and tied at the trailer, he stood alongside the elder. Even from her place on the porch, Tara noted how he politely deferred to Tom. When the three merged up a gentle slope toward a small, five-stall barn, Tara followed, unnoticed.

She continued to hang back when they reached the stallion's stall, but positioned herself where she could see everything. The stall door had open bars on the top half. Inside, a small beam of light reflected off a dark eye. The rest of the face was hidden in shadow. Aware of human presence, the stallion began to shift nervously, uttering low, guttural noises—half grunt, half whinny. As Tom approached, a large body suddenly loomed into view and leaned forcefully against the door with a loud bang. Fortunately, the door was bolted.

"Does he try and run you over when you go to halter him?" Tom asked Jolene in a manner void of alarm, the tone in his voice intimating that he already knew the answer.

"I've had a lot of trouble with that, Tom."

"Well," he continued softly, "we'll see if we can't have him stand back and wait quietly to be haltered this time. It would be good for him to learn to have enough respect for a person so that you could go in and out of there without much trouble."

Jolene nodded emphatically, eyes widening into a smile. Tara couldn't imagine what Tom would do. She knew the stallion could be disciplined through intimidation and force. But Tom had said the horse could learn to "wait quietly," implying that it was possible to have him be *willing* to do so. Right now, she could see that he was pretty much into being agitated.

As Tom moved closer to the stall, the stallion jammed his head up to the narrow bars, nose protruding. Something appeared in Tom's hand—a long, thin metal rod about two or three feet long with a plastic bag tied to one end. Tom reached up and tapped the stallion's nose with the bag. Startled, he snorted and wheeled around, back out of view. Tom took a few steps back, but soon the stallion approached again. Again, Tom moved toward the stallion. The stallion's head and ears pricked forward, but he stood solidly, not yielding his ground. This time, Tom casually reached up with just his hand in front of the stallion's nose, pausing a moment before thumping the front of the long face with his fingers. Again, the stallion wheeled back.

Tom stepped back as well. Tara squinted, not understanding the forward and backwards movement between man and horse. But this time, the stallion stayed where he was, half-hidden in the shadows. She moved in closer to see him better. The dark silhouette of his head and neck were raised in attention, ears moving back and forth, looking like he didn't know what to do. This time, when Tom moved toward the stall, the stallion's ears pricked forward, then he stepped back. Tara recognized his acquiescent demeanor, somehow achieved in only a few minutes with extraordinarily little effort from Tom.

"Now," Tom said to the quiet man, "do you want to take this halter and see if he'll let you put it on?" It wasn't really a question.

Without hesitation, the quiet man softly, but deftly took the halter made of rope—as opposed to the more widely used nylon or leather versions—from the elder's hand, and in two strides was at the stallion's door. As he went to open it, his movement slowed and became cautious, eyes locked on the dark face. Tara was afraid for him.

Although Tom remained safely outside the doorway, he was well within sight of the stallion. As the quiet man went to slip the halter over the long nose, the stallion reached sideways to bite the elbow near his face. But Tom's hand was already raised in warning to the horse who, before teeth could meet flesh, pricked his ears forward in sudden attention. In a few moments, he had been haltered without incident.

The quiet man did not lead the horse out of the stall the usual way. Instead of walking by the stallion's shoulder, as was the custom everywhere Tara had been, the quiet man was about twelve feet in front, holding a long rope attached to the halter. As the big, dark bay turned out of his stall, excitement overwhelmed him, and he leapt forward. But before his front feet landed back on the ground, the quiet man jerked his arm up, sending a ripple through the long lead rope. Tara admired his reflexes.

Almost instantaneously, the ripple flipped a metal bull snap connecting the lead to the halter underneath the stallion's chin. The bump of the snap against his flesh surprised the horse so much that, in his effort to scramble back away from it, he lost his footing and landed on his rear in a sitting position, looking like a huge dog on a leash. It was a rare and awkward pose for a horse and would have been utterly comical had it not been for the necessity of remaining vigilant in a potentially dangerous situation. Tara rocked to the balls of her feet, ready to jump out of the way of another explosion as the stallion stood up, looked around, and snorted before shaking himself and licking his lips. Still crouching, Tara heard a chuckle. She turned to see Tom smiling and nodding his head.

"That's fine now. You just go right on," he said to the quiet man as he and Jolene followed horse and handler out to the yard. Tara, supposing she could relax now, followed as well. "That's why I like to see a person lead out a-ways from the horse," Tom turned sideways to encompass man and horse in front of him, Jolene beside him and Tara in the rear. "Most people just think I do things backwards, but in times like these, a person is much safer some distance from the horse if they know how to flip that rope."

When they came out into an open, flat surface Tom held the long lead while the quiet man hoisted the saddle onto the high back without any trouble. It was when he was astride that everything became...not anything Tara could explain. They were trying to get the horse to move forward. Or were they? The quiet man's leg would press in on the horse's sides. The stallion's ears would lay flat back against his head, and instead of walking forward, he'd raise a hind leg to kick at the pressure.

"Now take your leg off," Tom said, over and over, and then they'd wait. And wait. And wait. The stallion, still looking sullen, hadn't moved.

Tara shifted her weight from one foot to the other, stifled a yawn, looked out at the rocky cliffs that came straight up out of the ground on the other side of the valley, then back again and sighed. She told herself she wasn't bored. Her lids got heavy as the sun warmed her.

The next thing she knew, the stallion was walking down to the arena. When Tom asked the quiet man for a trot, the horse didn't hesitate. Soon he had rolled into a canter, ears pricked forward, completely unperturbed by the human on his back or the legs that hung down either side of his barrel. Tara woke up.

"Now fold your arms," Tom said to the quiet man, who dropped the reins entirely and folded his arms across his chest. The stallion cantered on. Tara stood gaping.

"Does anyone else want to ride him?" Tom said to a small crowd of bystanders from around the neighborhood who had been silently trickling in during the past hour, somehow having heard that he would be there. Apparently, none of them had felt awkward about inviting themselves onto Jolene's property unannounced. Then, Tom looked straight at Tara.

"Do you?"

She froze for a moment, then snapped her dry mouth shut and shook her head. Of all those people, why had he chosen her? They hadn't ever been formally introduced. And how had he known that she rode? She wasn't dressed for it. She knew intuitively that Tom would not have asked such a thing of a stranger had he not been sure of the change in the stallion, but she did not trust what she was seeing. Did not understand it. His gaze paused on her face for an endless moment, blue eyes reaching in beneath her sunglasses. But he did not press her and turned back to the stallion, now standing quietly before them, head and neck relaxed in a lowered position.

Tom received no takers, and while the bystanders murmured amongst themselves, the quiet man dismounted and led the stallion back to his stall. He returned leading the three-year-old gray Lipizzaner who had never been saddled. Emerging from her fog, Tara wished she had followed him to see how he'd managed to get the halter on by himself. Now they stood in the open area where they had been before, the young colt tossing his head and pinning his ears. Tom stood a good distance in front of the gray, holding a long lead line while the quiet man fixed a soft, well-used braided rawhide rope around his girth where a cinch would be tightened to hold a saddle in place.

"When they get broken in and used like that one," Tom talked to the crowd as he nodded at the rope in the quiet man's fingers, "they're softer against a horse's hide."

Tom had the quiet man gradually move the rope back until it slid over the white rump and landed on the ground, encircling both hind feet. He then urged the horse forward with the lead line until one hind foot had stepped over the rope while the quiet man pulled the noose snug around the other foot. When the colt felt the rope around his ankle, he kicked out. Tom came around to help the quiet man hold the lariat, both men leaning their hips calmly into the line, steadying the flailing leg.

"What's Tom doing?" she asked another cowboy standing next to her who was nodding as if he knew something.

"He's lettin' the horse run into his own pressure, is what he's doin'."

Tara wasn't sure she understood, and again they waited. Suddenly, or so it seemed, the ropes were removed and the colt was saddled without trouble. Then the quiet man was astride. The horse remained bridleless, ridden for the first time with only the halter and lead rope as he walked easily around the unfenced yard. The colt's ears were no longer pinned but relaxed and forward, his head low, breathing calm. She checked her watch. Only 3 1/2 hours since Tom had first arrived this morning. Was it possible?

All the years that she had spent with these animals, becoming highly skilled and proficient in her sport flooded her mind, and she felt an odd sinking. She tried reminding herself that she was a capable, successful trainer with students of her own. But that persona, a source of security only a moment before, had suddenly become a source of agitation. The shifting of her weight from one foot to the other became an effort to calm herself down instead of an effort to stay awake, until in spite of her fidgeting, the realization surfaced. Compared to this quiet, unpretentious cowboy who would otherwise simply blend into the scenery, she knew nothing.

~parallel worlds~

When there is no center and no circumference,
then there is truth.

Bruce Lee
The Tao of Jeet Kune Do

She knew nothing.

The small crowd was milling about, but Tara separated herself, avoiding conversation. Jolene walked with Tom back to his car, crouching on one knee while he sat talking to her from the back of his opened car trunk. The quiet man had already briefly ridden his Paint around the yard, letting him get used to new sights before loading him back into his trailer and pulling down the drive. Others were beginning to follow suit.

Tara was sitting back at the porch steps when Tom stood to close his trunk where he stowed his rope, halter, flag, and extra jacket. Jolene called in her direction. "I've got another horse to ride and a lesson to teach. You're welcome to watch or make yourself at home. Maybe we could catch a movie later on, when I'm finished."

Tara nodded. "Sounds good."

Jolene turned toward the barn. Tom got in his car and drove away. Tara got up and went inside, removing her shoes in the kitchen. Wooden floors creaked under her socked feet as she wandered into the den, a room instantly cozy with carpeted floors and walls lined with books. She caught the word "dressage" in a number of titles and pulled down a thick hardcover filled with pictures of the Spanish Riding School in Vienna. Sitting sideways in a thickly cushioned chair, she draped her legs over its soft arm and slowly turned the pages, letting her eyes rest on the meticulously groomed Lipizzaner stallions and the manicured arena with chandeliers hanging from the ceiling.

She hadn't realized how absorbed she'd become until the sound of boots came clomping up the back porch steps. She closed the book with her finger wedged between the pages and saw that she was already three-quarters of the way through.

"Do you think what Tom does could be applied to dressage?" she asked Jolene after her friend had removed her boots and come in to join her, sprawling her arms and legs across the carpet.

"I think what Tom does is great for behavior modification. I don't know how much he knows about dressage, really."

Tara nodded, opening the book again to the next page and a new set of pictures.

"Feel like going to a movie?" Jolene asked.

"Sure," Tara snapped the book shut and swung her legs off the chair. "That'll be a nice change."

Jolene grabbed her car keys and stepped into a pair of clogs, obviously unconcerned about wearing her riding breeches out in public. The two of them bounced down the stairs.

Tara was in no hurry to leave the following morning as she sat at the round breakfast table in the kitchen, sipping tea and eating toasted bagels with peanut butter.

"I'm thinking about retiring my Thoroughbred." She was surprised to hear herself say the words, and a moment later regretted it. If she were to retire him, it would mean the end of things, at least for a long time. She could not afford to buy another horse of equal caliber, nor take the time off to search for one less expensive. Procuring a sponsor was risky, and the mere thought of the energy it would take to find one exhausted her. And then there was the loan that she had stooped to beg her father for, covering the remaining expenses of her horse's transatlantic flight to Germany. It had not yet been paid off. Her Thoroughbred wasn't too old to compete. Didn't she owe it to her parents to keep trying?

"If you had it to do over, would you still go to Germany?" Jolene broke into her thoughts.

"No!" Tara's emphatic tone slipped out before she could censor it. "I—" She glanced at her friend, and thinking of her own ride the day before, paused to make her words more deliberate. "I would never want to put my horse through that again."

The drive home felt long and laborious, and dread was already seeping into her senses as she thought of the workweek ahead.

Tomorrow, Friday, would be her Monday, and when the alarm actually went off the next morning, she once again found herself fighting the inevitable. Itching to leave the arena after her final lesson of the day, she walked through the parking lot in the direction of her Thoroughbred's paddock. Halfway there, she slowed, feeling the ache of the upward climb in her legs. *Today I will remain detached*, she said to herself, wanting to be alone for this ride, not knowing what it was going to take to conquer whatever still plagued her and this horse.

In a few minutes, she had him saddled and bridled. Leading him just outside the barn doors, she swung on and rode back down to the covered arena. Once inside the gate, she urged him forward into a trot. *Today I will remain detached*, she repeated to herself, and her attentions were immediately pulled into the feel of every footfall, silently gauging how his unified weight shifted over his center of gravity. Her breath came in time with the rhythm of his stride, and the rest of her life was forgotten. She barely noticed the swirling cyclone of sand blown through the arena's entry, indirect light making the tiny earthen particles shimmer as they sped through the air. Then, out of the cyclone, he appeared.

She noticed his eyes first; great liquidy pools of blue rushing toward her, encompassing her entire range of vision before moving back to where she could see his entire image. Rich, dark brown hair with auburn highlights was cut about two inches in length, its style modern and typical of a businessman — parted on one side and layered all around. Yet it crowned the most exquisite face she had ever seen, softly chiseled into perfect symmetry.

Her ability to view the back of his head — although he continued to face her — felt completely normal, so utterly absorbed was she in every detail of his appearance. But what she saw transported her into a renewed sense of awe. Every hair on his head was combed in perfect order, as if each strand had its pre-appointed place. When her attention moved back to the front of his face, she saw that the same was true of his short and neatly trimmed beard, lining a square jaw that make-up and plastic surgery couldn't have made more beautiful.

As her perspective changed again to a position farther away, she noted his robe — long and white with purple trim, then edged in gold piping. It didn't occur to her to question the contrast between his ancient attire and the modern appearance of his face — a face that suddenly looked angry, so stern and persistent was his gaze. As she took in his stare, her sense of open wonder turned to dread, and she had a terrible feeling of being in trouble. But in the next moment, a great warmth moved through her, or tried to, pushing its way up her sternum and prying open her chest, which had come to feel like heavy steel doors. Sorrow welled up inside her, and she felt like crying.

Then he vanished. The air was still, and she was staring at nothing. Had it only been a dream? A figment of her imagination? But at that moment, her gelding, still trotting, lifted his head and neck, pricked his ears forward and veered hard to the side, avoiding whatever would have been there.

Her horse had shied in order to avoid…nothing?

She brought him to a walk, her heart slowly pounding thick blood through her veins. She needed to think, wondering at the heaviness inside. The image had seemed to linger such a long time, long enough for her to notice every minute detail, yet only long enough for her horse to take a few steps. How long was that? Two seconds, maybe three? And those eyes, melting through her, holding her gaze. She remembered the blue pools, stern, yet not angry, the way one would look in deep concentration. *Remember who you are*, they had said to her. *Remember who you are.*

She dropped the reins and let her horse walk on his own, her eyes roaming from side to side without registering the surrounding world. A vague memory of a similar experience slowly came into focus. How old had she been? Five? Six? She'd been standing in front of the full-length mirror that hung on the back of her bedroom door, seeing the reflection of her naked skin. The look in her mother's eyes, staring from behind her, told her she was bad. But after her mother had left the room, a ray of sunlight filtered in through the trees outside her shuttered windows. She turned to face it, instantly thrilled by the dance of leafy shadows against the white walls of her room.

What do you want, Tara?

Without having to look up, she saw several grown-up faces of men and women hovering above her in a circle, speaking silently into her mind. She didn't recognize any of them, but their presence seemed perfectly normal, and she understood it was necessary to answer their question right away. Otherwise, it would be too late, the outside world pulling at her, making her live by its rules.

"I want to live with horses," she answered.

More than that. More than that.

She stood for a moment, sensing an urge and following it inward. The feeling grew stronger and stronger until, with a rush, she knew what it was, but unsure of what word to use.

"I want to be *wise*," it came to her then, and she said the word aloud to the faces as their image faded. Warmth poured out of her, and she felt them smiling. A heat inside filled her up again. She repeated it to herself, wanting to hold onto the feeling as her body cooled and she became aware of her outstretched hand, limp and clammy where her fingers had stayed curled around the shirt still hanging from their grasp. Startled back into the world, she quickly dressed, knowing it was not safe to keep her mother waiting.

Tara didn't know how long she had been sitting in one spot when she found herself blinking down at her hands resting on the pommel, fingers barely holding the reins. At some point, her gelding had come to a stop and was standing at the far end of the arena, a hind foot cocked in resting position. She closed her eyes and became aware of her own breathing. At length, she turned and rode back up to the barn.

8

~shift~

What we do to survive is often different from what we may need to do
in order to live.

—Rachel Naomi Remen, M.D.
Kitchen Table Wisdom

The clock outside Tara's office read one o'clock in the afternoon.
She had canceled today's afternoon lessons and now strolled the barn
aisles in search of a wheelbarrow amid old pipes, rotting lumber and
tools left to lie in the dirt where stalls should have been. A startling
creak and groan of the long metal roof made her jump. Looking across
the valley, the once solid hills appeared to undulate before her. Her
feet registered the soft bump and roll of the ground below. Twenty-
odd seconds of shaking seemed like minutes. Was anything in the
world actually the way it appeared to the human eye — or the way she
had been taught to perceive it?

She hadn't even thought to move from beneath the old roof to a
place free of falling debris, should it occur. The earthquake itself
seemed a minor shift compared to the decision she had recently made.
She resumed her search for a wheelbarrow, noting how her lack of
alarm sharply contrasted her elementary school days when she and
forty classmates had, on a regular basis, flung their chairs backwards
in a panic to dive head first under their desks, the screech of metal legs
sounding across the linoleum floor. They'd been instructed to bury
their eyes into both knees pressing into the hard ground, and fold their
hands over the backs of their heads. Arms draped over ears shielded
them from the possibility of loud explosions. They'd waited in silence,
hoping that the word "drop," quietly spoken mid-sentence by the
teacher, meant this was only another drill, and that the earth would
never actually come unglued, or another atom bomb fall — until

nothing happened, and they were allowed to crawl back out and find their seats again.

When her first big earthquake actually struck, she'd been a teenager at home in bed, abruptly awakened before dawn by a roaring so loud down the canyon she hadn't been able to hear herself screaming. Running blindly down the dark hallway, she met her mother at the seven-foot-tall sliding glass doors that spanned the entire back living room wall. After taking turns fumbling at the latch with desperate, shaky fingers, they had finally been able to push the doors wide and plunge to the outside where they stood clutching each other's arms, transfixed by pool water lapping up over the rim in waves and washing their bare feet.

"Oh, look!" her mother yelped when the earth was still.

Tara followed her mother's gaze to the wall of glass, still intact and directly behind them. In their relief to be outside, they hadn't considered their close proximity should it have shattered.

"We could have been killed," her mother added before glancing back at Tara, her eyes having barely rested on her daughter's form before she let out a hoot. Glancing down at herself, Tara realized she was stark naked, in plain view of the neighbors.

It had been one of the few times she and her mother had laughed together.

An aftershock sent another creak through the old roof, spooking Tara out of reverie and back into action. Hefting two saddles off their racks, she let them fall, spoon-fashion, into the only wheelbarrow she had found with a good tire. She pulled brushes out of their boxes, a horse blanket off the shelf, and a bridle off its hook. With her pile as high as she could balance, she tipped and rolled the one-wheeler cautiously along the barn aisle and down the ramp to the hard-packed adobe. The wheel gathered momentum, and dry dust churned underneath her feet. She leaned all the way back, legs scrambling to prevent a runaway to her truck and horse trailer, which were already hitched together.

She had not ridden her gelding for two weeks—not since seeing the "spirit in robes," as she called him. And, instead of returning her phone messages that night, she'd dialed an eighty-year-old man who'd handled two stallions and roped a calf in a way she couldn't explain. She hadn't expected him to answer the phone himself, thinking he was too big a legend not to have a secretary or publicity agent handling his affairs. But there he'd been on the other end of the line, his normally quiet tone sounding rough and to the point while she crouched over her phone on the living room rug, yelling to overcome his faded hearing.

"I was wondering if I could set up a time to work with you. I'm having trouble with one of my horses."

"Well," he gave a long pause, "I've learned to tell people that it's prob'ly best if they don't come down here."

Silence.

"But—" she'd stammered.

"'Cause generally what happens is they don't get from me what it was they were expecting."

"But I'd still—"

"And after awhile, they begin to figure out that they prob'ly woulda been better off if they'da never gone to the trouble in the first place."

Silence.

"I'd still like to come." She'd been furious at herself for not thinking of a better argument.

More silence.

"Well, then, I suppose that'd be all right."

She hurriedly loaded the gear into the trailer compartment and checked the electrical connection to the old but reliable 1976 Chevy pickup that she used for hauling horses. She felt that at any moment she might be caught with her hand inside the cookie jar, and imagined the disapproving looks from the "higher ups" in her sport who considered cowboys incompetent when it came to the exclusive refinement of dressage. Needless to say, she had not mentioned this trip or her association with Tom to any of her peers.

With everything set to go, she walked over to the paddock to halter her Thoroughbred. Even before she'd finished wrapping his legs for the trailer ride, she was thinking about loading him inside.

Not as bad as it used to be, she tried to cheer herself, remembering the days when she'd needed another person to stand behind him with a broom to chase him in. But he still required a chain threaded through his halter and over his nose in case he planted his feet. After fastening the brass links to his lead rope, she led him to the parking lot, and sure enough, the moment he saw the open trailer door, he pulled back, his breath hissing through the narrow slits of his nostrils as the chain tightened around them. Stronger than she, he dragged her back with him before she thought to let go of the lead rope, knowing his resistance would only escalate if she continued to hang on. Finally, he stood still a good distance from the trailer.

She hesitated before pulling the top links over his nose and under his top lip. But at length, she felt she had no other choice and reached her hand toward his face. Knowing what was coming, her gelding threw his head high and almost out of reach of her fingertips, the whites of his eyes showing as he rolled his eyes toward the back of his head. Still, she managed to slip the chain into his mouth. Luckily, this time, he followed her inside his narrow compartment without incident.

After letting herself out through an escape doorway on the side of the trailer, she ran to the back to fasten the butt bars and close the back door before he could think to back out. But no sooner had he been enclosed than he began to neigh loudly, stomping his feet on the rubber matting. She ran to the cab to start the engine before he kicked at the metal sides; he would keep his feet planted as long as they were moving. After fastening her seat belt and exhaling loudly, she moved the rig cautiously over the uneven ground onto the winding road that led away from the barn.

Her watch read 2:15. It was a three-hour drive to Tom's, and the first half required many changes of lanes through the swarming Bay Area traffic. Eventually, the freeway flowed eastward, thinning dramatically as they reached Interstate 5 and the unembellished flatlands of central California. She took in a deep breath, loosening her fingers from around the wheel, unaware she'd been gripping them so tightly, and thought ahead to what it might be like to work with Tom. Tomorrow, she'd be joining a clinic with a group of other people and their horses at the ranch where he and his wife had recently settled, and she was glad she'd made a point to come a day early to work with him one on one.

A dimming light still held over the western horizon as she exited the interstate, and drove past almond orchards and cotton fields and eventually came around the final curve to Wesland Ranch. Here, the landowners had agreed to make room for the ever-swelling influx of people wanting to work with Tom. She turned in over a flat, metal bridge with no side rails. It was a twelve-foot drop to the creek below should she lose control of the wheel or misjudge the amount of room she had on either side. But she drove on, passing a solid-looking ranch house on the right before swinging left onto an open gravel lot. At one end of the lot stood a mobile home, and at the other a prefabricated barn where she parked the truck.

Tom had obviously seen her drive in because, by the time she stepped out of the cab, he was already waiting a few feet away in a golf cart he had driven from around the mobile home.

"Ah, yah," he nodded as she came over to formally introduce herself for the first time. "I remember you."

She didn't have time for a lengthy introduction as the sound of stomping inside the trailer made her turn and run back to unload her horse. The familiar blast of hot air hit her face when she opened the upper side door to the manger where he was tied, his body lathered and trembling as he bellowed and flipped his head up and down. She stood on her tiptoes, struggling to reach his head and unhook the halter clip.

After opening the back doors, she stood to one side as he came flying out backwards, grabbing his lead rope before he could run away. Tom, saying nothing about the manner in which she unloaded her horse, or the sweat that covered his body, indicated the direction she was to take him. He followed her in the cart as, horse in hand, she walked toward a large field where most of the riding took place. Inserted in the middle of the surrounding fence line stood an ordinary gate made from a standard rectangular galvanized pipe panel. She thought nothing of it — until it opened. When she and her gelding were several yards away, Tom pressed a remote button inside the cart. Circular gears that looked like those fitted on a bicycle churned at one end. At the opposite end, the gate swung up vertically, instead of to and fro, the way one normally would.

"Wow," she exclaimed aloud as she passed through without needing to slow or alter a stride. Tom drew her attention to a push-button opener attached to the supporting post about as high as a horse's back. A mounted rider could easily reach it from either side and open the gate without having to dismount. She nodded at him, simultaneously raising her eyebrows. It had taken someone a fair amount of thought and know-how to come up with a design as unique and appropriate to the world of horses as that.

To keep from spooking her horse, Tom followed Tara through the gate at a careful distance before closing the panel behind himself, just in time to keep the loose horses in the field from escaping as they came forward to investigate the unfamiliar human and the one-like-them in tow. She smiled a thank you. He barely nodded in return as he drove past her to the arena. In time, she would learn that, for Tom, such synchronized action was a way of life and didn't require additional commentary.

He parked the cart next to an arena that was fenced in by a series of pipe panels linked to form a large oval. Attached to the arena at one end was a sixty-foot-diameter round pen made from the same material. Tara had never worked in one before, but once inside, Tom instructed her to unbuckle the leather halter and let her horse loose. The pen allowed him to move freely without the attachments of lines or ropes while keeping her in close proximity to him. She stood in the middle, behind Tom, who sat on a swivel stool. Rather than focusing immediately on her gelding, he made a point of showing her the stool's attached canvas pockets, used for holding water, gloves, and a booklet of poems and mind teasers. Tara wondered about the booklet, but not wanting to appear stupid, nodded as if it was a normal piece of equipment to bring out around the horses. Meanwhile, her gelding trotted and cantered around them in the sandy footing. She turned on one foot as Tom swiveled on his stool and pointed things out to her.

"Do you see how Blackie likes to carry his head to the outside? See how he dips his nose in towards his chest when he breaks over to the lope? See how he carries a kink in his tail? Notice how Blackie sags his right shoulder going in that direction?"

She smiled at his use of the generic "Blackie." Her gelding's show name was actually Mozart, indicating the fluid and rhythmical motion of his stride, but the name had always felt somewhat pretentious for everyday use, and she'd never used it. "Blackie" was simple. Friendly.

It then struck her how commonplace the things Tom mentioned about her gelding were. The way he held his head, tail, and shoulders and how he placed his weight were things all horses did, things she took for granted, things she would try to fix so that her horse balanced himself into a particular way of going—a way that met the standards of training in dressage. But Tom wasn't trying to fix them. At the same time, they seemed to take on more importance in that he deliberately mentioned them. She narrowed her eyes, confused. Yet something in his manner calmed her, reassured her. It dawned on her that she was standing beside a man considered by many to be the greatest horseman of all time. An uncensored, high-pitched squeal escaped her as she crouched to fling her arms about his neck. He laughed.

They stayed in the round pen for nearly an hour. In that time, Tom hadn't tried to alter anything about her horse's way of going, saying it would be better to wait until morning before doing anything specific. Without questioning, Tara haltered and led him back to the portable barn used for guest horses.

"What do I owe you for this evening?" She asked after putting her horse in an empty stall.

"Well, why don't we just wait until after tomorrow and see what comes of it?"

Tara paused and cocked her head. "Okay."

After Tom was sure she could find water and feed for her horse, he climbed back into the cart and waved good-bye, his arm held high as he turned the wheel toward the mobile home.

She unhitched the truck from her trailer, leaving her tack locked inside overnight. She would be staying only a few miles away at a hotel recommended by Willa, the ranch owner. Opening the door to the cab of the truck, she lifted a leg to the floorboard. But something caught her attention and she paused, pulling her foot back out. It took a moment to realize that it was the absence of activity and background noise summoning her. She stood quietly, feeling a palpable stillness all around. White stars were already visible in a blue sky rapidly turning dark. A light breeze made them blink in and out, in and out while evening crickets screeched faintly in time with their twinkling.

As far as the eye could see in every direction, the land went out flat into neighboring farms beyond the road that ran alongside the ranch. To the west, pastureland rolled steadily upward across the interstate and on into the foothills, miles away. The last standing pools of spring rain had evaporated in the creek bed that ran along the ranch's eastern border. From there, already drying grasses fanned out forever into a blanket of gold. Tara lingered until all light faded.

9

~self preservation~

Next Sunday Barnum was as bad as he had ever been. He refused to stand, and Laura had to wait for a third stop before she could leap into the buggy. Then he reared and tried to run, pulling so hard that after a time Almanzo complained, "He is pulling this buggy by the bit and my arms."

"Let me try," Laura offered. "It will rest your arms."

"All right," Almanzo agreed. "For a minute, but you'll have to hold hard."

He let go of the lines when she had a firm grip on them, just behind his. Laura's arms took the force of Barnum's pull; his strength flowed up the lines with the thrill she had felt before... Barnum sensed the change of drivers and stretched his neck a little farther, feeling the bit; then his trot became slower. He turned the corner by the livery barn, and dropped into a walk.

Barnum was walking. Almanzo was silent and Laura hardly breathed. A little by a tiny little she eased on the lines. Barnum went on walking. The wild horse, the runaway, who never before had been seen to walk when hitched to a buggy, walked the whole length of Main Street. He reached out twice, feeling the bit with his mouth and, finding it to his liking, arched his neck and walked proudly on.

Almanzo said, low, "Better tighten the lines a little so he won't get the jump on you."

"No," Laura answered. "I am going to let him carry the bit easily. I think he likes it."

All along the street, everyone stopped to stare...

"Well, I'll be darned! How did you do it?" he asked then. "I've been trying ever since I've had him to get him to walk. What did you do?"

"I didn't do anything," Laura said. "He is really a gentle horse."

—Laura Ingalls Wilder
These Happy Golden Years

Tara was the first to arrive back at Wesland Ranch early the next morning. Tom's wife was setting up a table just outside the panel gate, getting ready to accept auditing fees from others coming to watch the day's events. Before tacking up to ride, Tara walked over and briefly introduced herself, then headed for the barn. By the time she reemerged, horse in tow, the quiet grounds were crawling with activity. Clinic participants revved the engines of their dually trucks over the metal bridge and hauled long, goose-necked horse trailers into the yard. Auditors with out-of-state license plates parked their cars outside the gate, left in its open position, and walked in on foot. Some had children in tow. Most greeted Tom with smiles, handshakes, and hugs, apparently knowing him from before, while he sat near the arena on his swivel stool, getting a 360° view.

Deciding to use the name Tom had given him, Tara led Blackie into the arena and mounted, watching the surrounding field quickly fill with horses, riders, and handlers. Some joined her in the arena where she now sat. Only two others rode in English saddles, and she was the only dressage rider. Tom, however, seemed indifferent to what equipment the horses came dressed in. Human bodies of all shapes and sizes mingled and chattered against a background of hoof beats and squeaking leather.

Tom began by pointing out the creek bed, nodding as some maneuvered their mounts through the rocky, uneven ground. "Horses'll pay attention to where they put their feet if they want to make it out of there without causin' a wreck." His backside shook as he laughed at his own speech.

Tara quickly assessed that most of the other riders were neither as skilled as she, nor had her experience. Yet they could let their reins loose, and their horses didn't seem nervous or want to run off. Meanwhile, all the commotion was agitating Blackie, and she let him move about the sandy arena.

Before long, a woman came in on a gaited horse. Its high-stepping action made Blackie stop dead in his tracks. Flinging his head high in the air, he stood in iron tenseness, body trembling, gaze riveted on the strange beast. Then he bolted. Not knowing what Tom would want her to do she turned him back hard, only to have him bolt again as the woman, oblivious to Tara's dilemma, kept her horse going. Although Tom was seated just outside the fence and had a clear view of her through the open bars, he was occupied in conversation and seemed not to notice. Others did, however. People she'd never met were standing up and watching her ride out of control. Hot humiliation reddened her face. Normally she would have jerked on the reins and punished his sides with her spurs. But she knew this was not what Tom would want her to do, and so remained at a complete loss when Blackie bolted one more time.

Why doesn't Tom say something? She felt a fragile loosening inside. And was the woman riding the gaited horse truly that clueless that she couldn't stop her horse for a moment out of courtesy? Indeed, the woman maintained her focus straight ahead, not looking at Tara or anyone around her.

"Let's have the lady walk her horse for a minute," Tom's voice, barely perceptible, could at last be heard over the commotion. He apparently used the generic on people, too, regarding the woman on the gaited horse as if he'd been observing the situation all along.

Everything went quiet. "Let's have Tara bring her horse inside the round pen," his soft tone suddenly distinct in the still air.

Relieved, Tara nodded and maneuvered Blackie, now running sideways to escape the other horse, over to the end of the arena.

"Looks like ol' Blackie's need for self-preservation has kicked in pretty strong," Tom said to her as she slid past where he sat. His words seemed to justify the horse's actions. She stared straight ahead, not knowing how to respond.

A gate let them into the adjoining round pen where she and Tom had been the evening before. Tom's soft voice instructed her to dismount and remove the bridle. Instinctively she rolled up the stirrups on her dressage saddle so they wouldn't bang her gelding's sides or snag on the railing. Then Tom handed her a "flag" — his name for the stick with the plastic bag tied to one end — that she had seen him use on Jolene's stallion. Standing in the middle, Tara flapped the flag in the air to direct Blackie around the pen. He moved off, sullenly at first. But when the gaited horse began to move again in the large arena, Blackie exploded, all fours straight off the ground. His back humped like a camel with such force that it popped the stitching on her billet straps clean off, and she stood helpless, watching her good dressage saddle get slammed to the ground.

"Oookaaay," she heard Tom droll as she quickly snatched her saddle out of the dirt before climbing through the fence to safety, maneuvering the bulky weight with her, and trying to avoid entanglement with stomping feet that sent dust billowing into her face and lungs. "Now, if you'd like to come here for a moment." Tom's voice was still calm, his gaze steady as she found a place to set her saddle before walking over to him. Her knee-high boots had trapped the heat of her body, and now that her movement slowed, turned her into a living oven. Rivulets of sweat ran down her skin, itching everywhere.

"Let's let someone else ruin their tack on this horse for the time being," he almost whispered at her, as if softening the blow.

"I don't mind riding him, Tom," she heard a pleading tone in her voice. Tom nodded his head in response, but his eyes were diverted.

"You're too precious," he said, looking back at her.

Frustration only added to her physical heat. She trained horses for a living and couldn't shirk from this horse because of some old-fashioned idea that women were less able to cope. But Tom had already asked the lady with the gaited horse to stop for a moment and now directed a cowboy in blue jeans into the arena with a heavy western saddle and Tara's horse in tow.

She recognized the cowboy immediately as the quiet man who had helped with Jolene's stallions a few weeks before. He soon had his saddle on Blackie and was fastening the buckles on the bridle she'd left hanging on the fence. He swung on, and as the gaited horse started up again, Blackie bolted. But instead of trying to hold him back, the quiet man urged him on! Tara took in a quick breath. But to her amazement, her horse only ran a few strides before craning his neck to keep an eye on the gaited horse.

"Now, just let him follow that horse," Tom called, and the quiet man allowed Blackie to turn behind the other.

"You see," Tom now spoke to Tara, "he doesn't want to buck or run off any more than you want him to. It's just that he doesn't know what else to do in a situation where he perceives danger."

Tara looked at Tom, then back to her gelding. She didn't understand. She knew a horse's first means of self-defense was its ability to run from predators. It was how the species had survived for millions of years as an herbivore. But her horse wasn't in any danger. He was safe in the arena, surrounded by his own kind.

"Now," Tom continued, "by letting Blackie follow that other horse, the other horse will always be moving away from him. That way it won't seem as threatening, and as time goes on, he'll have a chance to gain some confidence."

Tara cocked her head. Something in what Tom said made sense. She looked back at the quiet man. When Blackie got close to the gaited horse, he raised his head and scooted sideways. But already, his curiosity was enticing him to follow again when the distance was right.

Although the quiet man went along with her horse on a loose rein, Tara saw that this kind of riding wasn't just a matter of sitting idle and following blindly. The quiet man rode with a relaxed seat, but his eyes were alert and focused, hands raised slightly, one on each rein, ready for any unpredictable move.

"Now, he might not be ready for that," Tom interjected, just as Blackie began to pass to the inside of the gaited horse. And sure enough, he bolted again. Again, the quiet man went with him, and then turned him back until he had slowed behind the gaited horse again.

"You let the horse do as much as possible on his own without losing him, but you're there to direct and support when necessary," Tom was saying.

Tara understood the words, but wasn't sure she would know what to do if she were the one riding. She continued to watch intently, unaware of how long she remained in that crouched position beside Tom until Blackie suddenly, or so it seemed, lowered his head and neck and came to rest quietly in the center while the gaited horse sped around him.

"Now, do you want to try?"

She looked up and met his eyes. Nodding, she rose instantly, and in a few strides was at her horse and sitting in a stranger's saddle. She nodded her thanks to the quiet man, but he turned to leave without responding. There was no time to dwell on the man's lack of social skills, however. Instantly she felt a tightening of muscles underneath her as Blackie sensed the change in riders. The gaited horse came around to her end of the arena, but instead of bolting, he seemed to know what to do, and without prompting from her, began following behind. After watching the quiet man, she knew she could let him. It occurred to her that this had been the underlying reason Tom had suggested the quiet man ride in the first place.

Letting her horse move where he wanted was a different way of riding. Her whole life, she had been taught that she had to make a horse go where she wanted to go in order to be in control, to be "the boss." Now she was afraid that using her reins and legs for control would only mess things up, get in Blackie's way. Indeed, he seemed to be more in control of himself. Steadier. Less likely to become upset. In fact, he stayed quiet the rest of the morning while Tom focused on others outside the arena.

At the lunch break, Tara rode him back to the guest barn to hose off dried sweat caked over his coat with a thick layer of dust. The weather was warm enough to leave him to dry in the stall with a ration of hay, and she walked back out to the smell of barbecue. Disoriented and queasy, she found an empty straw bale amid a row of others, and sat, waiting for her stomach to settle and the food line to dwindle. Everyone around her seemed to know someone else, or had come with someone else. She knew no one except Tom, who was surrounded by people, their eager chatter filling the air.

When the line shrank, she got up from her seat and walked to the table, separated a clean paper plate out of a stack of others, and rummaged inside a bag for a plastic fork. She fell in line next to a large man with a bushy mustache that extended beyond the outline of a face shaded by a broad-brimmed hat. His hands were thick and calloused. A rancher's hands. Someone who used horses to earn a living.

"About six months ago, I come 'round to work with Tom," he was saying to a couple standing in front of him. "My mare, why, she used to work me up som'n' terrible until I finally realized I had to see things the way she did before I was gonna git anywhere. Funny thing is, life is better at home now, too—gittin' along with my wife, even with my kids." He shook his head, a smile spreading across his face. "Hell, people are no different." Then he laughed while his friends nodded silently.

Tara caught herself staring at him and quickly turned away. Probably not the type to go in for family counseling, she mused. But he had found a fellow cowboy. She turned toward the crowd mingling in the yard. Tom, dressed in baggy jeans and Hush Puppies, looked nothing like the touted image of the Marlborough Man. Only the long-sleeved shirt and cowboy hat gave away his cultural orientation as he sat among the others, smaller than ever on his swivel stool, calmly and quietly nodding his head and smiling at the never-ending flock of people towering around him.

"After his folks passed away in the mid-fifties," the rancher was saying while they spooned beans and salad onto their plates, "Tom traveled around, visiting his brothers, who went on to do some ranching in Nevada and California. Well, the hired hands could never figure out why Tom preferred to ride the ones who had the least amount of handling." The rancher smiled at his friends, eyes twinkling like he might be getting ready to tell a joke.

"'Not as much to undo,' Tom would say," the rancher continued. "One time, I heard he went into a corral full of ranch stock just brought in from the hills. Old Tom picked out a colt the other fellas hadn't been able to lay a hand on, let alone saddle or ride.

"'Maybe you want to try out another besides that one,' one of the men said.

"'Naw, he'll be all right,' says Tom. 'He might be a little scared, but this one won't buck, he'll just run.'

"Well, o'course the men eyed each other. They'd all ridden these broncs, knew what it was to be slammed into the dirt. And you know, in those days, there weren't no helicopter to come pick you up if you split your head open or punctured a lung. So they all hung around to watch, figurin' he might need some help keepin' from bein' trampled to death when he bit the dust.

"But the way I was told it," the rancher now stood out of the way at the end of the long table, waiting for his friends, his plate piled high with food. Tara put one lettuce leaf at a time onto her plate, buying time to hear the rest of the story. "Tom only took a minute to tighten the cinch. Then he swung on, holding a single lead rope off the halter. Sure enough, the horse never bucked. He jus' ran around the corral, dodging the other loose horses left and right. Why, Tom, o'course, did nothing to try and stop him. He went along for the ride until the colt settled, then rode right out the gate as if that horse had been used to a person on his back his whole life, ready for a day's work. I understand the expression on the faces of the other fellas was a sight to behold," and he burst out in uproarious laughter.

He was still laughing as he and his friends walked off, plates in hand. Tara found another empty bale of straw and ate by herself. She finished in five minutes and left the yard to check on Blackie. Leaning against his stall door, she looked in to watch him chew his hay. In a few minutes, she'd need to get him ready for the afternoon ride, but when the time came, she hadn't moved from her spot, mesmerized by the rhythmic rotation of his jaw. The thought of riding seemed overwhelming. She forced herself to pluck the bridle from its hook anyway, and then hesitated again. His muscles would be feeling the morning's workout, she told herself, and watched him munch for a while longer. At length, she returned the bridle to its hook and walked back out to the crowd.

Seeing a space next to Tom, she sat cross-legged on the hard ground at his feet and took in what was happening around her. Every rider and handler in the arena and out in the yard was doing something different with his or her horse. She wondered how Tom kept track of it all. Suddenly, a big bay colt bolted and ran to the end of his line. The man who had been leading him was being pulled behind, the long lead rope slipping through his hands. As he tightened his grip, the horse kept pulling, causing his boots to scud across the hard-packed ground, as if on skis, before he could get his footing and pull the horse back under control.

"Looks like we'll be able to make a project out of that," Tom said.

Tara looked up at him, waiting for him to say more. But Tom remained quietly observant, even as the colt bolted again. Minutes passed, and still he said nothing. Tara felt a sharp ache in her feet. Glancing toward the bottom of her boots, she realized she'd been clenching her toes. The colt bolted again.

"Looks like he was pretty good at doing this before he came here, Andy," Tom finally called to the handler after he had ended up at the far end of the field. "Be aware of the whole horse, and you'll want to make sure to stay out at the end of that fifteen-foot rope, where you'll have some distance between you and his flying hooves."

Tara frowned. "Tom?" She heard the exasperation in her own voice. "What is Andy supposed to do?"

Without taking his eyes from Andy and the colt, Tom barely raised a hand off his thigh where it had been resting, gently silencing her. "Now get ready," he called to Andy, instead. "He's gonna get a build up pretty quick."

Tara glanced back at the colt. He seemed to be slowing down, not "building up." She frowned again. Half a minute later, he bolted. She opened her mouth to speak, but hesitated. Then, unable to contain herself, she dared again. "Tom, how do you know he's going to run off like that so far before he actually does?" She had seen the horse's expression change right before he took off—a common ability acquired by most horsemen. But she hadn't seen it as early as when Tom had warned Andy.

This time, Tom turned to her as if to say something, but instead bent both arms at the elbow and tucked them in against his torso. Tensing all of his muscles, he scrunched his body into a ball and made his face into a grimace. She stared at him, waiting for an explanation, but he turned back to Andy and the colt.

Sighing heavily, she squinted and concentrated on the young horse to see if she could see anything like a cringe. It felt as if she stared a long time, all the while vaguely aware of Tom's occasional comment in the background. Finally, she released her gaze and rubbed her eyes. Her feet had gone numb, and her back ached. After shifting her position, she glanced up again, and there! She'd seen something. But now it was gone already, and she realized she was focusing once again on the horse's body. What she had seen for that fleeting second had more to do with his demeanor or internal posturing.

"When there's something you don't want to have happen, be aware of what happens before the thing you don't want to have happen, happens," Tom emphasized as the colt bolted again.

"But, Tom, what is Andy supposed to do to correct the colt?" It had slipped out before Tara could catch herself.

"Well, now," Tom turned to her, "once a thing has happened, it's too late to try and fix it, 'cause it's already come and gone."

It took a moment for that to sink in. Tom waited until her eyes came back into focus. "Otherwise you just end up punishing the horse, which don't amount to much," he added.

"Because the horse gets sour?" Tara wanted to make sure she was following him.

"Well, now, could be." He paused. "Punishment is liable to backfire on the person doing the punishing as well as being useless to the horse, so it's a waste of effort, as far as I'm concerned."

Tom sat up and looked around at the crowd. "Sometimes it takes a willingness on the part of the person to be creative in their thinking," he was speaking to everyone now, "instead of just relying on what they've always done to get their point across in a way that isn't working." There was a sudden quiet among the auditors, as if a switch had been shut off, followed by a spattering of nervous laughter. Tara felt a hot rush of blood fill her cheeks, thinking of all the times she had become engaged in a battle of wills with Blackie.

Tom paused another moment to focus on Andy before continuing. "So, instead of trying to correct something, I like to get a person thinking about redirecting. That way, when something goes wrong, the person isn't spending their time worryin' about what's already taken place, but searches for another way to approach the situation."

Andy, having been surprised so often by the colt, was now flipping the rope as Tara had seen the quiet man do at Jolene's. Other times, he turned the colt in a new direction, never letting too much time pass before he changed what he was doing. His constant repositioning, although awkwardly executed, kept the colt's eyes and ears on him, instead of on everything else.

"Feel, timing, and balance," Tom nodded. "Now we're seeing things shape up."

Tara felt a headache coming on, and lowering her head to her chest, rubbed small circles over her temples. It was all so new. Out of the corner of her eye, she saw Tom pull something out of his shirt pocket. She turned her head and stared as he held a nylon string high so that everyone could see it. The string was tied to itself in a simple knot, forming a loop about a foot long.

"Is there anyone who hasn't tried this before?" He looked around, and soon several volunteers came up beside him. Tara sunk lower into the ground and scooted her seat out of the way. Tom instructed one of the men to hold up both of their index fingers close enough together for him to suspend the string around them. To a woman, he explained how to work the string itself with the index and middle fingers of one hand. The "trick," he told them, could be memorized in steps. After following the steps, the woman working the string had to connect her middle finger to the man's index finger, the string knotted through both of their hands. The last step, however, caused it to "magically" slip free without disconnecting their fingers.

"Now, you might want to try that again to see how well you observed the way it was done the first time," he said before shuffling his feet in small side steps, swiveling his chair back around to the riders. Apparently, he was going to leave them to figure it out for themselves. While the newcomers stood contemplating their befuddled hands, he pulled a booklet out of the stool's canvas pockets. Tara recognized the book of mind teasers and poems he had shown her the night before.

"Has anyone read this?" He now held the booklet up high to both nodding and head shaking. Opening the paper copy, he began to read. Tara glanced at the faces around her but saw no surprised expressions. Was there no one else wondering why Tom was suddenly reciting poetry at a horse clinic?

"When you get what you want in your struggle for self
And the world makes you king for a day,
Just go to a mirror and look at yourself,
And see what that man has to say.

"For it isn't your father or mother or wife
Whose judgment upon you must pass,
The fellow whose verdict counts most in your life
Is the one staring back from the glass.

Tara noted that, after the first line, he had rested the hand that held the booklet in his lap and was narrating from memory.

"You may be like Jack Horner and chisel a plum
And think you're a wonderful guy,
But the man in the glass says you're only a bum
If you can't look him straight in the eye.

"He's the fellow to please, never mind all the rest,
For he's with you clear up to the end.
And you've passed your most dangerous, difficult test
If the man in the glass is your friend.

"You may fool the whole world down the pathway of years
And get pats on the back as you pass,
But your final reward will be heartaches and tears
If you've cheated the man in the glass."

A sprinkling of hand clapping could be heard amid the chatter of others who weren't really listening. Tara stood and walked around to the back to stretch her legs. Cowboy hats nodded at her, and she smiled in return, headache fading. Off to the side, near the horse trailers, she recognized the quiet man standing by himself, watching from a distance.

"My name is Tara." She walked over to him, holding out her hand. "Sorry to startle you," she added when he suddenly turned to her, unfolding his arms in quick reflex. He nodded and shook her hand. "You did a nice job with my gelding. Thanks for riding him."

"Oh, sure," having recovered his voice, he sounded friendly.

"I actually saw you once before over at Jolene's—" she was hoping he'd remember and watched him cock his head. "In Carmel, with the two stallions…"

"Oh, yeah, I remember. Yeah, that was a lot of fun."

Tara was surprised at how suddenly animated he was. "I learned a lot watching you and Tom that day," she said, knowing she hadn't understood anything about what she'd been looking at.

"There's always something to learn around old Tom, that's for sure," he said while picking his hat off his head and combing his hair with his left hand. Tara saw a flash of gold metal as it caught the sunlight. She hid her disappointment well, she thought, as they talked for a few minutes more. When a friend of his came up, diverting his attention, she left to stand among the other spectators. Most of the riders were dismounted next to their horses in the middle of the arena. Their mounts' heads hung from the withers, and a calm had settled over the crowd. Things were winding down.

As the sun rested low in the sky, horses were led back to their trailers to be unsaddled and loaded. Tara stayed back, trying to act as if she belonged, feeling anything but. Still, she waited until the last trailer had turned down the drive, and the last person had closed their car door and driven off the ranch.

"What do I owe you, Tom?"

"Well, it'll be sixty dollars for today…"

"For the whole day?" Tara was incredulous; it was less than what she would have paid her dressage trainer for a forty-five-minute lesson.

"Well, I believe you only rode Blackie for half the day."

She shook her head. "And what about yesterday?"

"Well, now," he nodded his head, as if to counteract the wagging of her own. "We'll just call it even."

"No way!"

"Let's see here—" He walked toward the gate. "Better shut this gate before I forget."

She walked with him toward her truck and trailer, grabbed her planner off the front seat, and wrote him a check for $120, a substantial amount for her, but nothing for all he had given. She handed him the check and hugged him good-bye, her squeeze causing his hearing aid to sound a high-pitched squeal. He laughed again. She paused to look at him. Even after working a full day outside in the dirt and dust, he had a clean smell, like the air around him.

The light of another day was fading as she went to halter Blackie. Tom climbed into his golf cart, but stopped halfway to his house, watching from a distance as she loaded her horse, with some difficulty, into the trailer. She climbed into the cab, waved at him through her window, and guided her rig over the metal bridge and onto the unfamiliar road that lay ahead.

10

~learning~

You cannot add to a vessel already full. First you must empty the contents, then there will be room for the new.

–Wm. W. Walter
The Sickle

June arrived, and with it days that grew warmer and longer. Every week on her days off, Tara drove inland, away from cooler ocean breezes, to spend as much time as possible with Tom. In addition to Blackie, her clients had, one by one, consented to having their horses hauled down to see "the cowboy," until nearly all of them had made at least one trip.

"What does he teach you?" they'd ask her, wanting to know what was so special about him.

"Well, umm, you do a lot of turns and walking over things with your horse," she'd attempt, realizing that anything she might say sounded like nothing, still wondering how much about Tom she herself understood. Most people tried to be polite about her efforts, nodding at her explanations with empty stares or distracted eyes. Yet she was glad when another Wednesday arrived, and she found herself, once again, forgoing a day of rest to maneuver her rig through busy lanes and connecting interstates that took her east, then south to Wesland.

By the time she pulled in the drive, the early morning fog had already burned off, and as was often typical of a California sky, the sun rose unshielded in a background of solid blue. Quickly unloading Blackie, she wasted no time in tacking him up and riding him out to the arena. Tom followed in the cart, opening the vertical field gate for her with his remote. She smiled to herself, remembering her reaction when Willa, the ranch owner, informed her that he had invented and built the gate himself.

"This ain't the only one, you know," Willa had said. "There are others like it he designed for friends and family at other places."

In light of this and his other inventions, one being his swivel stool, Tara had been dumbfounded to learn he hadn't completed the eighth grade.

"Well, I preferred being outside with the animals, where life was real," had been his matter-of-fact answer to her wide-eyed stare, referring to his family's homestead in Oregon.

By the eighth grade, she had just been getting used to the idea of regurgitating data for term papers and final exams. She'd spent her days inside square, gray cement buildings stacked in tight rows that prevented any real sunlight from entering the line of windows along one side. Already on track to go to college, as all of her classmates had been, she studied everything but what she had a real passion for. It was what had been expected, what everyone else in her family had done.

On high school graduation day she stood, weighted in cap and gown, in a line of twelve hundred fellow look-a-like graduates, knowing practically no one and terrified of the world—a world light years from Tom, focused and bent over his gears under the unsheltered sky, patiently willing a screwdriver to work in his leathered hands. For him, the inspiration to create something invented in his own mind had always had room to thrive and be realized into form. She watched him park the golf cart next to the arena with his back to the sun, and felt a spontaneous surge of envy. He nodded for her to let herself inside the gate.

Bringing Blackie alongside the fence, she leaned sideways out of the saddle and fumbled with the manual latch. Blackie squirmed and sidestepped, making it difficult for her to maneuver the lever and swing the gate open without dismounting. But after several tries, she and her horse were inside.

"Now, it's whatever you want to do," Tom said to her, sitting outside the fence. So far, he hadn't asked her for anything that would cause her gelding's tension to surface, encouraging her to ride on a long rein and keep cues and movements simple and to a minimum.

She began with a warm up routine in the sandy arena, checking off each segment in her head. First the left side at a walk, then the right side. Then the trot. Then the canter. When she finished, Tom suggested she ride outside. She slouched at the request, wanting to know what would happen if she tried more advanced dressage movements.

"Tom, one thing I've always had trouble with is his canter pirouettes. I was wondering if you would watch how he steps with his hind feet while I swing his front end around them."

"Well," Tom nodded, "there's a lot we can do to prepare for that." And the next thing she knew, she was riding down into the dry creek bed, Blackie stumbling over the rocks.

"Just leave him on a loose rein and let him work it out," Tom said under the shade of the golf cart parked on the ledge overlooking the bottom.

But Blackie stumbled so often in the bed and up the bank that Tara wondered if he needed to be shod and bent over his shoulder to gaze down at his feet. The hoof walls were smooth and trim, reminding her that the shoer had been out only two weeks before.

"I don't know why he's doing that," she said to Tom who merely nodded, his face expressionless.

She sighed and rode up onto the flat surface as he pointed to six tires lying on the ground, lined up in a row. As horse and rider approached, Blackie shied sideways, not wanting to go anywhere near the rubber doughnuts. Tara used her legs in a rapid motion to urge him in closer.

"Nuh, nuh."

Tara looked up at Tom who was perched forward on the edge of his seat, one hand raised, his palm facing toward her. She stopped.

"Now, you'll just ride around them."

She stared at him for a moment, but eventually did as asked. After a few laps around the tires in each direction, Blackie stopped on his own and extended his neck to the ground. After a few snorts, he inched closer to explore the strange objects with his heavy breath.

"We'll wait until he gets a feel for them with his nose," Tom said. As usual, Tom was in no hurry, sitting back in his golf cart with outstretched legs, feet up on the dash and hands folded loosely in his lap. "You see there?"

When she looked down again, the Thoroughbred was dragging his nose across the black rubber, painting moisture from his nostrils in random swirls and brush strokes. She could feel by the way her seat melded into his back that the tension in his body was gone. This time, when she used her legs to urge him to step across, he didn't hesitate.

After walking back and forth over the tires from all directions, she tried riding the long way through, from one end of the line to the other.

"When the person stays in time with the horse, the horse will stay in step with the rider, and learn to put his feet right through the center of each tire."

But Blackie snaked his body from side to side instead, avoiding the doughnuts entirely. Tom's chuckle made her more determined, and after many tries, she managed to pick up her rein just as he was picking up a front leg. The rein, used at that moment, caused him to step sideways. Flop! His foot landed flat on the dark rubber.

"There!" Tom was enthusiastic. "You see, you got there earlier that time, in time with his feet."

"But I thought I wanted him to step in the middle of the tire."

"W-e-e-e-ll," Tom laughed the word in rapid staccato, "if he doesn't want to put his feet anywhere near the things in the first place, you'll settle for the fact that you got more than what you had before. Later on, as your timing improves, you can worry about going to the next—" and rather than finishing his sentence in words, Tom did what he so often did, and made a gesture with his arms, inviting her to finish the thought. She frowned, but nodded silently.

"Now, do you want to take a break?" He brought his feet down and leaned forward onto his knees, looking intently at her.

She gave a start. "Why, no, Tom! I'm not tired. I'd like to get as much done while I'm here as I can," she said, still thinking how much she wanted his help with the canter pirouettes.

"Sure," he nodded again before asking about Lena. "How's she gettin' along?" It had been nearly two weeks since Tara and her assistant had come down together for the day.

"Pretty good."

"Do you remember what happened when you were here last?" Tom leaned back again in the golf cart, tipping his hat high on his forehead while replacing his feet on the dash. Tara nodded, but turned her gelding to face him directly, knowing he would retell the story anyway.

"She thought she'd try riding with that plastic flag in her hand." He paused. "Well, when she tried to run it along the top of the fence there," he pointed his thumb over his shoulder to the arena behind him, "her sorrel wasn't sure he liked that very much." He paused again, waiting for another nod. "But, he was doin' all right until the flag got stuck in the fence, and Lena tried to pull it out."

Pause.

"When it finally came out, it came pretty quick and just popped him right there on the nose." His eyes were already twinkling. "Why, when that big horse saw that thing come at him, he decided he'd just about had enough."

When the plastic flag had accidentally flapped Lena's horse in the face, he had wheeled, bucked, and dumped her on the ground, then stood with his nose drooped over her forehead as if he couldn't figure out how she'd gotten there. Lena, normally polite and soft spoken around Tom, glared up at the sorrel from her heaped position in the sand and spontaneously uttered, "Why, you little shit."

"Ha, ha, ha," Tom punched the air. "I never thought she knew how to say those kinds of words. Ha, ha, ha." His face was tipped back, mouth frozen open. The expression infected Tara, and she was soon giggling along with him. When their laughter quieted, a welcome breeze came in from the west and made the leaves rustle.

"Did you ever get hurt by a horse, Tom?"

"Sure," he gave a single nod and paused, eyes fixed on Tara. She waited.

"There was a time," he looked past the Wesland fence line onto neighboring fields, "after my brothers and sisters had left home—"

"How many of you were there?"

"There were four of us boys and four girls."

She nodded, wondering if they had been anything like him.

"I stayed on the place, tending to the ranch and my folks, who were gettin' on in years. I only had one hired hand to help out there—" he paused to reach for a bottle of water. After a long sip, he eyed her. "So you can imagine there was some things to do around the place."

She nodded again.

"I'd been riding out in poor weather." He screwed the top on his water bottle. "My horse, well, he kinda slipped out from underneath me and fell on my leg." He set the water bottle down. "Now, the way that horse fell, it broke my ankle in such a way that I had to have a cast clear up past my knee."

"How long were you in the hospital?"

"About a fortnight," he looked at her. "Pretty much all I could think about was how much was piling up at home." He shifted his position. "They wanted to keep me there longer, but I managed to convince the doctors that I'd take real good care of my leg, see."

She nodded.

"Well, I made my way out the door on crutches. Promised myself I'd wait at least another week before trying to ride."

Tara smiled at the way his shoulders shook with soft laughter, and was already picturing what came next. A few short days later, he'd asked the hand to saddle a gentle mare. She could picture him working his way over uneven ground to the barn on crutches where the mare had stood, ready and waiting. He had shaken his head in response to the workman's offer to give him a leg up.

"I might find myself quite a distance from help," he had said, pointing to the surrounding hills with his eyes. "I need to know, now, before I start out, that I'm capable, should something happen."

The fact that he had broken his left leg meant mounting from the customary left side of the horse was impossible. But Tom, never having limited himself to customary fashion, did not hesitate to work his way around to the off side of the mare, where he propped both crutches under his left arm for support.

"I had to weight my bad leg, you see," he said, "and barely managed to hop high enough to catch my right foot in the right-hand stirrup." But after letting the crutches fall to the ground he'd grabbed the horn of his roping saddle and swung on, riding for weeks with that cast halfway up to his hip. Tara winced at the thought.

"Ooookaaay." Tom was fumbling under his sleeve to look at his watch. Tara narrowed her eyes at the gesture, having already learned that he cared little about time. "Guess we should head in for lunch."

Tara stared down at her horse's mane. Once again, he'd managed to get her to stop before she'd intended. When she looked up, he had already backed the golf cart out of her path and was waiting for her to head back. As she reached the front of the barn, she dismounted and led Blackie into his stall to be untacked. Tom was still waiting in the cart when she reemerged, and after motioning her to take the passenger seat, drove her back to the house.

His mobile home was a solid and well-built "double wide" with an adjoining dining room, separate kitchen, hallway, two bedrooms, and two baths. Each room was fully carpeted, tidy, and clean. A well-cushioned couch was set along one wall of the living room, which was lined in simulated wood paneling, giving it a 1950s look. Photographs of a younger Tom, some alongside his brothers, and some with others he had worked with over the years, hung above bookshelves along the opposite wall. Daylight filtered in through the large corner windows and made the room homey.

"I have everything I need," he had said earlier that morning, gesturing to his surroundings with a circular motion of his fingertips, the palms of his hands open towards the sky.

His lifestyle was a far cry from what it could have been had he been interested in self-promotion and making money. He certainly could have, Tara realized. Yet he continued to charge nominal fees in exchange for endless hours given to those who descended upon him, with no regard for what day of the week it was.

"What was it like where you were raised?" Many people asked that question, wanting to know what in his upbringing had allowed him to become the horseman he was.

"Good summer country," was how he'd answered them, and politely ignoring their need to idolize him, he'd emphasized that a house built with no electricity or indoor plumbing had offered a much easier living during the time of year that produced warm weather and the slow passing of daylight hours.

"I've got some salad here." Tom's voice made her turn abruptly from a picture hanging on the living room wall. She walked over to help him set food on the table. His wife, a few years younger than he, had her own horses and often left for the day to ride on some of their neighbors' ranches. But just as often, she made sure there was something ready for Tom and whoever might show up to eat—giving Tara insight as to what it might be like to share a home and husband with the rest of the world.

It was one-thirty in the afternoon by the time they finished eating, and Tara found herself in the living room slumped into one of Tom's recliners, tilted back with her feet up, the same as he was doing on the twin model. She gazed at him through heavy eyelids, thinking she ought to be riding and making use of her day. But it seemed that the more time she spent here, the more this drowsy sensation weighted her limbs, melting every inch of her into the chair.

"I can't teach a person anything, and I never liked the idea of calling myself a teacher," Tom was saying, his voice permeating her senses, "but if there is a willingness, maybe I can help someone learn something. Learning has to come from the inside of a person, same as it does for the horse."

He took a deep breath and swallowed.

"I usually tell people," he continued, "that it's here where they're exposed to new or different things. But it's at home where the real learning takes place, where a person has to figure things out for themselves."

She had to think about that. If she were trying to learn from someone, she wanted as much instruction as possible to make sure she wouldn't do anything wrong.

"Do you like walnuts?" he interjected.

She frowned, not understanding the segue, but nodded.

"Well, you know they grow walnuts here on the place." He paused again. "Two or three days ago, Willa brought me over a pretty good-sized box full," he said.

Ignoring Tara's blank expression, Tom got up from his chair and motioned for her to follow him through the back sliding glass doors. At one end of the wooden deck sat a picnic table fully shaded by an awning. On top of the table sat a box full of walnuts. Now she understood. Tom wanted help shelling the walnuts.

"There was a time when I would have set down to shell a box this size in one or two sessions," he said, slowly turning to her. "But now I figure that what I don't finish in one sitting will still be there the next time I get ready to do some more."

"I'd be happy to help you with them, Tom."

"Well, let's see now."

He moved without hurry to the table, then sat down slowly and positioned himself by adjusting the height of his bench seat with a pillow. After motioning for Tara to take a seat beside him, he took care to arrange a place between his feet for an empty box.

"This is where the shells will fall," he said, pointing to the box.

He then carefully placed the box of walnuts within an arm's length and reached for a wooden block lying on the table. The block had an indentation in the middle, "Carved 'specially to hold a walnut." He turned toward her, his eyes, now looking startlingly brown in the shade, fixed on her face while his hand hovered over the block, motioning to it.

"Now, there's a way," he noted, "that a person can shell a walnut so that they end up with two whole halves instead of just pieces," and he placed an unshelled walnut "pointy side up" in the indentation carved in the wood and began tapping the nut around the top with a hammer.

"Not too heavy, not too light," he said, and emerged with two whole walnut halves, their wavy ridges reminding Tara of miniature human brains. "Now, you give that a try."

She was reaching for the hammer almost before the words were out of his mouth, and placing a walnut on the wooden block, tapped around the head of it a few times. As she picked away pieces of shell, the nut exposed itself into numerous crumbs.

"It might take a few tries." Tom stared at the broken walnut.

Accustomed to using a nutcracker, she silently questioned Tom's method with the hammer, but she could see that if she were to help him, she'd have to do it the way he wanted. She reached inside the box for another. Then another, and then another. Her astonishing lack of success finally caused her to pause as she examined yet another shell in hand, her thumb sliding over the curves and valleys of its exterior. She looked at Tom and waited for him to tell her what she was doing wrong. He said nothing and nodded for her to continue. She turned back to the walnut.

"Not too heavy, not too light," he repeated. She stopped for a moment, realizing she'd heard him say that the first time. But had she?

It then occurred to her to try tapping the head of the nut in different ways. In five more tries, she realized each shell was responding differently to the weight and action of the hammer. If she hammered too hard, the nut crumbled along with the shell. If she hit too soft, not enough happened. The thing was, what was too hard for one shell seemed too soft for another, and vice versa. She took in a deep breath.

The next walnut had her full attention. She began to tap softly, then gradually harder on certain spots where the shell was less yielding, making adjustments as she went. After picking away the broken pieces of shell, there emerged two complete walnut halves.

"I did it!" She sat up abruptly.

"Now, I'll just let you tackle a few of those for a while," Tom said, easing himself away from the table. "Then I'll be back to see how you're gettin' along," and he shuffled his way through the glass doors.

With renewed enthusiasm, Tara decided to crack most of the walnuts for Tom. But in less than fifteen minutes, an aching stiffness ran up her shoulders and back. The hammer had become heavy, and she had trouble controlling its action, getting a lot more crumbs than halves. She looked at the still full box of walnuts, and her insides dragged. This was going to take a long time.

"Do you think that's about enough for today?" Tom suddenly reemerged.

She looked up, surprised. "I'd be happy to do more for you, Tom," she lied. But he was already turning back into the house, shaking his head.

"I expect they'll still be there tomorrow."

Feeling guilty, Tara got up and followed him back into the house. In two strides, her long legs caught up to his deliberate pace and made her slow abruptly.

"A person can get kinda sore doin' what they're not accustomed to," he eyed her.

She remained silent.

"When a person gets sore, he's not liable to be able to concentrate on what he set out to do."

There seemed to be something he was trying to tell her. She stood on the spot as he made his way back to the recliner. Shouldn't she be out riding? Reluctantly, she followed him back to her chair.

"People oftentimes ask me why their horse isn't doing things the way they'd like," he said, out of the blue. "Most likely, that question is followed by them wondering how things could be better." And he paused to look at her. Was he referring to the question she had asked earlier that morning about getting Blackie better at canter pirouettes?

"When I ask them more about what's taking place between them and their horse," he continued, "it usually turns out that they've been spending a lot of time training on the horse."

Tara squirmed in her seat.

"Everything I learned," he went on again, "I learned from the horse. So I wouldn't call myself a trainer, the same way I don't care to call myself a teacher."

He took a longer pause this time, while a frown slowly increased the line between Tara's eyebrows.

"I like to try and figure out a way to present myself to the horse, so that what I'm asking for is understandable to the horse. That way, the horse is happy, and I'm happy."

She was still frowning.

"Now, I suppose you want to ride some more this afternoon," he said.

Silence.

"Sure, Tom," her voice was weak when the words finally came out. She rose hesitantly from her chair, her legs reacquiring that lead feeling. As she opened the door to step outside, she turned back with an urge to ask another question, but Tom's eyes were already closed, head tilted back against the chair, mouth open, and a slight snore escaping with his breath. She left to tack up her gelding, assuming she'd be riding alone for a while. But just after she'd let herself into the arena, she saw the golf cart speeding through the pasture gate toward her. *Now that's timing*, she thought.

"You'll just start out on a loose rein, like you were starting from the beginning," he said to her as she moved off at a trot.

"And don't try and do anything fancy," he added, almost yelling to make sure she heard him across the arena.

She felt an inner twinge, but went on without argument, holding the reins loose at the buckle. Blackie stretched his head and neck out long, and feeling unrestricted, lengthened his stride. Tom then had her change direction, make transitions from trot to canter and back again. Without the use of her reins, she had to rely solely on her seat.

"Now make a circle at this end," Tom called to her.

Tara picked up her reins and coordinated various parts of her body, as she was accustomed to doing — multi-tasking.

"Remember that you're not here to make a day's wages."

She hesitated. Okay, so she was trying to do too much too fast. She dropped her reins again and with that, Blackie leaned into the turn.

"You'll want him to round out nicely in the circle."

She let out an exasperated breath. In dressage, bending a horse's body through a circle was one of the most basic of exercises. When the horse could bend in alignment with the circle's circumference, he would be balanced evenly on all fours instead of leaning into the turn like a motorcycle, the way Blackie was doing now. Balancing him evenly on all fours was something she could do — on a shorter rein. She made numerous attempts to achieve that same balance with a loose rein, but at length, was completely out of breath and had to stop. An agitated heat consumed her. Tom was chuckling again.

"Sometimes a person needs to learn to do less in order to get more."

Now what does he mean by that? She felt stupid. Only, Tom was smiling, as if he was pleased with her, and shook his head when she asked to try again.

"Naw, this horse has had enough for one day. But it'll be something you can work out at home."

She slumped heavily in the saddle.

"Now, when I was born, I was very small and wasn't expected to live," he said slowly, evenly, gazing at her pursed lips.

Are we still having the same conversation?

"So, I didn't have a lot of power to manhandle a horse. Still don't. But like I said before, I'd find a way to present myself to the horse so that the horse'd be happy and I'd be happy. Now, when that gets to working, they'll work their heart out for you."

She understood the words, but had no idea what he was talking about. In spite of his other problems, Blackie had never shied away from hard work.

Tom's eyes registered the confusion on her face. "I often tell people that life begins at eighty. Most of them think that when you're my age, you're too feeble to get along by yourself, so they offer to do everything for you. Then, if you say something they think is strange, they assume your mind has gone and don't bother you about it. The way I look at it, that's a pretty good deal."

She tried not to, but couldn't help smiling back. The sun moved slowly in the direction of the hills, and as Tom turned the golf cart around, she reluctantly opened the arena gate and rode toward the barn. Tom sat with her as she untacked Blackie by the trailer.

"What's the place like where you work?" he asked.

She told him.

"How many horses you got to work with?"

"Well, I have eight to ten horses in training, then about twice that many more people to give lessons to every week."

"I guess that keeps you pretty busy."

"It sure does," she said with emphasis, without stopping the actions of her fingers that were unbuckling the bridle straps to remove the headstall from around Blackie's ears. After she carried her gear back to the trailer and got everything set to go, Tom, as he often did, watched her load Blackie.

"Well, now," he said, after she'd managed to walk her horse in on the second try with just the chain around his nose, "sometimes just getting the job done is good enough." He leaned back in the cart. "And that's okay as far as it goes."

He paused as Tara looked at him.

"Sometimes that's all you can hope for in a situation," he added, nodding and smiling at her.

She was confused again, waiting for him to say more, but realizing there was nothing more he intended to say, she walked up to give him an awkward hug. As she headed down the drive, he waved to her. Returning the gesture, she realized how much he reminded her of Mr. Gloss, her high school driver's training instructor. Mr. Gloss had been the only teacher in all her years at school whom she remembered with any fondness. For some reason, he had liked her from the moment she'd gotten into the driver's seat for the first time. After she had uneasily started the ignition and turned onto the busy, four-lane thoroughfare surrounding her Los Angeles high school, he'd directed her onto a quiet, tree-lined residential street. There he'd rested his hand on her shoulder and laughed in delighted amusement when she, cradling the wheel in both hands, had involuntarily ducked her head while driving under a canopy of low hanging branches. The car's solid roof had, of course, made her action foolish. But with his simple gesture, Mr. Gloss had allowed her to feel all right inside anyway.

Tara smiled and made her way toward the interstate.

11

~omen~

Whatever is meant to be, will be—but then,
what isn't meant to be sometimes happens anyway.

—Anonymous

"I'd like to go again," Lena said to Tara one afternoon as they sat outside her office. Tara was recounting the latest trip to Tom's while scratching Wet Paw behind the ears. The tabby walked back and forth between them, his legs wobbling over thighs that couldn't offer a flat surface.

Tara reached down to the floor where she had set her planner and began thumbing through the days of the month, grabbing the cat before he smeared his dirty paws over the clean pages.

"We could go down on the tenth and stay a couple of days." Tara looked up.

"Great."

It was a Saturday morning when they loaded Blackie and Lena's big red Thoroughbred and drove southeast at a steady sixty miles per hour. Tara and Lena shouted their conversation in order to be heard above the rush of incoming air that leaked through the Chevy's dry, eroded rubber window sealing. The cab remained noisy until they exited the freeway and turned east again, moving in the same direction as the prevailing winds.

"Whoa! Is that what I think it is?" Tara's foot flew off the accelerator. The truck's engine chugged and backfired as its heavy gears, the trailer, and two horses in tow wound their speed down in a hurry.

Lena craned forward to get a better look from her side. "Look at that," her tone was matter-of-fact.

"I didn't know bald eagles lived around here!" It was difficult for Tara to notice creatures of the air without remembering a brief affair she'd had with a man from a local Audubon Society years before.

Later, she thought it ironic that just before she'd met him, she had begun noticing the stealth of a great white egret as it hunted the marshy areas adjacent to the public arena where she used to ride. It was only after they'd become involved that she'd realized that the bird was an emblem of the society itself. The relationship had ended badly, but Rodney's enthusiastic attention to the skies had rubbed off on her, and today was one of the times she didn't regret it.

The eagle was flying parallel with the rig and headed in the same direction, low and straight, wings moving powerfully, rhythmically, up and down. Its steady gaze gave it the same stern aura Tara had seen replicated on coins, flags, and countless memorabilia over the years. But to see one real and alive for the first time was more than she would have imagined.

"Don't tell me. Is that a ribbon trailing behind its body?"

"What *is* that?" Lena echoed.

Whatever it was appeared to be some kind of cosmic joke. Tara half expected to see "E Pluribus Unum" written on the side of the fluttering object, like one of those advertisements flown overhead by a hired plane. *In Many, One*, she repeated the Latin words to herself, liking that particular translation. It reminded her of the way Tom viewed the world, seeing the good in everyone he met.

"It's a snake!" She spat the words, her mood changing to one of foreboding as she watched the creature being held captive in the eagle's claws and flapping helplessly in the wind.

"Nothin' but a scavenger," Mark Twain had once said of the bird that he saw as unfit to represent a nation. It was suddenly hard to shake those words, even as she turned her rig south and sped on for the last leg of their journey.

When they pulled into the long drive at Wesland, Tara parked the truck's nose under the leafy overhang of a willow tree. Even a June sun in Central California would make the cab melt. She checked her watch. Only nine-thirty, and she was already struggling against that moving-through-molasses sensation. She wanted to put her head back or lie down in the cab, but Tom was already swinging around the mobile home in his golf cart and coming toward them. Dry dirt, sand, and pebbles flew out from under the wheels and made a grating sound. His speed startled her. She still didn't expect him to do what he did at his age. Lena laughed.

Tom pulled up near the driver's side and, as Tara stepped out of the truck, swung his hat high overhead, inviting her in. She reached under the golf cart's plastic canopy to give him a soft kiss on the lips. After she stood back, he motioned her in again, but she slapped him on the arm.

"You're gonna get a reputation for being a dirty old man!"

He raised his elbow in front of his face to fend off her blows and laughed, nodding his head. "Well, what have you gals brought down today?"

They went around to the back of the trailer, and after unloading the horses, both women saddled up and rode in the field all morning. By the time they broke for lunch and walked back to the house, Tom had already set the table. Tara instinctively navigated toward the kitchen and stirred a large pot of bean stew he had prepared early that morning, then ladled it into bowls while Lena brought out bread, butter, and cheese.

"I'd like to buy a few copies of your book, Tom," Tara said as they sat around the dining table and talked between mouthfuls.

"A few, did you say?" Tom looked up from his beans.

Tara nodded. "And would you be able to sign them for me?"

"Well, now," he set his spoon down, and sat back in his chair. "Over the years, I've gotten quite a few comments about the book." He cleared his throat. Tara leaned forward, anticipating a testimonial. "I've found that most people have trouble understanding a lot of what's written."

Tara narrowed her eyes as he looked straight at her.

"I don't suppose you plan on keeping all of those copies for yourself?" he asked.

She smiled again. "No, I have a couple of other people in mind, as well."

"Well," he cleared his throat a second time, "I have some copies here that you're welcome to give me your money for. Might lighten your pockets some." He turned to get a smile and a nod out of Lena before turning back to Tara. "But maybe you could save yourself and the others some trouble by not taking the books with you when you leave." His gaze was still steady when she cocked her head. "That way," he went on, "you'll save yourself having to haul all that heavy weight, and at the same time, you won't get any complaints from your friends when they try to read something they can't understand."

Tara blinked in silence, her eyes fixed on Tom. He and Lena were already snickering by the time she got the joke.

"All right, all right!" She felt her face grow hot.

"Well," Tom was obviously enjoying the tease, "in giving me the money while saving yourself the trouble of reading the book, you'll be doin' us both a favor. That's a win-win situation, don't you think?"

They all laughed.

After lunch, they rode out into the back pasture. Tara tried to take Blackie across a ditch in the uneven ground, but he balked.

"Why does he always do this, Tom?"

"Let's let Lena ride out in front," he answered, and only when the sorrel passed her and shuffled without hesitation down the slope did Blackie consent to go. It seemed too easy, but Tom reassured her. "He'll get so that he goes for you whether there's another horse there or not."

Tara nodded glumly. Shouldn't he just obey her because she asked? How else would she ever know what to expect, or what she could rely on? But they continued to ride over bumps and hills and in and out of the creek bed with Lena in the lead until the end of the day.

There was still plenty of daylight left by the time the horses had been stalled and fed. When the women emerged from the barn, Willa had come out of the main house and was talking to Tom, sitting beside him in his golf cart parked outside his mobile home. A light breeze and the chirping of birds felt soothing as Tara and Lena came up to join them. Tom had set the brake and put his legs up, crossing his ankles on the dash. Tara smiled at the way he always seemed content to be wherever he was, and was disappointed when their conversation was interrupted by the sound of a diesel engine rumbling over the metal bridge.

"Now, who's this?" Willa leaned towards Tom, putting on her most accusatory tone. Tara turned to see a gray dually hauling a matching gooseneck stock trailer. When it stopped alongside the ranch house, the driver remained seated at the wheel, appearing to be logging miles into a book, leaving the engine to idle.

"Oh!" Tom looked surprised. "Well, I believe this might be the fellow from Montana."

"The fella from Montana." Willa kept her stern demeanor.

Tom avoided her eyes and nodded matter-of-factly. "Yah. I believe he called last night."

"You believe he called last night."

Tom nodded again, still avoiding her eyes. "Yuh."

The driver's face took on the full light of the sun as he stepped out of the cab. A very good-looking cowboy in jeans and black hat began walking toward them.

He looks really young, Tara was already cautioning herself.

"Well, since you didn't bother to tell me, is this one leaving his horses overnight?" She heard Willa's voice behind her.

Tom, sinking deeper into the seat of the golf cart, began to nod his head in rhythm with silent laughter. "I forgot," he peeked at Willa out of the corner of his eye, looking sheepish. "I believe he's planning to leave his horses here a few days," he looked away, then back at her again.

"A few *days*?" Willa shook her head for added impact. "Well, he's come this far, I can't exactly turn him away now, can I?"

"I don't believe that'd be very neighborly," Tom whispered now, so their conversation would stay out of earshot of the approaching stranger.

They were all silent and stared at the cowboy walking toward them. As he got nearer, he slowed his step, looking from one to the other. Tara waited for someone to greet him, but still in a teasing mood, not even Tom made a move to say hello or be welcoming. She thought the poor guy might turn around and go back to his truck, but he kept coming, although more hesitant with every footfall. He nodded at her. She returned the gesture and smiled.

"I'm looking for Mr. Dorrance," he almost whispered.

How polite, Tara mused. *Mr. Dorrance.* But before she could answer him, Tom was already leaning forward. Looking relieved, the stranger smiled broadly, and calling himself Rio, quickly bent over the front of the cart to shake Tom's outstretched hand.

"I'm Tara," she said, and offered him her own. She was startled by the rough strength in his grasp after noting the sensitive caution in his approach.

"I believe you mentioned you wanted to have your horses stay over a few days," Tom spoke again.

"Well, maybe for the night, if that's all right. I might be coming back through here again in a week or two to stay a couple of days."

Tom nodded. "Well, you'll need to confirm that with the boss lady here," he said, a teasing mood returning.

"How many you got?" Willa's shorthand referred to the number of Rio's horses.

"Three."

"They all go together?"

"I have them all riding loose in the trailer now."

"You can keep them in the paddock next to my horses. I'll just go get my chestnut to make room for yours," Willa's tone was friendly as she swiveled off her seat and walked down the drive toward one of the permanent barns.

"You travel this way often?" Tom asked him.

"I'm on my way to southern California to deliver a horse. Been wanting to work with you for a long time and thought I'd stop by now that I had the chance."

"You got a place out there in Montana?"

Rio gave a single nod. "My parents run a working cow ranch outside of Bozeman. Me and my brothers try and act useful." All seriousness had left his face. Tara realized he felt right at home here *among his people*, suddenly self-conscious of her dressage breeches.

"Where in southern California are you headed?" she tried to join in.

"Down near Orange County," his eyes were soft when he looked at her.

She had hoped she'd know of someone there to mention, but as she was struggling to recall, Willa walked up leading a stocky Quarter Horse.

"Maybe Tara'd like to help me take Willa's chestnut over to the north pasture while Rio unloads his," Tom said, nodding at Willa.

Taking the cue, Tara climbed into the cart next to Tom and took Willa's horse in hand, freeing the owner to show Rio where to stable his three. Tom started the cart off slow to give Tara a chance to make sure the horse would follow without pulling her out of her seat. But the horse came easily, and soon they had picked up speed, the chestnut trotting to keep up along a graveled two-track that led off the main driveway. Tara turned in her seat to make sure the lead line stayed clear of the wheels and got a direct view of the others still standing where she and Tom had left them. Lena and Willa were engaged in conversation. Rio stood slightly apart, gazing after her. Even at that distance, their eyes locked, and the light from the setting sun reflected a glint in his dark eyes.

12

~willing communication~

I know that you believe you understand what you think I said,
but I am not sure you realize that what you heard is not what I meant.

— Anonymous

"Where did you stay last night?" Tara asked Rio the next morning as he led a small chestnut mare to the tying post outside the paddock where his horses had been stabled overnight.

"At the motel. Didn't get much sleep, though. The walls were thinner than paper." His eyes surveyed an adjacent pasture that contained five more of Willa's horses, engrossed in their grazing. The lush field had obviously been irrigated, and it contrasted the surrounding landscape, which was already seasonally brittle.

"Try the Inn next time. That's where we stay," she said, walking in the opposite direction, her head turned back over her shoulder so he could hear. She had spied his western saddle left sitting on the ground by the fence and reached down to pick it up. Its heaviness nearly took her breath away, but she remained stoic while attempting to carry and not drag it back over to him.

"You've either been taught good manners or are just naturally kind," he said softly, taking the saddle from her and swinging it up easily over his mare's back.

"It's no trouble," she replied, holding the gate open for him as he rode into the pasture with the other horses. She latched the gate behind him and hiked around the perimeter toward Tom and Willa, sitting in the golf cart at the opposite end. Lena was perched on the cart's hood and Andy, whom Tara recognized from Tom's clinic months before, had joined them and now stood alongside to watch.

"I'd like this mare to be more relaxed, Tom, especially working around other horses," Rio was explaining when Tara reached them.

Tom nodded and pointed toward the loose bodies grazing in the field. "Let's see what happens when you ride with the herd for a bit."

Rio rode the mare toward the other horses. She seemed fine until threatening looks and pinned ears warned her not to invade their territory, and she quickened her step.

"Now, when you feel her get anxious, you'll turn her," Tom said.

The mare, trying to avoid the others, moved into a trot as Rio wove her in and around them. She was still trotting when Tom's voice broke the silence.

"Okay, that's enough," he said. Another minute went by, and the mare was still trotting.

"That's enough," Tom said again and waited. Tara wondered why Rio didn't just stop his horse.

"That's *enough*," Tom said louder, and then to the group, "The parrot keeps talking until the message gets through."

The mare kept trotting.

"I said, THAT'S ENOUGH!" The unlikely boom in Tom's voice made Tara stand straight.

Rio leaned back in his saddle, picked up the reins, and pulled the mare down to a walk, letting out a groan that could be heard easily from fifty yards away. Tara recognized the sound. She had heard it inside herself countless times.

"Tom, why didn't you just tell him to stop?" Andy asked the question on everybody's mind.

"Because if I'da told him to stop, then he would have stopped, like he ended up doing anyway," Tom answered matter-of-factly. "But I didn't want him to stop," he added, and then paused for a moment, taking in everyone's stares.

"You see, if I say something real specific to a person, most likely, I'll get too much of an exacting response." He paused briefly before adding, "Which tends to keep a person from taking in the bigger picture." He paused fully to more silence. Tara wondered what the bigger picture was.

"Before the man got started," Tom was referring to Rio, "I believe he told me he wanted his horse to settle around the other horses." He waited, looking from one person to the next. "So I was looking for a way to make a suggestion about how he might go about doing that, without imposing a preset idea on him as to what would best help his horse."

"I thought you wanted him to stop," Andy admitted. The group nodded.

"Sure you did. That's what most people would think. And most people think that what they're thinking is what I mean." Pause. "But I'm trying to help a person go beyond what they're assuming is supposed to take place." Tom's hands had become animated as he turned in the golf cart to face them, nodding as if willing them to understand, his arms forming a large circle. *A globe*, Tara thought. *The big picture.*

"But I'm still not sure I understand how to have this mare stay quiet as she gets close to the others." Rio had ridden up to them and stopped near the fence.

"Well, earlier, I mentioned you might turn her when she got quick." Tom looked at Rio, then at everyone else. "If you had done a little more of that away from the other horses, directing the mare that way might have given her enough confidence to slow her feet and settle. Maybe not for very long to start with, but you could build on that, you see."

Everyone was nodding except Tara. She herself had thought of Tom's suggestion to turn the mare as a mechanical exercise, a technique, or a formula applied to get a specific, physical response that could be memorized and used again in the same way another time. Not as a means by which to give the horse a change of heart, a sense of how to calm down. The latter was a living, breathing thing, used for this situation. Not necessarily for every situation.

"Tom, is it okay to just pick up the reins to slow her down?" Rio asked.

Tara knew why he had asked the question. Many who had worked with Tom, or one of his protégés, often reinterpreted or oversimplified what he said, telling their students they shouldn't ever have to use the reins to stop a horse, relying on their seat and legs instead.

"Well, it's whatever best gets it across to the horse at that moment." Tom, as usual, didn't deny or endorse any particular idea, and ended with his stock phrase, "It all depends."

Tara's mind quickly sped back to her years at school, then to modern television, advertisements, political speeches. Day after day, millions of ideas were spoon-fed to the masses the same way supermarkets sold meats and vegetables—prepackaged, washed, and weighed. One size fits all. It was the "miracle" of contemporary marketing, requiring no one to think or feel, or risk an original concept.

Rio made a second attempt with his mare and rode between the other horses.

"Now, you'll adjust to fit the situation," Tom called out to him.

Tara admired Rio, knowing what it took to be out there, to admit he didn't have all the answers, letting his ego take a back seat to learning something new. How unlike the well-known trainer who had brought his horse down to Tom for some pointers a few weeks before. The trainer had rarely been around Tom, although he advertised himself as a student, and was well known for the training equipment he sold all over the world—special halters, bits, bridle attachments, reins—convincing those that purchased his merchandise that it worked better than what they had already. The day he came to Wesland, Tom immediately recognized his need to show off, and so made no comment, except to nod politely at the fancy maneuvers the man made on his horse.

"I figured the last thing he'd want is me tellin' him that there wasn't anything he was doing that actually amounted to much," Tom had said to Tara afterward.

"But, Tom, aren't you ever tempted to just tell people they're full of it?" She knew that at the very least, he could have politely tortured the trainer with the truth.

"Now that's a waste of my time and effort," he had said without hesitation. "I'm not here to try and change anyone. That's up to them."

The trainer had left for home the same day. A week later, it had gotten back to her that he had dubbed Tom a "poor communicator" when asked by his following how his session with the master had gone. "He doesn't know how to explain things."

It was what many people said about Tom.

Tara's attention returned to Rio and his mare with the sound of Tom's staccato "Yuh. Yuh. Yuh." He was nodding even as the mare became nervous near the herd. This time, Rio turned her away. After she had settled and was walking, he turned her back to test her confidence. When she got anxious, he turned her away again. It seemed so easy now. So obvious.

"Now that's fine," Tom said. "This is just one example of how you can give a horse exposure, just enough to where you don't lose her. It's similar to working with a young horse that's not used to being touched. There might be a spot on its body where it can tolerate your hand, but when you move beyond that place, it gets troubled. Then you have to come back to where it can tolerate you until you gain its trust."

Rio was nodding. Tara squirmed. The mare hadn't yet completely relaxed.

"Now, it won't matter if she does things perfect today. It's more important that a person learn what it takes to help a horse through those areas where they're troubled, and build on that."

Tara shifted her position again. It wasn't the first time that Tom had talked about building on something.

"You'll come right along with this," Tom continued, speaking to Rio. Tara looked at the elder, wondering how he had learned to be so sure of himself.

The group was quiet, resting in the filtered shade of a cluster of tall oak and elm trees. At length, Tom drove the cart back to the house where his wife had laden the table with place settings and food for lunch. They listened to Willa tell ranch stories while passing bread, butter, soup, and salad. Tara was disappointed when, not much more than an hour later, people began to rise from the table, "finishing up the chores" before the day's end.

"Looks like I better be getting ready to head out, too," Rio announced, standing next to the door.

"You're not staying another day?" Tara had forgotten he'd only planned to stay overnight.

"I've got to head south to deliver a horse, maybe pick up another, and be back in Penwood before next weekend."

"Penwood? That's near where I live! What'll you be doing up there?"

"I signed up to ride in a clinic." He then shrugged in response to her stare. "I've only paid for one day, in case I don't like it."

Tara started to speak, but stopped herself just in time, realizing that the clinic Rio referred to was being taught by the same trainer who had referred to Tom as a poor communicator. Finding herself with her mouth open, she quickly strove to say something other than what she was thinking.

"Oh."

"I'd been hearing the name of the guy who's putting it on so much that I thought I should see for myself."

"Well," Tara knew better than to spread negative gossip regarding a fellow professional. "You might find that you know quite a lot about what he has to say already," knowing that Rio had at least as much skill with a horse as the trainer, and that he'd be wasting his money.

Andy had already left, and Lena was outside, heading for the barn by the time Tom came over to them. Rio extended his hand.

"Thank you for helping me out. I hope I might be able to come back sometime."

"Well, just give a call before you do," Tom nodded his consent.

"Do you need help loading up?" Tara asked, knowing he was perfectly capable of loading his well-seasoned travelers himself.

"I'd love some."

They walked out to the paddock where his horses were stabled. He pointed out the three he would be taking, and Tara took two halters hanging beside the gate. The small Quarter Horses haltered easily and walked in tandem up to the roomy stock trailer, stepping inside without hesitation. After they were turned loose, Rio closed the tailgate and latched it shut.

"Good luck with your travels," Tara said and held out her hand. "Do you expect to be back this way?" She prepared herself for his grip as his hand took hers.

"Depending on how things go, I might come through here on my way back to Montana, but—" He shrugged, and she knew that any hoping was useless.

She waved as he climbed into his cab, started the truck engine, and wrote something in his logbook—then waited until he looked up, waved in return, and accelerated slowly down the drive. She forced herself not to follow his rig with her eyes as she walked back to the barn to meet Lena, who was getting her horse ready for their afternoon rides.

"That guy seems nice," was all she ventured that evening after they had finished for the day and were back at the hotel.

"Sexy butt," was Lena's uncensored reply.

Tara sighed heavily, admiring the easy manner of her friend who had met her husband at a bar a couple of years earlier. Tara never expected to meet any men herself while spending most of every day in a profession dominated by women. Besides, dressage was not exactly a draw for males brought up in a society that placed high value on the old macho image. That fact was what made it even more astonishing that, over the past sixty-five years, Tom's soft approach and quiet ways had been so well received in cowboy culture. "Breaking tradition, not horses," *People Magazine* had written. "The Marlboro Man Loses His Spurs," read the front page of the *New York Times*. "Leader of a quiet revolution," *Equus Magazine* had dubbed him.

As she lay in bed that night, eyes wide open, listening to Lena's sleep-regulated breathing, she remembered that Tom hadn't married until his fifties. *Maybe there's hope for me yet,* she mused. But secretly, she wondered if she was capable of anything like marriage. Being attracted to men had been the easy part. The difficulty had come with actually being around them. What was said or left unsaid had consistently and inevitably terrified her, disappointed her, humiliated her, offended her. It had never turned out the way she'd imagined it should.

In an effort to be practical about finding a healthy relationship, she'd recently attended a dating workshop, chancing an assigned hour or more of uninterrupted time with a male participant each week. She had even announced her willingness to date them all again after the workshop was over, in an effort to get to know them better. By then, she had at least learned that the initial hit of so-called "good chemistry" wasn't what made a relationship last over time. But then, the man that had taken her up on her offer hadn't ended up being someone she could muster any interest in anyway.

And then there was Steve. He'd had an open and frank way of talking about himself. No, not just of talking about himself, she realized, but disclosing what was going on inside. He could articulate how he felt. It was what had put her at ease and made her feel normal around the male sex for the first time she could remember. In fact, she'd felt so normal that, for the first year, she hadn't even noticed that she'd become his secret—until it became apparent that he was never going to leave his wife in spite of his supposed love for her. She'd had to be hit with the ensuing "maybe he loves you—sorta kinda—in his own way, but not enough" torture before she had been willing to cast hope aside and admit what a deceitful situation she'd been in all along.

She rolled over and looked at the clock. It was late. She rolled onto her other side. Sleep seemed impossible, but at some point it must have overtaken her because the next thing she knew, daylight was coming in through the hotel window.

13

~scratching the surface~

Love has more strength than an army, for one need not subdue an adversary;
an adversary can be transformed.

—Peace Pilgrim

When they arrived at Wesland, Tara turned Blackie out in the arena while she picked out his stall, filled his bucket with fresh water, and dragged a fresh bale of straw through the doorway for clean bedding. She was having a now familiar conversation with herself, one side trying to convince the other that her horse's more relaxed demeanor made up for her self-inflicted moratorium on competing. The uncertainty of if and when Tom might actually be able to help her with her dressage nagged at her, and she worked harder at loosening the compacted flakes of straw until the entire bale had been spread evenly. She finished just as the sound of a golf cart came up through the barn aisle.

"Well, now." Tom's distinct voice prompted Tara, pitchfork in hand, to move to the open door to greet him, the sweet aroma of fresh bedding still in her nostrils. But Tom was already standing by Lena's sorrel. "He's carrying on quite a bit now, isn't he?"

"He does this all the time when he's been separated from other horses," Lena said.

It took Tara a moment to realize that they were talking about the whinnying and pacing the sorrel had been doing since she'd taken Blackie out to the arena. She had completely tuned it out.

"Let's all come around to the outside where he can't see us," Tom said, backing in little steps toward the barn door, reaching out to give a tug on Lena's shirtsleeves, then Tara's, as he passed her standing outside the adjoining stall.

When they were all out from under the barn roof and out of the sorrel's sight, Tom turned his back to them and shuffled around in a circle, head bowed to the ground. The two women glanced at each other as he bent over to pick up small and medium sized stones out of the packed earth. When he had found a few, he walked back over and placed all but one in Lena's hand.

"Now," he said to her, "when your horse gets to carrying on, you'll just go up to his window and toss a pebble over in his direction, like this."

Tara and Lena poked their heads inside and watched him quickly shuffle up to the sorrel's stall before turning back to look at Lena.

"Make sure you do this, first," he said, lifting his arm up and down several times. Then he tossed the pebble gently through the bars.

Tara nearly burst out laughing. Surely, Tom didn't think that a tiny pebble, lobbed soft as a feather, was going to make a difference for this huge animal, so absorbed in his own rantings. "Stop crying, or I'll give you something to cry about," was the phrase that seemed to more aptly portray the intensity of what might be needed in this case. But Tom's quiet manner didn't even give the impression that he thought the sorrel was misbehaving. Yet, when the pebble plopped softly on the red hide, the horse turned abruptly and stood, ears pricked forward, silent, and momentarily distracted from his worries. Tara raised her eyebrows. *But will it last?*

Tom shuffled back toward them, reminding her of a toddler, the way their small bodies rocked from side to side, taking tentative steps. Or was it that babies reminded her of little old men, already wise and knowing?

When he rejoined them, the three of them waited, not speaking. In a few moments, the sorrel resumed his nervous pace. Tom nodded to Lena, who ran up to the stall door. After lifting her arm up and down, she tossed the pebble through the metal bars, and then tiptoed back. Again, they waited. She made several more runs before using up her pebbles.

"The next time," Tom said, before she could gather more, "you'll lift your arm like you were going to throw one, only you won't," Tom eyed both of them. "Have you noticed that there's a longer period between the times he gets worked up?"

Tara hadn't noticed, but nodded anyway along with Lena, who did as instructed. Tara peeked around to watch her lift her hand with no pebble in it and saw the sorrel turn, as if he was expecting it. Once his attention was focused on her, he became quiet. The next time, she just made herself visible and it had the same effect. Tom nodded.

"Well, now, I think that's gotten quite a bit better. Does Tara want to ride some?"

She nodded and returned to the arena to halter Blackie. As she was walking him back to the barn, Lena was leading her sorrel into the yard.

"What are you doing?" She wanted to know what Tom had in mind for her.

"Tying him to the pole," was Lena's shorthanded reply, referring to one of two tying poles stationed in the yard.

Tara was intrigued; tying a nervous horse could be dangerous. It was not uncommon for one to panic and pull back. She had once tied Blackie to a heavy log made into a tying post, only to watch helplessly as he dislodged it in a panic, even though it had been cemented into the ground. Fortunately, his lead line had snapped just in time. A horse dragging a heavy object in a wild frenzy could easily destroy itself and everything in its wake — including a human bystander.

But the tying poles at Wesland were different. Tom had explained that the twelve-foot-long, six-inch-thick, steel cylinders had been sunk nearly five feet into the ground. Four of those feet were in cement. The foot closest to the top was packed with earth "to prevent injury to a hoof, in case a horse pawed," he had emphasized. How rare that such forethought and care for the horse was as consistently put into practice as it was around Tom.

On the top of the pole was a wheel, attached horizontally, which rotated in either direction. Secured to the wheel was a large, heavy chain that hung down alongside the pole. The chain hung low enough for a person to reach and tie a horse to it, but high enough that it would be difficult to snag a leg if the horse reared. The height of the pole meant there was no leverage by which a horse could pull it up out of the ground, even if it stood on its hind legs. And because of the wheel at the top, a nervous horse could move around the pole without becoming wrapped tight — which would most likely send it into greater panic.

After Lena had tied her sorrel at the pole, Tom had her take a chair from the barn and sit just outside the circle her horse would make when he moved around it. Tom then asked Tara to ride down the field. After saddling Blackie, she rode away from the sorrel, who began his stormy pacing, calling after them as they moved into the distance. Now that she had stopped blocking the noise from her awareness, the harsh sound of his screams grated on her like chalk scraping on a blackboard. An ache in her jaw made her realize she'd been clenching her teeth. She turned in her saddle, watching the sorrel's whole body tremble, as if he would disintegrate, Blackie's presence the one thing that would hold him together. In spite of the warm day, a cold iciness came over her.

Mommy, can you come with me?

It was her own voice speaking inside her head, and with the words came the memory of her first day of kindergarten, years ago. She'd been looking forward to going to the big elementary school where her older sisters and brother had gone, until her mother parked alongside the curb and waited impatiently for her four-year-old daughter to open the car door and walk to her classroom. All by herself. Suddenly the world seemed way too big.

"Mommy, can you come with me?"

But the rigid jaw and frowning mouth of the woman sitting next to her did not soften. A black cloud lingered over her mother's head, and her eyes remained averted. The silent treatment. That's what her sisters called it — when there was too much anger for words.

Tara remembered looking down at her two feet as she turned sideways in her seat to set them on the curb, unsure if she could stand. She surprised herself when, pushing herself up, her legs held. Hearing the car door slam shut behind her, she put one trembling foot in front of the other and walked toward the wrought iron gate at the school's entrance. Stucco buildings loomed immense above her small frame. Cement walkways ran between rows of classrooms like a maze. At the gate, she turned to look behind her, but her mother had already left, other cars filling in the space alongside the curb where the familiar white station wagon had been only a few moments before.

She had barely gone down the first walkway and into the first turn before she knew she was lost. Older kids ran past, talking and shouting. How did they know where they were going? Pretending to be like them, she moved on toward a hedge where, through the branches, appeared a boy her own size. She turned toward an adjoining walkway, heart racing, to where he had been. A gate appeared off to the side. She went to it then, looked inside and, her whole body shaking, saw a teacher who was greeting other children like her, holding their mothers' hands.

Tara turned away from the sorrel, not wanting to feel herself thaw into the dull ache that was beginning to engulf her. But in a moment, she forced herself to turn back again, wanting to see what Tom would have Lena do with him. He was too far away for her to hear, but Lena stood up and raised her arm up and down several times. The sorrel jumped and snorted, swung his head around to his owner, and for a moment, stood perfectly still, forgetting about Blackie. Lena walked up to stroke his face and rub him behind the withers, offering herself in Blackie's place.

Tara faced front in her saddle again and looked out over the broad field before her, hot moisture oozing its way from the corners of her eyes. She blinked it back. Everywhere she looked, pastureland appeared to go on forever. But today, instead of soothing her, she felt an involuntary rush of fear, reminding her of the way she had felt walking out the gate at the end of the school day, the entryway stretching out wide and endless. Every afternoon, a sea of children clamored over its surface when the bell rang at three o'clock. A long line of cars waited to pull up by the curb and, one by one, take them all home. As always, she drifted over to a familiar spot off to the side under a young tree planted in a rare two-by-two-foot square patch of uncemented earth. She could still feel the cool, hard bark against her arms, and the way she had wrapped them around the narrow trunk, holding the tree to her, or her to it, while friends climbed into opened doors and drove away. When everyone had gone, the real dread set in, the huge span of cement empty. Silent.

One afternoon, the school principal noticed her standing next to the tree, and after locking the front double doors of the administration building, walked over to her.

"Is someone coming to pick you up?" Her voice sounded concerned, and for a moment, Tara thought this person was going to help her.

"Is your mother coming? Is someone coming to pick you up?"

The question had been asked a second time before Tara realized she hadn't answered it. She looked up into the eyes of the adult, wanting more than anything to shake her head, but felt a nod come out instead.

"Well, all right, then." The principal turned and walked away, car keys jangling from her fingertips.

The sound of a semi roaring down the interstate startled Tara to her senses. Had she really ridden this far? She quickly turned Blackie around and headed back, knowing she was out of sight of the sorrel. But her mood did not change with her change in direction, and she fought to piece together her memories. It wasn't until years later that she was able to make sense out of her sister Vera's offhanded mutterings about the men that had gone in and out of their parents' master bedroom, and understand what had kept her mother late those afternoons. But that day at school, when she'd finally seen the familiar, white station wagon drive up to the curb, her whole body had shaken with a great loosening of tension and an uncontrollable, high-pitched cry escaped her.

Lena's sorrel, agitated and covered with nervous sweat, saw her and Blackie reemerge and let go a piercing whinny.

"Oh, stop it! I was coming to get you," the black cloud had still been visible around her mother's face. Tara vaguely remembered a great struggle then as she sat in the car, panting and squirming until she could make herself quiet. At home again, she quickly pulled her clothes off, throwing urine-soaked tights deep into the laundry hamper before her mother could slap her for wetting her pants.

"Now toss a pebble at him." Tom's words carried on the breeze that floated in her direction and brought her mind into focus again. In the time it had taken her to ride out and back, Lena had been able to move her chair a greater distance from her horse. She stood again to raise her arm, but no pebble was necessary. The sorrel turned to face her. She went up to stroke his neck glistening with sweat, offering herself as company once more.

Tara rode away again, this time taking Tom's direction to position herself behind a cluster of trees and watch, unnoticed, through the branches. Lena crouched out of view behind a row of shrubs. Tom hid himself, too, sitting in his golf cart behind a stall stationed nearby in the field, leaning forward onto the wheel to peer out of the opening. The sorrel stood quietly, facing Lena's direction.

"You think that's about enough for today, Lena?" Tom called out.

Lena emerged from her hiding place and walked over to rub her horse's withers. Tara rode up as Tom drove his cart out to join them. He put the brake on, sat back, and brought his feet up on the dash, hands resting in his lap.

"Well, I read in the book," he began, referring to the book he had written, "where it talks a little about my time as a young person."

Tara, utterly drained, dropped the reins, and took her feet out of the stirrups to point her toes and let her legs dangle.

"In those days," he continued, "we had quite a bit of room there on the homestead." Swallow. "And even though there were eight children besides our two parents, a lot of times we'd find ourselves alone, working on one thing or another."

He gazed across the field and adjusted his hat. Tara fidgeted with Blackie's mane.

"Now, I was given certain responsibilities and guidelines, you see. So I couldn't just go out and do anything and everything that popped into my head. But within those guidelines, I had the freedom to explore and discover quite a lot for myself."

He looked from one to the other. Lena stood next to the sorrel, drawing lines in the dirt with the toe of her boot. Tara narrowed her eyes and stared at him.

"Well," he folded his arms, "when I was younger, I prob'ly took that pretty much for granted. But as I grew older and saw some of the ways other people lived, I began to realize that the security that had been provided for me, along with the opportunity I'd had to develop my own character, was as important to the horse as it had been to me."

Silence. He looked at Tara. Her eyes fell to the ground.

"Now, a lot of times people are interested to know something about my life as a young person. But I don't always figure that what I have to say will make a whole lot o' sense to them. It's just ancient history, unless a situation presents itself that makes my mentioning it worthwhile."

Both women looked up.

"I'll open the gate." Tom straightened in his seat to put the cart in gear, then swung it around and opened the pipe panel with his remote. They all made their way back to the barn. Tara remained quiet while they dismounted and packed the trailer, having decided to leave before lunch to beat the traffic. Blackie was much better about loading if there was another horse to ride alongside, and it wasn't long before both Thoroughbreds had been closed in and tied. Lena and Tara hugged Tom good-bye and climbed into the cab for the long drive home.

The shadows of tall trees fell long across the ground as they pulled into the driveway to the ranch, unloaded the horses, and hosed down the trailer. Their gear could be left locked inside until morning. Tara stopped briefly at her office to fill Wet Paw's cat bowl to the brim. She waved Lena a goodbye, then quickly drove home, parked the car, and dragged her sagging duffle bag along the ground, letting it bump up the brick steps before dropping it in the middle of the hallway, where it would lie until the following day.

14

~a crack in the armor~

Yes, our customs, habits, and early education hold us, as it were, with bands of steel.

—William. W. Walter
The Doctor's Daughter

Tara squinted, her eyes having a hard time adjusting to the bright August sunlight as she emerged from the shadows of the main barn. With head bowed and arms swinging, she hurriedly made her way across the yard, aiming for the paddocks and another horse to ride. The amount of effort it took to keep up with her day's schedule was, on most days, the fuel behind her complaints about her profession. Today, she experienced it as relief, a way to forget—and she pressed on.

Halfway to the paddocks, she nearly ran over Lena, who had intentionally blocked her path, compelling her to an abrupt halt. Her assistant was carrying an old, almost all-white calico in her arms. Little white paws stuck straight out as the cat allowed herself to be cradled passively on her back. Tara had only been vaguely aware of the ball of fur that seemed to always be curled up on a shelf just outside the clubhouse.

"She's covered with fleas." There was exasperation in Lena's voice, her eyes looking somberly at Tara. Concerned that the old cat might be too weak to survive the invasion, it was clear she was not moving until the complaint registered on her trainer's face. But Tara did not respond or change her expression, determined not to add one more responsibility to her life.

"These fleas are going to kill her," Lena pleaded. "Look how thin she is!"

The frailty of the old cat's frame finally caught Tara's attention and something in her softened. She sighed and nodded. It was obvious that the calico had received no real care for a long time, and she agreed to take the animal to the vet for a flea bath on her way home from work.

At the end of the day, she rummaged through the tool shed, which was strewn with old paint cans, chicken wire, pipes, leftover pieces of lumber, and things she couldn't identify. At length, a cat carrier emerged from under the rubble. With some effort, she pulled it free, hosed it down, and made a bed of clean towels inside. The cat, although wide-eyed when the metal doors snapped shut and held her captive, did not cry at the sound of the car's engine or the feel of the bumpy road, and soon Tara found herself cooing at "Snoozer" while steering with one hand and poking her fingers through the bars with the other. The cat remained calm in the strange, sterile clinic when Tara handed her over to the vet technician.

"She just sat there in the water the whole time," the woman said when Tara returned an hour later. "Probably doesn't have the energy for much else."

It seemed pointless to take Snoozer back to the ranch to become reinfested with fleas, so Tara brought her home. It was the first cat she'd had since leaving her parents' home at seventeen, and it wasn't long before the calico settled onto the back of her living room foldout couch, sleeping above her head every night on a towel that kept dirt and hair from staining the upholstery. In the mornings before work, she let the cat out for the day, saving her the extra chore of changing a litter box.

Weeks passed, and Tara was acutely aware of cooler air on her skin as she drove to the stables each morning and spent the day outdoors. When she came home, Snoozer would not have moved from her shady spot under the cedar tree in front of the house. In the evening, and again in the morning, the cat ate her portion of food without complaint, and after gazing up at Tara with steady eyes, softly purred while washing her multicolored face with white paws.

By late September, the rains had not yet come, and on a morning when Tara and Lena managed to slip away from their training schedule to spend another day at Tom's, the earth looked parched and brown. As they made their way inland, moisture continued to evaporate from the rivers and irrigated fields of the San Joaquin Valley, and a new layer of fog settled low to the ground.

When they arrived at Wesland, Tom was already out in the field, perched on his swivel stool, helping someone load a Paint mare into a horse trailer. Always interested in a new project, the two women stalled their horses and hurried outside, sliding their bodies through the narrow pipes of the panel gate and walking over the hard ground to sit at his feet.

"Now, she needs support before you come to that spot where she's stalling," Tom was telling two men who were doing the loading. "If Jay could approach the mare from the side while Rich brings her around again, you would provide the encouragement she needs."

The man Tom had called Rich walked his Paint toward the trailer for another attempt while Tom instructed Jay to act as a back up. Halfway there, the mare shied and pulled against the rope. Rich pretended to ignore it and leaned forward against her pull.

"What do you do when your horse is as stubborn as a mule, Tom?" he called out, keeping his head bowed. His body was nearly at a forty-five-degree tilt against the mare's weight. Tara hoped he wouldn't fall on his face if she suddenly unplanted her feet.

"Well, first of all, I've never seen a stubborn mule," Tom answered without raising his voice. "I've seen a mule shut down for awhile, to try and give the person time to figure out what the person should be doing." He paused, then added, "I usually tell people that a mule is just like a horse, only more so."

A long silence followed. Tara glanced at Tom and saw him look sideways. She followed his gaze and noticed a Border collie running out from behind the barn. She looked back at the mare, whose ears were cocked in that same direction, her head straining to get a glimpse of what was making all the noise.

"What's going on in one place might have a lot to do with what's happening in another," Tom said aloud. "I like to encourage people to be aware of everything around them."

Rich hadn't noticed his dog, but a woman standing off to the side had. She called to it while holding the truck door open until the collie came running up and jumped inside. In a moment, the mare relaxed and eased off the line.

"Now, you'll try again," Tom said.

The woman came over and stood next to Tom. While Rich made several more attempts to load his horse, she shifted her hands to her hips, then to the front of her belt buckle, then back to her hips, then again in front of her buckle, turning a wedding ring round and round on her finger.

"Tom," she finally ventured, her effort to control her voice obvious, "what keeps you from just yelling at him to pay attention? He isn't listening to you!"

"Well," Tom laughed, rocking back and releasing his focus. "There was a time when I was younger that I might have tried a lot harder to make things happen. But," he paused to glance at Rich, "I began to realize that while I was working real hard to find a way to explain things that would be of benefit to people, they were just waiting until I got through talking so they could ask about something they weren't ready for."

Tara registered the familiar deer-in-headlights stare coming from the woman's eyes. Tom waited. The woman blinked.

"Now I just present the information so that it's out there for anyone who might benefit," he continued, eying Tara sitting cross-legged in the dirt, "not necessarily those it's intended for."

"But we might be here all day," the woman persisted. "Isn't there any way you could just explain to him what he should be doing? Otherwise, he'll just do things the same way he's always done once he gets home."

"Well," Tom looked at his feet, "I sometimes tell people about the time when I was ten years of age, or so." He looked up and adjusted his hat. "Around that time, I was put in charge of the livestock, you see." He paused for a sip of water out of a bottle stationed on the dash of his cart. "If something went wrong with you or your horse," he continued, "there wasn't gonna be anyone around to get you out of a fix. But then again, if something happened," he cleared his throat, "you'd still have a twenty-five-mile walk home to figure it out for yourself." And, as if that hadn't carried enough impact, he added, "O' course, you might miss your supper."

The woman looked miserable. Tara looked at Tom and marveled, for the first time getting a sense of what it would mean for a ten-year-old boy to spend the slow hours of an era void of automation riding over more than 20,000 acres alone, checking fence line for holes and escape routes. She smiled to herself, recalling his comment about how the opportunity to study mathematics had come to him while memorizing the names and tag numbers of every one of the several hundred head of cattle his family owned.

Without knowing why, she no longer felt anxious for Rich to load the mare, although he managed to do so within the next hour. After securing the last latch on his trailer door, he brushed his hands together and came smiling over to Tom. To Tara, his apparent satisfaction was surreal as he shook the elder's hand, nodding his thanks as if he'd accomplished something. The Paint had physically gotten up into her compartment, but she'd remained defensive and resistant, and so had anything really changed?

Rich, his wife, and Jay climbed into the truck with the dog and drove away. Lena was silent, and Tara dug her chin into her knees tucked up against her chest.

"Well," Tom remarked, "I guess that's about all there is to that."

They broke for lunch before spending the remainder of the day riding out in the field. It was after dark by the time they had hauled the horses home and when Tara arrived back at the house, surprised by how happy she was to see Snoozer lying under the cedar tree in the black of night. On her way inside, she stooped to pick up the old feline, who weighed next to nothing, and walked up the porch steps to a soft purring over her left shoulder.

"You sweet thing."

In the morning, she stepped outside to an early gray chill that sent a shiver through her. Great billows of gray fog had blown in while she slept, winding a silent, fifteen-mile journey through redwood forests and over wind-swept adobe grasslands that stretched inland from the Pacific Ocean. Snoozer, standing in the doorway, paused to sniff the air, but instead of wandering outside, turned around and went back in. It occurred to Tara, knowing this to be unlike the cat, to allow the frail calico to stay inside. But that would mean setting up a litter box, and she was already late for work. Instead, she picked Snoozer up and placed her outside on the steps, ignoring soft meows and tender looks. A minute later, she had loaded her car and was driving out the gate for the barn.

When she returned home at day's end, Snoozer was not at the cedar tree. A quick look around the front yard revealed nothing. She ventured to the back of the property, picking her way more slowly through a row of tall eucalyptus that lined the property, her feet crunching over their beds of shed bark. Seeing no sign of the cat, she paused on her way back up the side lawns, gradually becoming cognizant of an odd feeling. It took her a moment to name the same dull helplessness she had felt when, at six years of age, her first childhood cat had not come home. No one had told her he had been hit by a car, even when she stood by the front door for several days after school, calling and calling. She remembered the moment when she had finally dared to ask.

"Mommy, where is he?"

"I thought you would just forget about him," had been the reply.

Such a simple answer. After all, she was only a child, her mother would often remind her later on, too young to know what was happening. But what she had quickly figured out after a few, quick sobs that had gone uncomforted, was that holding back tears was safer than risking open sorrow to someone who needed her to feel nothing.

Now a familiar lump grew larger in her throat as she called and called for Snoozer. With dusk approaching, she grabbed her flashlight and searched again the dark pockets and hiding places amid the trees, dried grasses, and thistles covering the acres surrounding the house, hoping to find nothing. And nothing she found, until at length, she resigned herself to go indoors for a few bites of cold chicken, a shower, and a troubled sleep.

She awoke to another gray dawn, numb and groggy. The fog had clung inland and remained low to the ground. Knowing she must face the inevitable, she put on sweat pants and a jacket and walked out the front door. She decided to go in a different direction from the night before and turned down the walkway to look outside the front gate. She continued along the tree-lined road until she came to a bridge she didn't recognize. She had only driven this way in her car and would have been accelerating too fast to notice it.

The bridge, almost entirely shrouded by shrubs, was built over a small, dry creek bed that acted as a runoff when the rains came. What she saw as she tiptoed to the edge and cautiously peered over the railing took her breath away. Snoozer lay rigid on the rocky floor below, her face frozen into a grimace. Ants had already begun their inspection of her open mouth and eyes as Tara skirted the railing and slid down the steep bank to wrap the soft fur in a towel. Clutching the stiff body in one arm, she clawed her way back up with the other. It was too late to say that she had made a mistake, that she should have paid attention to this cat's simplest of needs, that she was so very, very sorry, although she kept muttering these things over and over under her breath.

She didn't remember making her way back down the road. When she found herself inside her front gate, she stood for a moment before reluctantly letting Snoozer out of her arms to lie on the lawn while she walked to the tool shed at the side of the house. She was vaguely aware of groping in the dark for a shovel's cold handle pressed into her palm, of finding a cardboard box in which to lay the cat, of digging a hole in the far corner of the property. By the time she found herself back inside getting ready for work, a familiar numbness had consumed her. She had a full day ahead and forced herself blindly through her routines, every event passing in a blur until one more day had ended, and she was driving home again.

At the house, she sat outside alone on her front steps and stared into nothing, too tired to push away the flood of images she'd kept at bay until now. The face of another childhood cat flashed into her mind, the one she'd gotten after the first had been killed. Nicki had been small and black and the runt of the litter. Frightened of the world, she often hid under the heavy, antique desk against one side of the living room wall. When Tara felt the desperate urge for company, she often forced the cat into the open by batting at the furry flanks with a yardstick, even as the feline hissed and swatted vehemently with her paws. But the day the runt was herself to give birth, she ran up to the seven-year-old child, following her around the house. Thrilled to be needed, Tara watched as Crystal found a cardboard box to make a soft bed inside with towels. Somehow, her sister had known that the cat would need a quiet, out-of-the-way place to be, and soon five kittens of all colors had been born in the living room closet.

Tara's favorite, the one she kept, was a gray-striped male. Unlike his mother, Greld was calm and steady around people, purring softly at her touch. He came to sleep on her bed every night and greeted her at the front door when she came home from school each day. He even looked for her after she'd been overcome with the nameless recurring inner torment that often compelled her to hold him down with one hand and pound him with her other small fist, his sweet-tempered forbearance making him the only safe venue for her to reveal what she had never been allowed to say out loud.

She had not thought to stroke his soft fur or pay him a second glance when she left home at seventeen, nor had she noticed he was no longer at her parents' house during subsequent visits. At the time, it never occurred to her to ask how he died, or who had been the one to take him to the sterile veterinary office to be put out of his miseries. By then, she had learned that what she didn't notice couldn't affect her, a numbing fog ever providing a way for her to survive a life that hurt too much to go on living.

Self-preservation. Suddenly, the term Tom used so often had new meaning. *It allowed me to survive!*

Only now it was backfiring. Her unfeeling lack of awareness had consequences.

And now she had to feel that.

Which did she hate more? Feeling or not feeling? Both were an impossible price to pay.

The taste of bile permeated the inside of her mouth and her breath came in shallow gasps. Opening the screen door behind her, she slowly slid her seat backwards. Inside, she hugged her knees to her chest on the hallway floor where no one would see her. Burying her eyes into her knees, as if it were actually possible to be shielded from bombs and earthquakes, she cried the way she had learned to cry years ago: stomach heaving, body shaking, all in silence, so that no one need hear.

15

~seeds of denial~

The house is on fire, but like the story of the emperor with no clothes,
we are not supposed to look.

—John Bradshaw
On: The Family

Tara awoke with puffy eyes, and slowly remembering the events
of the day before, closed them against the unwanted pictures in her
mind. But closing her eyes only allowed herself to feel swallowed by a
vague nothingness, and she pushed herself out of bed. Opting to
forego her daily yoga routine, she got dressed and went to town, using
her day off to stock up on light bulbs at the hardware store and
groceries from the local market until fatigue prompted her to climb
back into her truck and head home. After haphazardly stuffing
perishables into her refrigerator, she wandered out to the tool shed to
find a trowel. A gate at the corner of the shed led to a quarter acre plot
where long beds of dirt had been formed earlier in the spring for a
garden. She walked over to the one cleared of summer's harvest and
dropped to her knees, driving her trowel wrist deep in dirt to loosen
the earth for a fall planting.

She had almost finished the row when she heard the rev of a
familiar engine pull in the drive. On a hunch, she walked back around
to the front yard, and sure enough, Jason, her neighbor, had made a
run to the ranch with his truck to have composted horse manure skip-
loaded into the long bed. He agreed to spare her a couple of
wheelbarrow loads for her vegetable plot, leaving him what was left to
put around the side yards and in his flower gardens.

An hour later, she was watering lettuce, broccoli, and chard seed
by hand, aware of herself taking in a deep breath for the first time that
day, feeling soothed by the smell of raw earth and the promise of what
would come. With some reluctance, she went back to the house to

scrub her nails and shuffle through her mail. All but a corner of a postcard lay hidden between bank statements and junk promotions, yet she recognized the return address at once. Parting the surrounding envelopes with her fingers, she slid the card free, as if needing to see it in its entirety to make it real.

Dear Tara, wishing you a happy Thanksgiving season filled with dreams come true. Love, Vera.

She rolled her eyes and tossed it back onto the table. The note allowed her sister to think she was "keeping in touch," although it communicated nothing. *You could at least be happy that she sent the card,* she reprimanded herself. But what won out was the feel of her teeth sinking into Vera's wide, soft arm when they were children. It was the kind of behavior she had been known for — and punished for — by her parents, no one empathizing with her struggle for equal status with her middle sister, four years older than she.

Having been the favorite child from the time she was born, Vera had grown into a model student, skipping half a grade before she was eight. By the time she was thirteen, she already knew how to converse suavely with their parents' friends and flash a seductive smile, her straight teeth accentuating a natural beauty made to stand out with well-applied make-up. At that age, she'd also been able to style her mother's hair as well as her own, and like her mother, looked forward to the evenings when their father came home to their house in the suburbs with an armful of sample designer dresses from his office in downtown Los Angeles. On such occasions, Tara, having always recoiled from her family's preoccupation with image, usually slipped out of sight and into her room.

In those days, girls were still required to wear dresses in public schools, but not usually comfortable in one, Tara was not always satisfied with what hung in her closet. Her reluctance to find something to wear each morning often prompted her superior sister to rummage through her clothes, picking out dresses for her to try while she sat on her bed, fuming and wanting to cry. Always well dressed herself, Vera often looked at Tara with the kind of smile a queen might bestow upon a subject, embellished with the affectations of her parents and their Hollywood friends who appeared at the house for martinis, ballroom dance parties, and other inebriated gatherings. Tara had hated her sister's presumed superiority, hated her sister, she thought — until the dream.

In the dream, she was eight or nine years old, yelling her rage at Vera with wide-mouthed abandon, behavior that, in real life, would have guaranteed her punishment. Her dream-life rantings brought no reaction from her sister, however, whose face remained mute with averted eyes. She felt her strength leave her then, there being nothing she could ever say or do to crack the facade. But then, without warning, Vera vomited, and Tara woke up, crying into the blackness of night. She had known then that she wasn't the only one in her family lost in a dark, dark place.

Tara stared at her pile of unopened mail as she emerged from reverie. Knowing that Vera had her own issues with the family didn't ease her frustration. She shook her head and distractedly reached for the phone bill, tearing it open with her fingers. She glanced at the contents.

"Forty-five dollars!"

Surely, some mistake had been made. But a close look at the list of calls revealed no mistake; she had forgotten about the call to her friend, Shelley, now living in Los Angeles. She heaved a sigh and slapped the piece of paper on the table. *This is not my day for mail.*

She rubbed a hand across her forehead, her fingers tracing the line etched between her eyebrows, absentmindedly reaching for Vera's card and walking it to the living room as if there might be something she'd missed the first time. She finished rereading the short line well before completing the five steps to her couch, where she flopped herself down and sank low into the corner pillows.

Her animosity toward Vera had diminished somewhat with age, yet there had always remained an unspoken distance between them. Besides exchanging a few intermittent remarks about their past over the years, they had never openly discussed the way things had been in their family. None of her siblings had. Tara got up and walked around the room. Maybe they were right to ignore everything. After all, their circumstances had changed when she'd turned seven. At least on the outside. She sat back down.

At age seven, she and both of her sisters had been sent to their grandparents' vacation home for the summer. The house, built long before she was born, sat along a quiet, tree-lined street in a small town nestled along the edge of Lake Michigan. She remembered feeling very adult that year, toting her own luggage up the worn wooden stairs to the bedroom shared with Vera. But her first impulse was to run outside, and even now, just thinking about the place conjured up a refuge of sights and smells provided by the lakeshore under an open sky. Mechanized street sweepers couldn't keep fine white sand from blowing over cement roads daring to encroach upon its beach, and the ooze of delicate white particles through her toes had always inspired a run, her feet scalloping fresh indents where they dug in hard.

The "big lake," as she and her siblings affectionately referred to the ocean of fresh water, was easily reached from anywhere in town, its presence transforming hot, humid air into soft breezes that sent whispering voices through the leaves of maple trees, promising nature's peace and a slowing of time. It never occurred to any of them to mind the absence of a television set—the natural world providing far greater mysteries and wonder. During regular sunset walks, the three sisters gazed at the multiple shades of blue water that blended with a sky that went on forever. They drew names on the sand that rose out of the lake into towering dunes with the same fineness, soft enough to accept the plunge of their bodies, smooth and firm enough to carry their weight, rolling and sliding down. Beyond the dunes, lush, green rolling woodlands and marshlands cradled the town.

The outside world of water and sand contrasted sharply with the rules of the house, where her grandparents insisted on a strict code of behavior and everyone's prompt arrival for meals served by the neighbor, hired on as private cook. Her grandmother sat at one end of the heavy oak dining table, lacquered thickly in black, acting weak and frail in comparison to her husband. At first glance, her demeanor gave the appearance of deference to his overbearing personality. But as everyone knew, she was not to be crossed, defiantly placing both elbows on the table—an action no one else was allowed—and slouching dramatically in open view. Her misery was further embellished at every meal with extreme belches blaring across the centerpiece, an event that never failed to elicit a startled look from any unprepared guest.

It was only through an offhanded conversation with a cousin, years later, that Tara learned her grandmother's gastric condition had not been some mysterious malady, but rather swallowed air, stored for her unique way of dominating the mealtime. Tara admired her cousin's ability to observe and question what everyone else had pretended was a normal event.

Grandfather's place was at the opposite end of the table, across from his wife. Tara, who was usually seated near his right elbow, used to dig her toes into the table's clawed feet, five times the size of her own, watching his rhythmic and deliberate intake of food, consumed in time with his heavy breathing. His eyes remained behind lowered lids that conveniently distanced him from the women that surrounded him. An old pendulum clock hung on the stained wall above his head, while cast iron irons, old Russian samovars, and other unrecognizable objects rested unmoving on antique wooden dressers stationed on all sides of the dining room, silently instructing her on another era.

At other times, Grandfather walked through the house with a booming voice and a heavy, arrhythmic gait, his prominent strength compromised somewhat by a leg shortened by childhood polio. Tara always made a point to move silently out of the way and become invisible, lest her unwanted presence ignite his wrath. Still, she had been told, she must love him because he was her grandfather. He did great things, they said, being an important Detroit lawyer who defended poor people, minorities, and social outcasts long before "civil rights" became a household term. Some form of pride mixed with terror as she kept vigil over his whereabouts.

It was during one of their regular evening meals that the phone's loud ring echoed sharply across the linoleum floor and bounced off the ancient wallpaper.

"Who would be calling right at this time?" Her grandfather's irritation was apparent as he kept eating, refusing to pick up the phone sitting on the small desk directly behind his elbow.

"Oh, for God's sake!" Her grandmother retorted, deliberately putting one hand on each side of her plate to push herself off the chair. The way her elbows bowed out from her chest reminded Tara of a bull terrier, a demeanor Grandmother held onto as she rounded her shoulders and shuffled her way behind where Vera was seated. "Someone's got to answer the damn phone!"

Her voice did not soften on the receiver, and her mood was punctuated by a sharp turn to her husband.

"It's Burt!" She referred to Tara's father.

"Oh!" Her grandfather instantly switched off his reserve and took the phone.

Grandmother turned and shuffled back to her seat, pronouncing the essence of the conversation.

"Your mother is in the hospital!" Even the mention of her own daughter did not change her tone. A minute after she sat down, her husband finished his brief conversation and hung up.

"Your mother has been admitted to St. Joseph's hospital in Los Angeles," he said in the same strong, matter-of-fact voice, eyes still averted.

Tara remembered the silence that had descended upon the table as her stomach hit the floor. She knew, without it ever being stated, that her mother's admission into the place where sick people went had to do with the black cloud she so often saw hovering around the familiar face. *At last*, she sighed to herself. Someone was finally doing something about it.

"The one thing I can't impress upon you girls enough," her grandfather's boom continued, spoon in hand, ready to scoop a portion of canned peaches into his mouth, "is for God's sake, don't ever say anything to anyone about this. Especially not to your mother." And he disappeared again behind lowered eyelids.

"No, absolutely not," her grandmother echoed. "Not a word!"

Tara stared at the other eyelids around the table, her newfound lightness fading. Utensils continued to shuffle food around on plates, everyone appearing to take the news and go on. And so, on she went as well, finishing dinner in silence, pulling herself up the stairs at bedtime and pretending to be lured into sleep by the sound of Crystal's lullabies.

The next morning she awoke late, and finding herself alone in the upstairs room she shared with Vera, dressed and went downstairs. Only Rose remained in the house, standing quietly in the kitchen and kneading bread dough on the counter.

"Can Gina play?" Tara asked about the cook's granddaughter, her best friend in town.

"I don't know what she has planned today. Why don't you go next door and see. The house is unlocked."

Tara eagerly flung herself through the kitchen screen door, but stopped short in front of the big maple, its grand canopy shading much of the lawn in the back yard. Halfway down the huge trunk was her favorite gray squirrel, its feet splayed wide in a momentary freeze, its tail bushing out from a sleek coat. Her grandmother had shown her how to let it take cookies from her hand, and she knew how important it was not to frighten it. But at her sudden movements, the squirrel leaped to the ground and scurried over the lawn. Thinking she could make up to him later, Tara resumed her way, tiptoeing through her grandmother's flowerbed and up to the stone wall dividing their yard from the neighbors'. She would have been in trouble had anyone seen her, but she hoisted herself onto the wide ledge anyway, assessing a landing spot before leaping over discarded tools and household junk left outside to rot amid unclipped thorny rosebushes. Collapsing in a heap on the other side, she felt pain shoot up her legs. Stifling a cry, she took a moment to rub an ankle and then, realizing she was unhurt, limped her way to the back porch. The weathered wooden slats creaked her entrance through the door and into the small, dark kitchen with a slanted floor. Many of the old houses in the village were like that, a contrast to the modern stuccos where she was from.

The house appeared empty and silent, her friend obviously not there. But the quiet drew her in. Tiptoeing into the living room, she was startled to see Gina's great-grandmother sitting in her rocker by the front window. Knowing the woman could barely see, she walked to within an inch of the chair, not believing anyone's face could be that wrinkled.

"Hi," Tara announced suddenly, wondering if it would come as a surprise to the elder.

"Good day." The great-grandmother had heard the soft crunch of Tara's feet over the faded carpet and answered in a voice both soft and rough. It was the familiar sound of an adult, always telling her what to do.

"Do you know who I am?"

"Why, yes. You're Nelson's granddaughter."

Tara, standing directly beside the arm of the chair, stared at the way the woman moved her lips made soft and flappy by a mouth void of teeth. Her eyes then strayed to the loose-fitting, old-fashioned summer dress—a soft fabric of pink flowers. Straps of undergarments, hinting of the mysterious secrets of adult women, lay exposed across the woman's shoulders.

"What's that?" Tara mocked a friendly voice, pressing her hand over a protruding collarbone.

"This?" The woman's bony finger rested at the top of her shoulder before running down along the white nylon strap. "Why, that's my slip."

"What's underneath it?"

To Tara's disbelief, the great-grandmother began naming pieces of underwear while Tara held the loosely fitted front neckline away from the protruding collarbone with a forefinger. The view was unrestricted down to the gray, curly hairs springing from both sides of white panties. She looked back at the wrinkled face, sensing the woman's frailty. For the first time in her life, she felt strong. Powerful.

"You're a stupid old woman, and I hate you, you old ninny."

The old woman's chest rose sharply. "Don't talk to me like that!"

But Tara couldn't stop.

"Go to hell! Go to hell! Go to hell," her voice grew louder with each repetition, saying the phrase over and over. She knew the words were especially bad. Where had she heard them? Learned them?

The elderly woman began to sob quietly, tears falling over her cheekbones like tiny waterfalls. Feeling the wind knocked from her, Tara stopped short. The woman's frank and open sorrow had taken her completely aback. She thought to run, to get away. But somehow, she wasn't able to move her legs, transfixed instead by the delicate droplets. It had to stop, she told herself. She had to make it stop.

"I'm sorry." She knew it was not enough.

"What?" The woman looked up, wiping her face with a plain white cloth.

"I'm sorry. I'm sorry I said those things." Tara felt sick, afraid of what others would say and do when they found out what she had done.

"Well then." The elder sighed heavily, resting back in her chair. Every limb in Tara's body was shaking.

"I'm all right now," the great-grandmother continued. "You said you were sorry. I won't tell no one, neither, that you made me cry."

Tara ran from the house, never to see the woman again.

At the end of summer, the three sisters flew home. They were greeted by their parents, who stood beside a brand new blue Ford Falcon outside of baggage claim at the Los Angeles airport. The black cloud was nowhere around her mother's features, only a pasted-on smile over her face. Tara thought she looked weak and frail. But from then on, life went on as normal. She was old enough by then to walk the mile to school, and after class or on weekends, friends came over to play in her room or in front of the living room fireplace with Barbie dolls, plastic horses, cards, chess, or one of her twenty board games, set up amid tidy furniture polished by the weekly housekeeper. They petted her cats, swam in her pool, and hiked with her in the hills behind the house that sat low in the canyon. It was all they ever knew of her life.

Then there were the presents, piled high each December under a fully decorated tree reaching all the way to the ceiling. Christmas Eve parties hosted friends and neighbors who caroled down the canyon, then filled the house with the usual inebriated pontifications that reflected their privileged social status. Tara wasn't able to escape the look in her sisters' eyes when they saw her neatly wrapped boxes of the latest toys on the market—things they hadn't received when they were her age. "Spoiled brat," Vera called her. But presents never filled the hole inside where the old ache had always been, and she had never felt fortunate.

Tara blinked. Her hands rested behind her head on the couch as she noted intricate patterns on her wall made by the shadows of the leaves of a cherry tree rustling in the breeze outside her window. She got up and went outside. Jason was breathing heavily as he shoveled the last barrow full of compost from his truck.

"Think I'll need one more load," he said as she walked up to see his progress. He hopped off the open tailgate and stood leaning on his shovel, spade to the ground. Sweat poured off his face and moistened his shirt around the collar and torso. "I'll prob'ly wait a few days, though," he smiled.

"I would think," Tara frowned at his balding head of gray hairs, knowing it was backbreaking labor. "Sure looks nice, though."

"Doesn't it?" The entire side yard, covered in roses of every color, had been blanketed with the rich, dark earth. "Keeps the weeds down and the soil moist."

Tara nodded. She often saw Jason outside for what seemed like hours at a time, hose in hand, watering each plant in spite of the extensive drip system he'd installed himself.

"Minerals in the water plug up the drip feeders after awhile, but I don't mind," he smiled. "Watering's my therapy." He set the shovel on top of the wheelbarrow to cart the last batch of compost to the corner of his lot.

Tara retrieved a pair of clippers from the tool shed and made a slow tour through the roses, gathering a bouquet before going back inside the house to wash breakfast dishes left on the counter. Afterwards, she set the vase in the middle of the table so she could smell the flowers as she pulled her checkbook out of her pack and sat with her stack of mail, paying bills. At the bottom of the stack was Vera's card. She slipped it among the rest of the empty envelopes and, grabbing the stack with both hands, tossed the pile into the recycle bin.

Taking a book off the shelf in the living room, she went back outside to take another look at her day's handiwork. Gardening was the closest she had come to feeling the way she felt at Tom's, a place where the frantic pace of the world became a distant memory. After peering over her beds one more time, as if by some miracle she might see green shoots already peeking through the rich earth, she sat on the lawn under the mimosa tree and read until dusk.

16

~details~

This world is not an illusion.
It is the concept we entertain of it that is the illusion.

—Joel Goldsmith
The Art of Spiritual Healing

"How would you gals like to step inside for a minute or two over a cup of coffee?" Tom greeted Tara and Lena late Tuesday morning as they stepped out of the truck at Wesland.

They readily agreed. A thick fog hung low and heavy to the ground, and the cold, damp air penetrated their clothes. After unloading the horses, Tara's Blackie and Lena's sorrel, they piled into the cart next to him and drove to the house. Inside, Tara made a beeline to the couch and curled her legs into the corner, thinking she would be content just to sit inside all day.

"That'll be Emerson," Tom nodded toward the corner of the room where, just outside the window, the sound of a diesel engine could be heard coming up the drive, "bringing some colts from over there on the east bay, not too far from you folks, I believe." He looked at Lena, who nodded in return. "I'll just go and tell him to come sit with us for a minute. By the time he finishes a cup of coffee, maybe that sun'll have made its way through the clouds."

The women had gotten up to make tea and were heading to the dining table when Tom came back up the front stairs, followed by a tall, lanky cowboy in jeans and wide silver belt buckle. Both men paused to stomp their feet free of debris before coming through the door. Tom introduced everyone, then stepped into the kitchen to pour Emerson a cup of coffee. Emerson removed his hat, revealing a thin crop of blond hair, the ends curling around his ears. His spurs chinked softly as he pulled a chair out from the table.

"Some horses I train for clients, and some I sell to customers," he reported after Tara had asked him about his stock horse operation. "Mostly Quarter Horses for reining and cow work."

He sat directly across from her, but looked just past her face, and she found herself staring at eyes that stared at some unknown endpoint. Tom handed him his coffee and sat at the end of the table, drinking nothing. Emerson looked at the dark liquid as he talked, then back up to no one in particular. Tom asked him about the colts he'd brought.

"Just two today, Tom," he answered. "But I also brought the older gelding I was telling you about—the one that's had a tendency to buck." He went on, recounting details of the horse's behavior and how the owner was afraid to ride him. Tara and Lena finished their tea in silence. Eventually, he paused to take a long swallow of coffee. Tom turned in his seat and nodded at the rays of sunlight filtering in through the windows. "Do you suppose we oughta go see how the horses are gettin' along?"

Tara and Lena rose simultaneously, and they all filed out the door, convening in a semicircle by Emerson's trailer parked in the field. After unloading two colts and turning them out in a paddock, he led a big chestnut gelding down the ramp.

"This is the one I was telling you about, Tom," Emerson said. "He's been known to buck pretty good."

"Well," Tom looked thoughtful, "you've often heard me speak about a horse's need to roll." He glanced around at them all. "A horse'll get a real good stretch through its loin and hind end when it rolls."

They all stood tongue-tied. It was one of Tom's typical non-answers that made it seem as if he had suddenly changed the subject, or hadn't heard or understood the topic of conversation. He remained quiet, taking in their stares. Then Tara smiled, recalling his comment about how people perceived the elderly.

"Now, you'll think about what a horse does when he gets down to roll," Tom went on quietly. "When he bends his knees—"

Tara followed his train of thought silently. First, the front legs would fold, causing the horse to bend to its knees. At this point, the hind end would still be in the air.

"Now that's one kind of stretch," Tom was saying.

Then, in order to buckle the hind legs, every leg joint would need to bend and flex. Every muscle, ligament, and tendon would need to stretch.

"I'm sure you've all seen how horses that are tight will often strain trying to bend the hind legs, and flop over onto their side instead," he continued. They all nodded. "Some can't even get down at all."

Suddenly, it all made sense. Horses that were tight over the back and in the rear tended to buck! Tara had often gotten the bucks out of a horse by longeing it or letting it run loose to "get the kinks out," but she'd never considered the possibility of doing something as simple as letting a horse roll. How much had she missed by not paying attention to these little details — all the things in life that appeared mundane?

"I've been meaning to ask you about lying a horse down, and whether or not this horse would be a good candidate, Tom," Emerson had finally regained his tongue, holding the big gelding at the end of its lead.

Tara's ears perked up. She had heard about such practices, picturing a person's ability to get a horse to lie down on command akin to a forced roll. It was a skill some bragged about using on horses that had severe behavioral problems. But again, Tom appeared to ignore the question.

"There are three areas where a horse can get bothered," he said. "You have to ask yourself whether or not the horse is comfortable in its surroundings, within itself, and with the person." He took them all in again with his eyes.

Just like people, Tara thought.

Tom then turned directly to Emerson. "Does he go to lie down when you turn him out by himself?"

"Tom, I've never seen this horse roll."

"Well," Tom responded, "I've oftentimes wondered what might be going on between a person and their horse that would keep that horse from doing something that's ordinarily so pleasant and natural."

Silence.

"Now," Tom broke in again. "Emerson can turn the big chestnut loose in the arena." He was already walking in that direction. Tara and Lena followed. "A lot of times, people don't want their horses to roll because they might get their hair all dirty after the person has just finished brushing them off," he continued when they had all reconvened by the arena gate, "or they've already got the saddle on."

"A lot of people think it's a bad habit for the horse to get into," Emerson added, "because the horse will decide to roll while the person is trying to lead it, or when they're riding."

"Well," Tom chuckled, "a lot of people haven't learned to accommodate the horse's need while at the same time gaining the horse's respect, so that the horse doesn't try and roll when it's an inconvenience to the person. Now, I like to get all that separated out and taken care of before there's a problem."

Silence.

Tom turned his focus back toward the arena. The others followed his gaze. "Now this horse," he said, speaking of the big chestnut, "doesn't appear to be in any hurry to roll."

"Like I said, Tom, I've never seen him roll on his own out in the arena," Emerson confirmed, "and even though he hasn't bucked in quite awhile since we've been working with him, he tossed his owner pretty good a few times in the past."

Tom was nodding his head. "And she's expecting that this horse'll come here to be laid down so that he won't buck anymore."

"I'll do whatever you think, Tom, but it did occur to me to tell her that that's what might happen here today."

"Well, sometimes, what a person thinks has happened does more for their confidence than what has actually occurred, or what's really necessary for the horse."

More silence. Tom checked his watch.

"Now, why don't we just leave him in here a while and get ourselves a bite to eat?"

They left the gelding free to roam the arena and walked back toward the house. As they sat around the table, Tara and Lena were quiet again as Emerson talked more about his various horses-in-training and the clients he worked with. Even the sudden blare of the telephone, its ringer set on high so that Tom would be sure to hear it, didn't distract him. Tara followed the elder with her eyes as he got up from the table to answer the call.

"Hullo," Tom's voice could be heard in the background. Tara had to concentrate on him in order to hear above Emerson's monologue. "Yeah," he said after a pause and glanced back at Tara. "Well, I think that'd be all right. You wanna come by this afternoon, you say?" He looked up again. "There are other folks here, Lena and Emerson—" Pause. "And Tara. All right, then, we'll see you in an hour or so." He hung up the phone.

Tara felt a nervous twinge in the pit of her stomach and kept her eyes riveted on Tom as he shuffled back to the table. Emerson's voice lulled.

"That was Rio. He'll be stopping by later this afternoon on his way up from southern California." As Tom began clearing dishes from the table, Tara jumped up to help him, any reluctance to be up and active suddenly vanishing. The rest of the group followed suit, and soon they were all clomping out the door.

"I think I'll just have a look at that chestnut of yours, Emerson," Tom remarked in an offhanded fashion. Tara and Lena, already heading toward the barn to saddle their horses, stopped dead in their tracks and looked at each other. In silent unison, they turned and followed Tom instead, climbing into the golf cart for a ride out to the arena.

The first thing that was apparent as they drove through the gate was the thick layer of dust blanketing the chestnut, making his coat a few shades lighter. He had obviously rolled in the sandy footing.

"Well, look at that," Lena exclaimed.

"Ya-ha-ha-ha," Tom laughed, setting the cart's brake and reclining in his seat. "It's interesting to note what a horse'll take care of all by itself by simply being allowed to be a horse."

They heard a scuffing behind them and turned to see Emerson catching up to them on foot. "Looks like you'll be able to tell the owner you laid this horse down after all," Tom said in a voice louder than normal.

Emerson looked toward the arena and slowed his steps, although he kept going until he was right up next to the fence, folding his arms through the pipe panels and nodding quietly. Smiling, Tara and Lena scooted from their seats to saddle their horses. Not long after they had mounted and were riding in the yard, Rio's gooseneck trailer pulled into the drive. In a few minutes, he had saddled a large chestnut, much like Emerson's, and was riding out to join them.

"Where'd you get him?" Tara asked about the horse, turning Blackie in a circle to ride up alongside.

"Oh, I had taken him down south to see if a trainer there could sell him for me." Then he looked at her and smiled. "Seems like maybe I was full of that thing called greed, and was asking more than he would bring."

Tara returned his smile and nodded. Southern California often brought inflated prices that allowed sellers to turn a horse over for a quick profit. "You must have made a couple of trips down there since I saw you last," she looked ahead and smiled again, noting his ability to self-reflect.

"Been down there a couple of times."

"What will you do with him now?"

"I think I'll take him back home to Montana with me, put a little more time into him, maybe try an' sell him again in a few months."

"Well, now." Tom had driven up beside them in the golf cart. "How's Rio this afternoon?"

"Fine, Tom."

"Did ya have a smooth drive on the way here?"

"It went pretty well," Rio was nodding and looking at the ground. Tara had the distinct impression that more had happened than he was letting on.

"Well," Tom sat back and folded his arms, "what would you like to do today?"

"I think I'll just ride him a little right now, Tom, then maybe see if I need help tomorrow."

"Okay," Tom adjusted his hat with a nonchalant motion of his hand, always ready to let anyone he worked with suit themselves. "That'll be fine."

For the remainder of the afternoon, Emerson rode the chestnut in the arena while Lena and Rio trotted over ground poles and rode down into the creek bed. For Tara, whether she stood with Blackie to watch from the sidelines or joined in with the others, everything that was going on around her had suddenly become fascinating.

17

~more than words can say~

Silence speaks with unceasing eloquence.

— Bhagavan Sri Ramana Maharishi

Tara rode Emerson's big chestnut somewhat awkwardly in the foggy morning breeze. His bulky western saddle, having molded to its owner's shape, was inflexible to her body and she had trouble overcoming its influence. Not in the mood to fight it, she allowed the big chestnut to stand quietly in the arena.

"It'll sound better," Tom had said when he'd suggested she ride him, "if the lady who owns him hears how another gal you barely knew didn't have any trouble at all."

Tara felt no hint of tension or need to buck coming from the chestnut, and wished for the comfort of another saddle so that she could do more with him. On the other hand, stopping allowed her to watch Emerson trying to saddle one of his other colts, a gray, outside the arena next to the field stalls. Tom was now holding him by the halter rope while Rio stood watching, hands stuffed into his jeans pockets.

Tara was thinking how much better he looked in his cowboy hat, although she hadn't minded looking at him last night at dinner, where he had politely removed it, revealing an already balding head. He had joined her and Lena at Anderson's Split Pea restaurant, holding the door open for them at the entrance before locating a square table big enough for three. She had just pulled her chair out to seat herself when she heard his voice.

She's a nice person.

She'd looked up and met his brown eyes, smiling into hers, then gave a start when she realized he hadn't actually said anything. At least, not aloud. Quickly lowering her gaze hadn't kept her face from growing hot.

It was the gray colt's first time being saddled and he was shifting nervously, even as Tom, somewhat tentative on arthritic knees, held him at the end of a long lead. His coat had already grown shaggy with the changing seasons and appeared dull from the mud that couldn't quite be groomed out with a brush and curry. Emerson threw a large, square saddle pad onto his back. The colt shied sideways, and Tom allowed him to drift over to the stall. The wall limited his sideways movement, but didn't quiet his trembling. Emerson pulled the pad off, tried to throw it on again, and then again, until Tom nodded his head and spoke to him.

Tara was too far away to hear what he said, but she saw Emerson look back over his shoulder and stop his arm mid-throw. The saddle pad hung limp in his hand as Rio walked up and took it from him. He stood where Emerson had stood, right beside the colt's shoulder. Both hands held the sides of the pad as he reached up and over the colt's back before releasing the woven cloth to settle softly across the withers. After pausing for a moment, he swung the pad off again, and then on and then off, as Emerson had done. His unhurried movements were smooth and soft as he reached over and down, all in one connected motion. Tara enjoyed watching him, admiring the feel he had with this sensitive animal. In three swings of the pad, the colt stood calmly. Then Rio took the heavy western saddle and swung it up, landing it neatly and gently on the broad back. The colt stood solid, licking his lips and chewing softly.

Tom had the two men switch places again. This time she saw a contrast in the way Emerson moved. His action was stilted in comparison to Rio's. Mechanical. Uncaring. By the second swing of his saddle pad, the colt was shifting his feet nervously. Tom, mirroring the wordless horses he worked with, said nothing as he motioned for Rio to take another turn. Again, Rio saddled the colt. Again, the colt calmed.

Tara remembered Tom talking about how a horse could learn to fill in for a person, given the right set of circumstances, and nodded, realizing that Rio would help this colt learn to become calm enough with the saddle to tolerate Emerson's lack of tact. The sun peeked through the fog and brightened the view before her. Then it occurred to her that Tom, who would never wish to offend a man who already thought he knew how to do things, was also using Rio to set an example to Emerson. If Emerson didn't become insulted because of a spoken criticism of his actions, he might be open to learning something new. She smiled to herself, remembering the walnuts. Months had passed before she'd realized that she hadn't been doing Tom any favors by cracking all those shells. Rather, he would use whatever was available to him to help someone learn to feel the best way to approach a situation.

"If I simply tell a person what to do, by the time they get home, they're likely to forget what I said or what it was good for. But if I can set up a situation so that a person can find it for themselves, then it has meaning for them, and they're likely to make use of it later on."

Tom's words echoed in her mind as she held her breath, waiting for the "Aha!" that would light Emerson's eyes when he saw what it was inside himself that could make a difference for this colt. She looked forward to that familiar exhilaration, the way it filled her each time she saw it happen for one of her students. Every time, it was a new discovery. Every time, it was her own.

This morning, like on any other day, she would have waited in that very spot forever. But in a few more tries, Tom stopped the men. The colt, having slipped and nearly fallen in an effort to get away from Emerson during the last round, needed a break. Tara sighed deeply, and the cold fog engulfed her. Emerson hadn't noticed anything. Hadn't changed anything. He would go on thinking the colt's tension was just the way the colt was—the same way people would go on thinking Tom didn't know how to explain things.

The young gray stood there, innocent, ears pricked forward, sensitive and alert to the people around him. He had never been overtly abused or physically uncared for. What would become of him, she wondered, knowing the answer. Like most children and animals she knew, he would have the harder road.

At lunch, they sat around the table, Emerson monologuing to Tom while Rio, Tara, and Lena sat quietly and ate. After the dishes had been cleared, Emerson loaded his cargo, *easily and without hesitation,* Tara noted, thinking of the trouble she had loading Blackie. Who was she to point the finger? She looked at Tom, shaking hands with Emerson. More than anyone, he deserved to be frustrated by all the people who took up his time but couldn't put into practice what they came here for, but he was not. The sun, finally burning off the morning fog, warmed their backs, and they waved Emerson out the drive.

Later in the afternoon, Tara stalled Blackie after her ride and came out to stand alongside Tom, seated in his cart and helping Lena as she rode her sorrel inside the arena. How long had she been standing there before feeling an impulse to look behind her? Rio stood near the bank of the creek, holding his horse and boring holes into the back of her head. She smiled and turned frontward again, as if it meant nothing.

As the sun went down, Rio rode to the paddocks at the other end of the drive, and Tara followed Lena back to the barn. She tossed alfalfa to the horses while Lena untacked the sorrel. After filling the water buckets in each stall, she stood in the aisle and inserted her foot into a bootjack, anxious for her feet to be relieved of another day's worth of aches and cramps. Unable to wriggle her sweaty calf out of the tight leather, she wrapped her arms around the back of her knee and tried pulling her leg up toward her chest, panting and straining. By then, Rio had walked back down to their end of the drive and stood just outside the barn overhang, talking with Tom before the elder waved and drove the cart back to the house.

"Where will you be staying tonight?" Tara, having finally wrenched her calf free of the boot, was still puffing.

"Well, last night I slept in my truck."

"Oh, no," she stood on her remaining booted leg, balancing the other socked foot off the ground. She realized he must have been trying to save money.

Rio shrugged. "It's not that bad. I just pulled into the Inn's parking lot. No one bothered me about it."

"You'd be welcome to stay with us." The words were out of her mouth before she could take them back. Rio shrugged his shoulders, but nodded.

Fortunately, Lena didn't complain, and Rio followed them to the hotel in his truck. Inside their room, they stopped to wash faces and hands, and dropped off their gear before climbing back into Tara's truck for the short drive down the street to a Chinese restaurant. The food was surprisingly fresh for a place so far from anywhere, and their conversation automatically drifted to horses and what it was like to be around Tom.

They split the bill three ways and walked in silence back through the parking lot, each finding their respective seats in the cab. Tara had just put the truck in gear when Lena cracked a joke; Tara snorted. "Don't get me started," she managed before an uncontrollable squeal escaped her as she attempted to maneuver around chunky potholes. Unable to watch the road, she quickly pressed down the heavy clutch with her foot and held it, letting the truck roll to a stop as the three of them punched out belly laughs over nothing. Eventually, she took the truck out of gear to cross her legs in the driver's seat. "I have to stop before I have an accident," she panted.

"No need to be drinking around you guys, is there?" Rio laughed again. None of them had had any alcohol with dinner.

Regaining her composure, Tara drove back across the street and found a parking spot near their room.

"I'll meet you up there," Rio called to them, showing up several minutes later with a guitar and his duffle bag. Inside the room, he perched himself on the edge of the bed, strumming softly while Tara sat on the floor sewing a snap onto her riding breeches. Lena fluffed the pillows against the backboard of the other bed, and with legs outstretched, absorbed herself in the pages of a magazine. By nine o'clock, they were all tired. Rio lay down on the floor, fully clothed, at the foot of Tara's bed and pulled a beach towel over himself, his socked feet sticking out from underneath. Tara peered over the edge and frowned.

"Is it all right down there?"

"Sure."

She couldn't imagine that it was, but when Lena turned out the light, she fell back onto her pillow, and they were all silent.

"Are you going to ride in that robe?" Rio teased the following morning as Tara packed her bag. Lena had been the first to claim the bathroom and was taking a shower.

"Maybe."

She hadn't seen him walk up behind her, but she wasn't really surprised when she felt him grab her arm, and, in one motion, push her face into the bed. She laughed loudly and wholeheartedly into the pillow, pretending to try to stop him while he, now straddling her backside, tickled her on both sides of her rib cage.

"Did you know that tickling is abusive?" Lena said, coming out of the bathroom.

Tara would have agreed, under any other circumstance.

"Maybe Tara wouldn't mind goin' up to the house to stir the pot o' beans I got on the stove," Tom said to Tara as she walked back out to the riding field from the barn. She had just stalled Blackie after a calm ride, and it was still well before noon. "I made it up special so we could have some for lunch," he finished.

"Sure, Tom," and without stopping, she made an about-face and headed for the mobile home. She almost ran into Rio, who had come into the field behind her from the paddocks.

"All right if I walk up to the house with you?" He strode beside her.

"Sure. You can help me get lunch ready. Hey, that looks like Portia," Tara referred to a neighbor who was making her way down the back steps of the house trailer. Just as she said it, she realized it wasn't a woman at all, but a man from PG&E to check the meters. Embarrassed, she laughed and flapped the back of her hand onto Rio's chest. He draped his arm across her back, squeezing her shoulder too hard. She winced.

"You need to take off those sunglasses once in awhile so you can see," he teased as they walked up the stairs together.

In the kitchen, she showed him where the utensils and plates were and enjoyed watching him set the table as she stirred the beans.

"You are a good person," the words came out spontaneously.

He smiled and shook his head. "I'm not a very nice person." She looked at him quizzically before he asked, "How long will you be staying here at Tom's?"

"We'll need to leave after lunch to beat the traffic." She smiled at his rapid change of subject. "How long are you staying?"

"Maybe another day or two."

"And then?"

Rio shrugged. "I'll head back home for awhile."

Tara knew something of the never-ending work to be done around a ranch. He would always be wanted home in time for starting more colts or haying or maintaining house and barns. "So you'll be there through the winter?"

"Yeah," he nodded. "Gotta help with the calving in February."

"You know, I'll be heading your way in the spring," she dared.

"Really?"

"Lena and her husband just bought a house in Colorado and will be moving there at the beginning of next year. I'd planned to visit them in May," she was already counting the months in her head, "and stop by to see some friends of mine in Billings, as well—make a vacation out of it."

Just then, Tom came through the door, and she filled the water glasses. Lena followed a few minutes later. They had a quiet, unanimated conversation, and after dragging it out as long as she could, Tara finally rose to help clear the table before hitching her truck and trailer. Out of the corner of her eye, she saw Tom gesture to Rio to help her while he and Lena followed.

She had backed the truck up to the trailer hitch when they arrived that morning, and now Rio crouched on hands and knees to hook the chains on one side. Tara needed to be on his other side to hook up the second set of chains, and placing her hand on his back, rested her weight against him for balance as she stepped over the hitch, enjoying the feel of solid muscle through his jacket.

"Fancy," he remarked at the hitch's configuration.

"Is it?" To her, the chains, battery wire, and electrical hookup looked commonplace.

Tom and Lena were saying their good-byes when Tara stood and left to bring the horses out of the barn. After Lena had loaded her sorrel, Tara put the chain over Blackie's nose. Thankfully, he walked into his slot in one try. The large bodies of the two big Thoroughbreds standing side by side filled every inch of space in the trailer.

"It's a good thing you have Quarter Horses," she said to Rio. "They all fit much more easily into your stock trailer."

Rio shrugged. "I've seen guys load up several warmbloods and pack them in without much trouble. It's a matter of what they get used to."

Of course. She nodded, feeling stupid. Then before she could think, she walked up to him and threw her arms around his neck, inadvertently sending his brimmed hat flapping to the ground.

"I'll miss you." Her face was turning hot again.

"Don't miss me too much," he answered, and stooped down to pick up his hat.

She pretended to ignore the comment and turned to stand in line behind Lena who was saying her good-byes to Tom. After making his hearing aid squeal, Tara walked to her truck, a voice telling her to keep moving. She opened the cab door and raised a foot to the floorboard.

"Be sure to get in touch when you come through Montana." It was Rio's voice behind her.

She turned around to face him. "All right," she answered evenly, taking in the now familiar glint emanating from his dark eyes.

Tara let her eyes wander over the freeway, the hills, and the sky throughout the drive home, a barrage of conflicting emotions swirling in the pit of her stomach. Just a few miles from their exit, a pair of headlights shone in her rear view mirror. With a start, she realized she was in the middle lane, holding back traffic. Turning on her blinker, she moved the rig over one lane to the right. A small truck with a camper shell on top passed her on the left, its back window revealing a large bumper sticker. "Go to the Eagles," it read, and she took in a quick breath.

"Look at that," she exclaimed to Lena, not caring that the sticker was, most likely, referring to the rock group that was performing in the Bay Area that coming weekend. She was thinking instead about the day she'd met Rio. "Remember the eagle we saw flying over us on the way to Tom's?"

Lena nodded matter-of-factly, unaware of any special meaning it might hold.

18

~secret's agony~

I could see people going about their lives, inhabitants of a normal, routine world, of which I was not a part.

—Andrea Bell
Dawson's Gift

November's cold afternoon breeze bit Tara's cheeks as she trotted Blackie around in the outdoor arena at work. Suddenly lured by the swaying of the trees, she changed course mid-stride and headed for the gate. Her normally busy afternoon had been lightened somewhat by two of her clients being away on vacation, and unencumbered by her usually strict time schedule, she unfastened the latch and rode toward the hills. The first rains of the season had come the week before, turning the regular clip-clop of her horse's hoof beats into a squishing sound over the slick, adobe soil.

Blackie had gotten good at standing quietly, allowing her to open another gate that led through the mares' pasture and into the rest of the three hundred-acre property. As they continued farther out, he stayed on the narrow trail that climbed steeply up toward the rock quarry, and kept his footing along the path, only inches wide, that skirted the side of the hill.

He's changing, she thought, and smiled while giving him a spontaneously affectionate rub on the neck.

Eventually, they dropped down into the shadows of many trees that canopied the dirt road running alongside a dry creek bed. Once they came up on level ground, the trail forked, one way going around the reservoir, the other leading through a ditch. She decided on the ditch. It would be a good opportunity to practice what they'd been working on at Tom's. But as they came to the edge of the drop-off, Blackie balked.

Instinctively, she began lightly tapping her legs on his sides, careful not to bump him with her spurs, but he backed up anyway. When he settled, she tried again, but he only flipped his head and threatened to rear. Stopping to think, she decided to maneuver him down sideways. When one side didn't work, she tried the other — but with no luck.

"Well," she said aloud, "since you like moving backwards, let's try going through backwards." But each time his hind feet came close to the edge, he swung his hindquarters deftly to the side before she could straighten him back.

She did try using her spurs then, and then her whip, when the spurs made him more agitated, knowing that if she used the whip hard enough, he would go. But nervous sweat was already beginning to slicken his coat, and the escalation of his angst was the very thing she was trying, after all this time, to avoid. Nearly two hours had come and gone when she threw down her reins and slid off his back. Feeling a slow burn in the pit of her stomach, she led him across on foot. He obeyed her then, but a frown remained on her face, pulling heavily at the sides of her mouth. He still hadn't *wanted* to go.

"It's Crystal," she heard her sister's voice talking into the machine as she pushed through the door to her apartment after work, arms laden with her pack and extra saddle pads from the ranch that needed washing. "Just calling to say hi. If I don't hear from you, I'll try calling back in a couple of days."

After freeing her arms, she moved to the sink to wash her hands. The clock on the wall said five-thirty. Seven-thirty, Iowa time.

"Is it a bad time to talk?" she asked, returning the call.

"Oh, no. I was just washing up the dishes from dinner," Crystal explained the hissing water in the background. "I wanted to check with you to see if you were still planning a trip to LA for Thanksgiving and when you might be going."

"I just got my tickets last week. I'm flying out on Wednesday the 25th, to visit Shelley and returning on Saturday — "

"Do you realize that Bob and I will be in LA that same day?"

"On Wednesday?"

"No, Saturday. We'll be spending the holidays here with his folks, then flying out to see Mom and Dad."

"Really? What time does your flight arrive?"

"Eleven-thirty."

"Wow, what a coincidence." Tara was impressed. Her flight left at 2:00 the same afternoon. It occurred to her that it was the second time this year that her sister had asked to see her in person. "Should we meet somewhere? I could come early and meet you at the gate."

"We could have lunch together, right there at the airport."

"Great!" Tara marked the date on her calendar, three weeks away.

In spite of the early rains, Tara managed to arrange a day between wet weather to spend at Tom's. Lena was busy packing for her move to Colorado, and without another horse to stand in the trailer compartment next to Blackie he loaded with some difficulty. Tara had to adjust to the long, predawn drive in the dark alone as well and shifted in her seat, not quite able to get comfortable. She pulled into the drive at Wesland an hour after sunrise. Tom was sitting casually in the golf cart just outside his house, talking to some cowboy standing alongside the cart with his back to her. Both men were dressed for cool weather, the cowboy standing, one knee cocked, with two hands stuffed inside the front pockets of his jeans. As she drove past, making a U-turn off the main drive, the men turned and waved, and her heart stopped. She hadn't recognized Rio from the back beneath his down jacket.

Instead of parking under the willow and out of the way, she stopped in the middle of the parking lane facing the portable barn and shut the engine off. The men were still talking when she unloaded Blackie and led him to the arena. When she turned him loose, he snorted, bucked, and ran while she stood hoping he wouldn't strain any muscles or tendons still cold from being pent up for three hours in the trailer. By the time he settled, the two men had driven over in the cart. Contrasting cowboy hats, Rio's dark and Tom's light, made the height difference between the two men obvious.

"And how's Tara this morning?" Tom spoke in his usual quiet, lighthearted way.

"Fine, Tom." She smiled and nodded to Rio, feeling her face flush. "What are you doing here? More horses to haul south?"

He nodded, returning her smile.

"Well, now, what did you want to do with Blackie today?" Tom asked.

"I'd like to work on loading him into the trailer."

"Ah, yah," he answered, nodding casually, as if he hadn't been waiting all this time for her to finally address the problem. He removed his hat to rub the back of his hand across his brow, his head of hair still surprisingly thick and black. "I see you've got your rig all set up," he nodded toward her truck and trailer. "We'll meet you over by the barn when you're ready."

Tara nodded, and in a few minutes led her horse back across the yard. At the trailer, Tom rummaged through a canvas bag for a rope halter with a long rope attached, the first time he'd made a move to change any of her equipment.

"Are those rope halters better than what he's got on?" Tara asked.

"Well, usually I see no need in using what the person isn't accustomed to. But this," he said, pulling out a wad of round spaghetti-like straps, "can be useful in situations where the horse needs more directing."

The rope halter fit around a horse's nose the same as hers, but she could see that it would be more severe if used forcefully—but also more effective in letting the person use less pressure to achieve the same results—without having to use a chain over the horse's nose.

"And this one has a longer rope attached, which gives a person more room at the end of the lead," Tom completed his thought and handed the rope halter to Rio, who nodded only once to indicate his willingness to load the horse "so Tara can watch." After replacing her halter with the one Tom had given him, Rio led Blackie to the back while Tara stood out of the way, next to Tom.

Her two-horse trailer had no ramp, which meant Blackie had to step up from the ground several inches and load straight forward into one of two narrow compartments. Tom made no comment about whether or not the trailer's design was better or worse than any other as Rio walked inside and disappeared up front by the feed manger. When the gelding was ready to come in, Rio would leave by the escape door on the side. There was room inside the narrow stall for only the person or the horse without risking the person being stepped on or crushed against the sides. Tara noticed that Tom hadn't suggested they move the dividing panel to give Blackie more room on the entry, even though she had seen him do so at other times for other horses.

Blackie followed Rio up to the trailer, but raised his head abruptly and planted his feet right before he stepped in, ears flicked backwards.

That horse is stubborn, is how she had been taught to judge such behavior. *Most horses will try to hurt you. Horses are the most willing creatures on earth. They'll only perform under threat of punishment. Horses want to please. They'll try to avoid doing what you tell them. Their brain is only the size of a pea, so they must be stupid. This one is real smart. He's acting this way just to get to me. He's being a bully. Horses are just lazy.*

Horses who didn't like loading into a trailer had their own behavioral litany. *They're claustrophobic. They don't like ramps. It's harder for them to step up and load without a ramp. They like riding backwards. They like riding at a slant. Never turn a horse backwards in a trailer. They don't like road noise.*

"Now, Rio, you just keep his head directed straight ahead, but otherwise have slack in the halter rope." As always, there was no ire or hurry in Tom's delivery.

Blackie remained planted on the spot, but Tom waited until he had lowered his head and neck and was chewing quietly, tongue slipping out between his lips. Tom then took his flag and used it to tap one of the front legs. The sensation startled Blackie, who snatched a foot off the ground. Tom then tapped the other leg and got the same reaction. He went back and forth calmly, from one to the other. Blackie alternately picked up his legs, marching in place. Then he stepped up into the trailer with his front feet and stopped, his body halfway in, hind feet trailing out behind and planted on the ground.

"You'll wait there a moment." Tom was talking again to Rio, who had positioned himself with one leg outside the escape door, his foot securely on the running board so he could move in or out easily. The sensitive, high-strung Thoroughbred seemed on the edge of wanting to back out. But when nothing happened, he lowered his head and chewed again. "Now reach out, easy, an' pet his head."

Rio stepped cautiously forward, slowly reaching out his hand so as not to disturb a fragile calm, and softly stroked the long face.

"We want him to learn that good things happen in there," Tom whispered to Tara.

In another minute, Blackie made a move to step out of the trailer.

"Just let him come out," Tom said firmly.

Tara was surprised, always having been taught that one should never let a horse back out of a trailer unless the person had asked it to. *That horse is playing games, being bull-headed, always fighting against me, calling the shots, being disobedient.* She herself had used such descriptive phrases many times. But the dark horse, feeling no restraint, backed out of the trailer and stood with his front feet just outside the step.

"Tom, wasn't that a bad thing that he just did?" Tara asked.

"Well, I don't usually like to talk about anything being bad—

there's no such thing, really. The horse is just doin' what he knows, same as the person."

Tara frowned as they let a minute or two pass, Blackie just standing quietly. Finally, Tom asked Rio to apply a soft pressure on the lead line. To Tara's surprise, he stepped up with his front feet without hesitation. When he backed out again, Rio let him, then asked him to step up again, then down again, then up again, and down and up and down—in and out of the trailer with his front feet a dozen or more times. Then, out of the blue, or so it appeared to Tara, Blackie just stopped and stood calmly with his front feet inside the trailer and made no more attempts to come out.

"You see," Tom said turning to Tara, "he's feeling better about that step with his front feet now, but he doesn't want to go all the way in because he's worried about what will happen when he has to back out of the trailer with his hind feet. He's liable to be a lot more concerned about himself when we start working on his hind end."

Tara nodded, but as usual, didn't understand. Why would the hind feet be any more trouble than the front? And if what Tom said was true, how had she missed knowing such a thing, especially after all the years Blackie had ridden in trailers? Might not her mentor's assessment be just another judgment on the list of assumptions that humans had about horses? How did he actually know that Blackie's so-called worry about his hind feet was what the horse was experiencing?

"Okay, Rio, you'll just ask him easy to come on out and take a tour around the yard a few times."

When Rio had made a big circle, Tom called to him again. "Now, you'll get yourself lined up and head straight for the trailer, as if Blackie's been doin' this his whole life."

Rio approached the trailer in a straight line, then stepped up and walked in as far as he could. The dark horse followed with his two front feet, then stopped quietly, already relaxed.

Tom moved toward his rump and began a similar tapping on the hind legs. "You see how he gets stuck in his movement?" he said to Tara

For the first time, Tara noticed that her horse paused for a split second after Tom's tap before snatching a leg off the ground in a jerky fashion. When she ran her eyes up to his rump, she saw the tension there as well, his tail clamped tight between two butt cheeks like a scared dog.

Tom stopped his tapping for a moment, then started up again, then paused again in intervals. Each time he started up, he intensified the tapping. Blackie was agitated, his breath coming quick and shallow. The odd thing was that he made no move to pull away, even as sweat began to lather his coat. Tara frowned again and looked at Tom, who remained perfectly calm, even though his tapping actions were now coming in rapid succession. He didn't seem to be trying to make the horse go anywhere, which further confused her. Still, Blackie was working harder, breath coming in irregular gasps, a dazed look in his eye, struggling, yet resigned. Tom continued tapping.

She suddenly felt tired, wanting some kind of relief, for this session to end, to be able to turn away or lie down. An old, familiar nausea swept through her and she felt dizzy. What was it?

Suddenly, she recoiled her bare foot with a jerk, having unsuspectingly stepped on a cold wet spot on the living room carpet. She looked up to see her mother clumsily weaving across the living room toward the master bedroom with a puffy face, eyes half closed. A hand was raised, revealing a bloody tampon dangling by a string in open view.

Crystal pushed a rag into Tara's six-year-old hand. "Here, you can help wipe it up."

Oh, no, not again. She desperately wanted to run. Instead, she dropped heavily to her hands and knees, a tightness in her chest making it hard to breathe. The pungent smell of her mother's urine stung her nose and filled her head. She was overcome with uncontrollable, silent gagging, like one of her cats trying to throw up a fur ball. Only nothing came out. Embarrassed, she glanced up to see if anyone had seen. Crystal was frowning, intently focused on scrubbing out a different spot in the carpet. Her father was sitting on the couch in front of her, but his face and torso were buried behind the newspaper. His crossed leg swung rhythmically, mindlessly, back and forth, back and forth, like a carefree child while his children wiped away his wife's body fluids. Holding her breath, Tara worked the rag frenetically back and forth over the urine several times, then ran from the room, slamming her bedroom door.

"Tara!" It was Crystal yelling. "Don't you dare slam that door!"

With a loud bang, Blackie jumped into the trailer, all four feet inside. Tara started, her breath coming quick and shallow, knees bent and torso angled forward, feeling a great urge to sit down.

"The darkest hour, just before the dawn." Tom turned to her while she tried to catch herself, making a supreme effort to look normal.

There was alfalfa hay in the manger for Blackie to eat, now that he was all the way inside. Rio stood outside the escape door, both feet on the running board, stroking the horse's neck through the opening. After letting Blackie stand quietly for some time, Tom motioned to Rio to back him out. As Rio pushed on Blackie's chest, the horse took a few gingerly steps back, but when his hind feet were just at the edge of the step, he stopped.

"You see, he knows that falloff is there, but he can't quite see it, and he hasn't learned to feel for that step," Tom said aloud. Tara nodded, remembering her horse doing the same thing at the ditch. Tom had been right after all.

Rio firmed the pressure on Blackie's chest with his hand and leaned into it.

"Sometimes they don't want to come out once they're in, or sometimes they'll run out backwards to try and get it over with," Tom continued.

Blackie crouched low, his whole body in tension. He stomped a few times in place before reluctantly setting a foot over the edge of the floorboards and down to the ground. Once he was out, he looked around with a bright expression. Tara let out a breath and felt her muscles go limp, blood running to her feet, pulling her down.

"Now, it's been quite some time that there's been this trouble spot. So, even though we're offering a better deal, it'll be a little while before that takes the place of the old pattern."

Tara, still in a daze, wondered if Tom was referring to her or the horse.

"The steps'll get so that they come up and down easy-like with the hind legs," he said to her as soft as a whisper, a hand in front of his face gently making up and down gestures as if conducting an orchestra in pianissimo. Calming. Soothing. Without judgment. Without punishment.

She nodded again, eyes glued to the ground. For once, she was relieved when Tom suggested they break for lunch. Without looking up, she nodded her thanks to Rio and, with horse in tow, left the two men for the barn and Blackie's stall. "I'll meet you inside," she managed over her shoulder before disappearing. They waved and climbed inside the golf cart.

She stalled Blackie and hung his halter outside the door. Halfway down the aisle on her way to the house, she hesitated and sat down heavily on a bale of straw that hugged the wall of the barn. Dried stems pushed through her breeches and poked at her skin, but she hardly noticed. She pulled air deep into her lungs, letting her head rest against the siding, closing her eyes to the outside world. Were other people's lives as secretive as hers, neatly hidden away so that nothing but nods and smiles escaped the surface? There had been few times in her life when what she felt on the inside actually matched what came out. And now, past events that she had tried so long to ignore seemed to pull at her, weigh her down, demanding to be felt. That was the difference. The memories were no longer just pictures in her mind.

The sun, hanging low to the south, angled in under the roof and washed over her. She sat there, disappointed at not having the presence of mind to take advantage of the opportunity to talk with Rio. But her body felt so heavy, and just the thought of getting up to join the men seemed impossible to contemplate until she heard the sound of golf cart wheels and realized she must have dozed off, missing lunch entirely. She quickly stood up from the bale of straw, rubbing her face into her hands before checking her watch. It was already one o'clock. She walked out to meet Tom and Rio, who were pulling up in front of the barn.

"When you didn't come in, we thought maybe you'd decided to take a little nap," Tom said.

She nodded, eyes downcast. Was there anything she did that he didn't know about already?

"Do you want to try loading Blackie once more before you go? That way, you'll be all set to leave in time." Tom smiled.

She nodded and turned to grab Blackie's leather halter, sliding the stall door open just enough to slip her body through sideways. Blackie's head was still deep in his alfalfa, and she had to pull hard on his mane to lure him away to fit the halter over his face.

Tom motioned to her to lead him up to her trailer. Rio stood back and watched while the horse stepped up and back, in and out of the trailer several times with his front feet. When he finally stood quiet, halfway inside, she saw the movement of Tom's arm through the trailer door, and knew he was tapping his hind legs again. Blackie was much less agitated this time, and it wasn't long before he stood on all fours inside the trailer. Tara's own feet stepped onto the running board, her hands reaching inside the escape door to rub the dark neck.

"Tom, what made you decide to use this particular way of loading him into the trailer?"

Tom looked up at her, resting both hands on the handle of his flag, which was pointed softly on the ground in front of him, as if it were a walking stick.

"Well," he said, "I've been around quite a few years, and in that time, I've tried quite a few things," he nodded. "Once in awhile, I'd find something that worked." He paused, looked to the side, and lifted a hand in preparation for another thought. Tara waited.

"I try and tell people that they haven't come here because they've got horse problems, even though that's what they're thinking." He paused with his mouth open, eyes twinkling as if he were about to laugh. "I tell them it's really the other way around — that their horse has a people problem."

She nodded and smiled, but turned her face back toward Blackie, leaning into him as she stroked his neck deeply, feeling small. Insignificant. The men waited. In a few minutes, she unloaded him again, stepping all the way through the trap door to follow him back outside. After walking around in a large arc, she tried loading him again. This time, he didn't hesitate and walked all the way in on the first try. Rio closed the back of the trailer. She closed the escape door, and then reached inside his manger to clip the tie strap to his halter. Although Blackie shifted his feet, he didn't paw or kick at the sides, so she didn't feel rushed to get the truck started.

She turned to Tom to wrap her arms around his neck, hanging her head limp on his shoulder for a moment before letting go. Feeling too awkward to say more, she could only wave at Rio before climbing into the cab. Both men were already in the cart heading back to the house as she pulled down the drive.

19

~naked~

The ego is a confusion of identification.

—*A Course in Miracles*

There were no lights on in the main house when Tara pulled in her driveway after dark, telling her the neighbors were not at home. Empty silence greeted her as she walked up the steps and the evening stretched ahead. She stood in the shower for a long time, soaking in the rapid fire of tiny droplets pelting her back, letting the day's images float through her mind—Tom tapping his flag, the kindness in his eyes, Rio's stare, leaving again. She had made the water very hot, and with steam still rising off her skin, she wrapped a towel around her head before going back out to sit naked on the couch to trim her toenails, smoothing tired feet with the palm of her hand.

My mother's feet.

She pulled the towel from her head, noting the long, blonde hair that had always contrasted with her siblings' short strands of jet-black and dark brown, her skinny arms and legs opposing their wider frames.

"The different one," they had called her.

But even as a child, she had known better, often sitting in front of her bedroom mirror connecting each part of her body to one of her parents. Her forehead belonged to her father. Her eyes and hands were most like her mother's. Her arms and legs belonged to her father.

My father's arms and legs.

It had been the ritual since she was ten. The year Crystal left home.

She rose from the couch and pulled on her sweats. Next to her answering machine and the blinking red light, she caught a glimpse of a phone number on a scrap of white envelope dotted with brown smudge marks. It was the handwriting of one of her clients, scrawled in heavy black ink. She picked up the paper and pressed it to her nose, detecting a faint earthen mustiness hinting of horse sweat and urine.

The number had been sitting in her pocket for weeks. Only a few days ago had she laid it in plain sight, not realizing until this moment that she was prepared to do anything with it.

"You're like a V-8 engine running on three cylinders," her client had said, writing the number on the partial envelope cupped in his hand. "A brilliant teacher, capable of doing most anything, but you're not getting anywhere." How odd that someone she was supposed to be helping was giving her advice. "I highly recommend you talk to this person." And then he'd handed her the number.

She had resisted the idea at first, thinking of the time years before when she had finally made the commitment to see a therapist, spending a sum of money she would need to go into debt for. How terrifying it had been, walking into that sterile office with cold, clammy hands, her stomach in knots.

"I just don't feel right," was what she'd said. "Sometimes I don't want to get out of bed in the morning."

"There. Now that you've said it, that's not so bad, is it?" The face sitting across from her had smiled. Had it been real? Tara still didn't know.

"But the bad feeling is still there," she'd tried again.

"Maybe it would help if you acted it out."

"What do you mean?"

"You could march around the room and express whatever feeling was inside. If you're angry, you might pretend you're a lion or a dragon, like this." The therapist had knotted her fists and stomped around, ranting some unintelligible phrase before sitting back down and waiting for Tara to try.

But Tara hadn't been able to force herself up from her seat. "I don't know that I can do that."

"Maybe you can't because there's nothing really there."

She remembered looking down at her hands in her lap. Had she made everything up, after all?

The following week, there had been longer periods of silence. Longer ones the week after that, and in two months, the counselor had declared there would be no more need for therapy.

Tara set down the piece of paper, and after smoothing its surface to better see the scrawl of black ink, picked up the phone and dialed the number. The recorded message sounded impersonal. She placed the phone back on its receiver and turned to walk around the apartment, hoping the movement would steady her shaky fingers.

She paused in front of her stereo system set among her bookshelves. Inside the tape deck was her latest recording of affirmations, "Guaranteed to lift you to a higher place, overcome the past, and get what you want in life," or so the self-help books said. She'd liked the idea at first, filling both sides of a cassette in first, second, and third person. *I am strong and happy. You are strong and happy. She is strong and happy.* It was something she could do for free and in the privacy of her own home, a different approach from the group sessions she'd attended during the late seventies, the era of burgeoning new therapies. At that time, she had been too embarrassed to speak in front of a group of strangers who would have analyzed her along with the twenty-something-year-old counselor-in-training. So, she'd opted for the greater anonymity of standing, lying, or crouching in an auditorium of a hundred or more, all crying, screaming, and raging together. In her emotional naiveté, such purging had allowed her to leave the sessions believing she had been healed, the nameless inner chaos having momentarily been exorcised. But the moment she'd landed back inside the familiar walls of her own home, she'd wasted no time in spooning cereal, cookies, or leftovers into her mouth—food the only thing that seemed to soothe the raw and open wounds that suddenly had no protection from the outside world.

Still in front of her stereo, Tara sighed and rubbed her face, thinking of the longer, more descriptive narratives she had recently recorded. *This tape is a gift to me, from me, to bring myself out of negative conditioning and unsupportive ways of thinking, feeling, and acting in my day-to-day life. I love my life and myself. You love your life and yourself. She loves her life and herself.* The tape was nearly forty-five minutes long, with Vaughn Williams' "The Lark Ascending" playing in the background.

But is it working?

She walked back to her phone, and glancing at the piece of paper still lying on her table, redialed the number. "I-I'd like to set an appointment," she stammered into the receiver and left her phone number.

"What are your qualifications as a therapist? I mean, how do you work?" Tara sat stiffly on the couch the following week, hands pinned under her thighs, trying to absorb the even gaze coming from Deedee across from her. She was not about to divulge anything until she had a better sense of this woman. Then, self-conscious of her own curtness, she added, "I've had a lot of therapy; most of it hasn't worked."

"I'd be happy to tell you about my background," Deedee smiled, and proceeded to rattle off an impressive history, which, if nothing else, indicated a lot of experience. "I have seen people get better," she closed to Tara's silence. "Why don't you begin by telling me a little bit about where you grew up, if you have any brothers and sisters—" and the rest of the session was taken up with the details of Tara's family structure, how many siblings she had, which order they came in, how old they were.

Not enough information to know if Deedee's the right person, Tara was thinking to herself at the hour's end, when the therapist asked if she'd like to set another appointment. How odd that it should be the unknown that made her agree to return. She needed to find out.

"Do you remember when you first knew there was a problem with your mother?" Deedee asked on their second visit.

Tara stared. It seemed she had always known, but like the rest of her family, had acted as if there had never been a problem. "I guess I realized I had been lying to myself sometime before I left for Germany."

Yes. In fact, she knew the exact moment. The year before she left to train overseas, she'd received the National Reserve Championship in recognition of her high show scores. On Blackie! Now, it seemed like someone else's life. But at the time, saving up for three tickets to the awards dinner to be held at the Santa Anita race track in Los Angeles was all she'd been able to think about, and their eventual purchase had left a noticeable dent in her savings.

On the afternoon of the event, she arrived at her parents' front steps and rang the bell, knowing they were expecting her—possibly already getting ready for the dinner. Waiting at the door, she became aware of how nervous she was, unable to imagine the evening ahead. Minutes passed before she realized no one had answered her second ring.

Startled, she looked to make sure a car was parked along the curb. Her parents' car was there. She rang the bell again. Still no answer. Setting her bag by her feet, she searched her wallet for a key. Feeling the small, cold metal object among her loose change, she gripped the head and inserted its silver points into the lock. Click!

The door opened wide, letting light pour into the dark living room and settle directly over an ashen white face, eyes closed on the couch pillow. How strange to see her mother still dressed in that pale blue bathrobe so late in the day. Her ensuing apology for disturbing her mother's sleep was cut short as the latter lifted her head, rolled over, and landed on the floor with a thud. A shaky arm reached out of the robe's wide sleeve to grab Tara's hand. Tara remembered staring at the swollen feet struggling to stand, then at the red eyes, puffy face, and uncombed hair. A long-forgotten putrid mixture of alcohol and urine wafted to her nostrils. She read her mother's slow movements and registered the drone of slurred speech.

Oh, no.

Before she could speak, a hand pulled her to the dining table, her mother's rough palm pressing against hers.

"Tara, there's something I must tell you." Her mother tried pulling her into the adjacent chair.

"What?" Tara refused to sit, defiantly pulling her hand away as she looked down at her mother's disheveled hair. Strands formerly dyed blonde had turned nearly all gray.

"You should know—" Her mother hadn't noticed her daughter's stiff reply. "No, you must never know."

You sound like an idiot! Tara had come within an inch of slapping the puffy face. Instead, she leaned toward her mother, and with dragon fire, shouted in a whisper, "Why don't you find someone who can help you?"

Big round tears formed in her mother's eyes and slid down her cheeks. "Because…You don't understand. Your father—" She glanced toward the adjoining room, warning Tara with a shake of her head that she didn't want him to hear their conversation. Tara couldn't imagine why it should matter, feeling the old rage smoldering inside.

"Why don't you find someone who can help you?" she said again, her voice still sizzling.

But as if a door had been slammed shut, her mother sat up, lifted her chin, and set her jaw. "There is no one who can help me."

Tara's wrath collapsed into another wad of frustration as her mother got up, staggered to her bedroom, and slammed the door. Drained and shaky, she found her father in the den, his head hidden behind his paper, a crossed leg swinging back and forth. Back and forth. He looked up when she approached.

"She's mad because I told her she couldn't go to your awards dinner."

Tara stared mutely at him before realizing that was the only explanation he was going to offer.

"You can take my car, if you like," he added. Then, reading her face, "Or I can take you—I can take you, drop you off, and come right back. I don't want to leave your mother for too long."

Her eyes became slits as she turned her head slightly and eyed him from their corners. He looked so confident and at peace, as though having an alcoholic wife made him feel better—stronger, perhaps. Of course, the polite thing would have been to go to the dinner and ceremony alone—never mind the tickets and the money she had sacrificed for them. But at the time, she couldn't bring herself to feel certain of the way there. She, who had driven across the United States and Canada several times during her teens just for fun. She, who had hauled Blackie up and down the state of California by herself to countless horse shows and seminars, was suddenly afraid of driving twenty-five miles across a city where she'd spent her entire childhood.

Her father barely spoke along the way. It hadn't occurred to her to break the silence, or to ask how, why, or when her mother had relapsed when he had acted as though nothing out of the ordinary had happened. Instead she'd let herself out of the car at the racetrack clubhouse in silence. As promised, he came back to pick her up after she had eaten and climbed onto the stage with the camera lights flashing to publish her picture inside a national magazine that neither parent would ever see. Or ask about.

"And how did that make you feel?" Deedee probed.

Tara shrugged, then shuddered involuntarily, the therapist's office seeming cold all of a sudden. "Life went on as usual, until—"

Until that hot summer afternoon in Santa Barbara when she'd been driving home from work in the old Volkswagen. She had been screaming that day, as she sometimes did, trying to find a way to rid herself of the nameless inner torment. She had often wished for the courage to point her car off a mountain or into a building, imagining it easier than slitting one's wrists, or taking an overdose of pills, or locking oneself in a garage, breathing exhaust fumes like a friend of hers had done. But in the end, she always chickened out, resorting to screaming and beating the steering wheel instead, rolling up the windows so that no one could hear. But finding herself not at all relieved that day, she tried opening the car window, seeking air to cool herself down. Steadying the steering wheel against her left knee, she placed one hand on the glass pane to pull it down while the other turned the handle. The tactic worked, but traffic had subsequently bottled and slowed, making fresh air useless while an uncomfortable sweat beaded over the surface of her skin.

Searching for another distraction, she fumbled with the radio. This she rarely did, the radio as old as the car itself, which made it difficult to distinguish harmonies from the constant buzz that emanated from the ancient speaker set into the hard metal dash. But on that day, she was determined to have music, and persevered over the power-on knob that had long ago lost its plastic grip, requiring her to pinch its metal spoke hard to overcome the resistance of its off position.

But it was not music she heard. Instead, a male voice, clear and audible, came blaring out of the speaker, well past her range of hearing. "Have you ever felt numb, empty, or sad? Is it hard for you to trust others? Do you feel responsible for other people's feelings? Do you feel unfulfilled in your personal life and at work? Do you feel inadequate or suffer from low self-esteem? Do you find it difficult to visit with your parents or other members of your family for more than a few minutes or hours? Do you have difficulty asking for what you want? Do you not know how to respond when people ask how you are feeling?"

She felt her heart beat too fast as a startling pain knifed its way into her stomach. "If any of these personality traits describe you, you may have come from an abusive, alcoholic, or dysfunctional family. For more information or referrals for treatment, please contact your local Al-anon organization today."

An empty parking space appeared in the long line of cars parked on the side of the busy thoroughfare. She swerved, cutting across a lane of traffic. Braking fast, she wedged herself in alongside the curb, nose first, not caring that her back fender still jutted into traffic as memories of herself at six blinded her to the present world. Suddenly, she had been tiptoeing across her bedroom, placing an ear next to the doorjamb to assess the safety of the outside world, creeping along the tiled floors in the hallway, silent on her bare feet. An inner voice had always told her not to be found. But the silence of another long afternoon eventually, inevitably called her from some closet where she had been playing—an uncontrollable, unquenchable longing pulling her out of hiding.

She usually found her mother in the kitchen, standing alone, facing the cupboards, one hand resting on the counter, the other holding a secret liquid in a morning's juice glass. Tara cautiously curled her body behind the door and peered in, mouth watering, imagining what it would be like to be wrapped in those arms, to feel their warmth on her skin.

"Mommy?"

Without answering, her mother brought glass to lips, the liquid silently disappearing.

"I remember being shocked to find myself back in my Volkswagen." Tara felt her chest rise and fall heavily and struggled to recount the last details to Deedee. "Like I'd been so absorbed in the memory I'd forgotten where I was, even though it couldn't have lasted very long, or maybe it did; actually, I don't really know if—"

"PTSD."

"What?"

"Post-traumatic stress disorder," Deedee said.

"You mean there's a name for it?"

Deedee nodded calmly, her brown eyes steadily holding Tara's gaze. "It's something that often happens to veterans, or people who have experienced severe trauma. It's also not uncommon in children from abusive families. Their survival mechanisms kick in to get them through the initial trauma, but it's not until later that their emotions can be processed." She tilted her head to the side. "Same thing happened to you."

Tara became conscious of her wide-open eyes staring at her therapist. She made herself blink, then frowned. "Well, it seems to be happening a lot lately." She pursed her lips. "You know, that day in my Volkswagen was the first time it ever occurred to me that my emotions might actually have an origin, that there might be a reason I felt the way I did." She fought to swallow back another lump in her throat.

"How old were you?"

"I was in my twenties already. Can you imagine being so clueless my whole life until then?"

"It was the only life you knew. What else were you going to think?"

Tara looked down at her hands, smiled, and shook her head. "You sound like Tom." She looked up again. "It's all the same, isn't it?"

"What is?"

"It's all the same. I mean, it doesn't matter what I do—whether I'm here or with the horses or washing dishes—it's all about the same thing. It's about—it's about—" Then she shook her head. "Lost my train of thought."

20

~circles~

What goes around, comes around.
What comes around, goes around.

— Proverb

Two days later, Tara flew into LAX, and after spending Thanksgiving with her friend, Shelley, she was back inside the terminal on Saturday morning, checking the monitors for her sister's flight. She felt a jolt as she caught the unmistakable blue eyes of her sister coming through the gate.

"How long has it been?" Crystal asked.

"I think more than two years. Hard to believe." Tara reached out to embrace the once familiar frame. Crystal's husband, who rarely spoke at social gatherings, gave Tara a silent nod.

The three of them walked along the busy concourse until they spotted a decent-looking restaurant off to one side where they sat at a small table near the entrance. The open-sided alcove did little to alleviate the chaos brought in by the steady stream of passengers filing past. Tara tried to concentrate on the bits and pieces of Crystal's life between glances at the menu, but she had trouble remembering if Crystal had said she was still teaching privately, or only for the public school system. Or had she said that she was thinking of acquiring new students? And was Bob, sitting silently beside her, working for a new district attorney, or had he become one?

In less than an hour, they finished eating, and after their plates had been cleared, Crystal leaned forward, looking Tara directly in the face, her voice softer than before. But suddenly, Tara heard every word.

"Why don't you come with us to see Mom and Dad?"

There was an intensity under the silkiness of her sister's tone that took Tara aback, telling her that Crystal had planned to ask the question all along.

"Well, I'm not really interested." Tara was determined to keep her voice as unruffled as her sister's.

"I think it would mean a lot to them if you came."

So what? Tara paused, desperately searching for another comeback. Why was everyone always considering how things would affect their parents, as if they were the only ones who mattered?

"How long has it been since you've seen them?"

Tara had to think again. It must have been after her return from Germany — when she'd come back to live in Santa Barbara. "You're wasting away here," her friend, Nell, had said after watching her try to restart her training business, struggling to stay afloat in a city rapidly consuming land for development. Every year, rising property values pushed another stable out of business.

Nell's counsel hadn't been what she'd wanted to hear. Ever since moving away from her parent's home, Santa Barbara had become a kind of oasis. The mountain range along the eastern edge of the city had often lured her into the predawn darkness on a horse to ride up the trail to drink in the reds, purples, and pinks of sunrise. The ocean on the opposite side had never been short of sunlight, reflecting sparkling diamonds off its surface during solitary gallops along the beach .

"You should at least go somewhere where all of your experience and knowledge will be put to use. Nothing's happening here for you," Nell had kept on. "Look at what you've been through. There's no one here who can appreciate your expertise."

Despite Tara's reticence, Nell's words had finally sunk in, and only a few months later, she'd made arrangements to stay with friends outside of San Francisco until she could reestablish herself as a trainer in northern California. Days before her move, she had driven her 1956 Volkswagen "Bug" to Los Angeles, knowing there would be strings attached if she actually kept the gift her parents had given her in high school. Her brother, Jed, had offered her a lift back to Santa Barbara, helping her recover the remaining odds and ends left buried in her parents' garage over the years.

It had been a friendly good-bye with her mother — the only one of her parents at home that day — the kind of interaction that had always belied the fact that there had ever been anything amiss between them. Climbing into the passenger seat of her brother's truck, she hadn't intended to look back. But as they'd pulled slowly away from the curb late that afternoon, she'd turned to see her mother still wearing the light blue terry cloth bathrobe, while standing on the curb like Mrs. Cleaver, waving them off from the City of Angels.

Tara had never premeditated not mentioning her move to her parents. But by the following week, when everything she owned had been packed into the back of her truck's long bed, she had yet to give word. It was still dark the morning she'd loaded her queen-sized mattress into one side of her horse trailer, Blackie into the other half, and accompanied by a red dawn, embarked on the five hundred-mile drive north.

"It's been nearly four years," she said to Crystal.

"What?" Her sister had been distracted by an argument between a man and woman, whose voices rose above the din as they moved down the concourse.

"It's been about four years since I've talked to them."

"I think it would be good if you came." It was Crystal's husband this time, his voice giving Tara a start. So many times, she had dreaded being alone in the same room with him, having to struggle to make conversation. Now he had spoken without prompting, and she felt helpless.

"Just come for an hour. We could bring you right back. You could take a later flight," Crystal attempted as Tara stared into her place mat. She had not expected this. Not from Crystal. "Maybe it would be a good opportunity for you to say what you have always wanted to say to Mom."

Tara's eyes flew back to her sister, remembering the months she had spent typing and retyping the ten-paged, single-spaced letter she sent to her parents two years ago. She still knew the first page by heart.

Dear Mom and Dad,

I am writing in the solitude of my room. Four walls enclose me, huddled at the head of my bed. They remind me of the many rooms I have had since the one in the house where I grew up. Countless pictures and memories from that time ignite the entanglement of emotion inside me. I imagine you to think that our estrangement has only existed over the last few years since we have not spoken. But for me, it has always been a part of my experience — something that became so commonplace over time that I forgot its original import. Only these moments of pain keep bringing me back to question what happened between us.

I have always told myself that if I could just come to some understanding of our situation, could just work through every problem I had, I would know what to say to you. I would know how to say just the right thing in just the right way to make it all O.K. But it scares me to dare speak to you as the person I really am, rather than the person who knew how not to make anyone feel uncomfortable, and to pretend that most of what happened in our family never happened. Or never mattered.

The letter recounted her experience. She had sent it first-class, having already made copies to send to each of her siblings, thinking she should let them know "the big one" might be coming, and that she was responsible, so they'd know whom to blame. It had been her last ditch effort to bare her soul to her parents. She had never heard back from them.

"I don't want to go," she said to Crystal in spite of an odd sense of guilt that suddenly panicked her. She did not feel strong saying it. She simply had nothing else to say.

Bob sighed heavily and sat back in his chair. Crystal's face fell, although her eyes continued to search the table for another argument. Tara was relieved to see a look of resignation finally imbue her expression.

"Well, we'd better go, then," was all she said.

Tara nodded as they stood up. Their hugs were brief. Tara exchanged nods with Bob before watching their backsides as they turned and walked towards the exit.

I was ten years old when Crystal moved away. Her feet moved mechanically toward her own terminal. When she reached the check-in counter, they were already calling rows for boarding. Standing in line, she pulled her ticket from the front pocket in her pack, suddenly unsure of what the point was in being there. In being anywhere. People clamored around her as they shuffled forward en mass. The noise became unbearable, and she ached to free her hands to cover her ears. But they would think she wasn't normal. And being normal was the important thing, wasn't it? Like her family.

The attendant took her ticket and ripped off the stub, which he then pushed firmly back into her palm. She walked down the mechanized ramp that took her to the plane's door, squeezed through the narrow aisles, and found her seat by the window. She had always known that Crystal's decision to move away from home had something to do with the day that she, Tara, set up a new jump in the backyard. By that time, pretending to be a horse had become a daily ritual, begun at every school recess when endless memorizations of historical dates and battles of war could finally be forgotten. Racing from the classroom, she rounded up friends who galloped with her over the fenced and padlocked black asphalt playground, imagining sweet smells of wild prairie land while defiantly whinnying into the Los Angeles smog that blocked the view of the surrounding mountains and made their lungs sore each day.

After school, she came home to rearrange picnic benches and chairs on the cement deck around the swimming pool where a lawn had once grown. These she hurdled barefoot, skinny arms and legs pumping, a long blonde mane flowing free behind her. Her rule had been that these solitary races had to be finished before the clang of the kitchen timer, stationed on top of the picnic table. With each lap, she set the wind-up spring to a narrower margin, challenging her own times.

One day, she created a new jump out of the old kitchen stool. The stool was higher than the other jumps, but she had cleared it once before and was surprised when she felt her toe catch on the back of it, causing her to fall head first onto the hard cement.

"Crystal!" she screamed.

But her mother came out instead, a look of distracted irritation flaring across her face.

"Who did you call for?"

Tara was too shaken to answer what she wouldn't have dared answer anyway. Her mother, seeing no broken bones, left her daughter bruised and scraped, and stormed back inside. Loud voices came from inside the kitchen.

"I want my children back!" Wasn't that what her mother had said? Then there were sounds of sobbing, steps running down the hall, Crystal's bedroom door slamming.

After Crystal left home, Tara heard no mention of her sister's name for weeks—or was it months?—until a neighbor taking her dog for a walk, spotted Tara and her mother driving home together. Flagging them down with a waving arm, the neighbor asked with unsuspecting interest about the oldest daughter, who had gone clear across the country to New York City.

"Well, she's doing quite well," was all her mother said, as if she had known.

Tara had merely sat silent in the passenger's seat, giving the neighbor an unsmiling nod once before looking away. Even at that time, she'd been unable to remember saying good-bye to that once reliable presence suddenly vanished from her world.

Her elbow was jostled as someone sat in the jet's narrow seat beside her. She heard a rustling noise, and then the click of a seat belt snapping shut as she pulled her arm off the shared armrest and into her lap. Tucking her chin into her opposite palm, she pressed her nose to the glass pane so that whoever it was next to her wouldn't try to make conversation. She closed her lids and felt moisture ooze from between her lashes.

"I wouldn't have survived without her," she'd croaked to her father years later, during one of her visits to see her parents. She had been reading in the living room while he rambled on to his wife in the kitchen, and had given little heed to his monologue, long since accustomed to tuning them out—until he mentioned Crystal's name.

"Why couldn't she have chosen someone else? Can you imagine living with a man like that?"

"Well, no," Tara's mother replied. "But, of course, growing up she'd never had the knack for attracting the right kind of people—"

"And she seemed to lack any kind of real ambition," her father finished the sentence for his wife, "same as her brother—"

It was the kind of "discussion" her parents often had about whichever child of theirs happened not to be present.

"I wouldn't have survived without her." She cleared her throat a second time, her words blunt and seething. Her father, having spun around to look in her direction, stopped talking mid-sentence, and Tara felt the rage in her eyes burning into his.

"Well," her father looked away quickly and nodded, fumbling for some recovery. "Yes, I'm sure she was a very good sister—" and disappeared around the corner into the kitchen, martini in hand, where her mother was busying herself with making dinner and not hearing—or pretending not to hear—her daughter's comment.

With eyes still closed, Tara felt the plane backing out of the gate, then humming down the runway. She felt the drop in her stomach as the plane lifted off. Why had it been so important to Crystal to keep up appearances with their parents all these years? The plane rose higher, and the minutes droned on to the sound of the jet engines.

"Would you like something to drink?" The flight attendant's voice made her jump.

"Apple juice, please." She managed a smile and pulled down her tray table. Her hands folded around the plastic cup the attendant held out to her, bringing it to her lips every few seconds as if she could sip the discomfort away. She glanced to her left. Fortunately, the man sitting next to her was engrossed in papers, writing furiously.

After the plane landed and taxied to the gate in San Francisco, she did not hurry as usual to be out of her seat. Instead, she sat until most everyone else had deplaned before grabbing her bag from the storage unit above her head and making her way down the aisle. She was the last one from her flight to walk through the gate, down the long length of the terminal, through baggage claim, and out to the curb where she sat, waiting for the airporter that would take her north. By now, Crystal and her husband would have arrived at their parents' house. She pictured her sister engaged in polite conversation, using the familiar calm but cheery gestures and facial expressions, hinting nothing about what she might really be feeling. Safe. Her sister would still be safe.

Nearly three hours later, Tara was home. She ate a quick dinner, and following a shower, crawled into bed to finish the book she had started weeks before. A sharp knock from the adjoining house made her start. She looked at the clock. It was past 9:30, but she got up anyway to answer the door that led from her apartment to her neighbors' hallway. There was nothing there except for a faint giggling that could be heard down the hall. Not in the mood for pranks, she closed the door and climbed back under the covers.

The knock came again. Again, she got up to answer the door. Again, she heard nothing but the echo of feet.

She ignored the next knock, figuring that Katie, the neighbors' five-year-old, was the culprit.

Boom! Boom! The sound hit Tara the wrong way. Stealing quietly up to her door, she waited for the next punch. As the small hand was about to land the second blow, Tara grabbed the knob and swung the door open before the child could run away.

"Katie, don't do that!"

She had only whispered the words, bent over a head of brown curls and wide blue eyes full of mischief. But the impact of her anger was unmistakable. Katie's clear and open smile vanished, red cheeks paled, radiance withered—like watching the life be sucked out of a flower through time-lapse photography. Katie ran down the hall, crying for her mother. Tara closed her eyes and let her forehead thump against the doorjamb, another lump lodging itself in her throat.

21

~letters~

The irony is that most people think they have to leave where they are
to get to where they want to be.
And so they leave heaven in order to get to heaven -
and go through hell.

— Neale Donald Walsch
Conversations with God

Dear Crystal,
I hope you had a nice visit in LA and a good flight home.

Tara looked up from her sheet of paper. The afternoon sun was coming in through the opened shutters at her kitchen table where she sat facing west, and the bare branches of the cherry trees outside her windows were the only thing that shielded her face from full light.

I appreciate your accommodations of my wishes to remain detached from visits with our parents, even though I know you don't fully understand my reasons, or find them necessary. It has been a difficult process over the years for me to understand myself. I find I am invisible, not only to our parents (which I now expect), but to my siblings as well, which carries with it a particular pain of its own, since I have always considered my relationship with you, Vera, and Jed to have some deeper basis in reality and not merely polite superficiality.

She hesitated and thought about bagging the whole idea. What little her siblings had shared about their family life had been limited to events, not anyone's feelings about those events, or how their lives had been influenced. Changed. Damaged. She put the pen down and leaned back into her chair. What was the use in trying to explain herself to Crystal when Crystal did not want to see what she herself had had to live through? What they had lived through together. Like the time the whole family had vacationed at the dude ranch in Solvang—the place where she had gotten to ride a horse twice in one week, proudly keeping her place with the adults along the trail. And she had trotted, that still having been a novelty at six, feeling the ground move past while breathing in a mixture of sage and chaparral made pungent in the warm summer air. She had loved the place for that reason, in spite of the hours she and Vera stayed locked in the rectangular hotel room when their parents left for some reason they wouldn't talk about, leaving her to think she would die from boredom with nothing to do but lie on the bed in her underwear, enduring the long afternoon heat.

The day they left for home again, her father and brother drove back in a separate car, leaving the women to ride in the white station wagon together. Vera sat in the front seat, next to her mother, who was at the wheel. Tara stretched out in the back seat, and resting her head on Crystal's lap, was lulled to sleep by the sound of wheels humming over the road. The next thing she remembered was sitting bolt upright to the sound of screaming.

"Mother, stop! Stop, stop, stop! Mother! Stop! We're going to be killed!" Crystal spat into the air.

She could still feel her fingers clutch the back of the slippery vinyl bench seat in front of her while the car veered around another turn. Outside the window, steep cliffs dropped off the edge of a winding mountain road. Straight ahead, she saw the side of her mother's face thrown back, tears streaming down her cheeks. "So what!" she yelled back. *How had she managed to see the road?* "So what?"

"Well, she did slow down after that," Crystal had said years later, as if that had made it all okay, and they could just forget about it.

How ironic, Tara shook her head. She probably understood her mother better than anyone did, having tasted many times the yearning to put an end to the backwash of indecipherable pain inflicted before she was old enough to know what it was or where it came from.

As if I know how to deal with it now.

She picked up her pen.

Leaving home became my one option for sanity, for I did not know what I felt or why I felt that way. After moving from the elderly man's home in Santa Barbara, I lived in a run-down Victorian that housed six other twenty to thirty-year-olds, barely making ends meet. I was proud of my poverty, my ability to live with nothing, the freedom I felt without the superficiality with which we had all been raised. Two of my housemates were male ex-convicts trying to go straight. Their backgrounds were so different from my privileged and cosmopolitan upbringing, but their presence always felt oddly familiar as I watched them search for a way to fit into a world that would never quite accommodate them.

What am I talking about?

With sudden intensity, she grabbed the paper in her hand, marched to her desk in the hallway, stuffed it in the drawer, and then went outside to take a walk. She wanted to get away from all thoughts of her family and the past. But by the time she got home, she had made up her mind, and before eating or showering, she pulled the unfinished letter out of the drawer.

> *The most difficult thing for me now is not knowing how to deal with the expectations of my siblings, who wish me to continue to be a part of a family that I consider insanely unhealthy. I do not know how else to tell you how lost and betrayed I feel amid all of you. I am neither a part of you nor apart from you, and I am both isolated from you and ever grateful for your love throughout my childhood, knowing that if I had not had you as a sister, I would not have survived the life I was given.*
>
> *Love, Tara*

She quickly folded the letter, stuffed it in an envelope, and marched it out to the mailbox before she could change her mind.

"You know," Deedee said on her following visit, "you could send that letter you wrote to your parents a second time."

Tara stared wearily at the therapist.

"Attach a cover letter." Deedee wasn't giving up. "And tell them that because you didn't get a response the first time, you're sending it again."

In the ensuing silence, Tara sank into the couch. She had trouble believing that if she hadn't gotten a response the first time, she had a right to be in their face yet again. But after the session's end, she found herself rummaging through her old files inside her desk drawer. It wasn't hard to find the bulk of ten pages, typed single-spaced with narrow margins, and stapled in the corner.

No sooner had she pulled it out of its folder than a familiar voice plagued her with doubt. Maybe she should just accept the way things were. What was done was done. She couldn't change any of it. And it had all occurred such a long time ago.

Well, no, actually. It's still happening — to me. Isn't that supposed to mean something?

In one motion, she stuffed the bulky stack of pages into her pack and went straight to the stationary store to make another copy. She was dismayed to see her hands shake while sealing a new envelope and weighing it at the post office.

I'm in my thirties, for God's sake.

As she slipped her cargo through the slot, preparing to let her truth be seen for the second time, she tried to ignore the fact that the weight inside her was not simultaneously lifted. If her parents had wanted to make up for the past, her absence should have been incentive enough, and they would have done so by now.

22

~searching~

There is no glimpse of the light without walking the path.
You can't get it from anyone else, nor can you give it to someone.

—Peace Pilgrim

Tara had already broken a sweat, working her legs furiously to get a five-year-old Hanoverian gelding into a trot in the arena at Tom's. The horse was massive, even for a warmblood, towering well above her head to more than seventeen hands at his withers. His bones were thick, like his cold-blooded draft horse ancestry, in spite of the infusion of hot Arabian and Thoroughbred bloodlines to refine his breed. The fact that he'd arrived at her training stables with large square patches on either side of his barrel, where hair had been worn off with spurs, made it clear that the trainer before her had had the same problem she was now having.

How odd, it occurred to her, that a human could cause a horse, evolved over millions of years to run as a primary means of survival and pleasure, to feel compelled to move forward only under threat of punishment within a fraction of its lifetime. Indeed, as she rode him without whip or spur, he remained unresponsive to her legs, which she continued to pound against his sides.

"Now you'll just stop there for a moment."

One line from Tom was all it took to make her realize that what she was doing wasn't "it." She stopped trying to make the horse go, and the gelding slowed to a miserable, lumbering jog. Her throat tightened, and sweat stung her eyes.

"Now you'll just bring the life up in your body," Tom continued.

She pursed her lips. *Isn't that what I've been doing?*

But then she realized that Tom had not said, "Pound him with your legs." Nor had he said to push the horse with her seat, or use her hand to make a slapping sound on her thigh, or cluck with her tongue.

In fact, he hadn't said anything specific about any of her body parts. She stopped to think for a moment, and the gelding slowed to a walk. He had only said, "Bring the life up." What did that mean?

She took a deep breath, then lifted her torso and threw her seat up out of the saddle, as if urging the horse into a flat-out run. To her surprise, the gelding moved forward. It didn't matter that he was only back to his slow lumbering jog. She hadn't expected anything from what felt like a hunk of dead meat underneath her. And even at that slow pace, the gelding's stride had a lot of spring. She posted higher out of the saddle, throwing her hips forward and back, up and down, trying to go with him. The gelding's ears flicked forward, then back to her, then forward again. Trees passed to the left, and the sound of his heavy steps was muffled in the sand.

"Now, stop riding forward," she heard Tom say. She relaxed and sat down in the saddle. The gelding slowed immediately to a walk. "Now bring the life back up."

The gelding's walking step gradually became bouncy until he broke over into another slow jog. Again, she lifted her seat high. She felt another response forward. It was not the lively step she wanted, but then, Tom had never asked her to try to get what she wanted.

"Now, keep on going right into the lope."

It took her a few tries before she figured out that she had to, once again, abandon all riding etiquette, and throw herself into her horse's movement, as if he were already cantering. When he finally broke over, he was slow. But Tara went with him on a loose rein, staying out of his way. After a few more tries, the gelding, feeling unrestricted, began to reach forward, his huge frame and platter feet becoming light and airy, covering the ground in open, round strides. Everything started to feel easy, and she could tell by his arched neck and forward ears that he liked it. In fact, he liked it so well he began moving into a gallop, nearly out of control. Instinctively, Tara gathered her reins, but the big horse barreled right on through, and they had no effect, even as she began to pull hard.

"You'll turn him in a circle at that end of the arena," she heard Tom's voice, "but leave slack in the reins."

Tara dropped her reins again, only picking up the inside one to turn the big horse into a circle. At first, she was afraid he might fall over. The arena was barely wide enough to encompass his stride, and he stumbled trying to gather his legs, although he then had to in order to make the turn.

"Can you feel him search for where to place his feet?"

"Yep."

"And you're letting it be his idea."

She nodded. Inside her head, a light bulb was going on.

"Now, wind the circle down."

Gradually, she turned the gelding in smaller and smaller circles until he naturally broke his gait to the trot, then the walk. It had been so simple. She would never have thought of it.

"Now you'll try the whole thing again," Tom directed.

In a few more tries, the gelding was moving up into the canter and down to the walk with the slightest influence. His body no longer felt like a stiff board, but soft and malleable. At the end of her ride, she brought him to a halt and stared at Tom, who was smiling at her. A door was opening, and she was going through it.

When she arrived home the following day, a stack of mail awaited her, and sorting through the pile, tightness gripped her throat and stomach when she recognized the handwriting on one of the envelopes. Except for a somewhat shaky line, the writing had looked the same for as long as she could remember. She opened the letter, wondering if her mother had been drinking when she wrote it.

Dear Tara,

I am so glad that you decided to mail us your letter again. Dad said he would write you, too, and I hope he does.

She let out a sigh.

For me, it was a great surprise to learn that the "you" you had always appeared to be is not the rather cold (tho' talented) daughter we had known.

She stopped short, a voice already telling her to stop reading.

It comforts me that at last I can explain what happened in your early years; explain events which occurred at that time, along with my thoughts and feelings, which I have supposed didn't interest you.

Tara's heart pounded blood into her head.

So I have decided to just list, in chronological order, the events as they occurred. They might give you some perspective.

The next two and a half pages did just that.

You were a messy little miracle when my pregnancy ended…
About a year and a half later…
By the time we went to Michigan…
I rode to Detroit with Hal and Harry…
As soon as we were back home…

Of course, Tara knew the events already. Her mother had talked of them ad nauseum over the years, but of course, she'd been intoxicated, so how would she remember? Before Tara could think about what she was doing, she pulled out her manual typewriter and began pounding on the keys.

Dear Mother,

I received your letter. It seems your only concern was to justify your actions. You mentioned, "Giving me some perspective," as if there were something wrong with me for not accepting your bad behavior. I wrote because I needed to tell you about my life and my experiences growing up in our family. Not only was there your abuse, but the years I endured watching my beautiful, so-capable and talented mother, overwhelmed by her own difficult history, slowly destroy herself with alcohol. I have watched her employ the so-called aid of a certain psychiatrist for the past six years with no sign of sobriety. As a result, I did not ever really have a mother, only the anguish I felt watching her deteriorate. And still, all this is nothing in comparison with the fact that these problems were treated as if they didn't exist or should have no effect on me.

Tara

Tara folded the letter and walked it out to the mailbox while her anger still burned, lest the old guilt overcome her and make her afraid. A week later, she received a reply.

Dear Tara,

After receiving your first long letter, I had thought you wanted a dialogue between us about the period in our lives when you were too young to understand what was happening. I was pleased, thinking that I could help you understand now.

Again, the voice told her not to go on.

Because of your obsession with calling me an alcoholic, I went into more detail than might have been necessary.

Tara read the rest in a blur.

*I know you were angry because I never told you. I would have, but...
At the time I asked every psychiatrist I saw. The answer was always the
same, to err on the side of waiting until you were mature enough to
cope... I simply never felt I knew you well enough to know. It was thirty
years ago. I will not answer any more hate mail.*

Yes. Thirty years ago. What had ever made her think that trying to
communicate with her parents now would work when it hadn't for
thirty years? She let the paper fall from her hand, watching it float to her
feet. She did not write again, nor would she receive any more letters.

"What was it she wouldn't tell you?" Deedee asked after reading
the letter at their next session.

Tara sat in her therapist's small, well-insulated office. Square walls
enveloped her in light gray. She looked at Deedee, not sure where to
begin. She herself had only found out four years ago, after returning
from Germany. It had been late summer, and deciding to take a break
from her training, she had turned Blackie out to pasture for a two-
month respite. At that time, both parents had been vacationing in the
house they'd built on her grandparents' lakefront property, land
divided between her mother and uncle after her grandparents passed
away. She'd been invited to join them, and after having been there
only a week, Vera phoned from Illinois. It was then that Tara learned
her sister was seeing a therapist.

"Someone who's helping me to remember things," Vera said on
the other end of the line. "I was wondering if you'd like to come down
for a visit."

"Sure," she replied casually, all the while staring wide-eyed,
knowing that Vera had been unable to remember anything before the
age of eleven.

"I was also thinking that maybe you'd be willing to come to one of
my therapy sessions with me. You remember everything."

She was tongue-tied. Was Vera giving her credit for something?
"I—I'd be happy to come."

Meanwhile, her mother, approaching seventy, wore the puffy face and droopy eyelids. Tara did as she and other members of her family had always done—acted as if nothing was the matter, all the while desperately clutching the semblance of calm she had learned to fabricate years before inside the cushioned walls of her own skin. And in the beginning, it worked. She stayed out late with friends, and then stayed in bed until mid-afternoon to escape the house without notice. Avoidance wasn't difficult, considering that her mother's thought processes matched her intoxicated lethargy.

Two nights before she was scheduled to drive south to visit Vera, friends invited both parents to dinner, and it seemed she would escape her mother entirely. But at the last minute, her father decided to go by himself. "She has a headache and isn't feeling well," is what he told his friends.

It was hard to believe they wouldn't know otherwise, but her parents had a way of making things seem what they weren't, and perhaps his friends were as much in the dark as she'd been for most of her life.

That evening, Tara tiptoed down the carpeted stairs as usual, assuming her mother had collapsed on her bed by eight o'clock. She grabbed her jacket, which was slung over a dining room chair, and was heading to the front door when a sound caught her up short.

"Where are you going?"

Tara jumped at the voice coming out of nowhere, then turned to see her mother move out of the shadows into the dim light of the entryway.

"I'm going to the Fletchers' house," she lied, referring to old family friends, hoping to circumvent the emotional edge in her mother's voice. But she had already seen the raised eyebrows and set jaw.

"You ungrateful ninny." The words came out seething. "Go to hell!"

In an instant, Tara was back in her closet, sitting on her shoes, the black cloud bending over her, an open mouth yelling those same words.

"Do you realize that your father—" Her mother weaved slightly, tilting her head and losing her train of thought. "Okay!" In open defiance, she suddenly shouted the words. "Let's have it out!"

Have what out? Tara's mind was reeling, searching for an explanation, knowing she was to blame, but having no idea for what. Then she went numb, and the too-familiar blank filled her mind. Thawing in the next moment, an actual thought formed, clear and simple. Why hadn't she thought of it before?

"I'll be happy to talk to you about anything when you haven't been drinking." She was surprised by her own words, her polite calm concealing the fact that her heart slammed against her chest.

"Oh, shit!" her mother seethed.

But Tara placed one hand on the doorknob, and while her mother struggled for another reply, she turned it in her hand.

Her mother kept searching.

She opened the door.

"You're not going anywhere until we have this out!" her mother suddenly spat as she staggered toward her daughter.

How huge a mere stagger had seemed.

Instinctively, Tara stepped back to get out of the way and found herself outside on the porch steps, then felt the knob wrenched from her hand as her mother grabbed the door and pulled it wide.

"This is YOUR problem!" she screamed into the night, "It's YOUR problem!" Then she slammed it shut in Tara's face.

Shaking through her whole body, she was forced to agree. The "problem," whatever it was, had been passed from her mother, right into her lap.

The question of whether or not to mention the episode to her father the next afternoon was answered when she was awakened from a nap by his stare. Opening her eyes from her curled position on the couch, she'd seen him, martini in hand, laughing silently behind closed lips in response to her startled and offended expression. She had been only too glad to be out of his sight at last and sitting with Vera in the therapist's office.

"What was that like?" Deedee asked her.

Tara shrugged. "Cordial. Polite." And then she thought to add, "Not anything like our childhood."

Deedee nodded for her to continue.

"But about halfway through the session, the therapist asked what our discussion had to do with me and the family secret. I had assumed she was referring to my parents' alcoholism, but before I could answer the question—" Her voice began to tremble, and she stopped, looking down at her hands.

"Before you could answer the question—" Deedee let a minute go by before urging Tara on.

"Before I could say anything, Vera turned to the therapist and smiled, as if to compliment the woman on her dress—" then Tara paused again, remembering every detail.

"Tara doesn't know the family secret."

Vera's tone had made it seem like it was a game of cards that Tara didn't know the score to, but at that moment, her blood went cold.

"Oh, my God," Vera's therapist looked at her, eyes wide, hand slapped over her mouth. "I thought they had told you."

A long moment of silence stiffened the atmosphere as she and the therapist locked eyes. Then words came spilling out as the profess-ional continued in a nervous, rambling chatter.

"Your parents should have told you. I'm not sure I want to be the one to tell you. It was your parents' responsibility. I had no idea."

A hurricane in Tara's mind made her deaf to the rest of the commentary and blind to the ensuing huddle with Vera. Her moment of equal status with Vera shattered, she did what she'd learned to do long before, and withdrew, concentrating on one single point inside herself.

What's the worst it could be?

I have some dreaded illness.

No, her other voice resumed, *Your parents didn't have an issue about physical health.*

What else? A pause. Nothing.

What else?

Then it came, falling heavy and sinking her deep and desperate into her chair. She looked at Vera. "I know what it is."

Her sister turned to her and nodded, still smiling, as if they were enjoying a Sunday brunch. Then, averting her eyes, she said, "You're your mother's daughter, but not your father's."

Click! Click! Click! Click! Files Tara never knew she had shuffled into order in her head. The yelling, the looks of disdain, the hatred coming from her parents' eyes. For the first time, her life made sense. She hadn't made everything up after all. Her heart had always known, and she had never actually been crazy, not the way they'd made her feel.

But a moment later, she gasped, a shock wave running through her. The hours, the years she had spent sitting in front of the mirror defining every detail of her features. Her arms and legs. Her father's arms and legs!

Suddenly, she found herself on the ceiling, looking down at herself, body cold. Stiff. Frozen.

Whose arms and legs are those? My God! Oh, my God. Those are not my father's arms and legs!

Those are not my arms and legs!

Silence roared everywhere.

These are not my arms and legs!

She slammed back into her chair, reaching over with one hand to stroke her other arm, freckled like no one else's in her family. It was like touching someone else.

"I'll tell you what I'll do," Vera's therapist began again.

Tara would never forget the effort it had taken to look up and meet the woman's eyes.

"I'll make myself available to you for therapy if you need someone to talk to." She said it as if it was a great gift offering, something outside her normal job. Tara managed a nod before being lulled back into the world of polite conversation.

Driving back to her sister's house, she and Vera barely spoke of the incident. She left a few days later, stumbling through the front door into her father's house by the lake.

"Why didn't you tell me?" was the first thing out of her mouth when she saw him sitting in his chair, reading the newspaper by the window.

"We did what we thought was best. We never intended for you to know. It would have been better if you had never known." His expression told her he'd been expecting the confrontation. Apparently, Vera had called to warn him.

Better for whom? Feeling a surge of frustration so wide that Tara forgot to breathe, she said, "But I did know. Inside, I always knew. But I thought I was crazy."

He brushed her off with a jerk of his head, squirming with obvious irritation. She wasn't grateful for all the things he and her mother had done for her. After all, he'd gone to work every day to give her a privileged life, he said, his crossed leg swinging back and forth, back and forth. She had no idea of what they had gone through, what they had had to endure.

For your own perverted decisions, Tara argued silently.

Then, looking at her face he added, "So, you don't owe me anything for the loan I gave you to fly your horse to Germany."

The last wind was taken from her lungs, reflecting the same futility she had felt every year at Christmas, sitting in front of a decorated tree and the latest Barbie doll, the newest play kitchen, stuffed animals, plastic horses, clothes, quilts. Looking at her father in silence, she got up and walked out of the room, out the front door, grabbing the keys to the car on her way.

She was surprised when he followed her. "What more do you want me to do?"

Upon hearing his words, she stopped and stood for a moment

before turning to face him. *Can't you just say you're sorry? That you did the wrong thing? That you knew better? That I mean more to you, after all this time, than some monetary payoff?*

"I should have known it was useless to try to talk to you," was what seemed more to the point.

He looked surprised, then offended. She read the look.

We allowed you to survive. Wasn't that enough?

Then, an epiphany flooded through her, filling every cell of her being. In that moment, she found herself in a state of complete empathy with every person she'd ever seen or read about in the news who had stood on rooftops or out in the streets, blasting the world and everyone in it with a machine gun. Most people assumed that kind of violence just came over people, out of the blue. But for Tara, in that one sweet moment, all such terrible and horrifying actions made absolute, perfect sense.

She turned then, and made her way to the car. In town, she stopped at the bank to withdraw the rest of her cash. Walking from the parking lot to the small square building, she looked up to see her father drive past. She knew he had seen her, but he'd pretended otherwise, keeping his face straight ahead.

It was the last time she had seen him.

"You could have ended up a psychotic." It was Deedee's voice, bringing her back.

Tara tried to imagine what it might feel like to know she had done something special by surviving her life, but she could not.

"You have to be a very strong person to have come out of that experience with your sanity intact," the therapist continued.

Tara looked away, feeling anything but strong. Or "intact."

Silence.

"What are you thinking?" Deedee persisted.

Tara shrugged. She hated this question, hated the discomfort of being asked to reveal what she had been coerced into being silent about her entire life.

"You've stopped breathing," her therapist said.

I'm still breathing. Tara clenched her jaw.

"Have you noticed it?"

Tara shook her head. *I'd be dead if I wasn't breathing.*

"I've noticed that it happens quite often."

"Whatever I'm doing, does it really make a difference?" The sarcasm in her voice didn't begin to express what she felt.

"Did you ever try to contact your biological father?"

"Yeah." Did she really want to go into this now? "I did a search on him. Took me a year." She looked up and took in Deedee's stare, then sighed and thought back, reluctantly recounting the details as they came to her.

Jed, her brother, twelve years older than she, had known her real father fairly well because, as Jed told her, "George Claiborne lived right across the street from us when I was a boy."

How convenient for my mother. Tara had rolled her eyes.

But Jed didn't mind recalling that George, who thought his lover's husband too effeminate in his fashion design world to know how to raise a son, used to take him out to shoot rifles. Jed also knew that he had been ten years her mother's junior, a police officer with the LAPD, and in the military during World War II. Tara wrote down every word that could turn into information for a search. Then she joined a birth relations support group, hired a private investigator, spent hours pouring through the genealogy library after work and waded through stacks of microfiche, trying to find a clue that led to a trail that led to the present. The fact that the name George Claiborne could have belonged to any one of a gazillion men didn't stop her from looking into the face of every sixty-year-old she saw, wondering.

Are you my real father?

In the grocery market or on the street corner, waiting for the light to change, she stared.

Are you my real father?

She pressed her face up to glass windows, peering into restaurants, the post office, the library.

Are you my real father? Are you? Or you?

She wondered what he looked like, if he'd known about her, or if she would know him if she saw him. But for a long time, all roads led nowhere.

"I went to the central office of the LAPD," the private investigator subsequently told her over the phone, "but their records burned in a fire several years ago. And there's no forwarding address given on the deed to his family's property at that time. It would sure help if we had a birth date. Doesn't anyone in your family know his birthday?"

Tara remembered howling into the phone. Why, yes. Of course. Her mother knew.

At the time, it had been inconceivable to think of asking her for it. But as the weeks dragged by, it seemed less and less of a bad idea, and one day, sitting alone in her room, she reached inside her desk drawer and pulled out a postcard.

Dear Mother,

I am writing to ask you for some information. Could you please send me the date of George Claiborne's birth?

Thank you! Tara

It sounded pleasant enough. She had even allowed herself to think that her mother, seeing the businesslike words, void of emotion, might actually respond. Until Jed called.

"What's going on?" were his first words.

"What do you mean, 'what's going on'?" She immediately tensed at the tone in his voice.

"Well, the other day, Mom pulled out a postcard with your handwriting on it. She wouldn't show it to me, but she began running around the pool flapping the card and screaming, 'She's ruining my life! She's ruining my life! Why is she trying to destroy my life?'" Her brother mimicked their mother's voice in a piercing falsetto.

Tara almost laughed aloud, but thought better of it and kept herself matter-of-fact. "I need to know his birthday."

"Why's that?" Knowing, without being told, whom Tara was referring to.

"Well, if I had his date of birth, the investigator could look him up in the DMV files, and I would have a way to contact him. Otherwise, it looks like he will be nearly impossible to find." She emphasized the word "nearly," determined not to give up hope.

There was an awkward silence between them.

"So—" She tried to think of something to fill the void. "I guess I won't ask Mother for any more information."

"I guess not."

Only days before her move to northern California, she spied a very thin book in the genealogy library. Could she have missed it all the times before? Quickly scanning its less than thirty pages, she found one piece of information she hadn't seen anywhere else—an address for the Social Security Administration. She hurriedly copied it down and rushed home to write a letter.

To Whom It May Concern,

It is my understanding that your department will sometimes forward mail to a lost family member, provided ample information is given to locate a current address.

She included a sketchy description of her birth father—name, approximate height, approximate age, possible place of birth, and his address thirty-three years before. She then listed her social security number and a letter to him, *left unsealed so your department can see it contains no derogatory information,* then reread the letter before mailing it. Whom was she kidding? Her less than scanty information would not be enough.

Two months went by, during which time she relocated to the northern end of the state, acquired new students, and looked for a place to live. Only weeks after moving into a new apartment, she retrieved a plain white envelope from the mailbox. Inside was a form letter, forwarded to her new address.

Dear Ms. Beacon,

 We have received your request to forward a letter to a missing person. We will search our records to determine if we have an address for this person. If an address is located, we will attempt to forward your letter. If an address is not located, we can take no further action, nor can we notify you of this fact. Therefore, we cannot assure you that your letter will be delivered, or that you will receive a reply. In any event, we cannot forward a second letter.

Tara sank to her bed, the last glimmer of hope going out of her. Three days later, the phone rang. It was before she had learned to let the answering machine screen her calls, and she found herself startled by a gruff male voice coming through the receiver.

"I'm calling for a Tamara Beacon." The voice spoke her full name, which she never used.

"I'm Tara."

"Well, yesterday I received a letter from the Social Security Administration saying you were trying to contact me, and I want to know why!"

His harsh tone promptly intimidated her into silence. *He's the wrong person! Is he not the right person? Jesus, I've gotten the wrong person! How can I possibly explain?*

"Well—" She took a deep breath, and then held it, trying to buy time. "I think you're my father."

Silence.

"Who were your parents?" His voice softened.

She told him, her heart thundering.

"Yes, I knew them. When were you born?"

And so the conversation began, a question leading to an answer that identified her to him, and he to her. He told her he had a very nice wife who knew he had conceived a child with another woman before he was married. In fact, she was sitting there with him, supporting his call. Calm settled over Tara, and she was assured he would find a way out to California from Louisiana to see her.

"Oh, and Tara?" he said, just before hanging up.

"Yes?"

"I love you."

"I love you!"

She hadn't hesitated to say the words before placing the receiver softly in its cradle. Then she screamed. She had finally found her prince.

~prince or pauper~

Children from alcoholic, incestuous, abusive, and other dysfunctional codependent families are hard put to know they are okay. Because they do not know that their parents' inability to love them has nothing to do with them, they naturally conclude that they are not being loved because they are somehow defective. Very early they absorb the core, shame-based ego belief that they are bad, wrong, unworthy, unlovable, unimportant, and inadequate, which sets the stage for their own internal disconnection.

—From: *Healing Your Aloneness*

"Did you actually get to meet your real father?" Deedee asked.

Tara nodded, continuing the story.

The day George Claiborne arrived in town she drove to meet him at his hotel. After finding her way through the corridors to room 201, he swung the door wide, revealing freckled cheeks and arms underneath a short-sleeved shirt, and she knew instantly whose arms and legs she had. He laughed when he saw her, pointing his finger at her curly hair, permed from its biological straightness. She quickly assessed that he didn't fit the wise and fatherly image, but he had no hesitation in talking about her mother.

"She used to drive around with a couple of bottles under the seat," he laughed in contrast to her silence before abruptly changing demeanor. "I knew the moment you were conceived." He and her mother had been together for three years.

"What about my father?" At the time, Tara had been unaware of the irony of the word. "Didn't he try to commit suicide when he found out my mother was pregnant with me, knowing I was your child?"

"I had forgotten about that." He sobered then, recalling how her mother, his lover, had run across the street to have him beat down the locked bathroom door to get her husband to the hospital and have his stomach pumped. "It was all a facade, him takin' those pills. He never intended to die. Just wanted sympathy."

He could be right, she thought, remembering many an evening meal when he had played the martyr, especially after a few drinks, because everyone had been trying to ignore his repeated monologues.

"No one in this family cares about me or anything I have to say," he'd punctuated before removing himself from the table and stomping into the bedroom. The tactic had worked well on Tara, sitting downcast in her chair, wringing her napkin into a wad.

"Wasn't your uncle a doctor?" George asked later when they drove out from the hotel to see the sights, stopping to walk through a local redwood park. Tara nodded, wondering if they'd met. "Your mother got him to give her something, to make her lose the baby." He spoke as if "the baby" hadn't been her.

"I guess it didn't work," she said quietly, knowing just how much she had infuriated her parents by having the audacity to pop into the world anyway.

"Why do you think everyone is so quiet here?" he suddenly asked, stopping and turning to her on the trail as if giving her a quiz. Both of them stood quietly and listened. Tara gazed up at the treetops. "Because of their reverence for nature." He didn't wait for her answer, but she nodded anyway. It was exactly how she felt.

With her head still tilted upward, she could barely see the sky due to the dense cluster of trees, and she noticed how straight and tall they stood, sheltered from storms and high winds by each other's presence. Like a family, she thought, remembering a morning in Los Angeles years before when she had woken with a start to wind and rain fiercely beating the windows of her bedroom and pounding the roof.

She had leapt out of bed, knowing her avocado tree was too young to withstand such a storm by itself. Racing out to the living room closet before dawn, she had groped around for her father's trench coat, sandwiched between others less waterproof. Wrapping it around her near naked body, she'd run outside into the back yard, where the top of her young tree was blowing nearly horizontal. Almost as slim as its width, she leaned into the trunk, feeling the force of its weight and the wind much stronger than she. She'd stayed there anyway, bare feet wedged into the mud, her cheek pressed into the smooth bark. Hot tears had been instantly cooled by the pelting rain that soaked through the coat. She hadn't noticed.

This was her tree, the one they'd said would never make it, would never grow from a mere seed, pierced with toothpicks and balanced in a glass of water in order to sprout roots before planting. It had grown anyway. She would not leave it to die.

An hour had passed. Maybe more. She had been nearly frozen before realizing that the wind had stopped and dawn had already lightened a gray sky. After one last embrace, she 'd peeled herself from her tree, which remained standing, roots firmly in the ground. Exhausted, but satisfied, she'd stopped briefly to slosh her feet in a puddle, watching the mud fall away before walking stiffly past the pool and into the house through the sliding glass doors. A light was on in the kitchen where her mother stood making coffee.

"Tara!" A high-pitched wail sirened when mother had seen daughter.

"I'm all right. I had to stand with my tree. The wind was blowing it over."

"Your father's good coat! You've nearly ruined it! What will he wear to work?"

Tara's neck had grown stiff from tilting her head back and looking at the treetops. When she blinked, moisture trickled out the sides of her eyes and down each temple. George, unaware of his daughter's silent travels, pulled out a picture from his wallet, showing one of two brothers she had never met, had never known existed. The young man caught in the frame had been playing the ham in front of the camera, tongue hanging out in a mock gag. Tara's own jaw fell. She had one just like it taken of her — sitting astride a horse.

"Do they know about me?" she eyed George then.

He nodded, looking solemn.

"And?" she pressed as he returned the photos to his wallet.

"They're not too happy with me right now."

She raised an eyebrow. *Or with me, more likely.* She had already prepared herself not to get excited about any future relations with her newfound siblings, as close in blood as those she'd grown up with.

"My father, your grandfather," he said to her when they arrived back at the hotel, "passed away not long after you were born. He thought of nothing but horses." He took a manila folder from his suitcase, and with thumb and forefinger, pulled out two eight-by-ten-inch sheets. She melted inside, looking at antique photographs of a grandfather she'd never met, dressed in military uniform, mounted on a cavalry horse.

"I'll never forget that moment," she said to Deedee. "It was the first time I hadn't felt like a freak." She paused for a moment, taking in the pastel walls of her therapist's office.

"I'm assuming you're no longer in contact with your biological father, since you've never talked about him before." Deedee was looking intently at her.

Tara looked back.

"But it seemed as though things had gone remarkably well up to this point. What happened?"

Tara wrinkled her nose and closed her eyes tight, remembering the phone calls from his wife.

"What's wrong?" she had asked after one of George's long-distance conversations that had left his face contorted.

"She's worried."

Tara waited for him to go on, but he would not.

"About what?" She couldn't let it drop.

He frowned, then sighed, then shrugged—and then sighed again, the same way she did, worry lines creasing his face.

"She says she'll commit suicide if I don't come home right away."

"What?"

He shrugged again. "She's accusing us of having an affair."

"You're kidding." Tara's outward calm again belied the bomb that sent her through the floor.

George's face froze into a grimace while she stood gaping at him, wondering what sort of fate could have conspired a moment such as this. She paced the room. She didn't want him to leave, not after all that had happened. Not with everything hanging this way.

"Hey," she turned suddenly, "why don't you invite her out here!" She waited to let it sink in. "Then she can see for herself what's going on, that I never wanted anything except to know who you are."

He cocked his head. "That's not a bad idea."

Tara was surprised at how quickly the ticket was bought. Two days later, they arrived at the airport to greet his wife at the gate. But during the awkward drive back to the hotel, May barely acknowledged her husband or his daughter while Tara and her father struggled to maintain a lighthearted chat.

At a market near the hotel, George stopped for groceries. "Talk to her," he mouthed silently to Tara in the back seat, secretly pointing to his wife as he hurried into the store. But May seized the moment to lash out.

"How could you possibly know you're his daughter? And it sure does seem as though y'all are havin' some sort of clandestine affair, not including me in your private conversations. You've treated me quite rudely."

Tara remembered the way May had turned her head away, lifting her nose slightly with down-turned eyes in an air of defiance, refusing to listen to further explanations. The next day, George had taken them both out to a tense lunch before depositing Tara in the middle of the stable yard at work, barely saying good-bye as he headed down the drive and back to Louisiana. She hadn't been able to do anything but bury her face in her hands and burst into tears.

"Did you ever see him again?" Deedee's soothing voice brought her back into the gray office.

She shook her head. "He kept in touch for a few months after he left. But when a year had passed, and I hadn't received any answer to my letters, it occurred to me that I should just stop writing. You know," tears filled her eyes, "how easy that is, to just stop a physical action like it has no meaning?" Her voice erupted into a nervous twitter. "How many children do you think are born into the world homeless every day? And here I was with three parents! Do you think any of them could have acted like one?"

There was a momentary silence between them.

"And have you spoken to your mother or father lately?"

"No."

Silence. Deedee waited.

"I had to stay away." A defensive edge cut into Tara's voice.

"I know."

"For my own sanity."

"I know. Did you think I would have a problem with that?"

"Everyone thinks I should talk to them, maintain a relationship with them," she said, thinking of Crystal, and then her cousin, who had driven all the way out from the Midwest the year before. "I'm worried about how guilty you'll feel," he had said, "if they die before you can make amends."

"Most people think you only feel miserable after your parents are gone," she said to Deedee. "But I lost my parents the day I was born, and I've always felt guilty for never having been the person they thought I should be." She set her jaw. "Most people think I'm doing a terrible thing."

"Most people don't have your parents. And no one else has your life."

24

~control~

People who dwell in the past lose an eye.
People who deny the past lose both eyes.

—Proverb

At daybreak, Tara rose out of bed and stepped in front of her large window to maneuver the shutter wand in her hand, watching the wide wooden slats slowly rotate to their open position. Bugs, the neighbor's elderly outdoor cat, was once again huddled on the narrow sill as she had been every morning of late, warding off the early January frost. Tara paused, wondering what it was about this particular morning that made her finally register the uncomplaining tenacity in the thin frame.

Without bothering to don a robe or a pair of shoes, she walked directly outside. The sudden cold of the brick walkway made her quicken her bare footsteps, and as she came around the corner, a startled cat leapt to the ground before Tara could catch her. Remembering that Bugs wasn't accustomed to being touched, she went back inside and rummaged through a cupboard for a can of cat food left over from when Snoozer was alive. Removing the lid with a hand held opener, she spooned a few bites into a bowl and set it just outside her door. By tomorrow, she thought, she could move the bowl inside, and voilá! Bugs could be sheltered by the warmth of the indoors.

But days passed, and Bugs continued to refuse eating any closer to the house than out on the steps. Thinking of the cold months still ahead, Tara persevered, and in a little over a week, managed to coax the cat just inside the door, but only for a couple of bites before the feline paced and howled with piercing resonance. Enduring the racket, Tara kept her inside just for a few minutes, *so that she gets used to being here*. But more days passed, and the pacing and carrying on increased.

After nearly two weeks, Tara could no longer stand the grating sound, and immediately after Bugs had gobbled down a few bites, opened the door and watched her run away.

Each day from then on, Tara stood with one hand on the door, ready to let the cat out. Standing in that same spot one morning in February, she noticed a blue jay hopping about on the bare branches of a cherry tree by the front steps. She watched how it cocked its head this way and that, fluttering from one spot to the next without rest. It balanced itself with perfect skill, and she smiled, wondering what it would be like to feel so at ease that high off the ground. When it flew away, her eyes lingered on the outside world and the way dark leafless branches contrasted with a blue sky growing light with sunshine. When she thought to look back at her feet, she saw an empty cat bowl and Bugs sitting on her haunches, gazing up at her while rolling a rough tongue contentedly around a yawning mouth. Tara didn't move or breathe while the cat began to lick her paws and wash her face. Another few minutes passed before she got up and stood calmly facing the door to be let out.

"Now, that's what I call a good cat lesson," Tom nodded to her after she'd told him the story while sitting opposite him on a recliner.

Then he was quiet, and she watched his eyelids grow heavy. A soft snoring, like a quiet purr, escaped his mouth hung open. She waited silently, and in what seemed less than a minute, he sat up in one motion.

"How's Lena doing?" He asked the question in a way that made it seem there hadn't been a lapse in their conversation.

"She moved to Colorado with her husband."

"They buy a house out there?"

"They did. I was planning a trip to see them in August." Her original plans to make the trip in May had already been thwarted by her work schedule.

"Uh-huh. Got any other plans for places to visit while you're in that part of the country?" A hint of a smile was emerging on his face.

"Well, I thought I'd check out some dressage barns in the area, see what people in the sport are up to."

"Uh-huh."

"And I have some other friends outside of Billings I thought I'd visit."

Silence.

"Wee-ll," he shifted forward, pushing the footrest back underneath the chair, sat up straight, then looked up at her, wide-eyed. "You put quite a sparkle in Rio's eye when he was here."

She blushed and turned her head to the side. The length of time it would be between the last time she'd seen him and her next opportunity had momentarily lost its impact.

"You got anyone to fill in for you now that Lena's gone?"

She looked back at Tom and smiled. He never failed to be polite when you really needed him to be. "I have a new working student who's helping me out," she sighed, relaxing into her seat again.

"Well, I suppose that lets you get away once in awhile."

She nodded.

Tom pointed his chin toward the corner window. "Willa told me this morning that she moved that small group of calves into the side pasture."

"Great!" Tara turned to look behind her. Although the pasture was blocked from her view, she knew the one Tom spoke of, and taking his cue, went outside to the barn to saddle Blackie.

He met her there in his golf cart before driving slowly beside her as she rode down the side road that stretched north between two pastures. Tom let her in on one side through a gate midway down the fence line where fifteen or twenty calves stood grazing in the field. She let her horse stand and snort at the brown and white creatures, remembering how he had gained confidence by following the gaited horse the year before. Tom eventually nodded, and she moved Blackie into a walk. The calves moved away from him easily, and he followed behind, around the pasture.

Soon she urged him into a trot. His hesitation vanished when the calves continued to move away, and she smiled. His ears were pricked forward, nostrils wide, curiosity making him game to follow. How odd she must look on a big, lanky Thoroughbred tacked up in dressage saddle and bridle, chasing cows around an open field. It was apparent that her horse's huge stride was unsuitable for this type of work, but when they passed Tom after another lap around at a canter, she flashed a big grin.

After maneuvering the calves into figure eights, she finished off by riding right through the middle of the herd, Blackie surrounded on all sides. He hadn't shown a hint of tension. "He's getting better, huh, Tom?" She panted at the elder.

"Well," Tom smiled up at her, "it looks as though he's startin' to figure out that life can be a pleasant experience after all."

She smiled back. There hadn't been one thing he'd said to her all day that she hadn't understood.

Tara wearily walked into her apartment the following day, still caked with dust and grit from her time at Tom's. Setting her pack down on the kitchen table, she rummaged through the mail left by her neighbors. Seeing nothing of interest, she washed her hands in the sink before grabbing a box of crackers to munch on while making her way over to her answering machine. Crystal's voice was quiet. Subdued. She noted the reluctance in her fingers as she punched the numbers on her phone to return the call.

"Hi, Crystal,"

"Hi, Tara. How are you?"

"I'm fine." Tara knew something was up. "How are you?"

"I'm fine."

Tara frowned. "But—" She waited for Crystal to continue.

"I wanted to tell you that Dad died."

Tara's mouth fell open. "Really?" She was shocked at herself, never having expected to feel such a weight lifting off her at hearing news as startling as this. Should she feel ashamed? "What happened?"

"Apparently, he died in his sleep. It seemed he had struggled without waking, then calmed again before passing away."

Tara hesitated, piecing together what must have happened. Her father had contracted tuberculosis working in the factories during World War II, and although he had outlived all the doctors who told him he wouldn't survive more than a year, his lungs had been badly scarred. By the time he turned eighty, there was barely any useable lung left with which to distribute oxygen throughout his body. "He must have been gasping for air." A silent groan knifed through her as she said it. As pleased as she was to have him so definitively out of her life, she had never wanted him to suffer.

"Maybe so. Are you all right?"

"Yeah. I'm okay."

There was such a long pause between them that Tara began to wonder if they had been disconnected. "Are you th—?"

"You know, Tara, I never expected that you should have gone with us to see Mom and Dad that day when we met at the airport," Crystal's voice was tentative.

Tara thought back to last November, then figured that maybe Crystal was worried about her feeling remorseful for not visiting her parents over Thanksgiving, and was trying to make her feel better. "Then why did you try so hard to get me to come?"

"We were just asking."

There was the "we" again. "Hmmmm." She tried to buy time while rolling her eyes and shaking her head. "Well, you could have fooled me." How was it possible to resolve anything with someone who wasn't willing to reveal what they were really feeling? "How is Mom doing?"

"Have you heard from Jed?" Crystal's voice was pensive.

"No."

"Apparently, she's not doing well."

"Oh?"

"She's not eating properly, or can't. Jed doesn't think she can go on like this much longer. She's pretty weak."

"Should she be in the hospital?"

"She won't go." There was exasperation in Crystal's voice.

"What do we need to do?"

"Well, I think that maybe she needs to have someone there at the house. But I know Jed doesn't want to be the one to do it, even though he still lives relatively close. He was going to try to find out if her insurance would pay to have someone come in to be with her. The problem is we don't know whether she would accept someone else in the house."

Tara knew her mother would never want to share her home with a stranger, or admit that she needed help.

"The other thing is," Crystal continued, "if her insurance doesn't pay for it, and we decide to do something about it, the cost would be left to us."

"Well, I could call and find out about that." Tara genuinely felt prepared to do some legwork from a distance. She didn't want to be in the same room with her mother, but she was not about to stand by and watch her die from neglect. "I'll make some calls and get right back to you."

"All right."

The next day, she managed to obtain a phone number from her therapist. One health care organization led to another, which led to another, which, several days later, finally put her in touch with a senior care organization based in Los Angeles. She spoke with an outgoing and knowledgeable social worker who agreed to make the trip to her mother's house and assess the situation first-hand. Once he had confirmed the worst, he and Tara set up a time for a conference call with her siblings.

"I don't understand what all the pressure is about," Jed said in response to their mobilization. "No one has done anything about her condition for years and now, all of a sudden, everyone acts so concerned."

Tara was surprised by his candor, made more poignant by the underlying fatigue in his voice. She had to remember that their collective family history had not been easy for him, either. But now that their father was no longer around to stop them from doing the right thing, she refused to be put off. Subsequently setting up a conference call with her sisters, the social worker agreed to report to Tara his weekly visits to their mother. He would charge on a per time basis. She would send the checks and be reimbursed by her siblings for their share of the cost.

Three weeks later, the inevitable happened. Crystal called to tell her that her mother's legs had finally given way, the advanced stages of alcoholism having made her unable to eat. Too weak to get up off the floor, she'd managed to crawl to a phone and call Jed, who had driven to the house that night. After carrying her to his car, he had taken her to the rehab center where Tara had already arranged to have her admitted. He'd lied when their mother asked him where they were going. But upon arriving at the center, the staff refused to admit her, saying they were unprepared to accept someone in as poor condition as she.

"But Jed didn't give up," Crystal continued. He had driven to the same hospital their mother had been to years before, when the three sisters had been sent away to spend the summer in Michigan. But times had changed and they, too, refused her. Alcoholism was not covered by her health insurance.

Tara was impressed by her brother's refusal to leave the grounds. While nurses brought orange juice into the lobby to keep their mother coherent, he'd pleaded with the doctors on her behalf. After two hours, they had come up with a diagnosis the insurance company would accept. Acute malnutrition. She'd been admitted that night.

A week later, Tara boarded a plane out of San Francisco, and after a fifty-minute flight, rented a car and drove to St. Joseph's hospital. Finding her way through the halls, she came to her mother's large and airy room. She stood beside the bed, watching the half-closed eyes, wondering if the woman lying there would recognize her daughter after all this time.

"Hello, Tara," her mother said, barely lifting her eyelids. She sounded neither aggravated nor surprised, but Tara could tell she was sober.

"How are you feeling?"

"Well, not too bad. Better than the first few days."

Tara could only imagine what withdrawal was like, even in the controlled environment of a hospital.

"I understand you're the one mostly responsible for putting me here," she said in the same even tone. Before Tara could ask if that was an accusation or a thank you, quick footsteps brushed behind her, and she turned to see a man in a white coat, tails fluttering softly around his pant legs.

"How are you this morning, Mrs. Beacon?" He said it a few feet from the bed, eyes scanning a hospital chart he held in front of him.

"Could I have some more Valium?"

"Of course," the doctor answered without hesitation, not yet looking directly at his patient. "It will take some time for the effects of the alcohol to wear off." He finally glanced in her direction. "We've been decreasing your dosage little by little, so you may be feeling that, as well."

Tara was amazed at his ability to get away with such open candor, even mentioning the word alcohol. Seeing the fatigue in her mother's face, she sat quietly on the edge of the bed until the nurses came in to take more tests. She left the hospital then, returning the next day before flying home again. She called once a week when her mother was moved to the hospital's patients-in-residence section downstairs, and two months later, returned to Los Angeles when her mother was fully discharged and living at home again. Their conversations were short. Polite.

"Nice day, huh?" Tara would say.

"Why, yes. It's so nice to see the sun," her mother would reply. Tara knew that any real discussion about their lives would never be possible.

Once home again in northern California, she received no phone calls from her mother. If they were going to speak to one another, Tara knew she would need to be the one to pick up the receiver and dial the number. *Nothing new*, she mused to herself while writing in her day planner the subsequent dates she'd need to make the calls—*so I won't conveniently forget.*

Each time they spoke, she expected to hear the familiar slur of speech over the line. But it seemed that, now that her father was gone, her mother had less trouble steering clear of the drink. How odd, then, that the sobriety she had always longed for was now the very thing that gave her less incentive to maintain her obligations. Her mother was all right and no longer needed such a close watch. *Physically, at least,* she thought to herself, thinking of the backlog of emotional wreckage that would never be brought to light or resolved.

Over the next few months, she found the effort to maintain the false front wearisome, and her calls became more infrequent. It was easy, then, to foresee the time when there would only be silence again between them.

25

~scavenger~

It is not easy to find happiness in ourselves,
and it is not possible to find it elsewhere.

—Agnes Replier

Tara leaned toward the window of the 727, getting a spectacular view from the air of the farmland surrounding Bozeman, Montana. Hues of greens and yellows lined the valley nestled among the mountains and reassured her that she was doing the right thing. It would make a good vacation, she told herself, to drive through this part of the country on her way to visit Lena. Had it been only chance that, right before she left California, someone she'd met at Tom's happened to mention that Rio would not be home at this time, as he had told her? Instead, she'd learned he was currently working for Rusty Gilmore, a cowboy who had worked a little with Tom in the past. Rusty was traveling the country, giving clinics on ranch roping, colt starting, and horsemanship. In a week, they would be convening in Wyoming. If she timed it right, she could stop in to say hello as she headed south to Colorado. If not, she shrugged as if it didn't matter, perhaps the inspiration of wilder, less populated areas would ease a restlessness that had been growing in her. But as the plane touched down on the unfamiliar landscape, the world suddenly seemed much too wide, and an old, familiar icy sweat broke out on her palms and under her armpits.

Somewhat shaky, she made her way to baggage claim, then rented a car and began her drive, allowing the ever-changing landscapes to distract her as she headed northwest toward Kalispel. Two days later, she looped back through Great Falls and then toward the southeast. Rather than drink in the vast expanses on either side of the road as she had expected to do, she pulled off the highway often to pore over maps of where she was headed. Postcards of where she'd just been littered her bedspread at night, as if they could fill the emptiness of each hotel room, the next one seeming more impersonal than the last.

It was late afternoon on the fifth day of her travels when she checked into a hotel outside of Billings. Taking advantage of the deserted hallways, she pulled on a swimsuit and walked to the far end of the building, where the blue reflections of a Jacuzzi beckoned from behind glass doors. She let herself into the poolroom and immediately submerged herself into the heat. A minute later, a slim man in blue swim trunks joined her, smiling as he eased himself into the water on the opposite side. As he was looking where to place his feet, Tara had a moment to take in a clean-shaven face that was nicely featured and topped with dark brown hair, well trimmed and combed.

"I'm a pharmacist from outside of Great Falls," Glen told her, "but I come down here two days a week. Gotta take the work where you can find it."

She nodded, then reading his gaze, replied, "Horse trainer," and for a moment enjoyed his unblinking, tongue-tied silence. It was a common response. No one ever expected her to do what she did.

"Would you be interested in going to dinner?" he asked after she had described the extended gardening seasons in California, and he had told her about the difficulties of starting a car engine during Montana winters.

She was mildly taken aback. He was quite a bit younger than she was, and she wasn't accustomed to trusting strangers. But then why was it, she wondered, that she never expected anyone to be interested in her? "I admire you," she finally answered. "I think it would take a lot of courage to ask someone you'd barely met out on a date."

Glen, now sitting on the pool's deck, looked down at his legs, dangling in the water. His hands curled around the ledge by his knees and gripped the red brick tighter. Dropping chin to chest he nodded, half-laughing, half-sighing. "Yeah. I'm sweatin' bullets right now."

Tara laughed, and deciding to trust her intuition, added, "Sure, I'll go out to dinner with you."

They walked the few blocks to the nearest restaurant and talked quietly over their meal. Although Glen seemed calm and kind, Tara was reminded that meeting someone for the first time had always been her most awkward activity, and she worked hard to think of things to say, things to ask him about, things to be interested in. When they made their way back to the hotel, the open look in his eyes told her she had a choice whether or not to extend their meeting. But the truth was she felt no enthusiasm for involving herself further with someone she'd never see again. When they reached her door, she said good-bye.

Now lonelier than ever in her solitary room, she spread her maps and postcards over the entire floor until, too tired to keep her eyes open, she changed into her pajamas, crawled under the covers, and went to sleep. She awoke to complete blackness. Glancing at the clock, she groaned. Only three hours had passed, and the grip of an icy chill was rapidly creeping through her like a fog rolling in over the hills at home. She didn't want to believe it. Hadn't these episodes been a childhood thing?

A new wave of heat in her head turned to cold sweat under her armpits and hands clenched tight. Attempts to reason away the thought that she must be going crazy weren't working, and soon she was on the floor in the bathroom, hugging her knees to her chest, rocking back and forth in the dark, biting her teeth into her kneecap. She found herself imagining riding a horse bareback as a child, an image that dissolved into the contours of the rocky paths she used to hike with friends through the canyons and dry creek beds behind the house where she grew up. Then she was lying flat on her belly in a clearing amid the chaparral's thick underbrush that pulled at her clothes and left stickers in her socks and jeans, her cheek and hands caressing the dry earth, drawing its power into her. The memories momentarily tricked her into thinking the fear was leaving, her body melting into involuntary sobs. But as soon as it left, it returned to grip her rigid again and again, and not even numbness would take it away.

At the first sign of light, she forced herself up, got dressed, and left the hotel, using movement and activity to distract her from wobbly legs as she invented reasons to drive straight through to Wyoming. The mind games finally worked, slowly pulling her away from the foggy clutches of the night as her car sped down the highway. It was still morning when she checked her bags into another hotel along Sheridan's main thoroughfare, and soon she was driving the few blocks to the fairgrounds. It had rained the day before, making it nearly impossible for twenty-five horses to work their way through the mud. She slowed the car as she drove past, craning her neck to catch a glimpse of the arena. Today the August sun and its warmth shone through puffy clouds floating across a royal blue sky. The footing would dry up in no time. She turned into the parking lot.

Once again, her hands grew cold as she stopped the car near the gate and walked toward the entrance. Under the archway, her feet slowed, and she thought of turning back. What was she doing here? But her feet kept moving up to the reception table. There was no one there to collect auditor's fees, so she continued unnoticed toward the grandstand. Her feet clanked up the aluminum stairs. When the muscles in her legs began to burn, she found an empty tier, and with her hand, swiped off chunks of dirt fallen from the boots of those who had already arrived. She sat on the hard metal surface, glad to be toward the top, where she could scan the crowd as well as the riders in the arena below. In a few minutes, she spotted Rio astride a Paint, young and green by the way he rode. In less than half an hour, he dismounted and led the horse through the back gate.

She sat in the same spot for over an hour, trying to focus on the activity before her. Suddenly Rio reappeared, this time in the stands to her right, talking with friends and playfully swinging the arm of a baby lying in a crib—like he'd had experience with that sort of thing. It was a side of him she hadn't seen. She turned away, still unsure if she wanted him to know she was here. It wasn't until he made his way down the long line of steps to the entrance, looking like he might be getting ready to leave the fairgrounds altogether, that she forced herself to stand and appear at ease as she walked to the bottom of the steps where he was now standing.

"Hi, Rio." The casual tone didn't sound like her.

He turned around, looked at her, and then leaned back, as if the surprise of her presence might knock him over. "Well, hey there." He suddenly came alive. "Gimme a big ol' hug." She threw her arms around his neck. "When did you get here?" he asked.

"Just this morning. Is there someone I need to pay?"

He pulled his lips to the side and rolled his eyes before shaking his head. "Say, I've got to help inside the arena for a bit. Are you gonna be here for awhile?"

She nodded. "Yeah. I'd like to watch some."

"Maybe we could get together for lunch. You could come along with the rest of us—around noontime."

"That sounds great!"

Tara climbed back up the stairs. The release of tension, added to the exhaustion from the night before, made her legs feel like jelly. She found a seat closer in, where she got a good view of the horses and people in the arena and was soon lost in watching a man trying to stay astride a bucking filly. In a few moments, he was flattened into the mud. Then he stood up, smiling, fortunately unhurt.

She was unaware of how long she had been sitting there when her gaze was pulled to the right. Rio was staring at her. She cocked her head. He motioned his hand for her to come down. She smiled and immediately rose to go down the steps.

"Would you mind holding this horse for me while I nail some shoes on?"

"I don't mind. You can shoe horses, too, huh?" She was genuinely impressed, although she realized that such diversity of skill was not uncommon on ranches too remote to call in a shoer or vet on a regular basis.

"I can usually get by," he said, bending over to pick up a hind foot.

Glad to be seated in the shade of the open doorway of a horse trailer, she held the lead rope belonging to a horse that appeared not to actually need holding. Talking was easy now, and they discussed the clinic and Rio's travels while he worked his way around each hoof, trimming the foot and tapping his hammer to drive in fresh nails. It wasn't long before their conversation drifted to Tom and the various ways one could look at the world, and for the first time in days, she felt her insides flowing smooth.

At lunch, Rio climbed into her rental, and they followed Rusty and a group of clinic participants to a local Mexican restaurant, lining both sides of two long tables pushed together. She and Rio split a taco salad and spent an hour in relaxed conversation with those sitting close by, their friendly company a welcome contrast to her past week of virtual solitude.

"What are your plans for the rest of the day?" Rio asked her.

"Well, I thought I might do some sightseeing this afternoon." She was aware of trying very hard not to appear needy.

He nodded, but to her relief, before she dropped him back at the fairgrounds, he suggested they meet for dinner. At six o'clock that evening, there was a knock on the door to her small hotel room. Jacket in hand, she turned the knob, ready to leave. But when she opened the door, Rio remained standing in the entryway, waiting for the fact that he wasn't going anywhere to register on her face.

"Do you want to come in?" She stood back, holding the door wide.

He came in and sat on the bed. "I'm not really hungry."

"Okay," she shrugged. "Make yourself at home," and closed the way behind her.

Seeing a magazine lying on the bed, he flopped onto his back and picked it up. "What's this?"

"It's a dressage magazine. Your favorite," she teased.

"Dre-saaaaaaaaaazh!" He rolled onto his belly while mimicking a snobbish tone with an upturned nose and began reading aloud the feature article. Tara sat on the bed next to him.

"I like her already," he said, speaking of the author, who was being somewhat self-effacing. A soft mist filled his eyes.

Don't be taken in by that, she warned herself.

"Dressage is pretty," he conceded, pointing to a picture of a horse in double bridle, the rider in shadbelly and top hat.

"Yes, it can be," she said softly, smiling at the way he looked carefully at each picture.

"What will you do now?" She knew when this clinic ended, so would his job.

"I'll be on the road a fair amount."

"Hauling horses?"

He nodded.

"Do you enjoy that?"

"Sometimes it gets lonely, but then I remember that I have my family and a lot of people who love me, so I don't dwell on it."

She wondered if he could really talk himself out of his loneliness, or if he was just hiding from it, like most people. The way she did. Their conversation faded until there was only the sound of crickets in the background.

"Do you ever just sit and listen to the night sounds?" he asked her.

"Mmmm," she nodded. "Sometimes, when it's this quiet, I can hear the sound of the air around me."

He looked at her. "The air?"

"Yeah." She kept her voice low but serious. "It's like a soft hissing."

She looked out at nothing and concentrated for a moment before she could hear it again. She didn't know how long she'd been like that, but when she looked down, Rio was sitting perfectly still, eyes closed.

Placing a hand softly on his arm, she said, "Do you need to get some sleep?"

"No, I was just listening to see if I could hear the air."

She couldn't believe he was actually trying to do such a crazy thing, and smiled at him appreciatively. He didn't talk too much, she noted, leaving space for another person to be a part of a dialog. It was deceiving, she later realized, because in spite of the fact that he could speak of things that had meaning for her, he never really exposed what he himself was feeling as he massaged her back, lulling her to sleep.

"I want to be close to you," she said when they finally turned out the lights.

"I'm not the person to try and be close to," he answered, and made no advances. Tara felt his weight, much greater than her own, sink the bed to one side, but she slid toward him anyway and wedged her back against his, enjoying the feel of his warmth.

In the morning, he stretched his arms wide outside the covers.

"Did you sleep all right?" she asked.

"I don't usually sleep that much. Too much to get out and do."

"Hmmmm," she nodded, feeling the ache in her neck and shoulders, the lack of rest weighting her own body. She rolled onto her other side to look at him.

"Go ahead. Push me out," he looked back.

Yes, push him out, her instincts told her. But on another impulse, she reached over his body, grabbed the arm that hung over the edge of the bed, and pulled him to her. He continued to roll until he was on top of her.

"Do you want to do this?" he asked her.

She had to think a moment, realizing that by "this" he meant "sex." She frowned. "I don't know."

But Rio didn't wait for her to think further and began moving over her. She felt him push one of her legs up, then the other, methodically, mechanically. The air went out of her as her insides fell. Rio was handling her the same unfeeling way that most men she had chosen to be with had. A moment later, she realized she'd stopped breathing.

Push him off you! It was her other voice. *The one I never listen to*, she thought, remembering the way she had pushed her father away when he came home from work each night, the smell of martini on his breath.

"Don't be rude to your father," her mother had condescended, voicing for him the hurt that creased his face, a voice that only gave him cause to grab her again and plaster an unwanted, wet kiss on her face.

She looked at Rio, but he had already closed his eyes, indicating his sojourn to some other place of his imagining, far away from her. In that instant, it became crystal clear how he had manipulated every moment with her to end up like this. She turned her head away, not wanting to breathe in his breath getting heavier, too self-conscious to make him stop after having let things go this far, even when everything in her was screaming, *No!*

"Your problem," a friend once told her, "is that you're always seeing the potential in people, not what they've actually made of themselves."

Rio had had great potential, she thought, remembering his sensitivity to the gray colt when she first met him at Tom's, aware of every nuance, every uncertainty of the animal. His responses had been respectful. Appropriate to the colt's needs. She would have given her life for someone like that. Where had he gone?

When he finished, she felt herself unclench her jaw, then watched as he rolled away from her to climb out of bed. Still in a fog, she could only stare as his mood turned jovial, then cringe again when he grabbed her, unasked, in a good-bye hug. It was still early in the morning after she shut the door behind him and climbed, exhausted, into the shower to scrub him off her. Why had she not been able to face the truth from the beginning? Why did she still feel such a pull toward men who were so deceivingly unavailable? What he had wanted, in the end, had had nothing to do with her. He may as well have been masturbating or rubbing up and down against a tree. Yet he held her in his talons anyway, picking apart his prey.

The signs had all been there, she realized, remembering the way he'd grabbed her hand too hard to shake it the day they'd first met, and the way he'd squeezed her shoulder too tight when she'd walked alongside him at Wesland. He had never been able to handle her the way he did the animals. A part of her felt sorry for him, knowing he'd traded in his heart for a few seconds of what lay between his legs. He'd thrown away a deeper connection, a real connection with another human being in exchange for body parts. The eagle turned scavenger. *And then who will he be?*

Surface workers, Tom's words echoed somewhere inside her mind.

She rubbed her face in her hands, feeling the numbness wearing off. An inner trembling threatened beneath the smooth surface of her skin as she toweled her body dry, noticing her feet and her hands. *My mother's hands.*

After shoving the last item into her duffle bag, she strode out of the hotel room and went directly to her car in the lot, looking straight at the ground, suddenly self-conscious of stares coming from other men stepping out of their rooms. Everything got thrown into a pile on the back seat of her rental. She would stop nowhere else, except to get gas midway to Lena's, briefly exposing puffy eyes to the public as she paid the cashier. Then she was anonymous once more, craving the privacy of the highway that turned her wheels too fast, allowing her to give way to hot tears that flowed all the way down the long drive to Colorado.

26

~secret of life~

"Rest in peace" is a blessing for the living, not the dead.
You can rest in peace only because you are awake.
The decision to wake is the reflection of the will to love,
since all healing involves replacing fear with love.

—*A Course in Miracles*

Tara arrived home after a long bus ride from the airport. Leaving her suitcase in the driveway, she called for Bugs. Her neighbors had cared for the cat during her time away, and in spite of it being almost night, she found the small round of fur curled up and sleeping at the base of a rose bush in the garden. She gently ran her hands over the dull coat, frowning at the ribs and bones so noticeable underneath. Cradling the small feline in one arm, she made her way to the house, grabbed her suitcase with the other, and rolled it up the steps. Inside, she left her baggage in the hall, and with cat in arm, found a comfortable place to sit on her rug. There she draped Bugs over her outstretched calves and silently combed for fleas while the cat buried her nose between her front paws. Stroking the soft fur felt soothing, an inner ache pouring out of her into the slow, deliberate motion.

Early the next morning, she dragged herself, exhausted and groggy, out to the barn, where she would need to spend the day acting pleasant to her customers. Every step seemed an effort, every horse an impossible energy demand. At the end of each lesson, she felt the dread of the next one coming right after. The minutes dragged on, and she counted the hours to the end of the day.

One day led to the next. Even the thought of riding with Tom could not shake the inner fatigue, and on the morning she was scheduled to drive to Wesland, she lingered in bed while the gray light of dawn revealed tiny bumps over the texturized coating on the ceiling. Eventually willing her legs to slide out from under the covers, she went through her morning routine by rote and left after the sun was already up in the sky.

She arrived at Wesland with the big Hanoverian. Since coming here with him the last time, she had learned to ride him more open and forward, allowing him to find his own balance and center of gravity by guidance, rather than coercion. As a result, his stride had blossomed, extending to its full potential. Seeing his ears prick forward with enthusiasm and watching the hair grow back along his now sensitive and responsive sides had initially made her smile. But somewhere along the way, his newfound energy and brilliance had become virtually uncontrollable. It was as if he had suddenly woken up, spooking at everything, and bolting away. He'd recently bucked off one of her students, and his owner had received a compression fracture in her vertebra after a fall.

How could such a good thing go wrong? The freedom she had finally learned to give him now seemed only to make him more distracted. Flighty, rather than happy, as he had seemed in the beginning. She now understood why trainers before her had held him in with the reins. But this, she knew, was not the answer, either. Somehow, his energy needed to be channeled, not squelched as it had been in the past.

In a few minutes, she had him tacked up and was riding on a loose rein through the gate and into the field that stretched all the way to the highway, Tom following at a safe distance in the cart. But before she had gotten as far as the arena, Tom spoke.

"Let's see what he does when you try and mount alongside the fence there," he said, pointing to the railing.

She dismounted inside the gate and led the gelding alongside the silver pipe panels. With one hand on the reins, she placed the other on the rail to pull herself up, rung by rung, until she was perched on top, facing away from Tom. She hesitated for a moment to find her balance. That brief time was all it took for the gelding to see something in the bushes and start to walk away. She managed to keep hold of one rein, which pulled his head around to her. But the bend in his neck created a torque in his body, which caused his haunches to swing in the opposite direction. Now there was too great a span between the two of them for her foot to reach the stirrup. She tried again. The same thing happened. On the third try, he walked away all together, pulling her off the rail as he went.

Tom was now talking to someone, and Tara heard their low murmurings behind her as she brought the big horse around to try again. In spite of the September morning coolness, sweat poured from under her armpits and down her forehead as she once again climbed the rail. Again, the gelding swung away. The murmuring continued.

After several more tries, she heard the familiar voice. "He likes to take over, doesn't he?" It was not a question.

She pursed her lips, heat boiling in her. Tom, and whoever was with him, had been watching her make a complete fool of herself the whole time. She sat on the fence looking straight ahead and heard his steps behind her, then felt his eighty-one-year-old body climbing slowly, but unfalteringly up the rungs beside her. But instead of sitting on the top rail, as she was doing, he stood astride, one leg to the inside several rungs down, the other on the outside. Taking both reins from her, he held them at an angle and pulled them toward his body, leaning back for leverage. Tara was amazed at the strength that emanated from him and the balance he was able to maintain. Although his action seemed crude and untidy, it worked. The horse, feeling an unyielding pressure from the reins, moved toward him and stood quietly.

"So many times, a person will miss an opportunity to benefit and learn from a situation when it presents itself because they're preoccupied with what they assume is supposed to be taking place, instead of what's actually happening." He handed her the reins and climbed back down. Then he added, "Now, a person, as well as a horse, needs some time to separate these things out."

She gritted her teeth and glared straight ahead, surmising that he meant she'd been expecting to maneuver this horse in a way that looked prettier. More professional. Well, all right, so she had.

"We'll wait until you're ready." Tom—and the stranger—were still looking at her. She knew by the way the back of her head felt.

She positioned her body on the fence the way he had done. When the horse tried to walk off, she leaned back hard and felt him run into the pressure of her reins. The power of his massive weight was intimidating, but she held her ground. Because of her less than stable position on the rail, she couldn't do more than wait until he responded, and suddenly she understood. So this was "letting the horse run into his own pressure!"

Finally, the big gelding stopped, but pushed his nose into the air, still trying to free himself from the reins. She held steady, waiting without trying. Without forcing. The gelding stepped back. She released the pressure. After a few times of that, he gave up. She placed her foot in the stirrup and swung on. The gelding stood. Then she turned to face Tom. Whoever had been talking to him was now walking toward the gate.

"It's respect that gets the response," Tom was perched forward in his golf cart, gazing up at her. His hands were raised in front of his chin, palms facing each other loosely, as if in prayer.

"Now, I read in the book where it talks about self-preservation," he said, referring again to his book, and paused to hold her gaze.

"Most people think I'm just talking about the physical part," he continued, "but there's another factor." He paused again.

Tara wondered if he wanted her to try to guess what he meant.

"The older I get," he was still holding her gaze, "the more I realize how important it is. But what I've come to see as the most important part, is usually what people have the hardest time realizing even exists."

Tara narrowed her eyes, knowing he intended for her to realize that she was one of those "people." She had often heard him talk about "the other factor" as being the horse's spirit, but somehow, his idea of what that meant and her idea of what it meant must not be the same. She stared at him, trying to think of what more he could have in mind. But all that came to her were images of Rio.

"Let's just ride him on out and see what happens," Tom broke the silence and opened the gate.

Riding this horse out in the open would normally put her on guard, but so firm was her trust in Tom that today she rode past the barn and the round pen on a loose rein, without reservation. When she passed the arena, however, the Hanoverian stopped suddenly, flung his head straight up in the air, pricked his ears forward, and went rigid with tension. She didn't see or hear anything unusual that might scare him, but by now she had learned that the way she saw the world and the way a horse did were not always the same.

"Now, he may try and turn back on you." Tom's voice was behind her. "If he does, you'll be ready to turn and face him back the way you were."

Sure enough, in the next moment, the gelding spun hard and tried to bolt toward the barn with such force that her torso fell horizontal. For a brief instant, she thanked herself for the years of yoga routines every morning and her subsequent flexibility that allowed her torso to bend while keeping her seat solid in the saddle. Before her horse could bolt back to the barn, she grabbed her right rein and turned him back around.

"Release! Release!" Tom was yelling to her. In her strain, she'd forgotten to let go of the pressure as the gelding responded to her turning rein. It was an uncomfortable moment, this letting go of her controls in the middle of a bolt. Then, before she had a chance to think, he spun again. Again, she took her rein to turn him.

"Now, you'll swap back and forth which rein you use. That way, he'll get practice turning both ways."

She almost laughed aloud before realizing he wasn't joking. Tom would expect her to think about the horse's betterment, not merely her own survival. She shook her head, but the suggestion worked, and the next time the horse blew, she was ready with the other rein. As she made herself release, the horse stalled out, but before he could spin again, he jumped in place, landing in a crouch, ears flicked backwards. Instantly, she knew he'd been startled by something behind him. Plunk! A rock scudded to the ground. Her eyes widened as she realized Tom was tossing pebbles with a calm, underhanded swing, landing them directly on the gelding's rump. Another one hit and the gelding, having paused briefly to discern what was happening, snorted and high-stepped forward two strides, and then stopped again.

Tara sat in readiness, hands spread wide on the reins, wondering what would happen. All was quiet behind her. The gelding's ears pricked forward. He was looking ahead again, but it seemed to Tara that it wasn't just fear causing him to react to whatever he saw out there, but him looking for something to do, something to occupy his mind. Then he spun. She turned him back, alternating reins. Letting go, she heard another "plunk," then another and another coming in more rapid succession, sometimes thumping on her backside when Tom's aim wasn't perfect.

Finally, the gelding leapt forward. She sat back and knew she was to let him go. He galloped a few strides, and then settled back, gave a sigh, and walked on without question. He could turn back at any time. But somehow, she knew that now he would not. Instead, he lowered his head, content to let his neck bob up and down in rhythm with his own stride. Tara let the reins drape loosely on either side, relaxing her seat and allowing her hips to swing along with the four-beat movement. It was a good feeling. They must have walked half a mile when she heard a faint call.

"Okaaaaaay. You can let him come on back now." She hadn't realized Tom had stopped following a while back.

She turned the Hanoverian around, thinking he would try to take advantage of the fact that he was heading for home and still on a loose rein. But he did not. A frown settled over her face. She knew that by tossing the pebbles, Tom had created a psychological barrier that made it difficult for the Hanoverian to race back to the barn. By using her turning rein, she had augmented that effort. But there was more to it than that. He was free to run now. But, for some reason, he no longer *wanted* to. Her eyes locked onto her mentor's as she approached him, questions burning in her mind.

"Tom, what was it about your use of the pebbles that made this horse come around like that? That made him want to go on, that made him want to settle down?" Then she hesitated for a moment, trying to think of a way to describe it. "That made him content to just be where he was — with me?"

"Why?" he gasped, looking up at her from his seat in the golf cart, an expression of incredulity sweeping over his face. "Why, because that's the way it works!"

She could barely contain herself. What did he *mean*, "That's the way it works'?" The way *what* worked? Her whole *life* hadn't worked, and she sat there in disbelief, letting the horse's feet stay planted in the ground, too stunned to know how to respond or what more to ask. Their eyes locked for another moment before Tom looked away, making her wonder if he was disappointed in her.

"Well, I suppose that'll be enough of that for today," he said and waited for her to walk ahead of him before turning his golf cart around to head back to the barn.

Spending a quiet day off at home, Tara was startled by the sound of a horn blaring outside the window. She jumped up to see Bugs sunning herself in the middle of the asphalt driveway, forcing the neighbor's large suburban to a halt. Its nose hovered over the tiny body, V-8 engine rumbling in idle. The cat eyed the behemoth calmly, and without ire, rose slowly and moved to the side of the road.

Tara marveled at how she would not be hurried or pushed by anyone. Even the other cats on the property and in the neighboring fields respectfully gave her a wide berth. She smiled, thinking of how Bugs had learned to come up the driveway at the sound of her truck, or come when she called her in from her favorite spot in the neighboring fields, acres away. Bugs had even learned to be content inside the house at night and to use the litter box in the closet.

But in spite of the extra care, the feline's health was faltering. She'd become steadily weaker and couldn't eat much. Still, during the day, she preferred the grasses, wind, and sky to the indoors, even when her exhaustion forced her to lie down several times before reaching her favorite spot across the creek. Finally, Tara had to carry her there each morning with bits of food tucked under her armpit and a bowl of water in her free hand, worrying that some animal would prey on her vulnerability. But at the end of the day, when Tara came looking for her, Bugs would not have moved from the spot, her eyes opening and closing contentedly, looking up without complaint.

She was in great pain the day she died, the vet arriving too late to ease her misery. Yet she purred as Tara stretched out beside her and stroked her limp body lying on the living room rug. It was hard to tell when her spirit left exactly, but her eyes became vacant quite a while before her belly stopped its heavy, rhythmic heaving. Out and in. Out and in. Tara closed her eyes. For once, she had been there when it mattered.

27

~wake up call~

A shadow appears on the ground on the side of a post opposite the sun.
But that shadow has no substance; it is no thing, nothing.
The shadow is merely the absence of light,
the absence of something,
a mere negation,
nothing;
yet it appears.

—Wm. W. Walter
The Doctor's Daughter

Clear days and the bright October sun contrasted Tara's mood as she became aware that it was more than her depression making her tired all the time. Her daily routine hadn't regained its ability to inspire her and the weeks following Bugs' death turned her initial fatigue into sickness. Her stomach hurt every time she ate, so she hardly ate. What she was able to put down ran right through her. Unaccustomed to being anything but strong and stalwart, she felt a jolt of fear when, several days in a row, she had to stay home from work, knowing she wasn't right, not knowing what was wrong.

Jamie, her new working student, drove her to a doctor while she sat hunched over in the passenger seat, trying to hold in place her insides that felt like quavering jelly.

"Acid reflux," the doctor shrugged after listening to the teary details of her symptoms. "An easy diagnosis. You really shouldn't have such an emotional reaction to this."

He put her on a "special" diet. "Things that are easy to digest," he said offhandedly while scribbling on a piece of paper. Avocados. Bananas. Rice. Tara looked perplexed. *Bananas?*

Only white basmati rice in small amounts ended up being tolerable.

When she had missed nearly a full month of work, a second doctor, after a five-minute consultation, gave her the same diagnosis.

"But why am I so weak?" It had to be more than stomach acid.

Without answering or looking her in the eye, he prescribed Prilosec.

"Take one tablet a day." He briskly handed her a slip of paper to be taken to a pharmacist.

After taking them as directed, she was plagued three days later by severe stomach cramps, shortness of breath, and insomnia.

"That drug can't give you that reaction," he said when she called him on his emergency line, feeling like she'd been run over by a truck.

The cramping stopped when she stopped taking the drug, but insomnia had already become the nightly ritual, along with heart palpitations, flu-like symptoms, and a yellow-green and gray tint to her face. It was 3:30 on a Tuesday morning when she grabbed a pen and notebook out of her desk.

Have been sinking for weeks. How can I get thru this mire when I don't know what I'm going through?

She decided to keep the notebook by her bed, hoping that writing her thoughts would help. Transferring longhand notes into edited screen pages helped her learn to use her new computer, and she spent time online, searching web site after web site for clues about her condition. But more weeks passed without any new insights, nor improvement.

"You may have to stop riding," the third doctor said.

She was determined not to, but soon found that she had to, and reluctantly turned Blackie out to pasture. Now too weak to drive, Jamie was forced to pick her up twice a week and take her to the ranch, where she propped herself up on the arena rail and taught for an hour before being driven home again. In January, she stood in stunned silence in front of her own naked image in the mirror. Her already thin arms had become sticks, and both breasts hung limp. Where muscle had once filled out her legs, a wide space carved out her inner thigh. She had not seen this coming. Turning from the mirror, she found her journal by her bed and read what she had written during the sleepless hours the night before, barely recognizing her own hand:

2:15 a.m. I've lost 25 lbs. and am down to less than 100. Fear of standing up for myself, standing alone, standing apart from my family. I am exhausted by carrying the burden of truth.

This time the pang that coursed through her was not so much of fear as what she often felt when Tom looked her in the eye, and she stared in eerie silence at the uncensored observations of her subconscious.

The click of the answering machine cut into her thoughts, and she waited to the end of her own recorded voice, sending its outgoing message into the room.

"Hi, Tara. Wanted to call—"

"Hi, Mimi," Tara picked up the receiver, recognizing the voice of one of her students.

"There you are," Mimi's voice crackled over her cell line, and Tara heard road noise in the background. "I wanted to call and find out when you'd be coming out to the ranch."

Tara opened her mouth, thinking something intelligible would find its way out. "I don't have any idea at this moment. It pretty much depends on when I'm strong enough."

"So you don't know when you'll be coming to work?"

"I-I just don't know what to tell you. I'm not certain enough of my condition, or how long it will take for me to get better."

"Well, I'd heard that you were out there last week, working with Carey, and thought maybe there'd be a way to work out a time." The jealousy in her student's voice took Tara by surprise.

"I've been coming out when I can, to help whoever is there. If you can give me an idea of when you'll be at the barn, I can try and time it that way."

"Well, then, I'll call you later about next weekend."

"All right."

"Take care."

"Bye." Tara hung up the phone, sat down, and reached for her journal.

10:30 a.m. Friday. Being a trainer seems to be all I've been good for all these years. The me that is me is still invisible to other people, and I make them angry when the "trainer" is no longer there for them. Tightness grips my heart, neck, shoulders, belly, spirit. I feel like someone kicked me in the stomach, then tossed me overboard and left me to die.

Two days later, Tom's wife called.

"We heard you were sick and wanted to see how you were doing."

Tara was speechless. How good that simple gesture felt. "How nice of you to call."

"Well, we haven't seen you for a while and wondered."

"Yeah, I've been pretty sick. But I do plan to get better. I'll get better," she repeated, just to make sure that she herself had heard it.

During their brief conversation, Tara's mind wandered over the time she had spent with Tom. How odd it seemed that, just a few short months ago, she had felt bored and frustrated by having to groom yet another horse, having done it thirty trillion times in her life, working as fast as she could to prepare for the more important action of riding. The more she had been able to ride in a day, the more money she could make. How good it suddenly seemed, in her inability to do anything, to remember the simple warmth of an animal's body, its patient life energy beneath her hands.

Rolling onto her knees, and then her feet, she shuffled to her desk, slightly hunched over, arms hugging her sore belly. Opening the drawer, she retrieved a clean sheet of paper.

Dear Crystal,

I appreciate how difficult it is to talk about the miseries of our family. I have always felt guilty for mentioning the subject in conversation with you, even though there were many times when I felt you were the only person who could, or would, listen.

"We have a very tight knit family," our father used to say. For a long time, I actually believed him. If one of our parents said it, it must be true, regardless of my own feelings to the contrary, which of course, couldn't be right. It seems we cannot relate honestly without that history coming up. It is so much a part of who we are. As much as the three of us sisters said we wanted to be closer, it has been easier to stay 3,000 miles apart rather than share the intrinsic pain of our common, if not alienated, history together—rather than risk being misunderstood or unacknowledged for our suffering. We were all so poorly treated as individuals.

It is not easy for me to write you such letters. A part of me still expects to be told to shut up. To say that I am sorry for the pain you also must have experienced seems like it barely scratches the surface. I don't know how to hope for better in the future, but somehow, in writing this letter, I feel compelled to try.

Love, Tara

How like her reflux her feelings had become, she thought as she sealed the envelope, the pain in her heart no longer able to be held completely at bay.

A gastroenterologist at a university hospital in San Francisco was recommended, and one February morning, her stomach was scoped. The miniature camera, whose pictures Tara watched live on the screen above her head, showed bile sloshing around in her ulcerated stomach and esophagus. Her new doctor prescribed Propulsid "to make the juices flow south." But her insurance didn't cover it and now, unable to work, she couldn't afford a tablet container larger than her thumb. While she had enough savings to pay for rent and food for a few months, she had to pay for everything else on credit. Already, one Visa was getting dangerously close to the limit.

Graciously, Jamie picked up the prescription at the drug store and paid the eighty dollars herself. Tara opened the vial, let one pill land in her palm, then stared at it a moment. Something cautioned her, and she got out a knife and cut it in half, guzzled it down with water and waited. How bad could half a dose be?

Fifteen minutes later, she was on the floor in a fetal position, rocking back and forth. .

"Look, you can make yourself tolerant to poison even," the doctor condescended in response to the fear and tension in her voice when she was able, four hours later, to reach for the phone and dial his direct line. "Take it in small doses until you develop a tolerance. This is the drug for you, hands down!"

Yes, anyone could learn to tolerate poison, she knew. A naturalist in Santa Barbara had told her about holding poisonous castor beans under his tongue to keep himself warm while camping at night. He had even developed immunity to poison oak by touching a small bit to his tongue over a period of time. Those things seemed to make practical sense. She set the Propulsid back in the cupboard.

On a recommendation from a friend, she made an appointment with an acupuncturist in town. Not thinking it would help, she almost didn't go. But by the time Jamie picked her up, it was too late to change her mind.

"This is an illness," he said to her, "that really worries people because of all the inexplicable physical sensations in the body," and went on to explain how one imbalance in the body could create another and then another. *At last,* she thought, as she slumped with relief back into her chair, *someone who takes me seriously and understands what's happening.*

"We should be able to see some consistent results after three sessions. If not, something more is going on."

She remained that day for treatment, lying on a table with needles up and down her back. After being allowed to sleep, she was instructed to turn over for another set of needles up and down her front. Three hours later, she left his office feeling better than she had in a long time, the internal swelling having abated. But over the long run, she was not regaining her strength, and toward the end of the month, she awoke from a nap unable to sit up. She tried again. She couldn't move. Her neighbors weren't home. There would be no one in close enough proximity to hear her yell for help. She could lift her arm, however, and groped for the phone behind her. Finding her receiver, she punched in the number of an old student who had recently moved to the other side of their property. The phone rang five times, and her heart sank.

"Hello?"

"Joan!"

"Hello?"

She hesitated. "This is Tara."

"Hi, Tara."

"I-I can't get up off of my couch." She tried to steady the quaver in her voice. "Would you be able to come over and cook a pot of rice for me?"

There was a brief pause. "Yeah. I'll be over in a minute."

How easy it would be to die, Tara thought, feeling her life energy slip away a little more each day. The sound of Joan's footsteps at the door, and then the subsequent sound of a pot placed on the stove and water set to boil encouraged her. She had not seen much of Joan lately, she realized, aware of her student's averted eyes as she sat opposite her on the floor while waiting for the rice to boil. Tara had always been the together one, the strong one, the one everyone else brought their troubles to. Now no one knew what to do with her.

"I'll come back to check on you in a few hours," Joan said after handing Tara a bowl of the cooked white kernels.

Tara nodded her thanks. But Joan never came back. For the first time in her life, Tara thought about the chronically ill, the wounded, the elderly. How many outcasts of her own society had she herself never given thought to?

Saturday. Feeling like a burdensome child, unlovable, a bad person. Dreary this time of year — dark, cold.

To pass the hours, she spent long afternoons reading on her couch. Her neighbors checked in on her regularly, twice scurrying her to the emergency room—once when she went blind from low blood sugar, the other when they, too, were fed up with her lack of progress.

"Eat ice cream," the doctors told her, as if getting well was just a matter of eating fat.

Ice cream? With the trouble I have metabolizing dairy foods? When they came home, her neighbors made a vanilla milk shake in their blender and brought it over. She sipped the creamy liquid until, fifteen minutes later she grabbed her stomach and crawled into bed, feeling like she would die.

In another week, the tests the acupuncturist had ordered came in. H-Pylori bacteria, intestinal parasites, sluggish gallbladder, toxic liver, low thyroid functioning, hormone imbalance. No wonder she felt bad. Although on most days she was strong enough to get up to feed herself, her generally weakened condition was affecting her heart, and she continued to be plagued by arrhythmia and palpitations as well.

"You can either take antibiotics and other allopathic medications for these conditions, or we try herbs," he told her.

"Herbs," she said without hesitation.

"The results won't be immediate," he cautioned. "For some, you won't feel the effects for three weeks."

"But maybe they won't destroy me in the process. It's worth a try."

March came and went. New tests showed that the H-Pylori bacteria were no longer present. Her acute pain subsided, but her weakness persisted. Then Vera called.

"We thought we'd come out for a visit."

Tara had to stop and register the implications of her sister's decision. "The whole family?" It slowly sank in that Vera had figured out the seriousness of her condition.

"Well, we can combine a trip to see Mom and some old friends of mine. Can you give me the numbers of some hotels in town?"

"Sure. When will you be out?"

"Probably toward the end of May."

Not quite two months away, Tara was figuring in her head.

"Do you want to see Mother while we're here?" Vera ventured.

"No."

"I was just asking. She'll be coming up to northern California for part of our stay."

"That's fine, but the answer is still no."

12:22 a.m. Dream: Two dogs are slaves on a leash, constantly being switched on the rump so that their sores never heal. I'm afraid of what everyone else thinks about me for not speaking to Mother. Lonely at night. I don't think I'm getting well.

It was a sunny day when Vera, her husband, and two children arrived with smiles and waves from the car windows as they drove into the driveway. The last time Tara had seen her niece had been several years before, carrying her home from the beach on one hip after a Fourth of July display on Lake Michigan. As they all climbed out of the car, she didn't recognize her nephew, now nine, although she knew it was him. Tara sat on the couch while the rest of them piled onto the folded futon and the floor, staying only half an hour before leaving to get settled at their hotel.

"We'll stop by tomorrow," Vera said as they left.

But the following day, her sister had to remain in bed, sleeping off a migraine. *Same as the last time she came to visit, years ago, in Santa Barbara,* Tara recalled. Vera had excused herself then, as well, from a planned outing to curl up under her bed covers for most of a day and night. Tara remembered how still she had looked, her head half buried into the pillows, eyes shut against the world.

So while Vera slept, Tara spent another day reading on her couch. Late in the afternoon, she tried to walk around the side yard, barely completing two laps before turning back and sitting under the mimosa tree to watch the leaves make patterns on the lawn. In the evening, her brother-in-law, niece, and nephew stopped by. She managed to cook them dinner, but finding herself too weak to sit at the table and eat, she got up in the middle of their conversation to lie down. Unable to think of a way to explain her actions, she nodded as they gathered their belongings and took their leave. In the morning, she slowly pushed a soapy sponge around on each of their plates left piled on the counter.

"Would you be willing to come to a therapy session with me?" Tara ventured to ask Vera the following day. She had been continuing her weekly sessions over the phone in spite of her inability to pay. "I have no doubt that you will pay it off when you're able," her therapist had responded when she tried to end the sessions.

"I'll have to think about it," Vera replied, eyes averted, "and let you know."

Tara nodded, already disappointed. But Vera did not let her know, and the day before the family was scheduled to leave, Tara asked again.

"Well—" Her sister's eyes glanced sideways. "When you came to my therapy session, it was for a specific purpose."

Tara looked at her. *And this isn't?* But she didn't argue. Nor did she have the heart to ask for a ride to see Deedee in person, knowing the family had planned the day for sightseeing.

"We'll be back around four o'clock," Vera said as Tara waited at the door, waving them off.

That afternoon, Tara stood facing the clock above her kitchen sink with the old pain in her stomach. Three o'clock, the dial read. At length, she opened the cupboard where the vial of Propulsid had sat for months. *Maybe I should try it again.* Fifteen minutes after taking a quarter of a dose, a burning sensation seared through her intestines. She could do nothing but lie in a ball on the floor and wait it out.

Half a dose—four hours. Quarter dose—two hours. She hoped her figuring was accurate. An hour later, she heard her sister and family come through the gate. She pushed herself up against the couch, and was propped there when they came in the door.

"It's the medicine," she groaned to Vera.

"Well, it'll wear off soon," her sister smiled, ushering her children into the living room. *You're always soooo dramatic,* Tara heard the ring of her mother's ridicule in Vera's tone.

As her family took their seats, the telephone rang. Tara had no inclination to answer, even as Crystal's voice broke in on the machine.

"Are you going to answer that?" Vera asked.

Tara shook her head, lying back onto the floor. Vera picked up the phone. They talked for twenty minutes, Vera's cheery tone filling the room as if nothing was happening.

2:30 a.m. Dream: I'm walking through a large mall. People have booths along each side of long corridors where they sell all manner of items. To my right stands an old, bony, unkempt mare. She is so weak she has to lean against the wall to hold herself up. Besides a halter bound loosely around sunken cheekbones, a rope winds around her fetlocks, keeping her tied away from the sun and sky and escape.

This horse was once something great, a grand creature, proud and capable. The current owners are capitalizing on its fame for their own fortune, not caring about the hopelessness and futility in the deer-like eyes. I look around me. Am I the only one who's noticing? The only one who bleeds inside for something unique? Special. Dying.

The following day, Vera and her family left. Tara stood gazing at the empty driveway long after they had gone, realizing that her relationship with her sister hadn't really changed since they were children. She felt the corners of her mouth pull down as a distant hope she'd hardly been aware of faded, reminding her of a summer long ago when the two of them had boarded a chartered bus full of unfamiliar faces from the city. The thought of spending a month at camp felt like a lifetime as Tara watched her sister leave her side to find a seat with other girls her own age. How come she had already known the camp songs they'd sung throughout the daylong journey to King's Canyon National Park, high in the Sierra Nevada wilderness?

Tara had never been in a place so remote. Only ten years old at the time, she was the youngest in her cabin nestled amid the giant sequoias. There less than a week, she awoke late one night with a gnawing in her gut. She sat up in bed, her arms involuntarily hugging her belly, trying to steady the shaking brought on by the aching cold that descended nightly upon the mountains more than seven thousand feet high. Although she shared a cabin with seven other campers and two counselors, on this night she heard no sounds, not even breathing. The solitude that engulfed her was more than she could bear, and before she could think, she swung her legs from under the covers to dangle over the side of her upper bunk. Groping her way in the dark, her legs wiggled toward the ladder at the edge of her pillow, her bare toes silently feeling their way down the steps. She walked, as if in a trance, to the canvas flap, and pushing it aside, went outside and down the wooden stairs. There was no moon; she could barely see. Huge dark shapes towered forever above her.

Soon she crossed the open quad under a sky blanketed with stars. Her feet took small steps over sandy, crushed granite, every limb stiff with cold and fear. She had been to her sister's cabin only once before in daylight and was not sure she could remember how to get there. It was all the way on the other side of camp, at the far edge. But whenever the thought came to her that she couldn't go on, the wrench in her stomach, like a hand crushing her belly, kept her moving through the cold, dry, thin air.

Her breath came in and out, quick and irregular. Popping noises erupted in the absolute silence, making her jump. Stopping in alarm, she listened intently before realizing it was only pinecones and debris that the giant trees let fall from their tined hands, marking her passage, chaperoning her way.

At last, two dark, square shapes loomed darker than the night in front of her. The permanent cabins where the older girls stayed looked more like hotels compared to the single-story square canvas tops on her side of the quad. She couldn't remember which one was Vera's, but before she could guess, the crushing hand seemed to pull her to the one on the left upstairs. She opened the solid door and yelled her sister's name in a raspy whisper.

There was a long, silent pause, her body weighted into the wooden floors. She called a second time.

"Tara?"

The familiar voice was like a miracle. Unable to see anything in the blackness, she felt her way toward the sound.

"What are you doing here?" Vera whispered, stunned and annoyed.

"I can't stand it. I had to find you."

"You should go back!"

"You can't send her away now." It was one of the other girls, hanging out over a top bunk in their direction. Tara melted with relief. The girl had stood up for her. "How did you ever find your way over here, anyway?"

"I don't know. Don't make me go back. I can't go back."

"Should we wake Buttons?" Vera asked the other girl about the more easy-going counselor, using her camp name. Thankfully, the strict one had gone away for the night.

"I don't think she'd wake up. She sleeps like a log. Anyway, she won't care."

"Okay, you can get in bed with me," Vera's resignation was music to her ears. "Just be quiet." Tara shook with relief when she slid in, spoon-fashion, and felt the heat and presence of her sister's body. But only a minute passed when Vera spoke again. "Tara, can you sleep in the upper bunk?"

It was the last thing she wanted to hear, spoken into the back of her head. "Which upper bunk?" She moaned the question.

"The one right above me. It's empty."

"Do I have to?"

"You keep movin' around, and I can't sleep."

"I'll be too alone," she half sobbed, reluctantly pulling herself from the covers.

"You'll be fine. You'll still be in the same room with the rest of us."

And so she slept in a stranger's bed, and by morning, she'd managed to regain a respectable numbness when confronted with the punishing tone of her sister's stricter counselor.

"What you did is against camp rules." The stern eyes bored into hers before she cast them to the ground. "I wouldn't have let you stay."

Tara bit her lip to keep from crying, but then remembered it was Sunday, the day all campers filed into the main lodge to schedule the week's activities. Looking up from the sign-up sheet to make sure no one was watching her, she took her pencil and circled five riding classes, more than twice the number that girls her age were allowed in one week. Trying to act nonchalant, she handed it to the counselor by the door, and to her astonishment, the schedule slipped by inspection. That night, she slept soundly, reassured by the thought of spending an afternoon with the horses the following day.

But the next morning, she found herself on hands and knees, sweating and pulling herself up the steep stairs that led over the kitchen to the infirmary. She had apparently contracted the stomach flu, which confined her to one of the cots lined up along white walls amid a row of other beds. Night fell once more, and she thought she would die.

"Doc!" She called into the dark the name of the elderly nurse who stayed with the sick campers.

"Go to the toilet in the bathroom," was the reply from the other bed.

But Tara groped her way to the nurse's side, instead — unable to bear emptying her dinner into the small, cold receptacle off to one corner all by herself. Nothing stayed down for the next two days. But by the third morning, she awoke, knowing she was well. The doctor, making his weekly rounds from Visalia, came in, and after looking her over, ordered her to stay for toast and tea. Weak, famished, and thirsty, Tara put off her urge to go immediately down the long hill to the stables, waiting instead for her food from the kitchen downstairs.

In an hour, it still hadn't arrived. Checking the clock above the door, she knew that her favorite riding class was well underway. She had already missed two others the day before. Making sure no one was watching, she stood quietly, shed the hospital gown, and pulled on her camp uniform. White shirt and blue denims hung more noticeably over her already lean and narrow body. Wondering if she would be able to leave without permission, she headed to the door and stood. But the nurse never looked up from her darning. Even then, the ease with which a child's meal could be forgotten made her pause until, finally, she left the room.

The doctor's words of caution to "take it easy for a couple of days," were far from her mind as she held the hand rail and forced her wobbling legs down the steep row of stairs to the bottom. Moving silently in sneakered feet between a cluster of cabins, she gained strength with each step. The day's activities had already begun and canvas-covered frames gaped empty and silent. Side flaps had been rolled up to invite fresh air to circulate over clean-swept floors and hand-smoothed army blankets folded neatly over bunk beds. Here she found a narrow path between a thick grove of redwoods—the short cut to the other side of the lake where the riding arena was. Campers were not allowed this way without supervision, but on that day, no one saw her.

The dirt path would normally have ended at the marshy edge of the lake had it not been for a long line of huge, floating logs chained together to continue the trail over the still, dark water to the opposite bank. It was too early in the day for water skiers or sailors to ruffle its surface, or to see her. Still, a slip of her foot would be easy, and she needed to be careful. Panting hard she kept her balance with arms outstretched, legs pumping as fast as she dared over the giant trees that had given up their lives for her. The bump and roll of their cylindrical bodies did not dislodge her, but she remembered the lapping of water at their base rippling outward in response to the simple action of her step. Everything she did in the world, she suddenly realized, had an impact. Beyond the tiny waves, the liquid darkness stretched on, reflecting the beauty of the surrounding world.

On firm ground again, she scrambled up the steep hill to the arena high above. Her fingers clawed into the loose and padded forest floor, every fiber of her being screaming of thirst. Feeling as if her body would explode, she pulled herself over the last crest to hear the familiar soft and rhythmic shuffle of hoof beats on sandy footing. A sudden confidence steadied her then, inspiring a final push to stand on level ground. There, in front of her, were horses moving gracefully at a trot around an arena lined with the great trees. Almond eyes looked at her standing suddenly among them, dark pools melting into her, questioning, but then accepting her presence. The dust that billowed its fine powder into the air from the churning of hooves erased all thought of herself, leaving only an all-consuming desire to ride and be one with them.

The sun was sinking low in the sky as Tara stood gazing after Vera, who had long since departed out the drive. In the end, it had always been animals and nature, not people, which had comforted her.

28

~from beds of decayed earth~

Because the tree is barren are you going to cut it down? Why not? There is no supply there—no visible supply. To all appearances the tree is barren. Ah, but you know better than that. You know that there is a Life-force operating in and through that tree, a Life-force that is forming the sap which will go up through the trunk, out into the branches, and which will later appear as the blossoms, and then later as the fruit. You are not misled by the appearance of a barren tree into believing that the tree has no supply of fruit or that the tree is useless.

—Joel Goldsmith
The Art of Spiritual Healing

Tara stepped inside the house, picked up her journal, and sat on her couch.

5/30: It occurred to me that perhaps my illness is not new, that I've been merely hiding it from myself all these years.

She reached over to set the notebook on her nightstand, and saw a folded sheet of paper wedged behind the lamp. Prying it free with her fingers, she recognized the most recent letter from Crystal that had been allowed to fall, unnoticed, weeks before. Prying it out, she unfolded the creased pages and reread the note.

Dear Tara,
I know you didn't intend for me to answer your letter, but I wanted to write — not really in response, but just as another voice in a dialogue.

No, not really in response. It was the way of her family.

You and I handle "family" matters in totally different ways. I now realize that our experiences as children were so different as to have been different lives. I fly out to California two weekends a year to visit Mom, and she stops by here on her way to Michigan. To me, the superficiality of the relationship with my mother is the relationship.

Exactly. That was the whole point. Crystal could rearrange her life to enable a superficial relationship with her mother, but not a real one with her sister. Tara felt a pang in her stomach, remembering herself in a huddle with both Crystal and Vera, the way they used to converge on certain Friday nights, excitedly counting up three dollars apiece, the amount they needed for an hour's horseback ride through Griffith Park the following morning. It had been one of the rare events when the three of them had been unified in the same goal, filling Tara with a sense of possibility she hadn't felt since.

In the morning, pitch black before dawn, she would leap out of bed to run down the hall and lean on Crystal's familiar body, submerged in blankets and asleep like the dead, her enthusiasm refusing to be put off by irritated groans coming from that dark place until a forehead finally emerged and consented to rise. As a child, she had lived for those early morning rides before the city was awake, before any cars accompanied them on the newly built 134 Freeway, which ran the length of the San Fernando Valley, letting the dread of days past fall away and be forgotten.

They had always arrived at the stables before others came later in the day to use and overuse her favorites—before a weary, defeated look filled their eyes, glazing them over. She remembered shaking with anticipation to see the huge, four-legged creatures, to smell the pungent mix of sweat and ammonia from day old stall bedding before being hoisted onto round bodies that carried her along the trail. Confident with Crystal beside her, each bend in the path had been a new discovery of trees and birds and the smell of the earth while her body moved with the horse beneath her, its breath and warmth mingling with her own.

"We love you, but can you just get over it?" was now the underlying message from her sisters. "We've swept the past under the rug, neat and tidy. Why can't you?"

Setting Crystal's letter down, she walked to her kitchen cabinet and removed the vial of Propulsid from the shelf. She held it in her hand, rotating it in her palm so that the label faced away from her and little white pills showed through the opaque orange plastic. She would be jeopardizing her health, her life, by not taking this drug, the doctor would say. The pharmaceutical industry would back him up—regular people didn't know as much as chemists and doctors. How much easier, then, it would be if she could just go along? To question meant having to think about what this illness was really about. It meant having to sink beneath the numbness. To take responsibility for her life.

She turned the vial again and opened her hand. The round tube rolled out of her palm, over her fingers and fell from her outstretched arm. Plunk! It disappeared into the recycle bin.

That night, she couldn't sleep as a renewed pain in her body rose and fell in waves. She was losing this battle, losing her grip, and felt the silent, smothering cloud descend. Her hands went cold, and a familiar icy sweat broke out under her armpits. Dismayed, she felt her already fatigued muscles contract, and she sat hugging her knees to her chest on the floor with the old fear.

You could call your therapist's emergency line, something in her spoke. *How ridiculous. It's nearly midnight.* Ah, the familiar voice.

Besides, how would she ever explain what was happening to her? What if she couldn't be helped? Maybe suffering in silence was better than knowing she could never get better. *Just like my mother.*

She looked at her phone on the table. Was it even real? Maybe it wasn't actually there and would disappear if she tried to touch it. She reached an arm forward and upward to its perch, just to see. Her extended fingers felt the smooth coolness of its plastic surface. She picked up the receiver and held it in the palm of her left hand. Her right forefinger punched in the emergency number. At least she could think that much. An operator answered the phone. Her therapist had told her what to say to get through. A pause. Then the familiar voice was speaking into her ear. Tara answered, not knowing what she was saying, just that words were coming out.

"Tara, you're having intense anxiety right now," her therapist said calmly.

Her tone brought Tara up short. "You mean—a panic attack?" Another knife stunned its way into her gut—to actually name it for the first time.

Deedee's tone did not waver. "Caused by intense feelings of loneliness."

Loneliness? That's it? She shook her head. She had been lonely before, and hadn't felt like this.

"As a child, you were too young to know how to process what had happened to you, so in an effort to survive it, you separated yourself from the pain. Yet it remained—because it was unresolved—and reoccurred every time a situation arose that unconsciously reminded you of it in some way."

Tara felt herself trying to follow Deedee's words, to understand what she was saying.

"Tara," Deedee kept on, "given your history, it's completely understandable that you would feel this way."

A wave of sorrow washed through her in response to the soft tone behind her therapist's words. Suddenly, she remembered the first time she'd ever felt like this. Why had she never pieced it together before? She and Vera had arrived home from camp, late summer winds blowing through the trees, sending leaves fluttering through the canyon with hints of fall. The sun was setting into smoggy hues of brown and orange when, all at once, she hadn't known where she was, or rather, she knew where she was, but felt like she wasn't really there.

She walked out of the bedroom she no longer had to share with Vera, and stumbled into Crystal's room. Only it wasn't Crystal's room anymore. Crystal had left months before. Remember?

She turned around and moved through the hallway, into the kitchen that led to the remodeled den with a fireplace and bathroom of its own. Seeing no one there, she wandered toward her parents' bedroom at the other end of the house. There sat her mother in front of the mirror. Vera stood behind her head of dyed blonde hair, styling the curled wisps for a cocktail party later that evening, chatting about fashion, new shoes, and make-up. What was wrong with her that these things seemed to have no meaning?

She turned around and walked back out, hiding in her bathroom beside the toilet with the door locked. The cold ceramic bowl rubbing against her bare skin had helped her focus as she rocked back and forth, back and forth, back and forth, trying not to breathe, whispering silently some word or phrase over and over. Her fingernails turned white, seesawing into her palms, cutting the skin, layer by layer. Seeing the blood slowly surface had made her feel like she was there. Alive. Real.

"I don't feel good," is what she eventually dared aloud to her mother. The normally set jaw softened into a worried look, eyebrows knitted over the bridge of her nose.

"What can I get you, dear? Would you like me to call the doctor?"

In response to Tara's wordless shrug, an appointment had been made, another visit among the many for vaccinations or regular check-ups to locate physical, functional things that could be fixed the way their cavities had been filled, retainers fitted, and braces glued to their teeth. But going to the doctor that day or any other day revealed nothing, just as it had revealed nothing with Vera, taken to the hospital years earlier because of a chronic pain in her side that had lasted the better part of a year.

Tara had never been able to suffer the humiliation of admitting to anyone that she was going crazy. Instead, she finally asked her mother to take her shopping for new clothes before school started in the fall, pretending to be eager to be driven across town over unfeeling cement roads to the sterile department store sprawling across the face of the once-living earth. Her mother, enthusiastic about her daughter's apparent conversion to her world of normal interests, stepped lightly from the parking lot to the large glass double doors at Macy's, reaching for her youngest's hand and humming a tune. Tara remembered allowing her appendage to be swung back and forth only once before recoiling.

Back at the house, she secretly rummaged through her sister's drawer in the bathroom. After finding Vera's razor, she locked herself in and quietly shaved her legs without asking permission. The following Monday, she put on her first bra and pair of nylons, and at eleven years of age, entered junior high school. By then, she had nearly forgotten her oldest sister, forgotten that she had ever needed a mother. After school, youthful romping and imaginings had become too unsophisticated for her new world, and she would not be seen running around the pool in the back yard again.

"Tara?" It was Deedee's voice, bringing Tara back, the phone still to her ear.

"Yeah, I'm here."

"What I wanted to reiterate was that in order to separate from the dysfunction of your family — "

"I had to go to a place where they were not. And in that place, I was all alone. And that has been unbearable." Tara finished the thought for her. The fear was lessening its grip. She could feel it. "Are you sure this is right?" She wanted confirmation anyway.

"Yes. The other piece of it is this. Every time you've made a move toward autonomy from your family, or a move forward in your life, you've felt guilty."

Guilty? That didn't seem right, until she thought about how she'd rocked the boat by writing letters to her sisters and choosing to throw away the pills. "You mean that by talking about what happened, I was breaking the code of silence. And in so doing, I was removing myself from the family, from their dysfunction?"

"Yes."

"And when I make my own decisions, like my decision to detach myself from my mother, I feel like I'm being disloyal to them, leaving them all behind. Kind of like a survivor's guilt, like I'm the only one who has the chance to get out, but that I have no right to be better off than they are."

"Exactly. And so you punish yourself for it."

"By getting sick."

"Or by feeling miserable in some way."

The confidence in her therapist's voice steadied her. It reminded her of how she felt with Tom when he stated the obvious. It was so simple; she hadn't been able to recognize it.

"And by not resolving my feelings," Tara's thoughts were now coming one on top of another, "they remained hidden, but continued to agitate me. And all that agitation got reflected on my insides." She thought of her ulcerated stomach and esophagus. "You know, the things that happened in my family were bad. But that wasn't the worst part of it."

"I know."

"The worst part has been how everyone wanted to ignore the effect of what happened—the effect on me, but on themselves, too."

"Right."

Suddenly Tara had a moment of revelation. She felt hopeful, picturing herself strong and whole, smiling at her life. In the next moment, she was flooded with renewed fear. Did she really have the audacity to be well? The gall, the "guts," to be whole?

She was exhausted when she hung up the phone, but slept well that night. The next day, she felt better, trying to rest inside a fragile calm. The day after, she felt lost again, and worse the next day after that. Remembering her conversation with Deedee steadied her, and she felt better again. Days turned into weeks, weeks into months, and healing came slowly. By August, she could walk a quarter of a mile and drive again. By September, she was working short days. Her slow movements and the necessity of many breaks during the day allowed her time to scratch Wet Paw behind the ears, or hold him on her lap as she rested on the bench beside her office. What a nice cat he was. Why had she never noticed before? Or cared? She decided to bring him home after work each day, where he could spend the nights sleeping on the foot of the bed, keeping her company with his soft purr.

In October, she received a letter from her mother. *"I heard you were ill and thought this might help,"* the card read. Enclosed was a check for one hundred dollars.

Money is what she has to offer, Tara tried to reason with herself, feeling heavily weighted by the $15,000 debt she had accumulated to date. At the same time, she knew if she spent it, there would be a different kind of price to pay — placations and emotional obligations. Secrecy. The requirement to abandon herself.

That's double payment. She stared at the check. *Send it back!* She was momentarily stunned by her own idea. *I could send it back. How blasphemous.* Then she pictured the look on her mother's face and knew she could not. Sighing heavily, she looked for somewhere to set the piece of paper as if it were a hot potato, not ready to just throw it in the trash, not wanting to give it residence, either. At length, she let it lie precariously upon her desk. Maybe it would just blow away when she opened the front door.

"Just spend the money," Jamie said the following day at work. "Think of it as payback for all your pain and suffering."

But money would pay back nothing. Change nothing. The disconnect rampant in her family would still be thriving. A disconnect that had begun generations ago, something she had learned the night she'd found out that her grandfather had been diagnosed with cancer. Her mother had worn a distracted look while rummaging the cupboards for the right-sized iron skillet to sauté onions for meat.

"I guess now that he's dying, he'll be coming out here to visit," was all she said over the ensuing clank of pots and pans.

Only fourteen at the time, Tara read her mother's undertone of dread laced with a sense of obligation, and then tiptoed out of the way as the desired skillet finally emerged and was slapped down on the burner. She then listened to her mother's mutterings about the night her grandfather used the back of his gruff hand to knock his sixteen-year-old daughter to the ground after she'd arrived home from a date fifteen minutes late one night. Tara realized then that she had never remembered her mother and her grandfather actually having a conversation in all the years they'd spent in Michigan together. What would it be like to have him on their turf?

She should have guessed that her grandmother would be the one to come through the deboarding gate at the airport in a wheelchair, as if she herself had born the illness.

"I'm dizzy, dizzy. So very dizzy," she had warbled in a whimpering sort of way while her eighty-year-old husband rolled her down the concourse himself. But by the next sentence, the whimpering tone had turned sour, her grandmother's face frowning. "I don't know why he wants to go to all the trouble to fly out here to California and drag me along with him," she said, as if he hadn't been right beside her, standing perfectly erect in suit and tie. "He's never been interested in coming here before."

Tara looked away from the dry, wrinkled face heavily powdered and rolled her eyes. But the absence of a rebuttal lured them back to her grandfather. He had merely smiled in response, serenity imbued in the smooth, clean-shaven face. Tara remembered staring. Something had changed.

At dinner that evening, her grandfather sat at the round glass table with the rest of the family, seemingly content to be a part of the background instead of at the head. Tara had never seen him touch anyone. He had certainly never paid much attention to his youngest granddaughter. Yet he was reluctant to let go his embrace of her the night before he said good-bye. Her heart had gone out to him then, knowing she would never see him again. But for her mother, who ignored his newfound overtures of affection, the change in him had not come in time. He had never learned to acknowledge or apologize for the past. She had never learned to voice her pain, except when she drank and acquired the uninhibited audacity to inflict her fiery torment upon her children.

For several days running, Tara walked in her apartment door after work and saw the check from her mother still sitting on her desk. On the fourth day, she picked it up and sat on her couch. It was dusk. She was working harder than she should, she knew, to pay off her debts. She felt her students demanding more energy than she could give. How ironic, she thought, that she had been previously diagnosed with parasites. No one could relate to how much effort and energy it took just for her to stand, to walk, let alone drive herself to work and teach. Let alone try to ride. She stared outside her windows. In spite of her recent revelations about her family and subsequent improvements in her health, she felt consumed by a great fatigue.

It had already rained early in the season, and distant clouds dotted a blue sky. The setting sun cast a golden light over young sprouts of green grass covering the hillsides. A horse grazed peacefully in a neighboring pasture. A light breeze made the tree across the drive sway its branches slowly. Gracefully.

Let your mother live her own life. They were actual words spoken quietly but prominently in her mind. The voice sounded so familiar, although she could not name it. *You are not responsible for her happiness. Let her be responsible for this,* it continued while she gazed out onto the world, some part of her merging with its beauty.

All I want, she said to herself, her whole being feeling the ache of longing, *is to get well. That's all I want.*

All that matters, was the immediate reply from the voice, *is the process. That is all that matters.*

It was not what she wanted to hear. But she had to admit she was traveling down some path, and instinctively knew that it was important to travel the whole length of it. The less she missed along the way, the better off she'd be in the end. And in order to not miss anything, she could not be in a rush. Not even to get well.

She pictured Tom then, sitting on his swivel stool in an absence of hurry, his understanding of people and animals so great he barely needed words or movement to interact with them—or to be effective! It was as if all extraneous action had been chiseled away and what was left was so streamlined, it appeared invisible to most people, as if he wasn't doing anything. Efficiency, real efficiency, it suddenly dawned on her, had nothing to do with time management or striving towards higher productivity. It came with being willing and able to accept whatever presented itself, and to deal with that, learn from that. It came with letting go.

She got up off her chair, went to her dining table, and placed the check on top, smoothing it over the cool surface with both hands and looking at the familiar handwriting of a mother she still knew by heart. Then she grabbed it again, tore it up, and watched the pieces fall on the floor like confetti. It seemed the lesser of all evils, allowing herself the autonomy she needed without rubbing her mother's nose in it by sending it back.

She returned to the couch, and without thinking, began beating the pillows lying beside her. Then she burst into tears. Heaving sobs made her feel that she was falling into a bottomless pit. Suddenly self-conscious, she wiped her eyes. Understanding parts of her life intellectually wasn't the same as having to deal with her feelings about it. In this, she felt completely inept, never before having allowed herself to feel anything in its entirety.

It was evening by the time she walked the red brick pathway that ran alongside her apartment to the mailbox. The ground was moist from the rain. She didn't want to admit that she still hoped for a reply from Vera in response to a letter she had lately written, although she knew in her heart that she would not receive one. Under the light of the full moon, she shuffled through her mail. No letter. How long would it take her to accept that no one in her family wanted to hear about her pain, *lest I remind them of their own, perhaps?* After all, if Vera's therapist hadn't made the mistake of leaking her true origins, they would have all been willing to let her live in secret forever. How much easier, then, to keep her out of sight and mind, rather than face the dilemma she posed to them.

She now understood Crystal's need to leave home all those years ago and, as much as it hurt, for leaving her when she was only ten. Crystal herself had not yet been an adult, so what other choice did she have? But Crystal was older now and had made her list of priorities. Tara knew her name was not at the top of that list.

It was late, and the world was quiet. Asleep. Mail still in hand, she stood under two cherry trees by the side of the road. Discolored leaves lay piled at the base of their trunks from last year's shedding. She felt the weight of her body like lead, her life the color of mud. At that moment, a light spot at the edge of the rotting foliage caught her eye and made her peer closely. Three naked ladies were blooming together, late in the season. Two stood side by side, the other somewhat apart and facing at a different angle. The moonlight cast a soft sheen over their pale pink petals. How delicate they appeared — the first blooms to emerge out of the shell-shocked earth in parts of Europe after World War II, so she had been told. It was hard to fathom how anything so vulnerable could dare rise up in such a place.

Tara pictured herself with Vera and Crystal, walking along the shores of Lake Michigan, writing their names in the sand. Like these flowers, they had come from the same source, had been raised under the same roof, in the midst of a war zone. Surely, her sisters knew what that meant, as no one else could. Surely, they could find solace in confiding their individual pain to each other. But perhaps for them it was better to keep the distance, to maintain that smooth, unruffled exterior, acquired when you'd found a way to let the ones who'd ruined your life no longer disturb you. After all, tomorrow the heavy shoes of the masses, rushing to complete their to-do lists, maintain their image, their status, and their things, would trample the soft unfolding of petals, completely blind to the impact being delivered by their unfeeling action. How could anything of real value ever survive? Flowers in darkness they remained, unseen by each other or the rest of the sleeping world.

~genesis~

It's never too late to be who we might have been.

— George Elliot

January, the beginning of a new year, Tara thought as she reached up to hang a fresh calendar above her desk. It was getting late, and there was no moon. Nothing but the night revealed itself through the open slats of the shutters, and a quiet lull surrounded the house. For once, she was grateful for her aloneness and pulled out a massive, 1940s unabridged dictionary, the one she used whenever weighty thoughts pressed into her, the old word library reflecting the thoughtfulness of its era. Balancing the heavy and unwieldy open leaves on her lap, she sat cross-legged on her bed and turned the thinner than thin pages delicately, suppressing an eager shakiness in her fingers. Arriving at the definition of "nature" she read, "That which is the source or essence of life; creative force; the basic qualities of anything or quality of being, perhaps unchangeable."

When she had first watched Tom work with the two stallions nearly two years ago, she had hung back out of the way. From where she'd stood, those horses had been dangerous and in need of discipline. They would need to be made to behave in a different way. Wasn't that the way everything in life was accomplished? A person had to make it happen.

She understood how one could set up a pressure so that the horse could physically respond of its own choice. But she still didn't understand how Tom had gotten both stallions to change emotionally. Striking and kicking had ceased. Pinned ears had relaxed to an upright position. Snapping teeth had calmed to soft, contented chewing and tongues licking lips.

At the time, it had seemed like a miracle. Certainly many people described the things that Tom did as miracles. But he always insisted that what he did was natural. And if what he did was natural, it wasn't possible for anyone to achieve what he did with force; otherwise, it wouldn't be natural.

Of course, you could argue that force was natural. But force had created the stallions' bad behavior in the first place. And while it was possible for those horses to behave in such a horrible manner, she had seen that it wasn't necessary. The stallions had stopped trying to fight and pull away from the people in their presence because...because... One could say that they had learned to trust people, but what had made them want to trust, and in so short a time? By the end of a few short hours, every tension had left, leaving...what?

Tara closed her eyes and frowned, remembering herself in third grade when she'd been appointed "lunch monitor." Only fifteen minutes had been allotted for her classmates to eat before a forty-five-minute afternoon recess, and everyone had to be quiet in order to finish within that time. Leaving class early every day before noon, she had donned a sash, fitted diagonally across her chest, which had been a visible indicator to the other kids that she had the authority to enforce the rules.

She had taken her job very seriously, telling offending classmates to "put your head down" or "sit out recess on the bench" if any infractions occurred. It had made her feel important, she now realized, and the power she wielded had made the other kids go along with her—the way one could influence a horse. Taking a leadership role brought respect, allowed a horse to have confidence and feel secure that they could rely on you to make the decisions, just like people. At school, she'd received extra credit from her teachers for taking on that role. But while she had made the other kids do what she told them to, it hadn't made them like her very much, and they certainly wouldn't have done what she'd asked on their own, any more than Blackie would today.

Then, she recalled the afternoon of her last lunch patrol duty. She had spied two girls she'd never seen before. "You have to be quiet," she'd interrupted their conversation, noticing that neither of them had a lunch, as did all the other children.

They were still talking on her next round. "Put your heads down." She hovered over them then, standing by to make sure they complied, which they did, folding their arms into head rests on the table.

On her third round, she saw that they had simply turned toward each other in their prone position to continue their conversation. She set her jaw and marched over. "You have to sit out on the bench!"

The girls rose easily as she pointed to "the bench" stationed at the edge of the asphalt playground. There they sat with legs straddled on either side, facing each other and continuing their conversation. Tara remembered her hair bristling up the back of her neck, but no one had told her that kids couldn't talk out there, and so she walked on, swallowing her indignation until one of them raised an arm, waving her over.

"We were just wondering how long we should stay out here."

The friendly manner and lack of ire in the girl's voice brought Tara up short, and in that moment, her desire to see the two of them punished completely evaporated.

"Have you been going to school here long?" the other one asked when she hadn't answered.

Tara nodded. "Since kindergarten. Whose class are you in?"

"Oh, we don't really go here. We're just visiting."

"I didn't think I recognized you."

"Yeah," they'd both giggled.

Tara stood staring at them for a minute. "I guess you should sit here for a couple more minutes," unable to convince herself that there was actually any need.

"Okay," the girls chimed together.

She'd walked away then, but in a few feet turned back and stopped dead in her tracks. There was no one there! But there hadn't been time for them to run, and when she glanced at the playground, she didn't see them there, either.

The next day, she turned her sash into the principal's office.

"But we need you." Mrs. Julian looked surprised and cross. "Don't you want the extra credit?"

Of course she wanted the extra credit. But she had merely stared at the woman and shaken her head.

Self-preservation, Tom's words echoed in her mind.

Self-preservation? Tara opened her eyes. *Not of my physical body.*

Her legs were beginning to cramp from the weight of the heavy dictionary, and her thoughts were jamming. The two girls had changed her without trying, just as Tom had changed the stallions. There was something about his patience and self-assurance; he could afford to have it because—because he knew something she still didn't know. He knew how to get from point A to point B without making it happen.

Aargh! She was back at the beginning of her dilemma, eyes burning. A sigh escaped her as she closed the dictionary and set it on an end table. Undressing for bed, she noticed marks on her bare thighs where the heavy weight had made a deep impression during her contemplations. She reached over to turn off the light and heard a soft pattering on the roof. It was raining again, starting so lightly she hadn't noticed at first. Now it steadily increased until the rhythmic pounding lulled her to sleep, knowing it would wash the air clean and leave everything fresh for the morning.

The cool morning air made her shiver as she stepped out of her car and walked to the barn. By now, it had long been common knowledge that Tara, the classical dressage instructor who had trained in Germany, was working with some old cowboy. The good thing about that was that the people who didn't like the "different" aspect of her approach didn't bother coming to her in the first place. For clients that had been training with her since before she met Tom, it was a difficult transition.

"I'm supposed to halt at 'C' from the working trot," Sandra pointed out to her during their afternoon lesson. Sandra, the owner of the big Hanoverian that Tara had ridden at Tom's, now rode him in preparation for a show that would be coming up in the spring.

"That means you need to start the process of getting to the halt earlier, so that you're not pulling on your horse's mouth just to be able to do it."

"But aren't I supposed to be able to halt within two or three strides?"

"Eventually, that's what happens. But until you learn the timing and feel with your whole body, your horse won't learn how to respond the way you want." And then, in response to her student's sigh of exasperation, "It takes awhile to put this together."

"Well, how long does it take?"

"As long as it takes for you to learn how to ask."

Ouch! That was always the rub. And it didn't always sink in. The next time Sandra came around the corner of the standard-sized dressage court, Tara saw it coming; once again, the rider's tight arms strained to pull her horse to a stop.

"He won't do it!"

"That's because you're pulling on the reins."

"How else am I supposed to get him to stop?"

"You need to release the pressure when he slows down, so that he's rewarded for his effort to get to the halt. Then the next time you ask him to slow down, he's more apt to respond because he hasn't gone numb to your constant pulling. He knows he'll find relief from the pressure and a place of freedom if he complies with you." It was the fifth time she had said it.

"But that will take longer for him to stop."

"Exactly. So you need to start preparing him earlier."

"But he should halt in two steps!"

"And so he will. But it's not going to happen overnight."

"But I want him to do it now."

"I know," Tara said, closing her eyes and nodding. "I know."

The following week found her standing in the center of the big outdoor arena, watching a bay mare named Ellie gallop around her in a frenzy, scrambling through the turns before charging down the straightaway alongside the rail. Without saddle or bridle, every muscle in the mare's body was visible and bulged with strain. For the past half an hour, Tara's only move had been to come into her path with a plastic flag to turn her in the opposite direction, somewhat concerned about over-stressed tendons and ligaments. Sweat dripped off the brown belly, and Ellie, head braced toward the sky, breathed heavily through distended nostrils.

Tara turned slowly, following the mare with her eyes. By the time she checked her watch again, another twenty minutes had elapsed, and Ellie was just beginning to slow her pace. In a few more rounds, she finally broke to a trot. As she stretched her neck, nose low to the ground, the hard bulge of her muscles gave way to a rippling motion beneath the sweaty shine of her coat. Tara took a deep breath. It had been the same scenario for the past three days, ever since this horse had come into training—except that the first time, it had taken her nearly two hours to get to this point.

When at last the mare walked, she still had that hurried drive in her, where anything could set her off again. Her eyes rolled from side to side, watching everything in her range of vision: a bird perched on the fence, a shadow on the ground, another horse grazing on the hill behind the barn, the breeze rustling through the eucalyptus trees. Tara kept her movements to a minimum lest she disturb the fragile calm. A horse like this would often keep going, in spite of fatigue, pain, or dehydration.

"She's not that bad," Gina, a young college student and the mare's owner, had said to Tara when Ellie was delivered from San Jose the week before. "She just gets really tense."

There must be more to it than that, Tara narrowed her eyes and looked at Gina, who was now standing outside the arena, waiting for her lesson.

"This might take a while," Tara warned after letting Ellie cool, and then haltering her for Gina to lead to the smaller round pen. "But if you want to keep this mare, you need to be a part of the process as much as possible. I can help make some changes, but unless you learn what it takes to keep her settled, she'll just revert back to her old self after you take her home."

Gina produced a silent nod, her dark eyes solemn as she turned the mare loose in the round pen and watched her start to run. The pen provided no relief for the mare to straighten out of a turn, but kept her at a closer proximity for Gina's benefit. It wasn't yet apparent to Tara whether this young woman, fairly inexperienced around horses, would be up for this kind of project. A horse such as Ellie provided multiple challenges, and aside from the likely possibility of further mishandling if passed into the wrong hands, selling her could mean putting someone else's life at risk—or allowing the mare to find her way to the meat packer.

"She's reared on me a few times," Gina offered then, "and the last time, I came off pretty hard."

Tara looked away. *Here it comes,* she shook her head, *after the horse has already been sent here.* "So what happened?" Not sure she wanted to know.

"Well, we were on the trail with another horse and came to a narrow place. She just didn't want to go through that spot and started rearing when I tried to get her to go."

The mare was running nervously again, making Tara grateful for the pen's heavy steel construction. It stretched fifty feet in diameter and was solid from the ground to five feet up, making it impossible for a horse to snag a leg between open bars. Three feet above that was open steel piping, providing enough height to keep horses from jumping out, but allowing them to look out and "take in their surroundings," as Tom would say. The mare did just that, craning her neck to the outside, as if Gina wasn't there.

"Many times, a person will try and get the horse's attention too early," she heard Tom's voice again, "before the horse has had a chance to become comfortable in their environment, before they're ready to think about what the person is trying to get them to do."

"Okay, Gina," Tara spoke again, "our first 'goal' is going to be to give the mare a chance to settle on her own. So all you're going to do is keep her in this direction until we decide to change it."

Gina turned slowly to follow the movement of the mare. Tara noticed her rounded shoulders and the way her body sagged. Just then, the mare lifted her head, and snorting at something outside the pen, spun around, swinging her front end in toward the center. Gina shuffled back to avoid being run over.

"Now you need to use your flag to turn her back the way she was going!" Tara was surprised by the intensity of her own voice as she tried to inspire Gina to act quickly. Gina moved as if to act, then smiled and shrugged.

"Go ahead and try again," Tara said firmly. "Raise your flag so she can see it."

Gina backed up tentatively toward the railing before the mare came around again.

"Lift your flag higher, where she can see it," Tara inserted a second time before it was too late. Gina raised her arm just before Ellie, still moving with speed, completed a lap and swung into the turn where Gina stood. Noticing the human body in her path at the last moment, the mare deftly locked her forelegs in front of her with such force that the whole of her head and neck were flung down between her legs. After making a supreme effort to gather herself, she pushed to the inside and swung back in the other direction.

Tara's heart was beating fast, and she could see the unsettled look on Gina's face. It was obvious that her student was not accustomed to wielding this kind of power.

"Now, Gina, you need to be there earlier." Tara blushed as she heard Tom's words coming out of her mouth. But it was vital for Gina to be more definite in her actions so the mare would learn to respect her presence. It was vital for Gina's safety.

Ellie continued around for several more laps before it became necessary to turn her in the other direction so that she didn't over stress one side.

"Okay, Gina," Tara said, "you need to move with more fortitude when you decide to change the mare's direction." When the mare had passed one side of the round pen, Gina would have only a few moments to move back toward the rail, lift her flag, and wave the mare around. "All right, go now!" Tara yelled.

Gina's body was still soft, and she moved too slowly. How common this was of women, Tara thought. Always afraid of breaking something, of being bold. Of being noticed. At the last moment, Gina saw her precarious position and stepped back just in time to let the mare gallop by without running her over. At least she had done that much.

"You have to get bigger," Tara's voice was calmer now, more patient. This was going to take a while. "When you decide to insert yourself in the mare's path, you need to be committed to that decision, and be firm enough in your actions so that she will take you seriously."

Gina made another move. Tara, still outside the round pen, was with her. "Go on. Go on. Go on!"

This time, Gina ran to the open spot and lifted her flag. Tara saw an unlikely strength emerge from this mild-mannered person. The mare had seen it too, and turned in plenty of time.

"All right!" Tara nearly jumped out of her clothes, knotting her fists and throwing her arms high in the air. How utterly amazing to see an animal teach humans so much about what was missing in their life, requiring them to reach beyond their comfort zone and develop a part of themselves they never knew they had. More than that, she smiled to herself, her ability to see the potential in others, an apparent curse in her personal relationships, gave her a great advantage as a coach. She knew Gina was capable, even when Gina did not. With that confidence, she could convince her student to try something new. The horse would do the rest.

30

~true unity~

Horse, thou art truly a creature without equal, for thou fliest without wings, and conquerest without sword.

— The Koran

It was March before Tara felt strong enough to make another trip to Wesland. At noon, after her morning lessons, she pushed her office door open with an excited flurry and began to collect her things. Wet Paw, whom she brought with her to the barn during the day, greeted her with a coarse howl. Although she commonly felt inclined to pick him up and drape him over her shoulder to stroke his thick fur, today she merely eyeballed his food dish, and seeing it full, ignored him. Not ready to be put off, however, he jumped up and landed with muddy paws on top of her planner.

"Get off!" She pushed him roughly aside.

He lost his footing, and sliding over the side of her desk, scrambled wildly. Unable to latch his claws into the metal frame, he fell into a pile of empty cardboard boxes. The sight of him going over the edge like that made her freeze, realizing too late what she had done. She reached for him as he landed on the floor, wanting to make it up to him, but he ran past into the bushes outside, wide-eyed with fear. She closed her eyes.

Damn, I've done it again.

But she had no time to linger. Adon was standing at the door to help load Ellie into the trailer. Once inside her compartment, the mare stomped nervously, and throughout the long drive over freeways lined with the monotonous, unchanging pattern of reflector bumps, Tara felt the truck lag and the trailer sway whenever the mare pawed or shifted her position. At length, she turned onto the exit, and ten minutes later drove over the familiar metal bridge.

Just as he had always done in the past, Tom drove the golf cart out from underneath the trailer home's overhang to greet her. After parking the truck's nose under the willow tree, Tara stepped out of the cab to give him a hug.

"Been quite a while since you been over this way," he smiled.

"Way too long," she felt her throat tighten.

The sound of stomping feet inside the trailer made her turn.

"I'll just give you a minute to get unloaded while I head over —" and he nodded toward the arena.

"All right, Tom. I'll meet you there," and she unloaded the mare and led her out into the sun, over the gravel drive, and through the gate that led to the enclosed round pen. After turning Ellie loose, she sat with Tom in the golf cart, explaining what she knew of the horse.

"Are you feelin' well enough to work now?" he interrupted.

"Well, pretty much. I still get tired easily." She didn't mention how tired, or tell him about the waves of recurring pain in her belly, or the bouts of insomnia and periods of weakness.

"Well, I imagine it'll take some time to overcome some of these things." Then he remained quiet while she went on about the mare.

"She still gets nervous, Tom, especially when I try to ride her around obstacles and such. So I've gone back to square one — setting poles on the ground." She then told him about the hours she'd spent walking, leading, and riding over them. Ellie would either race across, or veer sideways with such force that Tara had trouble getting her back.

"You can learn so much about a horse just by observing them in their natural state," Tom inserted neatly.

Tara stopped, her mouth still open, poised for another explanation. She knew that Tom, never excessive with words, meant something by everything he said. She turned to look at Ellie for the first time that day and squirmed, at a loss as to how to fill the empty, silent space. The mare paced the railing, only stopping to lift her head high up over the pen when she spotted other horses in the neighboring pasture. She seemed completely oblivious to the humans sitting right outside the bars.

Tara looked back at Tom, whose eyes never left the mare. A movement past the outline of his profile caught her attention as his terrier bounded over to them. Deformed at birth, the dog only had the use of three legs, but it didn't slow her enthusiasm. She canter-hobbled eagerly in circles while Tom, seemingly unconcerned about continuing any more discussion about the mare, swished his flag over the dog's head. Just before the terrier could catch the plastic bag in her teeth, he quickly lifted it out of reach. Tara had always felt that the natural exuberance in dogs to want to be with people made it much easier to have a relationship with them. Horses were never that eager to be around you except when you had food.

As Tom kept the flag out of the dog's reach, she leapt after it in a frenzy. After several rounds, he let her grab it and chew, but flicked it back before she could tear it to shreds. One of Tom's win-win situations, Tara mused. The dog was delighted, and Tom still had his flag intact.

"Oookaaay," he sighed then. "Do you want to let yourself in the pen there?" It was one of his non-questions. Tara removed herself from the golf cart and went inside the round pen. "Now, you'll go up and pet the mare."

Tara moved toward Ellie, who continued to pace along the railing.

"When you get to her, you'll pet with your heart, not your hand," Tom said.

Tara paused, and then made another attempt, but the mare moved away again. Tom had her raise her arm up and down to deliberately drive the horse away. They remained at a walk, but continued in this manner for quite some time. Finally tired of being pushed around in circles Ellie stood still, allowing Tara to walk up and scratch her on the neck, then over her back and along the sides of her tail as Tom directed.

"All right, I'll say it again," she heard his voice. "Pet with your heart, not your hand."

Tara remembered when her love for horses had been so strong she couldn't wait to be in sight of any stable yard. Her strokes slowed and became softer.

"Now, back away and see what she does," Tom continued.

As usual, Ellie turned away and went off to the far side of the pen, looking to regain sight of the other horses. Then Tom had Tara move toward Ellie, then back again, then to the right, then left, then to her front, then to her rear.

"Now follow her," he said as the mare again moved away.

Tara felt the familiar sense of disorientation that always seemed to be a part of being around Tom. As usual, she didn't know what he was trying to get her to accomplish. And what did all this have to do with Ellie's phobia about ground poles?

Finally, the mare stopped.

"Now try again," Tom said, the tone in his voice never wavering from its calm delivery.

Once more, Tara moved to approach the mare, but in the first two steps, Ellie swung her head away, preparing to walk off.

"Use your kitten feet," Tom inserted.

She knew what he meant. She slowed and softened her step like the delicate, innocent footfalls of the many kittens she had cuddled over her lifetime. One small soft step after another. It seemed to take forever, but this time, the mare stood. When Tara was close, she raised an arm in the same slow manner she had used her feet, letting the soft quality settle along the mare's neck. Ellie stood for a moment, then raised and cocked her head in an unpleasant manner. Tara stopped, realizing that she had done something to cause that reaction.

"Try moving around to her withers."

Tara moved her hand to the withers and scratched there. The mare lowered her head with a soft eye and droopy eyelid. Then, for what seemed like a long time, Tara explored the mare's body, working her fingers over the sleek coat while watching Ellie's face for an expression to tell her when she found a pleasing spot.

"Now, back away."

She had almost forgotten that Tom had been sitting there, silent, without disturbing her discoveries. She took a step back. This time, the mare swung her head and neck around to look at her. Tara stood riveted, feeling the mare's interest in her for the first time.

"Now, you just turn and walk away."

Keeping her head over her shoulder to watch Ellie's reaction, Tara turned her body and walked away. The mare followed! All the morning's tensions ran from Tara as around the pen they went, horse following human, no halter or lead to coerce her. Ellie's head was hanging low, making her look like a large, docile dog. She realized then that the mare had lost all interest in the other horses. And she was relaxed!

When Tara stopped, Ellie stopped alongside her. Tara stroked her face, softly running the palms of her hands over the mare's brow.

"She's wanted to be this way her whole life," Tom's voice came through the calm air. "It's just that no one's ever given her the chance to know how to be with a person. It should be no different when you're on her back." And then his eyes twinkled, "Or stepping over poles on the ground."

Would it ever stop seeming that just when she thought she knew something, she had actually missed everything? Tom was leaning back, as usual, his feet propped up over the front of the golf cart. A barely discernible smile gave a look of pleasure to his browned face, still largely free of wrinkles, his kind attention making her eyes sting.

"You give a little now to gain more later." He paused, once more allowing for that quiet, empty space. This time, Tara felt herself soaking it in. "There's so much good in a horse that I rarely get to see come out. And it seems that unless a person is willing to spend this kind of time with the animal, they don't get to see it, either."

Pause.

"Now, you mentioned that you didn't understand what had taken place with those stallions a couple years back." He waited for Tara's nod. Neither she nor the mare had moved a hair. Tom coughed. Swallowed. "When you said that it seemed as though nothing was happening much of the time," he pointed in their direction, "a lot of this kind of thing was going on."

Tara narrowed her eyes and slowly nodded.

Tom's chest rose, his lungs filling with air before he exhaled, emotion quavering in his voice. "All I'm interested in is this," his arms gestured outward, encompassing her and the mare, "what's happening *between* the person and the horse. That's *all* I'm interested in. The rest is just for surface workers." His eyes bored holes through her, and she felt their weight.

The next day, Tom didn't ask Tara to walk the mare over ground poles, but had her walk over everything else — bridges, tires, uneven terrain, asphalt — things with which the mare had no history. It wasn't until the afternoon of the third day that Tara rode her over a pole on the ground. It was as if it hadn't been there.

"Now Tom, why couldn't I have figured that out myself?"

"Well, now," Tom paused and looked down a moment, then looked up and cocked his head. "Did I ever tell you the story about the two men — the younger man and the older man?"

Tara shook her head.

"Well, there was a young man and an old man. They were talking amongst themselves, and finally the younger man got around to asking the older man how he had come to be so successful.

"The older man answered, 'Why, by using good judgment.'

"Then the younger man asked, 'But how did you learn to have such good judgment?'

"And so the older man answered, 'Through experience.'

"Well, the younger man thought about that for quite a while, then he asked, 'But where did you get that kind of experience?'"

Tom paused and looked at Tara, nodding his head as if he thought she should know the ending by now. When she didn't answer, he went on.

"The older man thought a moment, and then finally admitted, 'Poor judgment.'"

Tara shook her head and smiled wearily. "Tom, I think I'm just a slow learner."

Late in the afternoon, Tara packed up her trailer and readied to leave. After squeezing Tom good-bye, she went over to Ellie's paddock and stood by the gate. Without prompting, the mare walked leisurely up to her from the back end of her pen and lowered her head into Tara's hands while resting a hind leg. Tara stroked the unhaltered face, smoothing her palm over the soft, brown eyes, and thought of a human child who would naturally come to its mother, not for fear of being punished, but for love, security, and comfort. Why had she, only a few hours ago, thought that what would motivate a horse—or any living thing—to be with a person should be so different from that?

After all her belongings had been packed, she led Ellie to the trailer. Throwing the lead rope over the mane, she let the mare walk into her compartment on her own, noting how she stepped up softly and easily before allowing herself to be enclosed on one side like a sardine. It dawned on Tara that she hadn't needed help this time. Something in her was changing. But it was happening with such a lack of drama, with such delicacy, she had barely detected it.

At work the following day, she rode Blackie out onto the trail. Their meanderings brought them back to the same ditch where they had been stuck the year before and, as had happened then, Blackie balked in front of it and tried to nibble the grass along the edge. Before thinking about what her next move should be, she began her usual clucking and leg flapping. He didn't budge. But a movement in the grasses startled him, and he spun hard in the opposite direction. As she picked up her rein to turn him back, he lost his footing. The buckling of his knees told her he was about to go down. The odd thing was that he seemed not to care, as if he was going down for a roll.

But it wasn't a good place for a roll. The ground was not level and there was a fall off on either side of the mound. Instinctively, Tara hit him firmly with her whip, not as a punishment, but out of a sincere wanting to inspire him to make the effort to gather his feet under himself. Blackie was indeed surprised, and in the next instant, he jumped up and landed in position, facing the ditch. Not wanting to further agitate her horse, Tara sat like stone, reins draped loosely about his neck while he shifted his feet.

Then something different happened. Blackie pricked his ears forward and looked across the ditch. Tara barely breathed while an eerie feeling moved through her. Had this actually been the first time he had looked across, or just the first time she'd noticed that he had?

After a moment, he looked away. Not wanting to loose his attention, Tara pressed her legs cautiously along his sides. He didn't move, but his head swung back to the ditch. This time, she did not push him on and instead remained quiet, giving him time to soak. Again, he looked away. Again, she pressed her legs. Again, he swung his head forward.

In her quiet observations, she realized that she could tell when he was going to look away, relating to his desire to ignore uncomfortable situations. It reminded her of her family, and the way she herself had refused to deal with things throughout her life.

Self-preservation!

Just before he looked away the next time, she legged him again, feeling a genuine wanting to support him, encourage him, be there with him. He took a step forward. She resisted an urge to leg him on and immediately released the pressure instead. He paused, looking straight ahead. She barely breathed, knowing that something was working. He was no longer her adversary. He was simply afraid!

It's just that he hadn't acted as if he was afraid. He had acted belligerent. Stubborn.

Self-preservation.

"To see a thing uncolored by one's own personal preferences and desires is to see it in its own pristine simplicity," Bruce Lee had once written. Now she understood that her horse was no different from her the day she had stood outside the auditorium after school and a pen had slipped from her notebook. The new boy in her fifth grade class had been standing there, too, and had leaned down to pick it up. He'd held it out to her, smiling and wanting to make conversation. But she had merely given him a look of fire with her ten-year-old eyes and snatched the pen from his hand, having already learned it was not safe to let down her guard around anyone.

Self-preservation.

She legged Blackie again, everything in her saying, "I am here." Again, he took a step. Again, she paused and in that moment of pause, she *saw* him thinking—ears moving back and forth, head and neck stretched low, nose pointed out over the ditch, nostrils flaring and relaxing, seeking to assess what was before him. For the first time, she understood how much he needed this kind of unpressured time.

It's respect that gets the response, she heard Tom's voice. She had always interpreted that to mean respect from the horse. Now she realized how it was truly a two-way street. She had been trying so hard to make Blackie go across, that in her efforts to get to her goal, she had become blind to what he needed from her.

There were standards and guidelines for me to operate within, but I had the freedom to develop my own character. Tom's voice again. Suddenly it made sense how important it was to know when to be there for someone, and when to get out of their way—as she had the day she rode the Hanoverian, and Tom had tossed the pebbles at them. She had not learned any such thing in her own family, a family she had assumed she needed to learn "those hard life lessons." It was a popular theory, circulated in self-help books and espoused by religious and spiritual "teachers" and motivational speakers. Now, she had to admit that going along with the idea had made her feel better, had made her feel like there was a good reason for all the terrible things that had happened in her life. In anyone's life. Yet if she honestly believed that, she would be advocating for child abuse.

In fact, maybe there wasn't, ultimately, a good reason for all that pain. Maybe more could be accomplished without it. After all, that pain had been man-made, not anything created by—this place. This other way of being.

She legged her horse again, supporting him, encouraging him. He crouched low. She released the pressure from his sides, letting him make his own decision. His feet shifted from side to side as his muscles contracted, waves of power surging underneath her. She resisted a desire to pick up the reins for control and grabbed a hunk of mane instead. Then, all four of his feet rocketed off the ground, and suddenly they were flying as he leapt across. She let him go. He had *wanted* to go.

A week later, she was back in the fields at Wesland, riding Blackie over uneven ground, testing his newfound confidence. Tom followed behind in the golf cart before they made their way up a steep incline. Tara didn't realize how high she and her horse had gotten until they reached the top. A fence line blocked them from going farther, and the only way around was to go back down the way they had come. Tom, sitting at the base of the hill far below, looked like a miniature doll, watching her. Blackie took one look at the steep slope and stopped. Tara waited, and then gave him her leg. He didn't move.

"Come over this way, where it's not so steep." Tom pointed to her left where, if she followed the ridge in the opposite direction, she would come to a more gradual slope. But she felt her horse was just pausing to get his bearings. His feet were dug in, but his attention was in front of him.

"I think he can make it, Tom," she called back and, with relief, saw him nod his approval.

"Then you'll wait for his feet, no matter if you miss your lunch."

She smiled. All pressure was off, and with his support, all doubt was erased from her mind. She was confident that her horse would sort it out if she let him. And all at once, just sitting there and waiting became a pleasure.

So this is patience!

She sat in awe of her own discovery. Patience! It had come when she knew, without a doubt, that everything would work out. And it would work out because that's how life, the real nature of life, was. It was how life worked, if she would just stay out of the way and not try to make it into something it wasn't by pushing it, manipulating it, coercing it. It was already as good as it would ever be. And now, here in this moment, that was better than she could have ever imagined.

In less than a minute, Blackie lowered his nose to the ground and crept forward. Tara fed him the reins and everything in her went with him, although outwardly, she sat perfectly still. A quarter of the way down, he gained his confidence and took bigger steps, more even and balanced as he crouched his hindquarters low and carried his weight back under himself, supporting her weight as well. His hooves skidded over the dry, hard surface. Rocks and pebbles avalanched around his feet with scraping and popping sounds. But what once would have sent him bolting now did not distract him, and he kept steadily on. At the bottom, she heard Tom chuckle.

"Well, now! A moment like that makes you think that together you could climb a telephone pole, or ride down a badger hole. You wouldn't do either one, but you feel like you could just the same."

She nodded, smiling ear to ear. That was exactly how it was. And she had never felt anything like it.

She was still beaming when they made their way back to the barn. They had stopped to chat just outside the gate when a car drove by and honked. One of the neighbors had seen them in plain view and waved as people often did while driving along the quiet lane that ran along the ranch's eastern edge. She and Tom waved back, and while her arm extended high in the air, she wondered if they had any idea what was going on right here in their own back yard—how big it was.

Epilogue

He looked like an Indian.... And his snow-white horse wore no saddle or bridle. The horse was free, he could go where he wanted to go, and he wanted to go with Big Jerry wherever Big Jerry wanted to ride. The horse and the man moved together as if they were one animal....

Laura let out her breath. "Oh, Mary! The snow-white horse and the tall, brown man, with such a black head and bright red shirt! The brown prairie all around—and they rode right into the sun as it was going down. They'll go on in the sun around the world."

Mary thought a moment. Then she said, "Laura, you know he couldn't ride into the sun. He's just riding along on the ground like anybody."

But Laura did not feel that she had told a lie. What she had said was true too. Somehow that moment when the beautiful, free pony and the wild man rode into the sun would last forever.

—Laura Ingalls Wilder
By the Shores of Silver Lake

Tara rode Blackie first thing in the morning before her lessons began. As he walked along, her body moved with the swing of his stride, and she could feel through her seat where he placed each foot. She had only a light contact on the reins, and it seemed natural to lift her right rein as his right foreleg stepped off the ground. Before she knew what she'd done, he swung his front end around, and voilá! He made a 90-degree turn — landing a perfect quarter pirouette.

She stopped to think. She hadn't practiced pirouettes since she first met Tom, remembering the hours at Wesland riding over the tires and stumbling down the creek bed. How little she had understood his genius. "Prepare to position for the transition," he had said so many times. It no longer seemed foreign to think that her horse must not only prepare for a movement, but also prepare for the position into the movement! Tom had known all along that Blackie hadn't ever been given the opportunity to understand where to put his feet to begin with, and that she had been lacking a necessary feel and awareness, in spite of all her training. Or because of all her training. What would have been the use of practicing a movement when all she would have been doing was reinforcing an old, unwanted pattern?

She walked on and tried again. This time, she felt her horse shift his weight onto his haunches, lightening his front end as he swung around. She'd hardly done anything, yet he seemed to know already what she wanted. She giggled. Had there ever been a need to doubt that she'd be able to ride dressage on him again?

Summer came and went. Along with hauling horses to Wesland, she found herself, on many weekends, hauling students' horses to shows. On one September morning, the alarm woke her out of a deep sleep before dawn. After a brief yoga routine, she drove to the stables and walked up the ramp to the old barn. Brenda was already putting leg wraps around the Hanoverian's thick canon bones, preparing him for the trailer ride.

"Good morning," she called to Tara, a smile on her face.

Tara smiled in return, marveling at her eighteen-year-old student's cheery demeanor right before a show. And not just any show. This was the championships! Throughout the latter part of the show season, Sandra had been generous enough to loan her gelding to Brenda, whose own horse had suffered an injury right after qualifying for the finals. What a test this would be, both for the Hanoverian and for Brenda, who had not had much time to practice on a new horse.

He loaded easily, although he whinnied en route to Sacramento when he found himself alone inside the horse trailer. When they unloaded him three hours later, he held his head high, ears pricked forward, not knowing where he was.

"Take him for a nice long walk around the grounds while I clean out the trailer and park the truck," Tara told Brenda before the horse could get fidgety standing in one spot. "Make sure he has a chance to look at everything."

They had arrived in plenty of time to get the horse settled in his stall. Brenda rode him later that evening as the sun was setting to help calm his nerves before her classes the following day. The horse looked good, Tara thought, forward and light in his rider's hand.

In the morning, she couldn't tell if she was more nervous for her student or the horse as he came out of his stall snorting, the tension in the air having its affect on him. Everything about this day was new.

She gave her student a leg up and they walked to the warm-up arena. Tara barely had to comment. Brenda had improved a lot during the year and had a nice feel for this horse. At the same time, the Hanoverian had learned to be soft and responsive, and so was no longer complicated to ride. Forty-five minutes later, their number was called, and Brenda entered the show ring. Tara could not help riding every stride, every turn, every movement. She was exhausted six minutes later when her student halted and saluted to the judge, indicating the end of their ride. The applause of the other spectators startled her, and she clapped with them.

"He could have been more forward," was Brenda's first comment to Tara as she rode out of the arena on a loose rein. "But," she added, smiling with a shrug, "he stayed with me."

"He sure did," Tara echoed, a swell of pride permeating her senses. "I have no idea what your score will be. Let's just wait until after your second ride before we check."

"That is, if I make the cutoff."

"Oh, yeah. Guess I was assuming you would."

There was a three-hour wait for them before the first set of rides was completed and the finalists would ride again, determining the winner. They walked back to the stabling area, untacked the Hanoverian in his stall, and gave him some afternoon feed.

"Should I watch the other riders, do you think?" Brenda's expressive face looked questioningly at Tara.

"Well, when I'm showing, I never like to distract myself by watching the others. But everyone is different."

"Maybe we could get something to eat."

"Good idea."

As they came back from the lunch pavilion, Tara stopped outside the show office to make sure that Brenda had made the cut.

"I'll meet you back at the stall," she said before walking inside, letting her student continue on to the barn to check on her horse.

It wasn't a surprise to see her student's name on the list of competitors to ride a second time. What surprised Tara were the scores. Having expected Brenda's ride to have received somewhere in the mid-sixty percentile, above average for a dressage test, she gaped at the seventy-one percent printed on the sheet, the highest score of the day.

"You did good," was all she said as she joined her student, who was already grooming the Hanoverian.

"You don't have to tell me," Brenda smiled at Tara, knowing her coach didn't like to distract her students with the idea that they were showing just to win a ribbon.

"It's the quality of what you feel going on between you and your horse that's important," Tara gave Brenda a hug, "not what somebody else thinks of you. Not even the judges."

After tacking up, Brenda rode the Hanoverian to the warm-up arena.

"Let him keep moving forward," Tara reminded her just before the pair was called in for their second test.

"It was a better ride," Brenda smiled after she'd finished.

"I thought so too."

Now there was just the wait before everyone had ridden and the final scores were posted.

There were five horses in the lineup when Brenda reached for her trophy. She set the bulky silver bowl on the pommel as she sat astride the Hanoverian who had already been donned with a championship wreath around his neck and a monogrammed wool cooler over his rump. Camera lights flashed.

"I was smiling the whole time I watched their ride," one of the judges said later in an interview for Chronicle of the Horse. And in that write-up that took more than two pages of fine print in single spacing, those were the words that Tara remembered.

Printed in the United States
82066LV00004B/39